THE PURPLE BIRD

Dylan Roche

Jan-Carol
Publishing, Inc

"every story needs a book"

Thanks for Reading! Enjoy!

Dylan Roche

The Purple Bird
Dylan Roche

Published February 2019
Little Creek Books
Imprint of Jan-Carol Publishing, Inc.
All rights reserved
Copyright © 2019 by Dylan Roche

ISBN: 978-1-945619-88-5
Library of Congress Control Number: 2019930659

You may contact the publisher:
Jan-Carol Publishing, Inc.
PO Box 701
Johnson City, TN 37605
publisher@jancarolpublishing.com
jancarolpublishing.com

To those who have always loved hearing my stories...
thank you for listening.

TABLE OF CONTENTS

CHAPTER 1
What Happened
in the Greenhouse

This couldn't have been happening. But it definitely was.

Still trembling from the shock of the past half-hour, James sighed and leaned up against the glass door of the abandoned greenhouse. It was the only place he could think of to hide. He wiped his sweat-drenched palms on his jeans and looked around. Maybe it was just the fear still coursing through his body, but something about the abandoned greenhouse reminded him of a haunted forest, something out of Grimm's fairy tales. Tangles of overgrown plants spilled out of moldy garden boxes and twisted upward around moldy trellises. Late afternoon sunlight poured in through the cracks in the grimy glass walls, catching the dust that floated in the air and gleaming against the heavy spiderwebs that hung over everything. It was a place long forgotten, a place that might have once been beautiful and full of life but was now a place of decay and death.

Stop it! This wasn't the time to let his overactive imagination get the best of him.

There wasn't anything about the greenhouse that could actually hurt him, was there? Mr. Birken, on the other hand...

"All right, James," he whispered to himself. "You're safe now."

He sighed.

"Yeah, right," he huffed. "As if you actually believe that."

1

He shook his head. *And how in the hell are you going to get home now? You're so stupid, James—God, you're so freaking dumb!*

If he were smarter, or more adept at escaping danger—whichever skill might have benefitted him more—he wouldn't need to be hiding in an abandoned and possibly haunted greenhouse at all. No, if he were smarter and more adept at escaping danger, he would have run away from the school and straight in the direction of his house.

But he hadn't done that. He had been so panicked that his only thought had been to get away from the school as fast as his unathletic body could go. It wasn't until he was on the other side of town that his wits came back to him, and there was no way at that point that he was going back past the school. No way.

But Mr. Birken? Of all people, Mr. Birken?

His chemistry teacher, the kinda-sorta intimidating but otherwise friendly Mr. Birken, with his oversized glasses and his beer belly. Mr. Birken, who, before that afternoon, James thought was only as bad as threatening to fail him for the semester. If only James could have guessed!

His mind flashed back to those awful minutes in the storage room. Mr. Birken's bellowing voice. That crazed expression on his face.

James shook his head as if that might dislodge the memory from his brain. "Gaaah!"

He surged forward, pacing up and down the rows between the garden boxes. If he didn't keep moving, his nervous energy was going to make him explode. He swiped a large cobweb out of his way as he went, kicked at a pile of dead leaves, then fell to his knees, gasping for breath. *Think, James. Use your head.*

A rustling erupted in the overgrowth a few feet away, and James leaped, his heart suddenly hammering in his chest even faster than before.

"Hello?" he called.

Nothing. No sign of anything. Maybe it had just been a rat or a squirrel. *Maybe it's Mr. Birken.*

No, for real though, it was stupid to think that Mr. Birken was in the greenhouse. There was no way he could have gotten so far ahead of James so quickly, no way he could be lurking in there and waiting for him. It wasn't logical—but then again, so little of what had happened that afternoon had been logical, and there was no telling what to believe or expect anymore.

The rustling came again, this time a few feet from where it had been the first time. The leaves on one of the nearby plants shook violently. Whatever was making that movement in the overgrowth was too big to be any kind of rodent.

"Who's there?!" he called.

But he wasn't sticking around to find out. Panic overtaking him, he bolted toward the door.

As he passed a mass of browning flora, something appeared in his periphery. He turned just as a purple *something* emerged from the leaves.

A pitiful cry escaped him as he tumbled backward into one of the flowerbeds. His shoulders hit the ground hard as he landed, knocking the wind out of him and sending up a cloud of dust and dirt.

Wasting not a second, he hoisted himself back up, just in time to come face to face with the strangest creature he had ever seen in his entire life.

Covered in purple feathers and fur, about three feet tall and stoutly built, it was too outlandish to be considered an animal but too innocent and adorable to be called a monster. The creature stood before him, blinking with pearly eyes over a large golden beak. It excitedly gave a flap of its purple wings as if waving at James to calm himself.

"Please, please," the thing said. "I won't hurt you."

"You can talk!" James pushed himself back a little bit, still startled, still a little breathless.

The creature shook its head, tossing aside the shaggy hairs of its mane that hung in its face. "Yes, yes, I can," it said. "I can talk."

James, his fear now replaced by curiosity, climbed to his feet and circled the birdlike creature, looking it up and down. The bird reached up with his wings and straightened the lapels of the shabby blue vest he wore, almost haughty in his demeanor, as if he did not like being made a spectacle. The act was almost comical—the vest, as well as a crudely knotted yellow necktie, hung on the bird like adult dress-ups worn by a toddler, and the vest was patched with fabric of so many colors and patterns that very little of its original blue silk was still visible, the overall effect being that of a miniature homeless person. A hobbit hobo, James might have said at any other time when he wasn't so overwhelmed.

"I—I know you're probably amazed right now," the bird stammered. "But you can't tell anyone that I'm here."

"Sorry," James said. "I just..." He was at a loss for words. "Man, this has been one weird afternoon."

"Well, that's the thing," the bird said. "If you were to tell anyone that you've seen me, then it will likely get even more weird. Weird and terrible."

James paused. Such an ominous warning from such a funny-looking creature. It was like watching one of the Muppets recite Stephen King. But this creature itself didn't strike him as malevolent. No, in fact, he seemed just as scared as James.

"Are you in some sort of trouble?" James ventured.

The bird became silent, shuffling his talons—which were clad in miniature leather loafers—and avoiding James's eyes.

James stepped forward and extended his hand. "My name is James."

"Archit," the bird replied, putting out his wing. "That's my name. Archit Birken."

James's stomach turned. "Birken?"

The air in the greenhouse suddenly became thick with tension. The two of them stared at each other, neither exactly sure of what to say.

The bird hesitated. "You know my uncle, don't you?"

"Yeah," James said. "You could say that. I know a little more about him than I care to, I guess." He had been so surprised to meet Archit that he had almost started to forget about what had happened in the storage room back at the school. Almost, but not totally.

Archit took a deep breath. "Then you know how dangerous he is—and you know why it's so important you tell nobody you saw me."

James wasn't even sure at this point whether it surprised him that this bizarre animal called Mr. Birken his uncle. "Wait," James said, the connection now dawning on him. "Uncle? So you're his nephew?"

Archit nodded.

James's stomach twisted as he remembered everything Mr. Birken had said. *My nephew has eluded me for far too long!* "He's coming after you," James said. "You know that, right?"

"Yes," Archit said. "And I've had a few close calls these last couple of months, and I can't have him find me."

"At least not until your sixteenth birthday, right?"

Archit stopped. He stared at James with uncomfortable intensity. "What?" he said.

James got the impression he had said something wrong. "Well, that's why he's hunting you, isn't it? Something about your sixteenth birthday?"

Before James could say another word, Archit took him by the arm with his wing and led him over to the nearest flowerbed. "James, what do you know?" Archit sat down beside him on the edge of the garden box. "I need you to tell me everything, James."

"I–"

"Everything."

James sighed. He looked at Archit, who was staring up at him with pleading eyes. Only one or two minutes of knowing this creature, and already James couldn't resist sympathy. He hated himself for being such a softie sometimes. Still, it sounded as if Archit had some context to everything that had happened. Maybe Archit could explain it all.

"All right," James said, taking a deep breath.

"And don't leave anything out," Archit said. "I need to know what happened to you. Everything."

"All right," James said. "Well, I guess it started with the fact that this had already been a really awful day…"

And that was the truth—it had been a really awful day up until four o'clock, at least. After that point, the day had started to get weird and frightening.

At four o'clock, James had been in the courtyard, moping and avoiding going home. Dejected didn't even begin to describe it, though that was the closest word he could think of.

There had been the decision of some friends to make an impromptu after-school trip to downtown Annapolis without him ("Sorry, we totally would have invited you, but we've got a full car already!").

Then there'd been the rebuff he got from the girl for whom he had actually managed to grow enough of a spine to ask to the homecoming dance ("You're a great guy, but c'mon, don't you want to go with a girl who's, y'know, into books and smart stuff like that?").

And then there had been missing out on a role in the school's fall play ("Freshmen rarely make the cut, so don't take it personally").

After all that, he dreaded the thought of going home and being around the house all afternoon. His mom would be stressing out over the fancy schmancy cocktail party she was throwing that evening, some stupid thing she did every fall to have all her neighbors and extended family over so that she could play Susie Homemaker. If he went straight home, he would just have to deal with her berating him. "I need to you stay out of the way while I'm cleaning, sweet pea," she would condescend to say. "I'm gonna need you to go upstairs and get cleaned up so you're ready when everyone gets here. Don't dawdle, all right? No, you can't eat anything; I've already tidied the kitchen."

And all night long, there'd be nothing to do except sit around with his sister, Margot, and their cousin Liz—the only other person at the party who would be their age—and be bored, at least when they weren't being forced to socialize with adults they barely knew.

So no way was he going straight home. Instead, he'd killed time by bumming around the school library, brushing through a few books and surfing the internet on one of the computers before migrating to the school courtyard to sit quietly and stew in his own bad mood.

Yeah, so his time might totally have been better spent going to a remedial study session for chemistry. Just earlier that day, in third period, Mr. Birken had told him he was in danger of failing—just one more reason the day had completely sucked.

"We have a midterm coming up on Monday," Mr. Birken had said, giving James an intense look over the rims of his glasses. "Maybe a little bit of after-school help today would do you some good."

Screw that, James had thought. The last thing he wanted to do after the day he'd had was to deal with Mr. Birken. Little could he have known just how much he would be dealing with Mr. Birken, whether he liked it or not.

What James would have given to get away from it all! To escape the mundane world of chemistry midterms and fair-weather friends, to get away from the quiet suburb that worshipped high school lacrosse and music videos. It didn't help that Margot, who was a senior, was Miss Life of the Party of her class, and his parents couldn't understand why James, their younger child, spent so much time reading Shakespeare instead of magazines and going to coffeehouses on Friday nights instead of football games. Why couldn't life be more like the way things were in fantasy novels or games of Dungeons & Dragons, where the opportunity for adventure always waited just around the corner, and even an inconsequential little nobody could still aspire to be a hero?

He hadn't realized, however, that he had moped the entire afternoon away. Four o'clock. That meant he had only an hour until his mom would start to freak out. Not that she would actually be worried about his well-being. No, she would just be upset that he wasn't going to be ready for the party by the time guests showed up.

"I guess you better get going, huh?" he said aloud to himself in a sullen tone, flicking his eyes between his watch and the glass doors to the court-yard. From what he could tell, the school was empty—no movement inside, not even a janitor. He looked down at his watch again, eyeing the minute hand as it moved slowly toward the twelve. The frame of the watch was busted. He had dropped it as he was taking it off for gym class. He rubbed his finger along the jagged piece of metal where the frame had split, wondering whether it were salvageable.

Pulling himself to his feet, James shouldered his backpack, resolved that it did him no good to stick around here any longer. At this point, he would be lucky if he weren't locked up in the school.

He headed inside and turned to make his way toward the lobby.

Then he remembered.

My chemistry textbook! He had left it in his locker.

"Shoot," he huffed. *I'm not gonna give Mr. Birken the satisfaction of failing me, that pompous piece of garbage.* Chemistry sucked, but the idea of losing to Mr. Birken sucked even more.

He headed back down the hall the other way. His locker was in a far back corridor, and there was a chance that if the custodians were already locking up certain wings, then he wouldn't be able to get to it.

As he made his way through the labyrinth of cold concrete walls and linoleum floors, he became aware of how eerily still the whole place was. He had never been in the school this late before. The overhead lights were off, silhouetting the shape of the lockers along the walls, and the squeak of his sneakers on the linoleum floor echoed all around him.

"Hello?" he called out, half-hoping that somebody might respond, that a friendly custodian might peek out from one of the classrooms and say, "Hey-o, I was closing up this place for the weekend, but if you're still here, I'll turn on the lights," or that an administrator might appear and say, "Oh, James, you're not supposed to be here this late, but if you have to go get your textbook, I suppose I can stand here and make sure nothing bad happens to you."

But none of that happened, and James's unease grew a little bit more the farther he went down the hall.

Then he smelled it. He paused, sniffing again. The smell of smoke. Something was burning.

He peeked into one of the nearby classrooms. Nobody in there, he observed, but the smell was stronger. He stepped inside, looking around for an electric socket that might have exploded or a candle that had been left unextinguished.

Nothing. He turned to go, but before he had taken more than two or three steps, there came muffled voices from what sounded like the back of the room—or else the next room over. He stopped, listening to the muted, monotonic intonation.

James sidled back out to the hallway to check what was happening in the next classroom over—but the classroom he had just come from was the last one at the end of the hall. The voices must have been coming from a crawlspace or something behind the wall. Or else he had imagined them.

He returned to the classroom, edging through the shadows toward the back corner. As he neared the corner, the muffled voices grew more distinct. He hadn't imagined them. They were coming from behind the wall.

Pressing his ear up against the plaster, he listened for a moment. He could hear distinct voices, but what they were saying, he couldn't make out.

There was a man bellowing, and some harsh, rasping voices that he couldn't determine to be male or female, adult or child, whatever they were.

James stepped back, taking in a long look at the wall from end to end. No door that might lead to another room or a closet. Only a bulletin board, a desk, and a tall nine-shelf bookcase.

It was with apprehension that James approached the bookcase, looking it up and down as if he were trying to gauge its weight in his head. He gripped the side of it and braced his feet against the floor, giving the shelf a tug.

Just as he thought: The bookcase pulled away to reveal what might have once been a closet. The mold-streaked door looked as if it had been forgotten by any staff member for a long time.

James gave the door handle a little wiggle and could tell it was unlocked. His stomach fluttering with nerves, he eased the door open and peered inside. It was one of the storage crawlspaces. He had helped a teacher move some books into a similar one in the English department the week prior.

But this one here in the science wing looked as if it had been forgotten. Or deliberately hidden.

Light came from around a bend in the corridor up ahead, and as did the voices, though still muffled. *If this one is like the English storage space, there will be a little room down at the end.* There was definitely somebody in there, but James wasn't sure that he was going to like what he found.

Holding his breath, he crept along the hall, taking soft steps to be sure he didn't make any noise. As he came to the end of the corridor, he pressed himself up against the wall and peered around the corner.

Whatever he had expected, it definitely wasn't the scene before him. Never in his wildest dreams could he have expected this.

Mr. Birken stood over a roaring fire built atop a concrete slab, his arms spread wide. He no longer wore his school clothes—the gray trousers, the finely pressed white shirt, the Windsor-knotted tie—and was instead dressed in long black robes and a blood-red cape. He stood tall over the flickering flames, his broad belly thrust forward and his face tilted upward, whispering something in a language James couldn't recognize.

"Oh," James heard himself gasp.

But if the gasp were audible, Mr. Birken didn't hear it. He was too busy conjuring something—probably a malevolent something, judging from the shapes that were forming in the black smoke above the fire. Red sparks flashed here and there, and a trio of serpentine figures took form. Three snakelike creatures with leathery wings began to circle the fire.

They hissed together in a chorus. "Why have you sssssummoned ussss here, Abaddon?"

James's heart hammered. He swallowed hard, listening intently to how Mr. Birken might respond.

"Welcome, my creatures of darkness."

"What do you want from usssss? Why do you conjure?"

The creatures swooped high and low, circling the fire, hissing, flipping their tails.

"To boast, of course," Mr. Birken said. "Why else? Tell me—am I not the most wicked and evil of all the creatures of darkness."

The creatures hissed wildly and their eyes lit up with red sparks again. "You're not one of ussss," they cried. "You are not one of ussss!"

"You lie!" Mr. Birken shouted.

"We do not. Your power issss weak. Your cursssse issss breaking." At this, the demons began to cackle maniacally. The sound of it sent a chill down James's spine. Should he make a break for it, get out of there before he was caught? Terror and morbid curiosity had him paralyzed.

Mr. Birken sneered. "What do you mean by this, to say that my curse is breaking?"

"It has already begun," the demons hissed. "On his next birthday, your nephew shall turn sixteen."

"No!" Mr. Birken shouted. "It cannot be!"

"You cannot sssstop it. You cannot sssstop it." The demons hissed and cackled as they swept through the air, circling Mr. Birken tauntingly.

"You have a vissssitor, Abaddon," they hissed.

A *visitor*? James realized they meant him, but it was too late. Mr. Birken glanced in his direction, and their eyes made contact for a brief instant. Moved by sheer terror, James turned and ran, bolting toward the outside world as quickly as he could.

Mr. Birken roared angrily. Intense heat erupted on James's back, and he was thrown forward against the wall, taking a face full of decaying plaster as he toppled to the ground. He felt claws grasping at his arms, the ground scraping across his face—he was being dragged back into the storage room.

Mr. Birken loomed over him, looking down with a strange expression of mixed fury and sick delight. James pushed himself up and scooted backward. Shadows moved in the darkness behind his teacher—two feral teenagers crawling around on the floor like animals. They must have been what had dragged him back into the storage space.

"Well, well, well," Mr. Birken said. "A surprise guest. James Shannassy."

James's heart hammered in his chest so hard he thought he was going to puke. He held his breath, trying to keep down the bile burning at his throat.

Mr. Birken bellowed a deep laugh, tossing his head back with a sick, wide smile on his face. "I think we can find a use for you, Master Shannassy."

He swiped his arm through the air, summoning two thick black cords that curled around James, digging into his skin and tying him tightly. James gave a wretched little choking sound as the ropes caught tight around his diaphragm.

"That's better," Mr. Birken said. "We don't want you leaving too soon, now, do we?"

James stared around the room, taking in the candles, skulls, and other artifacts and ornaments of sorcery, all of them menacing in the low light of the little room. In the murky shadows behind Mr. Birken, the two feral children had slunk back to crates where they crouched like wolves, chewing on bones and glaring at James with flashes of red fire in their eyes. They looked familiar, as if he might have seen them around school before, but their ragged appearance and animal-like demeanor had rendered them unrecognizable.

Mr. Birken stepped toward James, crouching down. "What brings you in here, Master Shannassy?"

James choked back some of the vomit in his mouth. His whole body was shaking so badly he thought he might pass out. "I...I..."

Mr. Birken sneered, standing again. "Afraid, are you? You needn't be."

James trembled, wrenching at the ropes that bound his hands. He looked up into Mr. Birken's dark eyes. The only way he was going to get out of this was by keeping a clear head and acting fast. For now, he had to keep Mr. Birken talking, to distract him if he could.

"S-so...what are you, some kind of evil wizard or something?" It wasn't brilliant, and James sure as hell wished he had sounded braver when he said it, but he had read enough fantasy and sci-fi to know that the best way to outsmart a merciless villain was to get him on a bragging rant. If nothing else, it might buy him some time.

Mr. Birken let out another deep laugh. He turned and circled the fire.

James kept his eyes on Mr. Birken, fiddling with the ropes as best he could behind his back. If he were subtle enough, he might be able to use the jagged edge of his broken watch to saw through the binds without Mr. Birken's realizing what he was doing.

After a few tense seconds, Mr. Birken spoke. "I think I'll be needing your assistance, Master Shannassy." He drew out each word in a cold, sinister tone.

James noticed movement along the floor, and his blood ran cold. It was a long, hideous python weaving its way toward Mr. Birken. The large man stooped down to greet the serpent as if it were a puppy, cooing softly, "Yes, we will, precious, won't we? We'll be needing Master James's help."

James had to keep talking. "What's this all about? What were those monsters you were talking to?"

Mr. Birken stood, provoked by the question, his eyes flashing with fire. "My nephew has eluded me for far too long!" he shouted. "My curse will be broken, and my eminence among the creatures of darkness will be lost forever!" He raised his arms and shook his fists wildly, making the fire rage up in a sudden burst of green light and black smoke. The feral children behind him whined, frightened.

Mr. Birken approached James and crouched down near his face again. "And you are going to help me hunt him down." Mr. Birken's breath was hot and stinking against James's face, and a sheen of oily sweat gleamed on the big man's puffy cheeks.

James whimpered, closed his eyes, and tried to find words. Mr. Birken so close to him, the crackle of the fire, the growling of the ferals, the malevolent presence of the evil artifacts around them—it was all too much. "What if I don't want to?" he protested.

Mr. Birken stood, stepping back to the fire. "Oh, I don't think that will be a problem." He waved one of his hands over the flames and whispered again in the foreign language James again didn't recognize.

It was obvious what was coming next. Mr. Birken had prepared some spell to manipulate him, to force James to do his bidding.

"That's why you're a teacher, isn't it?!" James looked at the two pathetic kids crouched in the shadows. "And they're...they're..."

"They're just here for a little after-school study session, just like the one I encouraged you to come to, Master Shannassy." Mr. Birken gave James a sick little grin, a thin-lipped slice of malevolence that spread across his face, and he gazed greedily at him with black, soulless eyes. "I told you that you were failing, but I never expected you to drop by in quite this fashion."

Dizziness set in on James again, stronger this time. If only the cord behind his back would part a little more easily, or if only the jagged metal would have been a bit more efficient! He couldn't delay Mr. Birken much longer, he could tell.

Mr. Birken continued. "These two behind you, they're not the academic type, of course. Slackers, you might say. But they know they can come to me as a source of something they might need."

"Drugs?"

"Ha! You think a great wizard controls his minions by use of opioids and narcotics? No, my potions are a bit stronger, though every bit as addictive. When it wears off, they'll remember nothing—except to keep coming to me for it."

Mr. Birken crossed to a table in the corner where Bunsen burners bubbled and smoked mysterious substances in beakers. "And a chemistry teacher at a public school in an affluent area always has easy access to the best equipment," he said as he lifted one of the bottles and held it to the firelight. "Combined with teenagers with a bit too much spare time and too little supervision after school—why, it's every evil overlord's dream, isn't it?" He laughed.

This is it, James thought. Mr. Birken was going to possess him, or maybe worse—after all, James knew too much now. What was to stop Mr. Birken from doing away with him entirely?

Mr. Birken lumbered around the fire, his red cape dragging behind him across the filthy floor. "Well, now, Master Shannassy," he said, holding out the frothing potion. "Open up your mouth."

James sawed furiously at the rope behind his back. It was slackening. *Almost there.*

Mr. Birken stooped down in front of him, reaching forward to grab James's face and force his mouth open. James jerked his head away, resisting, giving the rope two or three more tugs. By some good grace, the ropes gave way at that very momen. James twisted his hands free, lifted his leg, and delivered a swift kick to Mr. Birken's large belly.

With a deep bellow of surprise, Mr. Birken stumbled backward, his feet twisted in the length of his cape. For a moment, he teetered back and forth, trying to recapture his balance. Then he went down hard, falling backward into the roaring fire.

James sprang to his feet and took off down the passageway. Behind him, Mr. Birken screamed in pain and fury, but James wasn't stopping to look back. Trembling with terror, he bounded back to the empty classroom, then raced back through the school and out the doors into the open afternoon air. He fled the property, not stopping to catch his breath or his bearings until he found refuge in the abandoned greenhouse.

By the time he'd finished recounting it all to Archit, the bird was restless with excitement. "This can mean only one thing," Archit said, getting to his feet.

"*What* can mean only one thing?" James asked.

Archit hesitated for a second. "Look, James," he said, "I need you to remember carefully. 'On his next birthday, he'll turn sixteen.' You're sure that's what his oracle said?"

"Absolutely."

"You might have been confused. You were in a lot of danger, and you were really scared."

"I know what I heard," James insisted. "Trust me, every second of my time in that storage closet is branded on my brain. I'm scarred for life."

Archit pressed his wings against his head, trying to think. "Oh, what does this mean?"

"What does *what* mean?" James asked.

"Look, it's complicated," Archit said. "And truthfully, the less you know, the better."

James scoffed. "Well, I'm involved now. Don't I deserve an explanation?"

"Yes, of course you do. But I need to get you home safely first."

"Get me home?" It wasn't exactly the priority that James was expecting. Five minutes ago, he had wanted nothing more than to be home, safe, and out of danger, but since talking to Archit...

"Yes, get you home," Archit said. "Do you think you can stay out of trouble there?"

"And what? Just hope all this goes back to normal? Do you really expect your uncle to forget that I know all of this?"

Archit shook his head as he moved toward the door to the greenhouse. "No, but you'd be in a lot more danger with me." He turned back, gesturing with his wing for James to follow. "Come on, there's no use talking about this in here. We need to act quickly." He made for the door. "Who knows what my uncle might be up to while we're sitting here shooting the breeze..."

"Oh, that's comforting," James said.

Archit swung the door open and scurried across the lawn to hide behind one of the bushes. James paused for a moment in the doorway and then, still somewhat unsure, followed the bird. It was cool outside the greenhouse, and the shadows of the trees were getting longer. It would be only another hour or so until it was dark.

"So, what exactly is your plan?" James asked as he knelt next to Archit.

Archit peered out between the leaves of the bushes, looking up and down the street. James couldn't deny that the bird's lack of explanation was beginning to irritate him a little.

"Hold on," Archit said, reaching into the pocket of his vest. "I have just what we need in here."

"What do we need?"

Archit drew out a small pouch. "Here 'tis."

James stared. Something inside the bag was glowing. The silk exterior shifted from pink to blue and back again.

"Whoa," James said. "What is that?"

"Fairy dust, of course."

James rolled his eyes. "Oh, of course. Why didn't I think of that?"

"Don't get sarcastic," Archit said. "I thought you were getting used to weird things happening."

James couldn't argue with that. He looked down at the bag again. "Where'd you get it?" he ventured.

"I stumbled upon a fairy council years ago," Archit said. "It was a reward for a good deed I did them."

James couldn't tell whether that was true or not—but if not, then Archit must have had some good reason for not making full disclosure.

"Now," Archit continued, "there's not much left. Just enough for maybe two more spells, as long as they don't need to last long. And I'm going to need some to open up the doorway between the worlds."

"Huh?" James said. "*The doorway between the worlds?*" This afternoon had gone from horror story to fairytale to ancient myth pretty quickly.

"I can't open it up until tomorrow morning," Archit said. "It's a spell that needs to be performed at dawn. But we'll be able to use a bit of it for getting you home."

"You mean, like, teleportation?"

"Nothing so elaborate," Archit said. "But I think the fairies have established a precedent for this one at least. You're familiar with the story of the little cinder maid?"

"You mean Cinderella?" James said.

"Exactly," Archit said. "And look! There are a few pumpkins on the front stoop of that house over there." He turned and pointed at one of the houses across the street.

"How lucky we are that it's October and I need a coach to get home," James said, unable to resist sarcasm again.

"We're not doing a coach," Archit said. "That'd be too conspicuous."

"Oh, and you think stealing pumpkins in the middle of the afternoon isn't going to draw attention?" But James had to admit there wasn't a car in the driveway of the house Archit had indicated, and all the blinds in the windows were drawn.

"Stop hesitating," Archit said. "Just go."

James wasn't necessarily sure why he was doing as he was told, but he figured he had to trust Archit. He stood and eased his way out from behind the bush, looking all around for witnesses. Considering he was on the run from an evil wizard, he thought that getting caught stealing a pumpkin should have been the least of his concerns. Even so, an extraordinary adventure was one thing, and petty theft was another. He didn't want to be busted for something so commonplace with everything else going on.

He tried to look as casual as possible as he walked up the driveway to the house across the street, but he was pretty sure anyone who might have been watching would have instantly assumed him guilty of *something*, just based on how nervous and jittery he was.

As he paused at the bottom step leading up to the front stoop, he looked up at the house just to be sure nobody was watching him through the windows. No sign of anyone.

"What are you waiting for?" Archit hissed from the bushes across the street. "The apocalypse?"

James turned but didn't shout back. It would draw too much attention. Still, it was easy for Archit to be confident when Archit was hiding in a bush and James was the one who was about to steal something.

"What the worst that can happen?" he said to himself as he reached forward, grabbed the pumpkin, and spun back around toward Archit. Clutching the gourd to his chest as if someone might try to tackle him and take it back, James sprinted back across the street and ducked behind the bush with Archit. "Got it."

"Good," Archit said. "Glad to see it wasn't too great a challenge." His beak cracked into a smile, and he gave a little laugh. For the first time that afternoon, James wasn't stressed out or scared.

"All right," James said. "Let's see this magic in action."

"Stand back," Archit said, crouching over the pumpkin and pouring some of the dust onto the end of his wing. "Here goes nothing."

He shook his wing and James watched the glittering powder fall over the orange skin of the gourd.

Nothing happened. James blinked. Maybe the dust wasn't really magic, or maybe Archit had done something wrong. After all, it wasn't as if there were any reason to believe Archit even knew how to—

But before James could let his doubts get the better of him, the pumpkin began to glow and its skin began to pulse a little bit. James gasped, watching it grow before his very eyes, its shape changing slightly as it did, a glass windshield forming across its front and tires popping out from its bottom. A bright orange car took shape, and the last few flashes of fairy dust fell away to the ground as the transformation completed itself.

"Whoa!" James said.

"Not bad," Archit said. "But it's not going to last long. We probably have fifteen minutes at most."

James chuckled. "What, not until midnight?"

"I'm not that strong a magician," Archit said, as if he had missed the joke completely.

The two of them hesitated for a moment, neither making a move for the driver's side.

"Can't you drive?" James asked, but he already knew the answer.

"Nah, I'm not tall enough to reach the pedal," Archit said. "I thought you could."

"No, I don't have my license yet."

Archit grumbled and looked around at the yard. "What we need is a squirrel."

Before James could question how they would even get close enough to a squirrel to enchant it, Archit had started back toward one of the trees beside the greenhouse. "There's one!"

James followed, but Archit turned and held his wing up, signaling him to stay back. "Not too much movement," Archit said.

Archit dipped his wingtip into the pouch again and flung a puff of glitter into the air. The effect again came quickly. The squirrel, which had turned and begun to flee upon Archit's approach, shifted and morphed into the form of a stocky middle-aged man dressed in a gray suit.

"Well, not bad," Archit said.

The man, who seconds before had been a squirrel, looked around. His mannerisms were still rodent-like. "What's happened?"

"You're a chauffeur now," Archit said, as if this should have been easy to understand. "We need you to drive. Come on, and hurry. We have only fifteen minutes or so before you change back."

"Change back?" the chauffeur squeaked.

"That's right, you'll be a squirrel again soon," Archit said. "No need to worry."

James smiled awkwardly at the chauffeur, trying to be friendly. "Hi."

Archit pointed to the pumpkin car. "Come on, everyone," he said. "No dawdling. Let's get in."

James didn't have to be told twice. The last thing he wanted after the horror of the afternoon was to be stranded in the middle of town with a pumpkin, a squirrel, and a talking purple bird. There was no way he could explain *that* to anyone, let alone what he knew about Mr. Birken's being an evil wizard on top of all of it.

He opened the back passenger-side door and climbed inside. The yellow-orange pleather upholstery was cool and clammy, maybe because it had all been pumpkin guts only moments before. Archit went around to the other side and climbed in next to him.

"Do you know how to get to Fairview?" James asked the chauffeur. "The neighborhood?"

"Fairview?" the chauffeur repeated.

"Yeah," James said, wondering whether the squirrel knew the area well enough to identify different neighborhoods. James didn't know what to believe or expect any more. "Across town," he described. "Waterfront community. Lots of Cape Cod cottages."

"Ah, yes," the chauffeur said. "Right. So, then, here we go."

And they were off. James looked at his watch. It was quarter to five. If Archit's prediction about their fifteen-minute time constraint were correct, they had until five, at best. In any case, that was far too late for James to be getting home. He doubted his mother would notice he was missing. She would be too busy getting ready for the party—but Margot would be aware. She was probably already wondering where he was, because he didn't meet her at her car after school. She would have assumed he went downtown with some friends to get pizza or something earlier. By now, she would be irritated that he wasn't home and that she might be stuck covering for him.

James looked over at Archit, who was staring out the window in pensive silence.

"So...uh..." James hesitated. "Look, I know this is a touchy subject, and I'm sure you're tired of my asking about it..."

"No, that's all right," Archit said, still looking out the window. "You deserve to know." He turned back to James. "I have to go see somebody. Somebody wise and powerful, who I hope might be able to explain all of this."

"But I don't understand. What could be so significant about a sixteenth birthday?"

"Because by all possibility, I shouldn't *have* a sixteenth birthday."

James didn't even know how to respond to that. "What? How?"

"I'm a figment creature," Archit said. "Do you know what that means?"

"Like, a figment of the imagination?" James said.

"Exactly. Never born, never aging, never dying. You see, I don't even think I'm part of this world of reality."

James wondered whether that were supposed to make sense to him, because it definitely didn't. Even as an avid mythology buff—or so he liked to consider himself—he was having a little trouble wrapping his mind around this. "Oh."

Archit struggled to find the next words. "I say 'I think' because...well, I remember aging when I was younger. But that was a different time, a happier time, and when my uncle cursed me..." He sighed. "Look, I could explain all this, but it would take a while."

"Maybe I should come with you," James suggested.

"What?"

"I mean, I can't really just stick around here, can I?" It was only a matter of time before Mr. Birken came for James. He was better off going with Archit and seeing this through to the end. *Besides*, James thought, *we're in this together now.*

"I see what you're saying," Archit replied. "But it'll be dangerous."

"It can't be any more dangerous than what I encountered this afternoon," James said. Talking bravely made him a little less nervous. "And we're stronger sticking with each other, right?"

"Yes, I suppose we are," Archit said. "But you don't have to go for my sake. I've been dealing with this for hundreds of years now, so I'm not afraid to go on alone."

"No, I want to go," James said. What was he saying? What exactly was he agreeing to? It gave him a rush of excitement to think this was actually happening. "But we have to wait until late tonight," he added quickly. "If I don't put in an appearance at this party tonight, my parents will wonder where I am, and they'll come looking for me before we have a chance to get away."

"That's all right. We can't cross the border between worlds until dawn anyway."

There was that phrase again—the border between worlds. "Oh, man," James said. "Is this really happening?"

Archit laughed. "Yeah. But I hope you're this enthusiastic when the going gets tough."

"I'll try to be."

The car began to slow. James looked out the window, realizing that they had already reached his street. "This is my house coming up at the end of the block."

"Will you pull over at this last house up ahead?" Archit asked the chauffeur.

The car slowed as it approached the cedar-shingled house at the top of the hill. The place was so familiar and comforting, yet so detached from James all at the same time. It was a funny feeling that he couldn't quite understand—this might be last time he was going to be home for a long while, but he didn't mind at all. No, in a way, he was almost excited to be leaving it behind.

When the car stopped, the two of them climbed out of the backseat and stood momentarily on the street, looking up at the house before they headed up the hill.

This was it. James had been waiting his entire life for something like this. Fifteen years of being a pathetic little nobody in a small town where nothing ever happened, and now he was setting off on the adventure of a lifetime!

Am I ready for this?

If he weren't ready for it, did he really care? He was with Archit, and Archit knew what he was doing.

Sure, he had known the purple bird for all of a half-hour max, but he could already tell that Archit was brave, tough, streetsmart, and headstrong. Archit was an *adventurer*. And maybe James would prove himself to be one too.

Maybe Archit felt the same sense of relief and gratitude that James did. Maybe, just maybe, the bird was happy to have a companion who would help him brave whatever lay ahead.

CHAPTER 2
Explaining the Inexplicable

I think the best plan," James said to Archit as they walked around the house to the backyard, "is to get you upstairs to the rec room. Nobody'll go up there, so you'll be safe to hang out until it's time for us to leave."

"Sounds great," Archit said.

James paused as they approached a window, peeked inside to be sure nobody was there, then proceeded.

"Why are you being so cautious?" Archit asked. "I thought you lived here."

"I do. But we don't need to be running into my parents right now. It won't make this escapade any easier."

"Ah," Archit said.

"Besides, if they see you, they'll freak out."

"Well, that's the strange thing about being imaginary: It's only sometimes that people actually see you."

James paused. "Huh? But I saw you."

"Yes," Archit said. "But you looked right at me. We directly confronted each other in the greenhouse, remember? Besides, you had already encountered my uncle, so your resistance to the supernatural was worn down, you might say."

That was a weak argument as far as James was concerned. "So you're telling me my parents wouldn't be able to see you?" James asked.

"Hard to say," Archit shrugged. "I mean, better safe than sorry. I wouldn't call attention to myself, and I certainly wouldn't go up to them and introduce myself. But it's weird. I don't think people notice me unless they're forced to."

"Oh."

"I couldn't have avoided human society for hundreds of years if it were so easy to see me," Archit said.

Not very convincing. Still, James turned the corner of the house with slightly less hesitancy and went into the backyard.

He pointed up at the dormer leading to the converted attic space they used as a rec room. "There," he said to Archit.

"What?"

"That window. That's the rec room up there." He pointed from the window to the branch of a nearby tree that grew dangerously close to the roof. "Dangerously close" was the phrase his mom used when she described it, whenever she mentioned that they needed to have it cut down. James was grateful she hadn't yet gotten around to doing so. "You can climb that tree up onto the roof and climb in the window."

"Or I could fly up."

James paused. "You can fly?"

"Of course." Archit spread his wings as if to demonstrate.

"Duh," James laughed. "Of course you can! I knew that."

This made things simpler. James could go inside by himself, head up to the rec room, open the window, and let Archit in that way. No problem at all! "Great," he said aloud.

The sound of a screen door opening around the side of the house interrupted his laughter, and his sister's voice cut through the air. "James!"

"Hide," James hissed. Even if Archit were confident that people couldn't see him, it didn't hurt to be cautious.

But Archit was one step ahead of him. James whirled around just in time to catch a glimpse of Archit disappearing behind a bush of azaleas.

James turned back just as Margot appeared around the side of the house, walking across the lawn, her wavy brown hair streaming behind her as she made a confident stride toward him. She might have been mainstream, but Margot always came off as cool and collected. James couldn't help envying her for it.

"There you are," she said. "I was wondering when you'd get home."

James tried to act natural. "Hiya, Margot," he said. He couldn't have sounded more idiotic if he had tried. "What's up?"

"I could be asking you the same thing," she said, pushing up her sleeve to look pointedly at her watch. "It's past five o'clock. You need to get inside and get ready for the party. Or did you forget?"

James surveyed her casual ensemble—distressed jeans and a long-sleeved T-shirt. "You're not ready either," he said.

"Yeah, but I'm gonna have to do my hair and makeup before I change clothes," she said. "I figure I could do you a favor and let you get in and out of the bathroom first. Come on."

Awkward silence. James hesitated, not wanting to leave Archit alone outside. If they split up, there was no telling what trouble Archit might get into, or how they were ever going to reconnect once James was inside the house. "You go on. I'll be right behind you."

Sure, he was being a little paranoid. Maybe Margot would just suspect he had been smoking and that's why he was acting so weird. *Oh, God,* he thought, *I never thought I'd ever wish for this, but please let her think that I've been smoking.*

Margot gave him a strange look. "What were you doing out here?"

"Nothing."

"And who were you talking to?"

"Whom," James corrected her. "Nobody. Come on, let's head into the house..."

But Margot was already brushing past him and walking toward the azaleas where Archit had hidden.

"Margot," James said, trying to distract her.

"I thought I saw..."

It was too late. Margot pulled back one of the branches and came face to face with Archit, just as James had done back in the greenhouse.

"Auuugghh!" she screamed

James's stomach sank as Margot's scream rose. It rivaled Fay Wray's when she had first set eyes on King Kong. So much for being inconspicuous!

"Margot!" he shouted.

His sister stumbled backward, tripping over a lawn ornament behind her and landing hard on the grass.

James didn't waste a second. "Come on!" he shouted to Archit, bolting toward a nearby tree and shimmying upward. Archit spread his wings and swooped after him.

James pulled himself from branch to branch, making his way toward the outspread bough that reached "dangerously close" to the rooftop. He looked down at Margot, whose eyes bulged with dumbfounded wonder. "James, what are you doing?!" she called.

He looked back to the rooftop and the dormer leading into the rec room. There was nothing to be gained by dawdling—he took a deep breath and pushed himself off the branch. For a moment, he flew through the air, his heart hammering. Then he slammed against the roof. He flailed for a moment to catch his balance on the grainy shingles, then scrambled forward to the dormer. His fingers fumbled with the edge of the window screen as he tried to wriggle it free.

Suddenly, he heard the kitchen door opening from around the side of the house, followed by footsteps on the patio.

"Come on!" James hissed at Archit.

Tugging the screen free, James tossed it over his shoulder and shoved the window open. A wave of relief went through him as he heaved himself into the room, Archit close behind him. It took only a second for James to gain his bearings on the rec room floor before he pulled himself upward and peered out the window just in time to see his mother and Zoe, her hired cleaning lady, come running into sight.

"What's going on?" Mrs. Shannassy asked, going to Margot, who was still distraught and looking up at James with wide-eyed bafflement.

"Oh, Mom," James shouted. "Sorry!"

Mrs. Shannassy looked up at him. "James, what in the world…"

"My bad, Mom!" He chuckled, trying to feign nonchalance as best he could when he was out of breath. "I was trying to get this window open and accidently knocked the screen out. Took Margot by surprise and nearly scared her to death, I think." Then he quickly added, "Sorry, Margot."

Zoe went and put a consoling arm around Margot. "Poor thing."

Mrs. Shannassy looked between her children, first up at James and then over at Margot. "You two *are* going to behave yourselves tonight, right?"

Margot glared up at James savagely, and he tried his best to make his laugh casual. "Yeah, of course we are," he said.

"All right then," Mrs. Shannassy said. Something in her tone suggested it really wasn't all right but she would worry about that when she wasn't worried about receiving guests in less than an hour. "You'll help me put the screen back in tomorrow, won't you, baby doll?"

"Sure," James said. "Sorry about that."

He pulled his head back inside. As he pushed the window closed, he could hear his mother consoling Margot. "Are you all right, sweet pea? I know he's an irritant, but..."

The window clicked shut, cutting off the sound of her voice. James watched as Margot shot one last dirty look at him, pulled away from Mrs. Shannassy, and stormed toward the house. Mrs. Shannassy and Zoe exchanged tired looks and a few words.

James turned to Archit, who had taken care to stand a safe distance away from the window and stay out of sight.

James sighed. "Man, that was a close one."

"I'll say. For a sheltered resident of the suburbs, you do find yourself in plenty of trouble. First my uncle and then this?"

James shrugged. "It's not normally like this. It's usually pretty quiet."

Footsteps sounded on the stairs outside the rec room door—angry footsteps. James's eyes went wide. "That's Margot."

But Archit was already diving behind one of the sofas to hide, and just in the nick of time too.

The door swung open and there stood Margot, fuming in such a way that James was surprised steam wasn't coming out her nostrils and ears. He threw his hands up defensively. "Margot, I know what you're probably thinking..."

"Oh, really? Then what am I thinking, James?"

27

James stammered. "You didn't tell Mom, did you?"

"Are you kidding me? No, she's swamped getting ready for this party tonight. She doesn't have time to have me committed."

James forced a laugh. "Committed. That's funny."

Margot huffed. "James, what was that thing? That purple bird that was in the bushes?" She paused, her expression changing. "Oh my gosh! It's in here, isn't it? It came in the window with you!"

This was going nowhere good, James could tell. He was grateful that before he could respond, Archit stepped out from behind the sofa. "Hello," he said in a timid voice. In the entire hour that James and Archit had known each other, James had never seen Archit look or act timid.

Margot whimpered. "Cripes, it can talk?"

Archit and James looked at each other, unsure of how to respond to that. Archit sighed. "Look, I'm sorry we startled you, Margot..."

"And it knows my name. I must be losing my mind. I must be hallucinating, and I don't even remember eating anything funny!" Margot sank down on the sofa.

"Margot," James said, trying to bring her back to reality. "Will you calm down for a second? I'm not going to sit here and try to explain the inexplicable if you're going to refuse to believe any of it."

She looked up at him. "What?!"

He worked up the best defensive tone he could muster against his big sister. "Are you going to listen to me?"

"I guess if I want an explanation for all this, I have to, don't I?"

"She's quite savvy, isn't she?" Archit observed to James.

"I don't think that's going to help, Archit," he replied.

Margot looked at Archit uneasily, though not as fearfully as she had moments before. "Jimmy, what is it?"

James hesitated. "Is it all right for me to tell her?" he asked Archit.

"No harm now, I suppose."

James sat down on the sofa next to Margot. "He's a figment, like of the imagination. I met him after school today."

"Huh?"

"You know Mr. Birken? The science teacher?"

"Yeah, I had him for physics last year."

"Well, I caught him practicing black magic in one of the storage rooms after school today."

After an awkward pause, Margot rolled her eyes. "Jimmy..."

"No, Margot, you have to believe me. Archit is his nephew, and Mr. Birken's on the hunt for him. Now he's after me too because I know about all this. So Archit and I are gonna have to leave tonight. We're going to find somebody who might be able to help him."

"You're *running away* tonight?" Margot asked, voice rising again.

"I know it sounds crazy, but you have to cover for me," James said.

Archit had to chime in at some point. "Margot, I know that this is a lot to take in," the bird said, "but James is in danger as much as I am. I need his help if I'm going to escape my uncle."

Margot didn't know what to say. She looked from James to Archit and back to James again. James hadn't even known it was possible for Margot to be speechless.

"Look," James said, seizing the chance to cut the conversation short. "I think it's for the best if we're ready for the party on time, so I'm gonna go shower and get dressed. Archit and I already agreed that I'm going to put in an appearance tonight so that nobody worries about where I am. Archit, will you be all right for a little bit while I go downstairs?"

"Yeah."

Margot wasn't so keen. "James..."

"We can talk about this later, Margot, if you really want to argue about it," he said. "But mark my words—I'm going."

CHAPTER 3
Escape from the Cocktail Party

For the past hour, Margot had been saying the same the same thing over and over again. "James, are you crazy? You can't go."

"Margot, for the last time, I'm going."

He turned back to the mirror and straightened his tie. The way Margot was pacing back and forth across the rec room was stressing him out, and he needed something to do to occupy himself. He had checked himself in the mirror and straightened his tie ten times in the last hour while the two of them bantered back and forth.

After cutting the conversation short the first time, he had gone downstairs to shower and douse himself in too much cologne, then done his best to run a comb through his shaggy brown hair. He had dressed in a gray suit with a white button-down shirt, adding an emerald-green power tie he had bought secondhand for a dollar the week before, then went back upstairs to relax in the rec room.

Or *try* to relax, at least. Margot had come up about a half-hour after him, dressed in a sophisticated crimson cocktail dress and pearls, her hair done up and bobby-pinned to perfection. Since then, it had just been one long back-and-forth as she tried to talk him out of leaving. For the first few minutes, James worried that she might actually go and tell their parents, but it was clear she had no such intentions. Protective though she might have been of him, she did have standards, and she wasn't about to go off and snitch to any adults, let alone tell anyone about Archit.

Frustrated by James's insistence, Margot huffed. "Are you seriously going to run off to *wherever* just because of some Martian bird?"

"Hey!" Archit looked up from the sofa, where he sat engaged in a copy of *Paradise Lost* that he'd borrowed from James's personal library.

"She didn't mean any offense," James said.

"Still. I'm not from Mars. I'm not even from outer space. I'm from Nalgordia, and that's another world entirely."

It was the first time James had heard it, but the name made his nerves prickle with excitement. "Nalgordia? Is that where we're going?"

"See," Margot exclaimed, "you don't even know where you're going with this thing. Nalgordia? Another world? James, I don't know what's going on here, but this is obviously some sort of joke."

"A joke?" James said, incredulous. "What do you mean, a joke?"

"I don't know, but I can't just let you go off on some inane excursion..."

James had always known Margot to be opinionated, but this was too much. "What are you going to do? Tell Mom?" Once he said it, he wished he hadn't put the idea in her head. "Please don't tell anyone, Margot. Just let me handle this. I can take care of myself."

Margot stared at him, frustrated. "Well, if there's no way I can stop you, I can at least go with you."

"*What?*" James and Archit said simultaneously.

Margot shook her head. "I can't just let you go running off by yourself, with no way of knowing what you're getting into or if you'll be safe. And if I can't stop you, I gotta go with you at least, y'know, to make sure you don't get into too much trouble." She crossed to the bureau and pulled out a bottle of wine she'd stolen from the caterers and stashed up there earlier. She and James were allowed one glass, and one glass only, on special occasions, but there was nobody to stop them if they snuck a bottle upstairs to enjoy away from the adults.

James turned to Archit. "Is that all right? If she comes with us?"

"Fine by me, as long as it ends this conversation; you two have been talking in circles for the last hour." Archit got up from the sofa and went to Margot, who was uncorking the wine and pouring herself a glass. "Pour me a glass, won't you?"

James wasn't so keen yet. "You said it was going to be dangerous though."

Margot lifted her glass to her lips and handed the bottle to Archit. "Ha! And you think you're tougher than me?" she said to James.

"Than *I*."

"Huh?"

"Tougher than I," James repeated.

Margot rolled her eyes, taking a long sip of her wine. "Oh, for Pete's sake, grammar cop." She sat down on the sofa.

James sighed. "Now the only question is...what are we going to tell Liz?"

Archit looked up from the glass of wine he'd poured himself. "Who?"

"Our cousin," James said. "She's going to be here tonight. She'll be wondering where we are if we both go sneaking off halfway through the party." James had been counting on slipping off by himself with Archit and leaving it to Margot to cover for him.

"What're you going to tell her?" Archit said.

"Beats me," Margot said. "This is you two's crackpot scheme."

"You know," James said, "if you can't be helpful—"

As if on cue, the sound of high heels on the stairs below interrupted his retort.

"That's probably Liz now," James said. He looked at Archit, realizing that they might be risking a reaction similar to Margot's. "Archit, hide. The closet."

Archit scurried toward the closet and ducked inside just as the door to the stairs creaked open and the face of a pretty blond girl peeked inside. "Hey, guys."

James smiled. He couldn't help it. No matter how stressed or upset he was, he couldn't not be happy to see her. "Hey, Liz!"

"Hey," Margot echoed.

"Your mom said you two were up here," she said as she came in. "She sent me up to tell you to come downstairs and socialize."

Mrs. Shannassy had always described Liz as the perfect child, lamenting the differences in their children when talking to her sister about how easy it must have been to be the mother of a girl who was polite, smart, accomplished, sweet, and pretty. As far as any adult was concerned, Liz was everything a teenager was supposed to be. James probably would have resented her for it if he didn't love her so much.

"Your ears must've been burning," he said as she came into the room. "We were just talking about you."

Margot took a sip of wine. "Just wondering how we were going to tell you about some errant B.S."

"Margot, can you not?" James said.

Margot shrugged, looking into her wine glass as if assessing the burgundy color with great interest.

Liz looked at the two of them, concerned. "Is something wrong? You both seem really uncomfortable."

James didn't know what to say. "Uh..."

Margot laughed. "I'm gonna let James handle this one. Do you want a glass of wine?"

"Sure. Do the adults know you're drinking up here?"

Ignoring the question, Margot stood up from the sofa and crossed to the bureau where the bottle was. "You'll probably need it."

"You need to slow down, Margot," James said. "You're already halfway done with that glass. If you're going to come, then I'm going to need you to drive."

"Going to come?" Liz said. "Where are you two going?"

James dreaded this part of the conversation. "Liz, I have to leave tonight. I, uh—oh, how do I even begin to explain this?"

"Don't look at me," Margot murmured into her wine glass.

"Shut up."

Liz looked from James to Margot. "Explain what?"

There was nothing else to do but be honest with Liz. Besides, James had always been able to trust her with everything else. "I have to leave tonight for an adventure," James said. "With my friend Archit. He's..."

Before James could say another word, the closet door creaked open and Archit peered forth from inside, his pearly eyes shining out against the shadows.

Liz took a step back, surprised. "Oh."

"His name's Archit, Liz," James rushed to explain. "I met him earlier this afternoon."

Archit took a few steps out from the closet, coming into the light so Liz could see him and making a low bow.

Liz smiled, belying any discomfort she might have felt. "Hi, Archit."

"Pleased to meet you, Liz," Archit replied.

Liz didn't seem frightened in the least, so James continued, throwing caution to the wind. "Archit's in trouble," he said. "Well, he hasn't explained it all to me yet, but…"

Archit took it from there. "James overheard something very crucial this afternoon." He paused. "We're off to see someone who might be able to explain it."

Then it was Margot's turn to interrupt. "And I'm going with them to make sure James doesn't get into any trouble."

Liz's face lit up. "Can I come too?"

"Huh?" James hadn't expected that.

"Well, I don't want to miss out on all the fun. You're not going to leave me here, are you?"

James couldn't think of how to protest. "We might be gone a few days."

"Good. Then it sounds like a real adventure."

Archit lifted his wings in protest, trying to slow the conversation before it got out of hand. "You girls should understand that this isn't some fun little road trip. It might be dangerous."

"That's fine," Liz said. "I'm tougher than I look."

James caught Margot's eye, noticing that she wasn't as enthusiastic. "I was telling Archit," he ventured, "that I think we should put in a short appearance downstairs and then duck out."

Archit nodded. "We can open the portal between this world and Nalgordia at dawn, and then we're on our way."

Liz looked from James to Archit. "Nalgordia?" she said.

"Doesn't it sound excellent?" James said.

"One of the last remaining worlds of magic," Archit explained.

"Magic?" Liz said. "James, what have you gotten us into?"

James wasn't sure how to approach this part of the conversation. "That's the other thing that I haven't gone into yet. My science teacher..."

He paused.

Liz looked concerned, and James always hated it when he upset Liz. "What is it?" she asked.

Margot rolled her eyes. "He thinks his chemistry teacher is an evil wizard."

Something clicked in James's head. "Wait! Archit, I just thought of something! You don't think your uncle would show up here tonight and try to stop us before we get away, do you?"

Archit's expression turned nervous. "He knows where you live?"

"Well, no. But I'm sure he could figure it out somehow if he really wanted to," James said. "I mean, the school has our address on file."

"No way! We're in public school," Margot said. "Our personal information is kept under lock and key."

"Not if you're a deranged wizard intent on obtaining it," James said.

"A what intent on whatting it?" Margot replied.

"He could find a way, I'm sure," James said.

"No, you're absolutely right, he could," Archit said. "In fact, I'm surprised he hasn't already. I think the sooner we get out of here, the better."

"And miss the party?" Margot said.

"Margot, we might miss our chance to get out of here altogether if we stay too long," James said. He turned to Archit. "We can tell the adults we're going for a walk. You can get out through the window and meet us out there, and..."

"No," Archit said, "it's too risky." He looked from James to Margot to Liz and back to James as he spoke. "If my uncle comes here for you, nobody can know you're gone. We need to keep this a secret as long as we can, if we can." His eyes moved to the means by which he and James had entered the room earlier that afternoon. "We'll all go out the window."

"What?" Margot said. "We're on the third floor!"

"She's right," James said. "Climbing that tree earlier was way too risky."

"And stupid," Margot added.

James went to the bureau. "This is where Mom keeps all the spare linens," he said, opening up one of the drawers. "Bedsheets and blankets. We can tie them together and make a rope ladder."

"Brilliant," Archit said.

"Are you sure it's safe?" Liz asked.

"This is a broken neck waiting to happen," Margot said.

James ignored Margot's protest and dumped an armful of sheets onto the floor. "Save your breath and help me with these." He began to knot two of them together.

"Now, be sure to tie it to something sturdy and heavy," Archit said.

Margot went to the bureau and put the wine away in the cabinet. "I have my keys," she said, pulling them out from a drawer. "We can take the car."

"Huh?!" James and Archit both looked at her, wide eyed.

"I had a hunch I'd never be able to talk you out of this, so I planned ahead."

James looked at Archit. "I guess she's serious about coming with us."

"My purse is in the car already," Margot said, "with my debit card and cellphone, in case we need them."

James laughed. He went behind the sofa and pulled out a small gym duffel he had stashed there after he got dressed. "I packed some supplies as well."

"Good," Archit said. "Now, before we head out of here—"

Liz's eyes suddenly went wide. "Shh!"

Footsteps on the stairs below. Voices.

"It's Mom!" James said.

He dashed forward and pushed the button lock on the handle of the door. "Quick," he hissed to the others. "The window!"

The four of them exchanged nervous glances, scared to speak lest they give themselves away. Their plans to escape were about to be thwarted and there was no way of stopping it. All they could do was charge ahead. There was no turning back now.

"My sweater," Margot whispered, gesturing toward the chair across the room. Liz grabbed the white cardigan draped over the back and handed it to Margot.

"Your heels," James said, pointing at the girls' feet to indicate the loud noise they would undoubtedly make on the hardwood floor if they tried to walk. They got his drift and reached down to slip off their heels.

"Come on," Archit whispered, waving them all toward the window.

The door rattled in the jamb. "That's funny," came Mrs. Shannassy's voice. "The door is locked."

Then the sound of their aunt's voice. "I thought you said the kids were up here."

"I thought they were," Mrs. Shannassy said. "Kids?!"

Archit wordlessly motioned toward the window.

"They might've locked it by accident," their aunt's voice came.

"Oh, you know how kids are," Mrs. Shannassy said.

"Do you have a key?"

"It's up here."

They could hear a scraping sound above the door, suggesting that Mrs. Shannassy was fumbling along the top of the jamb to find the key.

Margot reached for the bedsheet ladder, but James stopped her. "No," he whispered as quietly as he could. "I'll go first to be sure it's safe. If anyone's breaking a neck here, it's going to be me."

Margot gritted her teeth but didn't argue. There wasn't time. She nodded, urging her brother along.

James straddled the sill and ducked through the window, scurrying out onto the slope of the roof and toward the edge. The ground awaited twenty or thirty yards below. This was probably the third or fourth crazy, adventurous thing he'd done so far that day—far more than he normally would have on any other day. It probably wasn't going to be the last, not for several days to come.

"Careful." Margot's voice came from behind him. He looked over his shoulder as she and Liz came creeping across the roof toward him. Archit hovered in the air just outside the window, his eyes darting from inside the room to his companions and back again in a frenzied way that stressed James out.

"They're trying to unlock the door," Archit said.

James nodded. "Well, here goes nothing."

He tossed the bundle of tied-together linens over the edge of the roof and watched as they unfurled. The end dangled just a few feet above the ground.

James kicked his legs over the edge of the roof, gripped the bedsheets, and lowered himself down with his legs braced against the side of the house. He'd been on the climbing wall at summer camp a few years ago, but this was much more intense.

"Be careful," Margot whispered.

James cast her a sardonic look. "Thanks, I was planning on being as careless as possible while climbing down a bedsheet from a third-floor window."

Liz looked back through the dormer window into the house. "Guys, don't fight. We gotta hurry."

James shimmied downward, trying to keep his feet planted firmly against the house as he went. He was on the ground before he knew it.

"Safe," he whispered up to them.

Margot and Liz scurried down after him, whispering to each other in voices inaudible to James as they descended.

"Come on," Margot hissed as she reached the ground. "Run!"

"Your mom's got the key," Liz added. "She's gonna have the door open any second."

James spun around and dashed across the lawn toward the hill that sloped down to the street. The sound of Margot's and Liz's footsteps behind him seemed to mix with the rhythmic pounding of his heartbeat.

"Faster," Archit called as he flew alongside them.

Looking ahead down the sloping hill of the lawn, James could pick out Margot's car among the others parallel-parked along the street. *The car can't be close enough*, he thought. Never before had their yard seemed so big, never before that moment when all he could think about was getting out of the sightline of that third-floor window as quickly as possible.

He suddenly felt his foot hit a patch of damp leaves. Before he could register what was going on, he stumbled backward, sliding down the hill and bringing Margot down with him. "Whoa!" he shouted.

Archit swooped down, offering a wing to help him to his feet. Liz took

Margot's arm and pulled her up. They were back to running.

"Come *on!*" Archit said.

"Sorry," James whispered to Margot.

They reached the car and ducked behind it not a second too soon. Still breathless from the sprint, James peeked up over the hood of the car. A pool of light poured out the front door onto the front walk. Several recognizable silhouettes came out: Mrs. Shannassy and their aunt led the way, Mr. Shannassy and a few others following.

James ducked back behind the car, looking over at Margot, Liz, and Archit. They squatted on the pavement and leaned into the shadows with expressions that revealed their shared panic. At least he wasn't the only one who was freaking out!

The sound of his heart pounding in his ears nearly drowned out the distant voices of the adults up at the top of the hill. He couldn't make out what they were saying, but he could sense the panic in their tone.

"No, no, they can't be far." His mom suddenly raised her voice, calling out into the unresponsive darkness of the night. "Kids?!"

Hearing his mom shout for them—not aggressive, not angry, just worried—almost crushed him.

"James? Margot? Liz?"

But the only response was a cold silence in the dark night. He peeked back over the hood of the car and watched as his aunt tried to comfort his mom. He should have felt bad about it, but he couldn't risk telling her anything. Revealing himself to tell her how he had to run away on this adventure with Archit would, of course, mean having to explain everything about Mr. Birken.

The adults stood there for a while, conversing in low voices that drifted through the air in faint murmurs. James held his breath, half-expecting his mom and the others to start walking across the lawn to the cars so that they could start a search throughout the neighborhood.

He watched the adults turn their attention back toward the front door and respond to someone who must have been standing in the foyer. His aunt headed inside, and for a few more moments that dragged out like hours, the adults stood on the walkway, talking together.

"What's going on?" Margot whispered.

"Shh," James hissed, not taking his eyes off what was happening. Then he ventured in the softest of whispers, "They're still out on the front walkway."

"Do my parents look upset?" asked Liz. She sounded as if she were feeling the same guilt James was. He didn't respond. The adults were hard to read.

Mrs. Shannassy headed toward the house and the others followed. For a few seconds, everything was still. James hesitated, wondering whether they were going to come back out.

"They're gone," he said to the others.

A collective sigh.

"That was the clumsiest escape I've ever seen," Archit said with a shake of his head.

"This is ridiculous," Margot said to James. "You really owe me."

James ignored her. "Come on," he said, standing. "Let's get out of here before they come back." He bolted toward Margot's car and tugged at the door handle. "Margot," he said. "The keys—unlock the door."

The realization dawned on Margot in a way that James could read plainly in her face. "I don't have them," she said. "I...I must have dropped them... when we fell."

"What?" James said.

"It's all right," Liz said quickly.

"No, it's not all right," James said. "We need the car if we're going to get out of here." He looked up at the house. The adults would be back out at any second.

"We don't need the car," Archit said. "But I think we ought to put some distance between ourselves and your house as soon as we can, don't you agree?" He took off walking down the street, waving for the others to follow.

"Where to?" James asked, following with the girls just behind him.

"Somewhere else," Archit replied.

James wasn't going to question that. He exchanged a look with Margot and Liz to gauge their reaction. Liz still seemed enthusiastic—but Margot, not so much. It was probably too late for her to change her mind now. She was too far involved.

The four of them walked at a steady pace along the street. "We'll have to make camp somewhere out of sight," Archit said. "Somewhere no one will think to look for us. I was originally thinking we'd be able to drive the car somewhere outside of town..."

"Probably for the best anyway," Margot said. "If they called the cops, there'd be a search out for my car."

That didn't sit well with James. "You think they'll call the cops?"

"No," Liz said. "They won't want to raise a fuss over nothing. They'll assume we're sneaking out to go downtown or something. They'll be ready to yell at us when we get home, but they're not going to file a missing-persons report just yet."

"It sounds like we're in the clear," Archit observed.

They walked along in silence for a minute in the dark. The reality of the situation was finally sinking in for James. Archit, Mr. Birken, and the world of Nalgordia—he didn't know whether to be nervous or excited.

The streetlight threw long, veiny shadows along the street. Maybe it was just his imagination, but James could have sworn that some of the shadows looked like tendrils and claws reaching out to grab them. He knew this adventure wasn't going to be fun the entire time. The memory of Mr. Birken still scared him. He would probably have to face Mr. Birken again at some point.

With the adrenaline of escaping the rec room now beginning to wear off, James felt his stomach rumble. When was the last time he had eaten? It must have been back at fourth-period lunch, around half past eleven.

"You guys hungry?" he asked the others.

"Yeah," Margot and Liz chorused.

"Once we get out of the neighborhood," he said, "we should find a place to stop and eat. I brought some snacks for the road." He patted his soccer bag.

"What'd you bring?" Margot said.

"Peanut butter sandwiches, granola bars, apples, bananas."

Margot groaned. "Great."

"I was trying to get stuff that wouldn't spoil."

"It's all right, James," Liz chimed in. "But I think we're all pretty hungry. Maybe we should try to get something *substantial* before this whole adventure starts."

"Like what?" James said.

"Pizza," Margot suggested. "I have money." She reached into her bra and pulled out a small wad of bills. Fortunately, she hadn't put that in her car with her debit card and cellphone.

"I like the idea of stopping for dinner," Archit said. "It will give me a chance to explain everything. But I can't go inside anywhere. We'll have to take it outside."

"There are picnic tables along the bike trail," James said. "Nobody'll bother us there, I wouldn't think."

Just as he said that, a car turned from the intersection up ahead of them, its headlights illuminating the street. "Quick! Hide!" Archit exclaimed.

James ducked behind the trees closest to the shoulder, the others following him. They stood with bated breath as the car drove by. It likely wasn't anyone from their family—the car had come from the opposite direction—but James didn't want to be seen by anyone. A group of teenagers walking around in party attire might arouse suspicion.

"That was close," Margot said.

They stepped back out onto the road. "Do you think the adults will come looking for us?" Liz asked.

"Maybe," Margot said. "They know we're on foot and we can't be far off."

Nobody said anything as they digested that astute observation.

James broke the silence. "So...pizza?"

"Sure," Margot said.

Fifteen minutes later, James stood in the foyer of Luigi's, the local pizza shop. The others waited outside, just out of sight. Luigi's was warm and inviting, smelling richly of pasta, cheese, and the spices of homemade Italian cooking. James put his hands in his pockets and tried to look innocent while the employees behind the counter hustled and bustled in and out of the kitchen.

One of the guys stopped. "Can I help you?"

"Yeah," James said. "Can I—uh, may I get a large cheese pizza, please?"

"We have one coming out right now," the guy behind the counter said. He glanced toward the woodfire oven. "Hang on."

He scooted over to the oven and grabbed a paddle to extract a piping hot pizza glistening with molten mozzarella.

"Is that going to be it for you?"

James studied the fridge full of soda in the corner. "Four sodas, too," he said, sidling over to grab a bottle for each of them and taking them to the counter.

The cashier added the drinks to the pizza on the register, then said, "That'll be fifteen dollars even."

James pulled out the wad of bills Margot had given him and handed a twenty to the cashier, who examined the bill with the meticulous attention of someone who thought a teenage kid would try to rip him off. "You look sharp," the employee said as he opened the register and made change. "Where're you coming from?"

James had nearly forgotten he was still wearing the suit he'd intended to wear to the party. How unusual he must have looked, walking into a pizza parlor in a suit and tie. "Just a family reunion," he replied, a little apprehensive about the fact that he was revealing true details, but he couldn't think of a plausible lie on the spot. He hoped the police wouldn't come into Luigi's to question the staff about missing teenagers in party attire.

The man didn't reply. He handed over five one-dollar bills, lifted the pizza box, and passed it over the counter. "Enjoy."

James nodded, trying to look cool. Why he was trying to impress the guy working the counter at Luigi's he couldn't quite explain, but maybe if he looked tough and formidable enough, this guy wouldn't squeal on them to any cops who might stop by to question him. These, James thought with deprecating self-awareness, were the thoughts that only a paranoid nerd could have when he seriously rebels for the first time.

Stepping outside Luigi's, James took in the cool October night. The scent wafting up from the warm pizza box in his arms mingled with that of the crisp leaves. His stomach growled. Ready to sit down with the others and finally eat, he turned right and set off walking around the side of the building.

"That was fast," Margot said as he came around the back of the strip mall. She leaned against the side of the building with her arms crossed to keep warm, pulling her cardigan tightly around her. Liz and Archit, seated on a nearby bench, perked up as he approached.

"They were taking a cheese pizza out of the oven as I walked in," James explained. "I guess they're not selling much by the slice tonight, so they're apt to sell a whole pizza to anyone walking in off the street."

They crossed the ground behind the strip mall, walking through the trees and onto the bike trail. From the glow of the streetlamps around the parking lot on the other side of the building, James could just barely make out the picnic tables beside the path. He set the pizza box and bag of sodas down on one sitting a bit farther from the trail than the others.

"All right," he said. "Let's eat."

The four of them sat down and dug into the pizza ravenously. It might have been the best pizza James had ever eaten, but he devoured it too quickly to taste it, putting away half a slice in only a matter of seconds. "This is so good," he said.

"I bet they're eating garbage at the family reunion right now," Margot said.

James, feeling he'd been waiting far too long to get the details behind what happened to him earlier and why they were headed off on this adventure, figured he would cut to the chase. "All right, Archit. Are we going to hear this whole story or what?"

Archit hesitated, chewing his slice of pizza slowly. His beak made eating pizza a delicate maneuver. "I guess I can't put this off any longer, can I?"

"You don't have to tell us if you don't want to," Liz said.

"No, I need to," Archit said. "You all need to hear this if you're going to come along."

He sighed and set his slice of pizza down. "Very well. Where do I begin?" He looked at each of them.

"When I was little," he began, "back in the later part of the eighteenth century—as unbelievable as that sounds—I lived with a human who was the only father I had ever known. I don't know whether I actually had birth parents, or how I came to be separated from them. As a figment, I guess I was never actually born, so I must not have had parents—but as I told James earlier, I don't understand why I grew and aged until my fifteenth birthday."

"Didn't your father ever explain any of that to you?" Margot asked.

"Margot, please," James said. "Don't interrupt."

"No, it's all right," Archit said. "It's all a little confusing. I suppose I never questioned it while I was growing up. Why would I? It was the only normal I had ever known. I didn't have any of these questions until my uncle tried to curse me—but I'm getting ahead of myself."

Archit took a deep breath, as if he were steadying himself.

"Father and I lived in Oxford, where he worked as a professor at the university," he continued. "Few people in town knew about me; those who did always said my father was a little strange for keeping me as a son when they thought I ought to have been kept as a pet. Despite what some people might have said, my father was always cool and confident in everything he did. He didn't care what other people thought, and he always said that being able to think for yourself was the greatest strength you could have. He loved history and philosophy and poetry, and he would often read aloud to me from the Bible or Shakespeare or other classics, and he always took the time to answer my endless questions."

"So, it was just you, then?" James said. "As far as imaginary creatures go? You were the only one in town?"

"No, not exactly," Archit said. "There was Dromio. I guess you could say he was my only friend. Now that I look back on it, I don't know where he came from or how he found his way to our town and became my friend. He was just always around for as long as I could remember. Father used to say my guardian angel must have led him to me."

Archit sat quiet for a second, contemplating how to proceed. "Well," he said, "now that you understand what my life was like before all these... *complications*, for lack of a better word, I think you'll better understand the drastic shift my life took when my uncle became a part of it."

James set down his pizza and leaned forward, not wanting to miss a word.

"My uncle," Archit said. "My father's brother. He was my father's only living relative, but they weren't close, not on good terms. They never visited or even spoke, but they would occasionally exchange letters. In fact, from a very young age, I could tell that there was something wrong with my uncle. Even if my father didn't say so, I could tell that my uncle was a bad, bad person."

"And that's who you saw this afternoon, right, James?" Liz asked.

James nodded. "And I can vouch for what Archit says. Bad is an understatement."

"I never actually met my uncle for years," Archit continued, "until the day he finally came to visit. I'll never forget it. He arrived on the street outside our house in a black carriage drawn by sickly, abused-looking horses, attended by hunched footmen in hooded cloaks. One of them opened up the carriage door and helped him out, and I saw him look up at our house with vacant, listless eyes that gave me this feeling he had seen all the horrors of the world, all the nightmarish things that even the bravest people would fear, and he was merely jaded and unimpressed by even the darkest devilry.

"My father came to the window and looked over my shoulder, then told me to go wait in the parlor until my uncle had left. I obeyed, but I stayed attentive, hoping I might be able to overhear what they said. When my father answered the door, he and my uncle exchanged a few words, in whispers at first. Then they went back to my father's study so that they could talk more openly.

"After an hour, they came out. My uncle said, 'So, you will give what I said some consideration?'

"My father replied, 'I have considered it all I need to, and my answer is no.' Then he added, almost as if after some hesitation, 'I don't know to what dark coven you have given loyalty, but I won't be a part of it.'

"'George, be wise,' my uncle said. 'What I'm offering you brings great rewards.'

"'Perhaps in *this* life,' my father retorted with a note of finality in his voice. 'Now, please leave my home.'

"My uncle had been circling the foyer, and it was at that point that he peered into the parlor and noticed me sitting there, eavesdropping.

"'Abaddon,' I heard my father said, 'I must insist you leave.'

"'Hold on, George,' my uncle said as he ventured into the room and approached me.

"'Abaddon, leave him alone,' my father said.

"My uncle circled me where I sat in my chair, reaching forward to stroke my mane in a way that still makes my feathers shiver when I think about it. 'George, what is it?' he asked.

"'*He*,' my father emphasized, staying remarkably cool despite the situation. 'He is my son. His name is Archit.'

"'Your son?' my uncle scoffed. 'George, don't be stupid. Raising your pet as if it were a child?!'

"'Archit is no pet,' my father defended me. 'Now, Brother,' he addressed my uncle coldly, refusing to call him by name a third time, 'I have asked you plenty of times to leave my home.'

"'I will!' my uncle replied angrily, straightening to his full height. He bowed his head to me and flashed me a grin that would haunt my nightmares. I could tell his mind was at work, thinking of some evil plan that had to do with me.

"I thought I would talk it over with my father later that night when he was tucking me into bed. 'What were you talking about with Uncle Abaddon earlier today?' I asked.

"My father sighed. He said, 'This won't be easy to explain, but I think you deserve to know. I'll do my best.'

"He explained to me that, for years, my uncle had been sending him letters in the mail, but my father had been ignoring them. At last, my uncle had come to visit and discuss the matter in person.

"See, I learned then that since his youth, my uncle had been dabbling in black magic. My father thought this devilry was dangerous and discouraged my uncle from messing around with it. My uncle was using powers that he didn't fully understand, and he was using them for self-indulgent and malicious purposes. And now my uncle was encouraging my father to join him.

"My uncle had delved so deep into his sorcery that he had started to go crazy. He lived in hiding, in a dark castle in the mountains somewhere in Eastern Europe, and there, my uncle had dwelled in darkness and surrounded himself with demons and beasts, and focused on his studies of black magic.

"I couldn't believe it! My good father's own flesh and blood dabbling with evil spirits! I asked why my uncle was still coming to visit my father if my father had made it clear he had no interest in joining him.

"My father sighed and told me that my uncle had delved so deep into these terrible acts that all of what was good in him had dried up into dust and blown away. At first, I thought he was speaking metaphorically, but as he went on, I began to think that maybe this had literally happened. As my father said—and I could see the tears in his eyes when he said it—my uncle was no longer a human person. He was now like one of the evil creatures he so often trafficked with, like a demon or a monster from a myth or fairytale."

"Hold on," Margot said. "And this is Mr. Birken you're talking about? You're telling us that Mr. Birken isn't human? That he's some sort of monster?"

"That is exactly what I'm saying," Archit confirmed. "I know, he still looks human. But when he became an evil wizard, he found a way to throw off his mortality along with his soul. He became like something out of a nightmare. That's really the only way I know how to describe it."

James contemplated this. It didn't even come as a surprise.

"This news about my uncle was disturbing, to say the least," Archit continued, "but danger didn't seem really tangible to me when I had known such a peaceful life up until then, so I didn't let it bother me. By the next morning, I had forgotten about it. Life went on normally until one night, several weeks later. When I woke up from a nightmare that night, I couldn't get back to sleep. After enough time passed from my sleepless tossing and turning, I went in to wake up my father to see whether he could comfort me.

"I went into his room, but he didn't respond. He lay sprawled out on the bed. He'd been sleeping, I think—he was dressed in his nightclothes, and the medicine that he always took before bed was sitting on the table next to him. The window was open, and a cold breeze was coming in. I hurried to close it, latch it shut, and then draw the curtains. I shook my father, but he didn't respond.

"Now that I'm older, I understand what had happened. But when I was so young and innocent, it didn't make any sense to me. I didn't want to think that he had died. After all, he was all I had in the world, the only one to protect me. I'd never known anybody who died before. And he looked so peaceful the way he was lying on the bed, his eyes shut, his face all still.

"After a minute, Dromio came into the room. He had lived with us ever since that day when my uncle had come to visit, and it was a good thing, too—I needed somebody to comfort me that night. Dromio led me out into the sitting room and consoled me while I cried and cried.

"'Remember what your father always told you?' Dromio said. 'Remember what he said about humans?'

"And yes, I did remember. I haven't ever forgotten in all the years since. My father had told me that even though a person lives on the earth for only a short while, when people die, their spirits rise up out of their bodies and up higher than the sky to continue living happily forever in heaven.

"I took solace in that thought, but that solace was short-lived. Later that night, maybe three hours after midnight, my uncle arrived for what I thought at the time was just another visit.

"My uncle came in the front door and didn't bother to greet me. Instead, he acted as if he were all alone in the house, as if it were his. He moved about the house as if there were nothing rude or out of ordinary about his behavior. He took off his long gray coat and hung it on a peg by the door, then strode past me toward my father's bedroom. I heard the door shut and kept waiting to hear my uncle's cries of despair over his dead brother, but they never came. Eventually, my uncle came back out from the bedroom. He didn't even look sad.

"'He is dead, then,' he said in a matter-of-fact tone.

"My uncle sat down in a chair and stared at me. 'Now then, young Archit,' he said, 'your father is passed. You'd best come with me.'

"I didn't know how to tell my father's brother that I didn't trust him, that I didn't want to go anywhere with him. I didn't know how to state outright that he was a bad man, that he and my father didn't get along, and that I hardly knew him. I just couldn't say all that. I tried to be as kind as I could, as I knew my father would have wanted me to be. 'I'm going to stay here,' I said. 'Dromio is my friend and guardian. He will take care of me.'

"My uncle seemed taken aback by this response. 'Dromio?' he said. 'Archit, I don't know what your father told you, but the people of the town will not see it as such. They'll come for you when they realize your father is dead.'

"'I'm going to wait until somebody comes for me,' I told him. 'They'll send me somewhere where I'll be taken care of.'

"My uncle came and knelt next to me. He seemed oddly warm and kind for the bad person my father said that he was. 'Archit,' he said, 'it won't end that easily. You're different—you do know that, don't you? They won't treat you the same way that your father treated you.'

"I didn't know how to reply to that. I knew what he said was true.

"'You'd best come with me,' my uncle repeated. 'I'm your father's brother. It's the best thing.'

"He seemed genuine and kind. For the first time, I thought that maybe he really did care about me. I was his nephew, of course. Maybe he wasn't as bad as my father had always thought.

"I agreed to go with him, then went to my bedroom and collected the few belongings I had in a small suitcase. I was sad and scared, and while I packed my things up, I began to cry. Dromio came into my room and found me crying. 'Dromio,' I said, 'won't you come with me to my uncle's house? You're my only friend, the only one I have left, and I'd be so scared and sad to go by myself.'

"So Dromio agreed that he would come, and the two of us finished packing my suitcase together. I went to the sitting room, where my uncle was waiting. When I came in, he stood and nodded his head in my direction. 'Ready then, Archit?'

"'Dromio is going to come with us,' I told him.

"'That is out of the question,' said my uncle. 'Dromio? First he is going to protect you from the villagers, and now he is going to come with us? Did your father consider Dromio one of his children as well?'

"'No, sir,' I said, 'but he doesn't have any family, and he spends so much time with us that my father and I have accepted him as our own. He's not Father's child, but he's my best friend. Where I go, he goes.' This was the honest truth, and if my uncle had denied me of this, I don't think I would have gone with him.

"My uncle never gave us a word of approval, just a nod and a gesture for us to follow him outside to his waiting carriage. My uncle climbed into the carriage first, and Dromio and I clambered in and sat across from him.

"We rode the rest of the night and into the day, the three of us sitting in silence the whole time. Not one word was uttered, not even by me or Dromio. After a while, I found enough peace of mind or else was so exhausted that I fell asleep. I slept through the rest of the day and into the night. When I woke, the carriage bumped and jolted over what must have been very uneven terrain. I could hear the wind howling outside, and it occasionally pushed the carriage from side to side. I peered out the window to see we were traveling up a mountainside. A full moon shone brightly in the sky, illuminating the sea far below the cliffside. Violent waves crashed against the rocks many miles below us.

"'We are almost there,' my uncle said. His voice startled me; it was the first time he had spoken during the whole carriage ride. Then he said, 'See, here we come now.'

"We rounded a crag and I saw my uncle's home. Even if someone had warned me ahead of time, I never would have expected what I saw. It was a castle, but it looked almost as if it were part of the mountain itself, a collection of black stalagmites stabbing upward into the misty night sky, sharply pointed turrets bridged by stony walls.

"Gehenna, as the castle was called, was surrounded by a black iron gate overgrown with thorns. The grounds were a wasteland of weeds and deforestation dotted with wells of black water, thorn bushes, gargoyle statues, all through which nocturnal creatures roamed about to and fro.

"The carriage creaked to a stop and the three of us climbed out. My uncle led us across the grounds, past bogs and briars, to a tall set of doors where hunched, goblin-like servants greeted us.

"'This is my nephew,' my uncle said as we stepped into the foyer. 'He is the son of my brother, George, who has just died. Prepare comfortable quarters for my nephew, and see to it that breakfast is ready by sunrise. We'll rest for a short while, then have a welcoming meal for our newcomers.'

"And that was how my brief stay at Gehenna began, in the care of Uncle

Abaddon."

Archit paused, heaving a deep breath. He looked from James to Margot to Liz, then gazed down at the tabletop. He was trembling. The sight of it was like a punch to the stomach for James. He had been afraid of Mr. Birken that afternoon, sickened by the evil he had witnessed, but never could he have imagined what Archit had been through. He reached forward and put a hand comfortingly on Archit's shoulder.

"You all right?" he asked.

Archit looked suddenly self-aware and gave a shake of his head. "Yes. I'm sorry, I only meant to tell you about why the thought of a sixteenth birthday is so significant. Here I am, rambling on about every little detail when I probably could have said it all in a minute or two."

"It's all right," Liz said. "You're right to tell it to us like this. We want to hear it."

"We need to understand it the way you do," James added.

Archit looked up at them. "There's been so much of this that I've shoved to the back of my mind. It's like I'm remembering *all* of it for the first time in hundreds of years. I want the three of you to...to understand what we're up against."

A chill went through James, one that had little to do with the cold autumn night. He looked over his shoulder in the dark to be sure there was no sign of anyone approaching them. He turned back and felt the weight of everyone's discomfort set in on him.

"So...what happened after that?" he said.

Archit nodded and took a sip from his cola. "Much. Let's see—how do I continue this? There's a lot left to cover."

He sighed.

"After only a few days in my uncle's home, I began to feel much more comfortable. I admit, the ominous appearance of the castle had made me uneasy at first, and my uncle had a tendency to be cold or formidable at times—but I was given a luxurious room, my uncle surprised me with presents every day, and we had dessert for every meal. What was not to love about a place like that?

"My uncle frequently boasted about how happy he was that his 'brother's little foundling child' had come to live with him. I started to think that maybe my father had misunderstood his brother. Maybe my uncle wasn't as bad as my father had thought. This went on for several weeks, and with each passing day, I forgot more and more about the happy childhood I had led with my father and I grew more and more comfortable with my uncle.

"Dromio saw through all this gross deception, this false bond that my uncle was trying to form with me. Whether Dromio grew jealous or not, I can't say—but I know he must have been hurt. How could he not, when he was my true friend, forced to just stand by as I succumbed to my uncle's tricks?

"There were several times when he said to me that we could go for a walk on the castle grounds together, we could go exploring, or go to one of the rooms of the castle and draw pictures together, tell stories, put together jigsaw puzzles or something. But I wasn't interested unless my uncle was there to join us. After a while, I don't know how long exactly, I forgot about Dromio. He still lived in the castle with us, but I never paid him any regard. Looking back on it, I hate myself for being so stupid and mean."

Archit paused, and James didn't know what to say. *Hundreds of years later and these memories still hurt him,* James thought. *He's still broken up about it.*

Archit looked as if he were going to cry for a moment, but he took a deep breath and went on. "This is the important part," he said, looking at each of them in turn. "This is what I've been building up to. After months of deceiving me to earn my trust, my uncle told me one night that he would take me and Dromio to an amusement park. I was beside myself with excitement. I'd never been to an amusement park before. Father had never taken me on big, exciting outings because he didn't think I would fit in with the human children.

"The next morning, my uncle, Dromio, and I boarded the black carriage and set out for a long journey that lasted the entire afternoon. Looking back on it now, I remember passing the hours-long drive being cold and indifferent toward Dromio, and looking to my uncle as if he were my best friend. How could I have been so stupid as to become enamored of my uncle? I wanted belonging. I wanted to feel loved and protected, and that's what my uncle was for me then. Or so I thought.

"A little while before sunset, we pulled up to a busy, lively amusement park ablaze with colored lights and crowded with people of all ages, all of them dressed in costumes and masks.

"Where do I start? There were rollercoasters, carousels, and a Ferris wheel to ride. I spent the next few hours overjoyed, laughing, never sparing a second on a worrisome thought. All the while, Dromio must have been aching to share the fun with me, but I didn't think to worry about him when my uncle was introducing me to magicians, letting me play with exotic animals, or buying me colorful masks to wear.

"Around midnight, I started to get tired. I didn't realize it until I was riding the Ferris wheel for the fourth time that night, and with the slow and comforting movement of the cart as it rocked gently back and forth, I put my head against my uncle's shoulder and drifted off into a deep sleep.

"I have no idea how long I slept. All I know is that I awoke in a black pit, maybe a dungeon cell, deep in the catacombs of my uncle's castle. My uncle was there, but he looked as I'd never seen him look before. He was dressed in his wizarding garments—black robes, a flowing red cape, and a pointed hat—probably what he was wearing this afternoon when you saw him, James."

James nodded, but he didn't want to interrupt. He hung on Archit's every word, trying to follow where this story was going.

"I tried to move," Archit continued, "but I was chained by my neck and talons to the stone slab I had been lying on.

"A chorus of evil laughter erupted around me, and I saw that my uncle and I weren't alone in the room. Also present were his servants, all of them dressed in long black hoods and armed with torches.

"The room was also full of *monsters*. There was a host of animals, but animals like I'd never seen. Their bodies were twisted and they were larger than they should have been naturally. Their eyes glowed like fire and their teeth glistened like steel. There were wolves and crows, bats, snakes, cats, toads, and rats.

"There were also demons and dragons, ghouls, vampires, ogres, trolls, goblins, witches in black robes, swamp monsters with green scales, zombies with gray skin, imps, bogeymen, and even walking skeletons. They were the

54

creatures of the Night Scourge.

"When all of them took notice that I was awake and struggling against the chains, a hubbub erupted, several of them hissing or growling or cawing, others reaching forward with their hideous claws and gnarled hands.

"My uncle looked down at me. 'He's awake,' he announced to the others as he circled the table.

"'Where's Dromio?' I demanded. It was the first thing that came to my mind.

"'You've abandoned Dromio,' my uncle said, and a cold smile spread across his face.

"Hearing those words made me physically hurt. I hadn't abandoned Dromio! I hadn't left him behind! Why would my uncle suggest something like that? 'No,' I shouted, 'No! I haven't!'

"'You did,' my uncle demanded. 'You abandoned Dromio, and now he's been destroyed.'

"I couldn't believe it. I couldn't stand such a thought. 'You're a liar!' I shouted, feeling somehow bold despite the chain around my neck.

"My uncle heaved a sickening laugh. 'Oh, I'm a liar, am I?' he said. 'Rest assured, Archit—Dromio has been obliterated, and he'll never be able to save you! And now, you'll join us!'

"All of the monsters started cheering, their red eyes lit up with blood-thirsty anticipation. I struggled with the chains, but even if I'd managed to escape, I don't know what I would have done. Where would I have gone? There would have been no chance of escaping the situation I was in.

"'Do not struggle,' my uncle bellowed in a deep voice. He knelt down, rested his chin on the table, his face right next to mine. I could feel his hot breath on my face, and I winced. 'Archit,' he said, 'why do you struggle so, when you don't even understand what I have in store for you?'

"I didn't want to listen. I screamed and kept pulling at the chains. My uncle grabbed at my beak, trying to hold it shut to silence me.

"'Archit,' my uncle said, 'when this spell is finished, you will be immortal. You will be my servant forever and ever, for all time! And when I've sealed this fate on you, these witnesses—the creatures of the Night Scourge—will revere me above all others.'

"I began to shout and scream as Uncle Abaddon grabbed a torch from one of his servants with one hand and a sword with the other. 'Archit, do not struggle,' he shouted. 'I demand that you don't struggle! Don't you understand, Nephew? This could be the greatest curse I ever cast! You should be honored that I have chosen you!'

"I was so scared by the sight of him with the sword that I froze up, paralyzed from fear. He leaned down and dragged the silver blade of the sword along my side, drawing blood. He collected some of it in a glass phial, then shook my blood over the torch he held in his other hand. A legion of demons emerged from the flames, one rising up after another. They all had skull-shaped death heads with empty sockets for eyes, long serpentine tails, and bat-like wings. They circled overhead like buzzards, screaming in voices so shrill that I thought my blood would turn to ice.

"At some point during this ritual, I passed out. When I came to, I was still chained to the sacrificial table in the dungeon, but each of the monstrous slaves was at ease. They seemed to be whispering to each other, gossiping in hushed growls over what had just happened.

"I stared around in fear but didn't say anything. I didn't want any of them to notice that I was awake, or else they might take to torturing me again.

"After a while, my uncle came back into the room. He looked exhausted. His face was glistening with sweat, his clothes were disheveled, and his hair was in disarray. There was an expression on his face that I couldn't quite understand—not then and not even now, knowing what I have learned this afternoon.

"He didn't speak to me. Instead, he undid the chains, took me by the neck, and led me out of the room through a long, low hall. 'Where are we going?' I asked him. I was disturbed by the thought that I was trapped as a servant to this terrible man for the rest of eternity. At such a young age, I couldn't exactly comprehend such a thought.

"My uncle silently led me up a winding staircase, through many of the grand rooms in his castle, then up several more smaller winding staircases until we came to a room at the very top of the east tower. He shoved me inside.

"'You'll stay here,' he said. 'This will be your prison henceforth. Do not hold hope that you will ever see the light of day again.'

"With that, he shut the door, locked it, and forgot about me.

"I found myself all alone in the world—imprisoned in that bitterly cold tower up above my uncle's castle, locked away to never come out again.

"I wasn't the only thing put away up there—it looked as if my uncle reserved this room for hiding things he no longer needed or wanted, a place where he could put them out of his sight and not look at them anymore. There were old pieces of furniture, paintings, statues, and artifacts. There were wild beasts that had been killed and their heads mounted on the wall, their dead faces fixed in absent stares they would hold forever, in expressions that would never change. Just like me.

"There was an ancient grandfather clock with thirteen numbers on its face and seven different hands. It looked like it had long since stopped ticking. That was how time was for me now, too. Time didn't seem to exist; it was frozen. It didn't matter if there were thirteen different hours in a day or twelve. It didn't matter, because time would never affect me. I was now a prisoner of my uncle forever.

"I set my mind to escaping immediately. All night long, while the wind howled and shrieked outside the window, I dug through the detritus and packed a bag with anything useful I could find: maps, tools, and some trinkets that looked like they would fetch some money if I tried to pawn them. I packed it all in a small satchel, and managed to pick the lock on the door to the tower. It was so surprisingly easy that I couldn't believe it at first.

"After I stole some food from the kitchen, I let myself out the servants' entrance and crept across the yard. I had to be careful; I knew my uncle kept many wolves and crows as pets, and they would destroy me if they caught me trying to escape.

"But neither wolf nor crow nor any other guard disturbed me, and I left my uncle's castle grounds with tremendous ease, never to come back. All that night I ventured down the mountain, and I didn't rest until I'd reached the forest by the seaside.

"You have to understand that my life wasn't easy just because I'd escaped. I have since lived in hiding from my uncle, and from most of society.

I did a good deal of exploring by stowing away on ships and joining caravans, doing odd jobs for kind people in exchange for food or shelter. There were some people who were willing to accept me and not shriek at the sight, but I had to be careful. If somebody saw a giant purple bird, there would be talk about it, and my uncle would surely catch wind of it, wherever in the world he might be.

"And that is how my life has been for centuries. I have always been on the run, in hiding, but never aging or growing, despite the many years that go by."

Archit paused. "But now things might be different," he said. "From what you tell me, James, there very well might be hope for me."

Archit gave another heavy sigh as if reliving it all had worn him out.

James, struggling to digest what he had heard, looked at Margot and Liz. *Do they believe all this?* They both looked uncomfortable, as if they'd been tricked into watching an offensive movie and they weren't sure how to react.

But James had no doubt. He had experienced enough of it earlier in the day to know Archit wasn't exaggerating anything. Still, a few questions lingered.

"I don't get it though," he said at last. "Were you mortal before your uncle cursed you?"

"That's hard to say, isn't it?" Archit replied, as if that answer should have been obvious. "I'm not sure whether I was real or a figment of the imagination, or whether I was from this world or an imaginary realm. I mean, I grew up in the mortal world, raised by a human, but...I've never seen another creature like me before. Have you?"

"No," James said. Margot and Liz shook their heads.

"But if I were a figment of the imagination, then I wouldn't have aged and grown the way I remember doing when I was younger. And why would my uncle try to curse me with immortality if..."

"If you already were immortal," James finished.

"Exactly," Archit said. "For all these hundreds of years, I haven't aged or grown—or changed in any way really. I really *must* be cursed. Now you tell me that on my next birthday, I'll turn sixteen. Do you know what that means?"

James wasn't sure, but he ventured anyway. "It means...that maybe the curse has been broken?"

Archit nodded. "And if the curse is broken, then maybe I'm just like the other mortal creatures in this world. Maybe I'm...maybe I'm real, and not a figment of the imagination."

He paused.

"I know imaginary worlds seem exciting, but I don't belong in any of them," he continued. "I've spent many years living in Nalgordia, but it isn't my home the way the human world is—or *was*, I guess I should say. It's the only place I've ever been happy. This is where I'm meant to be. In the human world." He added as if to himself, "I'll have to ask her if it is possible."

"Her?" Liz said.

James had caught Archit's vague reference as well. "Who is it we're going with you to see?" he asked.

"We're going to the island of Nalgordia," said Archit. "It's a magical place, filled with all sorts of fantastic people: fairies and elves, witches and wizards, dragons and unicorns, and animals who wear clothes and live in houses. There are hippies and dinosaurs, too."

Hippies and dinosaurs? James had been ticking off in his head the many mythical creatures Archit had listed, but hippies and dinosaurs were...well, not exactly the mythical creatures he was used to hearing about. "Hippies?" he asked.

"That's who we're going to see," Archit said. "There's a commune of hippies that have made camp in the western woods. Their leader's name is Dawn Flower, and she's sort of a godmother to me. Her knowledge of the spirit world is renowned, and I'm thinking that she might be able to shed some light on all this about my sixteenth birthday approaching."

"And you have a plan on how we're going to get there?" Margot said. "I mean, like airfare or whatever. That's all taken care of?"

Archit laughed a little. "The transportation is taken care of, yes. We just need a place to lie low tonight until dawn."

James looked up and down the bike trail as far as he could see in the dark. "This seems as good a place as any."

"Will anyone bother us here, you think?" Liz said.

"No," James said. "Not likely." Several times, he had walked the bike trail at night with friends, and he had never seen anyone.

"Well, then we ought to get some rest," Archit said. "We have an early morning ahead of us. Unless you have any more questions for me."

The three kids exchanged nervous glances. "I think we're going to have a million questions in the coming days, but I can't think of any now," James said.

Archit nodded, understanding. "Just as well. You can ask them as they come to you."

James stood and went to the next picnic table. "The good news is we each have our own picnic table," he said, trying to look on the bright side.

Margot claimed the picnic table on the other side. "Great, my own picnic table. I'm sure I'll be comfortable now."

Liz laughed. "Margot," she scolded gently.

James thought of a response but yawned deeply and forgot what he was going to say. Exhaustion had come out of nowhere. He lay back, turning his head to watch the others settling atop the nearby picnic tables. "Goodnight," he whispered.

"Goodnight," the others chorused.

James closed his eyes. His body was exhausted, but now that he was settling down, his mind decided most unapologetically to wake up. Archit's story made him remember his encounter with Mr. Birken all the more vividly. Understanding what Mr. Birken had done to Archit, being informed on what they were up against, was supposed to make him more confident and more assured. It didn't. It just made him feel worse.

What if they weren't able to help Archit after all? And what sort of danger were they in by trying to help him, and practically subjecting themselves to Mr. Birken's evil? Was it worth the danger? He might have been better off not going, and just hoping that Mr. Birken would leave him alone as long as he kept his secret.

No, no—that was insane. He couldn't abandon Archit. Not after all this.

Would Margot be mad at him for dragging her on this adventure? Would Liz try to be the peacemaker and just end up getting upset in the process? And was it wrong of him to bring them into the danger, too? As much as he didn't want to endanger them, he felt so much safer knowing that they were there with him.

And his mom and dad, what were they thinking right now? Were they worried sick that the kids were missing? Was it wrong of him to have gone with Archit?

Archit. James felt a rush of gratitude at the thought of his new friend. On a day when James had needed to escape the real world more than ever, Archit had come into his life. A new friend. James was really lucky.

But Archit doesn't need a friend, James thought. *He needs a brave companion, a loyal sidekick. You really think you're up for that challenge? You can't even play a game of flag football! You really think you've got the guts to do something like this? You really think you're going to be any help to Archit when he finds out what a wimp you are, how pathetic and useless you are when the going gets tough?*

James rolled over on his side, almost as if the change in physical position would help him change his thoughts. Even though he was lying on a bumpy, wooden tabletop, and even though the October night was getting cold, he found himself slowly surrendering to sleep.

Whatever the next day would bring, he would find out soon enough.

CHAPTER 4
The Journey

"S st...James."

James opened his eyes to see Archit staring down at him, the far-off glow of streetlights casting odd shadows across his beaked face. James jumped, startled.

"Sorry," Archit whispered. "Didn't mean to scare you."

"That's all right." James looked up at the sky. It was still dark, but there was that faint haze to it that suggested daybreak was imminent.

"It's almost dawn," Archit said. "We've got to get moving if we're going to cross between worlds."

Crossing between worlds. James wasn't sure that he'd ever get used to hearing that.

"All right," he said to Archit, stretching as he spoke. Never before had he thought he could have so many aches and pains after a night's sleep. The bumpy wooden tabletop had been all kinds of uncomfortable. He felt as if somebody had taken a club to every muscle up and down his neck, shoulders, and back.

He crept over to Liz, who was sleeping with her head resting delicately on her arm. "Liz," he said. "It's time to get up."

She stirred. "Is it morning?"

"Close enough, I think," James said. He lifted his bag and threw the strap over one shoulder.

Margot, who'd been gently awakened by Archit, was pulling herself up off the tabletop with grumpy, labored stretches. "Who knew sleeping outside on a picnic table would be so sucky," she said sarcastically. "And so damn cold."

"It's all right, Margot," James said. "We're getting to the fun part now, right?"

"Not much time to waste though," Archit said. "Come on."

They walked along the bike trail, stopping where it intersected with the street. Everything around them stood still. James had never seen the town so quiet before. Neither a car nor a pedestrian broken the sleepy tranquility of the streets and shops.

"This way," Archit said. He headed down the sidewalk with what James thought was a little too much confidence for an imaginary figment meandering through a conservative little suburb, even in pre-dawn darkness.

Archit paused and surveyed the quiet streets around them. James shivered in the chilly morning air, and pulled his suit jacket tighter around his chest.

When they passed the library, Archit looked up at the large tree growing on the edge of the property. Something about it seemed to capture his attention. "This'll do," he said.

He circled the square of sidewalk directly under the tree's widespread branches. "All right, sit down, sit down," he said.

James knelt, followed by the girls. The three teens huddled together on the cold concrete. Archit looked over his shoulder at the sky through the tree branches. "Sunrise," he whispered to himself.

The sky, James noticed, was indeed growing faintly pink. He looked back at Archit, who was producing a glass bottle from the pocket of his vest, along with the sachet of fairy dust they had used just the day before.

"Water," Archit whispered to himself, uncorking the glass bottle and pouring it onto the concrete. "And fairy dust."

When the glittering dust hit the puddle of water, smoke began to rise. Liz gasped. James gazed transfixed on the swirling smoke.

Archit murmured something under his breath, waving his wings over the smoke several times. A brisk wind swept over them, rustling the branches of the tree overhead. The ground began to shake ever so slightly.

"What's happening?" James said.

It was over as quickly as it started.

When the smoke cleared, it revealed an iron ring fixed to the concrete where the puddle of water had been mere seconds before. Archit leaped to his feet. "Come on. The doorway between worlds will only stay here for a few seconds."

He gripped the iron ring with both wings and pulled hard. The concrete square of sidewalk swung upward like a trapdoor to reveal a deep, dark pit. A set of stone stairs led into the darkness below.

James didn't have to be told twice. He leaped forward and bounded down the stairs, turning only to see whether Margot and Liz were following.

"Oh, how amazing, Archit," Liz said. "What's down here?"

"Please tell me we're not headed into the sewers," Margot said.

"No time for that now," Archit said. "Hurry up. I'll explain all that later."

James started to get the feeling he would be hearing "I'll explain all that later" frequently on this trip. He didn't care, though. He was too excited.

Looking back, he watched Archit descend behind Margot and Liz, drawing the concrete slab of a trap door closed behind him. For a moment, they were in complete darkness. Before Margot and Liz could begin to protest, there was the sound of a match striking, and a faint glow emerged from the black as Archit lit the wick of a rusty old lantern.

"Hope I didn't frighten you," he said, looking up from the lantern and assessing the reaction of each of his companions.

"Not at all," James said. "Where are we?" He looked around at the stone walls slimy with moss, and the staircase that wound downward into shadows. Humidity hung in the air, and the sound of drips and splashes from down below suggested there was water at the bottom of the stairs.

"Let's go then," Archit said, holding the lantern up to illuminate the stairwell. He made no explanation for where the lantern had come from or where they were; he merely worked his way to the front of the group and led them down the spiraling stairs.

"Hold on," Margot said. "Where are you taking us?"

"To Nalgordia," Archit said. "We went over all this last night."

"I didn't know it was in the sewer," Margot retorted.

Archit didn't even dignify that with a response, and James couldn't blame him. As far as James could tell, this clearly wasn't the sewer. This ancient stairwell was leading somewhere that wasn't a part of their town, or even of the real world that he'd always known.

As they descended, Archit's lantern occasionally illuminated maps and tapestries that had been mounted on the wall. James stopped to look at one that depicted a group of people dressed in clothing made of flowers and spiderwebs, and they were speaking to a dog that stood up on its hind legs.

"What are these tapestries showing?" he asked.

"Nalgordian history," Archit said. "Hippies. Sinacshin. They were an important part of establishing this world. Oh, here we are."

They rounded the corner to find themselves at the foot of the stairs in a high-ceilinged stone tunnel through which ran a river of the clearest water James had ever seen. Light from the ornate overhead lamps shimmered on the lapping waves of the river as it flowed along at a rapid pace, splashing the slate-tiled walls.

"Cool," James said.

"And look!" Liz said, pointing toward the water. "Look down there."

Margot did a double take. "What the heck!?"

About ten or twelve feet below the surface of the crystal-clear water, a miniature ocean floor spread out along the bottom of the river as far as they could see in either direction. Brightly colored fish flicked between coral reefs and occasional pieces of debris, swimming around sunken rowboats overgrown with barnacles and abandoned treasure chests overflowing with glittering gold and jewels.

"Get used to stuff like this. There are lots of surprises ahead of you," Archit said. "This river leads through the cavern and out to the sea. There's a canoe up there, over this way. Follow me."

He set the lantern down at the foot of the stairs and proceeded down the tunnel, leading them along the rim of a stone walkway that bordered the river.

"James, this is really weird," Margot said.

"You were cool with all of it last night," James said. "You can't turn back now."

He began to follow Archit, and the girls followed him.

"I think we'd better go along with it, Margot," Liz said as they walked. "Archit won't let us get hurt."

"What, like you know?" Margot said. "James, what have you gotten us into?"

"Archit needs our help," James said. "And I'm going with him." Maybe if she really did want to flake out, she might still be able to make it up the stairway, but James didn't want to suggest it. He didn't want them splitting up, even if it meant she was going to bluntly air her reservations the whole time.

James turned his gaze toward the river again and watched a school of fish gracefully dart back and forth, a turtle stir in the sand, and an eel weave its way through holes in a sunken crate.

"Here we are," Archit said, stopping beside a rustic-looking wooden canoe bobbing in the water. A mossy rope tethered it to a nearby post. Archit knelt down and began to untie it. "We'll take the canoe from here," he continued, "out of the tunnel, and from there, we'll make our way across the sea and up another river that runs through the jungle."

"The jungle?" Margot said.

"Yes. Don't worry, we won't go in the jungle. It's too dangerous. But the river runs straight through it into Nalgordia. It'll take us a few hours, but we'll nap and rest up when we get there."

When Archit finished undoing the rope, he reached into the canoe to pull out two bamboo poles and handed one of them to James. "Here. We'll paddle. Everyone get in."

James had to hold the edge of the canoe to steady it as he stepped in, realizing as he did that he had no idea what he was doing. He'd been canoeing only once before, when he was in elementary school and his class took a field trip to a nature reserve. He hadn't been very good at it then, and he had a feeling he hadn't improved in the meantime. He hoped, however, he would be good enough at faking it so that Archit didn't think he was a complete loser. He had to be James the adventurer and trusty sidekick, not James the nerd who couldn't get anything right.

Margot and Liz climbed in behind him. "Man, oh, man," Margot sighed as she settled herself clumsily on the floor of the canoe. "I wasn't expecting to be canoeing this morning." James could tell she was trying to look grace-ful as she smoothed out the skirt of her cocktail dress.

Archit hopped in the back of the canoe and gave his bamboo pole a dramatic swing over his head, bringing it down with a splash into the river and dragging it through the water. "And we're *off!*"

The canoe skimmed along the river swiftly, moving with the tide, and James found it easy to keep up with paddling. He wanted to say something smart or inspiring to start a conversation, but nothing came to mind.

What are the adults back home thinking at this point? More than likely, his parents and aunt and uncle, along with all the others who were at the party, were abandoning any hope that the kids had only snuck out for the night. They would soon realize the kids were gone—and not coming back for a while. How long before word got out around town? What would everyone at school say on Monday, when he got back?

A sudden shout from Archit caught his attention. "James, look out!"

James looked up just in time to see a sharp gray rock jutting up out of the water as their canoe slammed straight into it. He tried to pull his pole out of the water to push off against the rock, but he was too late.

Everything seemed to go into slow motion as the canoe split almost in half. Water poured in, taking the vessel beneath the surface of the river. James felt himself pulled under as the canoe suddenly dropped from under him, and he flailed his arms and legs to pull himself back to the surface.

"Ugh!" he shouted.

The others splashed around him. "Way to go, Jimmy," said Margot, treading water aggressively.

"Stop, Margot," Liz pleaded. "It's not his fault."

"I'm sorry!" James said.

"It's all right, James," Archit said, tossing his dripping wet mane out his eyes and flailing his wings to tread water. "But we need to get out of here fast. Look down."

A shout escaped James's throat. Four sharks circled beneath them.

"Calm down," Archit said quickly. "They're just circling for now. As long as we aren't bleeding, or flailing around like we're injured..."

Something down at the bottom of the river caught James's eye. It looked like a sword, resting halfway buried beneath a pile of debris, its silver shaft glinting in the dim light from above. "Hold on," James called to the others. Before he could overthink the situation, James took a deep breath and plunged downward.

He opened his eyes to look around as he swam down to the floor of the river. The silence of being underwater felt overwhelming, particularly when he was so scared. If he could get at the sword, he might be able to protect himself and the others should a shark or something worse try to attack them.

Swimming proved more and more difficult the deeper he went. James flailed his arms and legs, but his clothes dragged, heavy with water, as did the sport bag still strapped over his shoulder.

Just as he reached the floor of the river and began trying to move closer to the pile of debris where the sword lay, something grabbed at him from behind.

James turned. A girl hovered in the water just behind him, her angelic face surrounded by a swirling mass of white-blond hair. "Quick," she said, her voice ringing clearly through the water. "Go back to the surface, back to your friends. Leave the shark to me."

A mermaid! She was a mermaid! With a flick of her fishtail, she circled around him, reaching for the sword. He watched dumbfounded as she glided through the water. For a moment, he nearly forgot to hold his breath.

He looked around to see several other mermaids peeping from the reefs, looking at him with great interest, whispering to one another in curious voices.

"Look!"

"Isn't it sweet? It's an Earthling boy."

"Why has it come beneath the surface?"

"I hear they cannot breathe underwater. It will surely drown."

The mermaid who had first spoken to him hushed the others. "He's come to protect his friends from the sharks. We must do this for him." She looked at James. "Go, boy! Must you wait until you run out of breath?"

James nodded to her as a way of indicating he understood, then pushed off the floor of the river and began kicking toward the surface. He couldn't tell whether he was weighed down too much by his wet clothes or just pathetically out of shape, but had the water been any deeper, he might not have made it.

He came up splashing and gasping for breath so violently that he startled Margot and she actually screamed.

"Don't do that!" she shouted.

"Sorry," he wheezed. "But the mermaid—there's a mermaid down there, and..."

"What?" Liz said. "A mermaid? A real mermaid?"

"Oh, baloney," Margot said. "It can't be."

"She's got a sword," James said. "She said she'll protect us from the sharks."

"A shark won't attack a mermaid with a sword," Archit said as if it were common knowledge.

James still panted for air. He looked down. The mermaid floated in the water just below them, sword held outward toward the sharks as if warning them not to get any closer.

"This is crazy," Margot said.

"Crazy or not, there's no turning back now, Margot," Archit said.

"I didn't say I wanted to turn back," Margot replied.

"Well, there's nothing to do but swim," Archit said.

James shucked off his blazer and kicked off his shoes, finding it a little easier to stay afloat that way. He watched as Margot peeled off her cardigan, and she and Liz both pulled off their high heels. He was pretty sure Margot grumbled something about how expensive the shoes had been.

"Come on, then," Archit called, throwing his wing forward in the direction of the cave's exit not a hundred yards away. "That way."

They thrashed through the water, grumbling and sputtering as they swam in their wet clothes. James kept an eye on the mermaid swimming steadfastly beneath them, brandishing her sword to defend them. The sharks all drew back when she approached. Merpeople must have been worthy swordsmen, or else the sharks would not have been so afraid. This was especially impressive considering how hard it must be to brandish a sword under water.

When they swam free of the dark tunnel and through the cavernous exit into daylight, they found themselves in a wide-open sea. The dazzling blue waters shimmered under the scorching white sun overhead. The air felt tropical: slightly humid, moved only by a slight, salty breeze.

"How beautiful," Liz said.

"Yeah, fabulous," Margot said with a roll of her eyes. "Where are we supposed to go from here?"

"There," Archit said, pointing at a patch of green in the distance that looked like an island. If it had been a only little closer...

"What?" James gasped. "How are we supposed to swim all that way?"

Archit looked a little offended. "Well, we're supposed to be in a canoe, remember?"

"Oh, dammit," James cursed.

"It's not your fault, James," Liz said.

"Don't swear," Archit said, glancing over his shoulder, suddenly paranoid. "Whatever you do, don't swear when you're in these waters. It attracts pirates."

"Huh?" James and the girls murmured.

"I don't know if it's true or not," Archit said. "It might just be a legend. But I've heard that if you say a curse word while sailing the Nalgordian Sea, the sound of it will draw pirates to you the way sharks are drawn to blood. It's like they can smell it, y'know...then they know that there are people around for them to plunder."

"But I wasn't that loud," James said. "And I've said far worse before."

"It doesn't matter," Archit said. "Even a single drop of blood spreads quickly in water."

"But they won't bother us, will they?" Margot said. "The pirates, I mean. We don't have anything for them to steal."

"I don't know," Archit said, "but they might take us prisoner. We'd better start making our way to shore."

With that, he turned and began to do what James would have described as dogpaddling had he ever imagined that a bird could dogpaddle. James turned back to Margot and Liz. They looked unhappy, and he couldn't say he blamed them. Stranded in the middle of the open sea without so much as a canoe, not to mention the threat of sharks and pirates. Maybe they were out of their league here, not that he wanted to admit it.

"I guess we're going to have to swim," he said, avoiding eye contact with Margot. He began to breaststroke after Archit.

Liz was the first to notice the ship. Her face distorted into a look of dread, and she raised a quivering finger out of the water to point at the horizon opposite the direction they were swimming.

An illustrious galleon perched on the waves, its red sails fat with wind. From its mast flew the Jolly Roger, the black skull and crossbones seeming to laugh cruelly at their misfortune.

"The red sails of the pirate king," Archit said, fear in his voice.

The pirate king? Did I hear that correctly? James thought.

There was no use swimming away; in no time, the ship had overtaken them. A dark cloud rolled across the sun as it came near. A small dinghy descended from the main ship, approaching them with little hops over the choppy water. The two pirates rowing the boat leered at the children, laughing nastily.

"What do we do, Archit?" James whimpered.

"Quiet, James," Archit said, not taking his gaze from the approaching dinghy. "There's no way we're going to outswim them. We need to be brave now."

In a moment, the group found themselves in the dinghy with two of the vilest and most disgusting men they had even seen. The first was thin, the other stout; both were stained with sunburn and dirt, their hair damp with sweat. Their sullied clothes smelled rank with body odor.

James trembled at the way their gnarly hands had grabbed him, dragging him out of the water and into the boat as if he were an object rather than a person. He sat next to Margot, dripping wet, trying not to look as scared as he felt.

"You're our prisoners now, you are," growled the stout one, glaring at them. His mouth curled into a gummy smile. "Wait 'til Cap'n Blackcrab gets a look at you."

Onboard the pirate ship, they found themselves under the calculating gaze of fifty cruel, devilish eyes set in greasy, sunburned faces. James could hear some of them whispering to each other, but he couldn't tell what they were saying. He pressed himself closer to Margot, feeling much less adventurous than he had an hour before. Liz took his hand as she edged closer to him and Margot.

James looked at Archit, who he could see was surveying the crowd as if sizing them up for a fight.

What's he going to do if this gets violent? Has he met these pirates on his adventures before, or just heard stories about them?

"Ah, unexpected guests," a voice purred from the balcony above.

They looked up to see a man who could have only been the pirate king himself. Exquisitely dressed, he exuded an effortless air of malice. The man's sun-bronzed face was accented by a greased black mustache and goatee, a startling contrast to the wig of elbow-length white curls that curtained his shoulders. His tricorn hat bore a large red plume that matched the color of his velvet coat and satin shoes exactly.

James got the sudden impression that this was not a man to be trifled with: a man who was as savage as he was dignified, a man who might sip champagne when he made prisoners walk the plank, or smoke cigars when he threw traitorous crewmen to the sharks.

"And who, pray, are you?" Captain Blackcrab asked, striding down the stairs. He examined them with unsettling interest, boy and girls and purple animal, all dripping wet and looking terribly frightened.

Archit took a step forward. "I—I am Archit Birken."

"Birken?" said Captain Blackcrab, looking amused.

"Yes, sir. You've heard of me, I assume?"

Captain Blackcrab chortled. "You wouldn't happen to be related to Lord Birken, the dark lord of the Night Scourge?"

"Yes," Archit said. "Abbadon Birken is my uncle. We're on a journey right now so that I can break one of his evil curses."

"On a journey?" said Blackcrab. "Not anymore, you are not."

James didn't like the way that sounded.

"Tell me, Archit," the pirate king continued, "how did you come to be lost at sea without any vessel to carry you?"

"Our canoe crashed into one of the rocks in the river between worlds," Archit said. "We've been swimming since then."

James marveled at how cool and collected Archit sounded under pressure. Maybe it was from all the adventuring the bird had done before, but James didn't think any amount of experience would ever help him sound as naturally confident as Archit. Maybe Archit would implore the pirate king and his crew to spare them. Maybe with the right offer—like a pardon from Dawn Flower, who sounded like somebody important in this land, and the pirate crew might yearn to be pardoned by someone important—the pirate king would set them free. Maybe he'd even be so gracious as to give them a dinghy, in which they might row to shore.

"Well," said the pirate king, flashing another devilish smile. James noticed he had a gold tooth studded with a ruby. "It is good fortune that we picked you up. We wouldn't want for you to perish at the teeth of the sharks. My crew is on a journey to the Isle of Konilos this next day, but the day after we have finished our journey, we shall see you safely to the shores of the Nalgordian beach."

"But..." Archit began to object, and James was surprised by the note of desperation in his voice.

"Silence," said the pirate king, raising a jeweled hand.

Why had Archit objected? Wasn't going to the Nalgordian beach part of his plan all along? What trick were the pirates playing on them that James hadn't followed?

Captain Blackcrab pointed a finger at Archit, eyeing him ferociously. "Be grateful, young Birken, of the favor I am doing you. If you'd like for us to kill you now instead, I would be delighted to have it done. When blood is spilled, it always gives my crew incentive to scrub the deck. Or, if you so choose, you can wait for us to take you to shore—you can perish there in the Jungle of Darkness."

There was a chorus of malicious laughter from the crew.

"Take the humans below deck," the pirate king commanded. "The bird too. Lock them up. We will continue our voyage for the Isle of Konilos, and will leave them on the Nalgordian shore tomorrow morning."

Emboldened by desperation as a few of the pirates moved in on them, James rushed forward to push them away, shouting to his companions as he did. "You guys, run!"

Whatever had possessed him to make him think this tactic would be successful was knocked out him quickly and forcibly by one of the pirates he'd rushed. The brute, whose sleeveless tunic showed off biceps nearly the size of James's head, grabbed the boy, stopping him so forcefully it nearly made James throw up.

Several other crewmen lunged forward to overtake Margot, Liz, and Archit before they could make similar moves to escape. Margot didn't hesitate to throw a punch, as James saw when the brutish pirate holding him grabbed his hair and forced his head up. "Don't think you'll get away so easy," the pirate growled in his ear.

Before the chaos could escalate further, Captain Blackcrab drew a gold revolver from inside his coat and fired a warning shot overhead.

Everyone quieted immediately, their attention turning to the pirate king. Archit, though restrained by one of the pirates, stood near enough to James to put his wing out and urge him to calm himself, not to act out again. James understood that much.

The pirate king strode forward and glared at each of the adventurers one by one. "Well, well, well," he said. "A bit bolder than I thought you were, aren't you? You were submissive when my crew pulled you out of the water. Why this brashness now?" He looked around at all of them, then wheeled on James. "And you—you're not the coward I thought you were, are you?"

James didn't reply, unable to find his voice.

"Or maybe you are." The pirate king turned away from him and looked at Archit. "This boy overestimates himself. You should keep an eye on him."

James's cheeks burned. He didn't need the pirate king to mock him openly in front of his entire crew, let alone in front of Archit.

Captain Blackcrab turned his attention to Margot and Liz. He looked long and hard at Liz, as if he enjoyed the resolute face she put on. "Take care of these ladies," he said to his men. "If I find out they were in any way mistreated, you will walk the plank bound in lead chains." He looked around at his crew. "Is that in any way unclear to any of you."

The crew was silent.

"You know the rules of my ship," he concluded.

The captain leaned in close to Liz and Margot. "If any of my crew should offend you," he said, politely, "please, let me know. I will not have a woman mistreated under my flags."

Captain Blackcrab turned and walked toward the stern of the ship. "Take them below," he called over his shoulder.

The pirate holding James in a headlock passed him off to two others, who each took him by an arm and shoved him through the door leading below deck. "No," James shouted, trying to pull himself away. "Where are you taking my sister and cousin? Margot! Liz! Archit!"

"It's no good shoutin'," one of the pirates growled, pushing him down a flight of stairs. They dragged him through a maze of passageways, all of them dark, dank, and smelling of stagnant sea water. Their grip on his arms was tight enough that James felt sure it would leave bruises.

Midway through one of the halls, they stopped just long enough to practically rip open a wooden door and toss James inside.

The door slamming behind him hit James on the back of the head, knocking him forward. Wincing in pain, he could hear the pirates walking off down the hall. Even though it was a futile effort, he got up and shook the door handle, hoping it would miraculously pop open. No such luck, of course. He was locked in.

His eyes adjusted to the darkness. By the look of things, he was locked up in a closet. His only company in the cramped space was a mildewed broom propped against the wall. He huddled in the corner, crossing his arms close to his chest. He was still sopping wet, and the chilly, damp closet wasn't helping.

Some adventure this was turning out to be. How did Archit plan to get them out of this mess? And if he couldn't—then what? Why had Archit seemed so disturbed at the thought of being left on the shore of Nalgordia? Hadn't they been headed that way? What was this Jungle of Darkness the captain had mentioned?

James banged his head backward on the wall, partly out of frustration, partly as a means of self-punishment for ever thinking he would make a worthy adventurer.

"Don't cry now," he told himself. "Whatever you do, don't cry."

He hit his head twice more, trying to focus more on the physical pain than on his fear and resentment.

Hours passed, and he managed to calm himself enough to drift off into a light sleep. The sound of scratching at the lock awakened him.

The pirates! They're back! He scrambled to his feet, bracing himself, trying to look brave.

The door swung open, and there stood Archit. What a relief! James let out a sigh.

"Archit. How—?"

"You all right?"

"Yeah...yeah, I guess so. How did you know where to find me?"

Archit shrugged. "This was the only door that was locked. I've been searching for a while now. They had me tied to a post down below in storage."

"Did you pick the lock just now?" James nodded toward the handle of the closet door.

Archit held up a thin, bent piece of black metal. It was a bobby pin, one of Margot's.

"Margot came and found me," Archit said. "She's waiting for us in her room. C'mon, we have to go get Liz."

Archit turned to go down the hall. James grabbed his bag and followed.

After turning two or three corners, they went up a short flight of stairs. The two of them held their breath at every noise as they crept along.

At the top of the stairs, Archit paused, peeking around the corner cautiously. "The crew is up in the galley. They're drinking, and...well, they're doing whatever pirates do. There shouldn't be any on these lower decks, but if there are, we need to run in opposite directions. Hide somewhere; go back to where they locked you up, and I'll come find you."

James didn't like the thought of that. "But..."

"But what?" Archit's tone told James everything he needed to know.

"All right," James said.

They passed through a dimly lit corridor, then went down another flight of stairs to a lower deck. They passed several doors, which Archit counted as they went by. Stopping at the third door, he looked back at James. "Margot said this is where Liz is."

Archit peered through the keyhole. "Liz? Are you in there?"

Silence. Then Liz's voice. "Archit?! Is that you?"

"Shh!" Archit whispered. "We need to whisper, Liz. We can't be too cautious. Hold tight. I'm going to get you out of there."

He deftly wiggled the bobby pin in the keyhole, twisting it back and forth. The door swung open in seconds.

Liz knelt just inside the door, looking frightened and more vulnerable than James had ever seen her look. "James! Archit!" she leaped to her feet and threw her arms around James, drawing him in for the most relieving hug he had ever known. Even if he had no idea how they were going to get out of this mess, it was good to be back together. Liz turned to Archit. "Thank you!"

Archit shushed her. "Don't forget. We're still prisoners, and we need to keep quiet."

Liz nodded.

James peered through the doorway. Liz had been locked up in a grand suite of a room. Whoever had owned this ship before the pirates commandeered it must have been very wealthy, maybe royalty or gentry.

"Come on," Archit said. "Back to Margot's room. We need to make this quick."

He proceeded down the hall, and James and Liz followed.

They went through several turns in the narrow corridors, several times stopping to assess which way to go. When they reached the end of one particularly long hall, he went up a short flight of stairs to the door of Margot's suite.

Archit pushed the door open cautiously, peering inside. "I found them," he whispered.

James and Liz followed Archit inside. Margot sat on the edge of the bed, her hair down, her brow furrowed with worry. At the sight of her brother and cousin, her face lit up.

"James," she said, going in and hugging him close. "Thank God you're all right."

She looked at Liz over James's shoulder. "You good?"

Liz nodded.

James looked around at Margot's suite. Like Liz, she had been imprisoned in an exquisite sleeping chamber. The bed was made of well-polished wood and covered in silk and linen. The windows that looked out onto the moonlit sea were curtained with velvet. In the corner was a dressing screen, a large chest, and a table with a wash basin and pitcher. "Nice place you have here," he laughed. "They stuck me in a broom closet."

"I found Archit down in storage," Margot said, "tied to a beam like cargo."

Archit moved to shut the door. "So," he said, turning back to them. "Now that we're reunited—let's talk escape."

"We can go tonight," Margot said. "Now. While they're drinking themselves into a stupor. We can take a rowboat from up on deck."

"It seems...hasty. What if they catch us?" James said.

"Not tonight," said Archit. "Tonight, they very likely would catch us. We'll wait until tomorrow. They'll all row ashore to barter with the islanders of Konilos. While they're away, we'll break out and take whatever rowboat remains."

"Won't they take all the rowboats ashore?" Liz said.

"There are seven rowboats onboard," said Archit. "The entire crew can fit into six, but the pirate king insists on carrying seven because seven is a lucky number."

"Will they all go?" James said. "Won't a few of them remain onboard? Maybe a few just to guard us?"

"I doubt it," said Archit. "Even if several are told to stay, they won't. No pirate in his right mind would miss a visit to Konilos, even if it meant defying the pirate king's orders."

"Why?" James said.

"The islanders are generous," Archit said. "If they're welcoming the pirates as their visitors, they're likely to prepare a feast, and they'll trade for any riches and treasures that the pirates bring with them. Pieces of eight might be traded for anything from rum to smokes to concubines. Believe me, there's no way any of them are missing out on that tomorrow."

"So that's the plan then?" James said. "You'll come for us tomorrow morning?"

"They'll be gone for most of the day," Archit said, sounding surprisingly confident. "We'll have plenty of time to seize the seventh dinghy, and we'll be halfway across the sea toward Nalgordia before they return." He added, "With any luck, they'll be drunk and exhausted when they come back to the ship. They won't have the wits to sail after us until the next morning."

"That's good," Liz said. "These pirates give me the creeps. They were looking at me and Margot all through dinner." She poured some water from the pitcher into the washbasin and splashed some of it onto her face.

"Dinner?" James asked.

"Captain's orders," Margot said with a roll of her eyes. "He insisted that Liz and I join him for dinner. I've been on some bad dates before, and this doesn't even begin to compare."

"Captain Blackcrab would never let one of his crew disrespect a woman," Archit said, as if that were some reassurance. "He may steal and kill, but he would never hurt a lady. Not even he is that immoral."

"It's still pervy and gross," said Margot. "I don't care if they won't touch me; I don't want them looking at me like I'm dessert."

Liz lifted the lid of the cedar chest to peek inside. "Oh!" she exclaimed, opening it farther to reveal piles of women's dresses. James saw silk and satin of all colors, lace trimmings, ribbons, and brocades.

"Wow," Margot observed. "Would you look at those!"

"I wonder who these belong to," Liz said.

"Maybe the wife of the commodore—or, y'know, whoever owned the ship before the pirates took over?" James suggested, looking to Archit for affirmation. "This must've been her room, right?"

"Well, I hope she doesn't mind if I borrow one," Liz said with a laugh. "I can't stand being in this soaking-wet dress anymore. I hope one of them fits."

She pulled out a mass of blue silk and satin brocade, taking it behind the screen to change.

"Is it all right if we hang out for a little while, Archit?" James asked. He was starting to feel comfortable for the first time in hours; he didn't want to go back to the broom closet right away.

"I think we're safe for a few minutes," Archit said, "as long as we leave ourselves plenty of time to get back into our prisons."

"Good," James said. His stomach rumbled. "You hungry?" He reached for his bag and pulled out a few peanut butter sandwiches, still safely water-proofed in their zip-close plastic bags. The rest of the day might have sucked, but at least their food wasn't soaked. James would take whatever blessings he could get at this point.

Archit took an apple and a peanut butter sandwich and began to eat. James offered the bag to Margot, who declined. "Dinner with the captain kind of killed any appetite I might have had," she said. James wasn't sure whether she referred to the food itself or to the company. He had a feeling it was the latter, but then again, he remembered a History Channel special he'd seen on pirates. He recalled something about rotten vegetables and overly salted meats.

James noticed that Archit looked pensive as he chewed his sandwich. "What's on your mind?"

"Nothing," Archit replied.

"Be honest," James said. "Is it something about the escape?"

"We really need this boat," Archit said, "now that we've lost the mermaid to protect us from the sharks."

Liz peeked out from behind the dressing screen. "All right, you guys have to swear you won't laugh," she said.

She came out in something that must have once belonged to a princess. Empire-waisted and flowy, the royal blue dress might have been from the medieval or Renaissance period, if James were remembering art history correctly. Liz just looked relieved to be wearing anything other than the wet dress she'd had on before.

"You look cute," Margot said.

Liz laughed.

"You do," Margot insisted. "I mean, you look like you're going out for Halloween, but besides that, I really like that dress on you."

"Thanks," she said with a roll of her eyes. She sat down on the bed next to Archit. James offered her an apple and a sandwich, which she accepted eagerly.

"Why's it so important that we have a boat?" James pressed on with

Archit. "What's this Jungle of Darkness the pirates were talking about?"

Archit sighed. "The Jungle of Darkness surrounds Nalgordia on all sides. There's no way to get there except by going through the jungle."

"Is it that dangerous?" James said. What a stupid question that was. Places didn't have names like the Jungle of Darkness for no reason.

"Nobody who goes in there comes out again," Archit said. "It's full of plants that spit poison, and it's patrolled by a monstrous beast. That's why it's nearly impossible to get to Nalgordia, and only the most seasoned transuniversal adventurers have ever done it."

"You mentioned a river earlier," Liz said. "Is that the only way to get there? Down the river?"

"Yes, exactly," said Archit. "There's a river that goes through the jungle. It's how the merfolk out at sea can get to the lagoons in Nalgordia. We need a boat or we're out of luck."

James thought for a minute, but he didn't want to say anything. Any ideas he had probably weren't worthwhile. Archit was the brains of this operation, and he hadn't yet given James any reason to doubt him. Besides, what idea could James have that Archit hadn't already considered several times over? "Don't worry," he said to Archit. "I know we can do this."

Archit nodded. "We can."

Everything was quiet for a moment. A heavy tension hung in the air.

"We better get back to our cells," Archit murmured, "before the pirates come back."

James nodded and looked at Liz and Margot. "You two'll be all right?"

"I don't think we have much of a choice," Margot said.

"We'll be fine," Liz said.

James and Liz followed Archit toward the door. Before they left, Archit turned to Margot. "You keep the bobby pin," he said, holding the bent pin out to her.

"I have plenty of them." She gestured toward the table with the pitcher and basin where she'd laid seven or eight bobby pins she'd fished out of her hair. "You keep that one just in case you need it, buddy."

Archit nodded and carefully hooked the pin onto one of the button-holes of his vest.

"You're going to come get us all in the morning?" Margot asked.

Archit paused. "How about you do it?" he suggested. "Watch from your window. When you see they're all getting off the ship and headed toward the island, come and get me."

"You got it," Margot said.

"Goodnight, Margot," James said.

"Goodnight, Jimmy," she said. "Liz, Archit."

"Goodnight," they whispered.

The three of them filed into the narrow passage outside Margot's suite. Archit and James walked Liz to her room in silence. Liz thanked them and gave them both hugs goodnight. James and Archit stayed while she went in and drew the curtains, then unmade the bed, preparing for sleep. It was hard for them to part, even with the knowledge that they'd be escaping the ship the next day.

When James and Archit left Liz, they returned to the broom cupboard where James had been locked up. James hated the thought of going back in there.

"You're sure this escape plan is going to work?" he said.

"Sure as anything," Archit said. He didn't sound convincing.

James nodded. "Well, then..." He wanted to say something encouraging, but the words wouldn't come. "Goodnight."

He went into the broom closet, closing the door behind him. He heard Archit picking at the lock to close it, then the fading footsteps as he went away. James was alone in the dark until morning.

Again, he began to feel scared. *Archit will get us out of this whole mess,* he thought. *Tomorrow, we'll be headed to Nalgordia and visiting Dawn Flower. I'll be home for school on Monday, and everything will go back to normal.*

Despite his fears, James nodded off to sleep. It wasn't a deep sleep, but it was sleep nevertheless.

Their escape commenced the next day just before noon. Late in the morning, James heard voices and footsteps and shuffling in the corridors outside the closet and on the deck above, signaling that the pirates were up and preparing to depart. Then the ship was still for a few minutes. He didn't know how long. It could have been ten minutes, but it felt like an hour.

Archit's whisper from the other side of the door was a welcome relief. "James."

"Archit!"

"It's time to go," Archit said.

With the sound of the bobby pin scraping in the lock, the door swung open. There stood Archit and Margot. *This escape is actually happening,* James thought, excited.

"C'mon," Archit said. "We still gotta go get Liz."

They walked down the hall, which was now bathed in the warm glow of sunlight streaming in from the stairs that led up to the deck.

"It took them long enough to set off this morning," Archit said as they walked along. "I was beginning to think you forgot about us, Margot. Or else that something had gone seriously wrong."

"No, it just took those jackholes forever to get up and get going," Margot said. "It must have been all the drinking last night."

"They wouldn't let a little morning-after sickness stop them from visiting Konilos," Archit said.

"Clearly, they've got C-team abilities at handling their liquor," Margot said.

They arrived at Liz's room and Archit began to fiddle with the lock. Liz was waiting for them, standing in the corner of the room, still wearing the blue dress from the night before.

"Ready?" Archit said.

"More than ever," Liz said.

"You guys want some breakfast?" James asked, pulling a few granola bars from his bag. *Rations are getting low,* he observed. *Let's hope we make it to Nalgordia soon, or we're not going to have enough to sustain ourselves.*

They walked out the galley door onto the deck of the ship to see the blue-green sea spread all around them, the waves twinkling in the bright sun. After being cooped up below deck, James relished the feeling of the warm sun on his face.

Archit indicated an island off to the side of the ship. "There's Konilos, there."

It looked beautiful, green palm fronds spread out over white sand. Still, the thought that the pirates were that close...

"Let's get out of here," James said.

Archit nodded. "To the lifeboat, then," he said. "Let's not dawdle."

The bird bounded across the deck toward the last remaining dinghy, which was set out on the deck as if it were waiting for them. Archit went to hoist the boat over the side of the ship. "Help me, James."

James took a deep breath and braced himself to seem tough. He went and tried to assist Archit in lifting the boat over the guardrail.

Margot and Liz ran forward too. "Here, Jimmy, let us help you," Margot said.

Archit looked at them incredulously. "This is men's work," he said.

Margot and Liz laughed as if Archit had been joking, and they continued to help hoist the dinghy over the side of the ship. James caught a fleeting look of disbelief on Archit's face.

It shouldn't have been a shock to them that escaping a pirate ship would not be an easy effort, even if the pirates were not aboard. As James would recognize in hindsight, the pirates might have had many detestable qualities—they were dirty, foul, dishonest, thievish, cutthroat, disloyal, and inclined to drunkenness—but they were not stupid, and they took their deviant trade seriously. Captain Blackcrab's pirate crew would not sit by and let their captives escape them. A pirate did not leave anyone alive. All it took was one pirate to spy them, and the escape plan was sunk like an enemy ship.

The escape started out well, however. Once the four of them successfully got the boat over the side of the ship, they climbed into the teetering, shaking dinghy and did their best to steady it as Archit lowered them into the water.

James picked up the oars from the floor of the rowboat, keeping one for himself and handing the other to Archit.

They had hardly paddled four or five strokes before a great commotion arose on the island. The pirates had returned to the beach to fetch a chest full of gold and rubies that they had left in their dinghy. That was when they saw their prisoners stealing away from the ship in one of the rowboats.

Captain Blackcrab grabbed his pistol and fired a smoking bullet into the air. "Capture them! Capture them, I said!" Once, then twice more, the captain fired his pistol into the air.

"Oh, no!" Archit gasped. "Row, James! Row!"

But the pirate crew obeyed their king's orders as quickly as the bullets had flown from his gun, and James's and Archit's meager rowing skills were no match for them. Within minutes, they were overtaken.

Chaos ensued. Three pirate dinghies approached, blocking three directions of escape.

"Keep going, James!" Archit shouted. "We haven't lost this yet."

James's arms strained at the oars, dragging them through the water with all his might. His hands tore and burned against the rough wood of the oar. Hot sweat formed in plump, salty beads on his forehead. "I'm trying," he heaved as he looked up to meet Archit's desperate face.

Despite their effort and panic, the dinghy just seemed to bob and teeter in the water, not going anywhere.

Captain Blackcrab's shouts continued. "Don't let them get away!"

The pirate king stood in a dinghy propelled by at least a dozen men, all of them looking like wild beasts ready to pounce as they rowed aggressively toward him.

"Archit?" James whimpered.

There was nothing to be done. The pirates were gaining fast, steadily approaching.

Blackcrab's dinghy reached the ship, and the pirate king scrambled up on deck to observe the scene as his other five rowboats surrounded the seventh. Archit looked more desperate than James had ever seen him look before.

James followed the sole impulse that came to him. As one of the pirates reached to grab him, James pulled his oar out of the water, gripped it with both hands, and swung it into the pirate's face with such force that he might have knocked out a few teeth. James himself was so shaken by this defense that he fell forward and landed like a bridge between the two boats.

There was a good deal of confused shaking, splashing, and fighting. The pirates all reached for James at once to punch, restrain, or stab him with their swords, but Margot threw a punch at the first pirate who reached for her brother, and Liz was quick to come to her aid.

The pirate James had struck dropped his sword to hold his broken nose, and Liz grabbed for it. She swung it viciously, but the pirates had surrounded the dinghy; it was a hopeless fight with four youths against half a pirate crew.

Margot pulled James to his feet. "You all right?"

But James was too distracted by the sight of Archit getting abused by the pirates. "Archit!" he called out.

As one pirate descended on Archit, Liz swung the sword with all her might, leaving a deep gash across the brute's face. The pirate turned and struck her, sending Liz spinning. Another pirate grabbed Archit around the neck and pulled him into a headlock, face in the man's sweaty armpit. James leaped to defend Archit, but his movement was too fast and uncoordinated. The boat floundered so badly that James fell backward into the water.

For a moment, James couldn't figure out which way was up. He flailed his arms around, trying to right himself and swim toward the surface. A pair of powerful hands grabbed him at the shoulders and he was ripped upward out of the water.

He had never been pulled so violently or so fast, and hardly had his senses fully registered what was happening before he found himself dragged over the rail of the pirate ship and onto the deck. He blinked the water out of his eyes and stared up at the crew of villains standing over him.

Before he could get to his feet, a fist forced him up by the collar. James spun around to see that the person grabbing him was the pirate king himself. James gasped.

"Well, well, well," the pirate king said.

Captain Blackcrab shoved him into the clutches of two pirates who stood nearby.

James looked back at the pirate king to see the golden pistol pointed at his face. His heart jumped into his throat.

His eyes darted to Liz and Margot, putting up a fight as they were manhandled onto the ship. Both girls struggled wildly, kicking and scratching fiercely. Liz caught a glimpse of James's precarious situation and froze, giving up her resistance. She batted at Margot, who was still struggling with one of the pirates. Margot turned, seeing what Liz saw, and stilled her fight as well.

A tense silence swept over everyone on the ship. Friend and foe alike froze and stared at Captain Blackcrab, who aimed the pistol steadily at James, only inches away.

"A daring escape plan," Blackcrab said, sounding somewhat proud of his captives. "I must say, you did take us by surprise." He laughed coldly, then turned to Margot and Liz.

"Ladies," he said, "you know that I would never disrespect you in any way. But I have no qualms about hurting your companion here."

With these words, the pirate king flashed James a gold-capped smile, then turned back to the girls. "Pull another trick like this and I'll serve you tea and biscuits while you watch my crew scrub his brains off the deck."

Margot whimpered.

"Understand—all of you," said the pirate king, looking from James to the girls to Archit, "that on this ship, my word is law." He lowered his pistol and slipped it back into his belt. "We have rightfully kidnapped you, and if you try to escape, we will not hesitate to commit murder. You shall not rebel against my rule again." He smiled and actually looked charming. "Then, we're all understood."

He nodded at the two crewmen holding James and they loosened their hold. James heaved a sigh of relief.

Captain Blackcrab turned his attention to the girls. The pirate holding Margot tightly under the armpits set her down as the captain strode over. Liz got to her feet, her eyes still focused downward to avoid the captain's gaze.

"That's a lovely dress you have on, milady," he said to Liz. "I dare say I recognize it."

Liz looked up nervously, trying to find her voice. "I found it in my room." She sounded polite but not meek. "I put it on because I was cold and wet."

Captain Blackcrab smiled. "It's a beautiful gown, isn't it?"

Liz didn't respond.

"I believe that it belonged to the daughter of a marquis. Her wardrobe would fetch us a good fortune in trade. But you may keep that dress...as a gift from the pirate king."

Liz smiled weakly, and James could tell she was trying to hide her disgust. "Thank you."

"It will be a pity," Captain Blackcrab said aloud to his crew, gesturing to Liz, "when such treasure-worthy fabrics are torn to shreds by the Beast of Darkness."

The response was mixed—some grumbled, others laughed heinously.

"Now," Captain Blackcrab continued, "it has been wonderful enjoying the company of our prisoners. But I'm afraid it's time for them to return to the lower decks. I want each of them to be guarded in their captivity—is that understood? Good. Get them out of my sight."

The two pirates grabbed James by each arm and dragged him back below deck, back to the broom cupboard. There was no chance for escape; even if they got the chance, the risk was too great.

The sound of the key turning in the lock signaled that he was trapped, alone, doomed. Another night of imprisonment lay ahead—and the next morning, they would have to face the Jungle of Darkness.

James managed to sleep that night, but for the second night in a row, he didn't sleep well. He curled himself into a ball, tucked his head into the corner, and fell asleep to the rocking of the ship against the waves. He was awakened several times by the sound of groaning deep within the belly of the ship or by the waves lapping up on the wall he leaned against. He sat up and listened for a while each time, then went back to sleep. If he had more room to do so, he might have tossed and turned.

He must have found peace at some point because he was sound asleep when somebody came kicking at the cupboard door. James startled awake and scrambled against the back wall of the cupboard. He heard the sound of keys rattling, and the door opened to reveal the corridor outside, sunlight framing the pirate who stood in the doorway. The pirate's stubbly face was red with sunburn, shadowed by dreadlocks, and accented with a toothless smile and nose ring.

"Good mornin', wretch."

James scrambled to his feet, unsure of what to say. "Time to go?"

"Cap'n Blackcrab's orders."

The pirate reached forward and put his hand around James's neck. James managed to grab his bag as he was dragged out of the cupboard and shoved down the corridor. James found himself feeling a little sick at the smell hanging around the pirate, a mix of sweaty body odor and rank halitosis.

They went up onto the deck of the ship, where a hot, bright sun hung just above the horizon. Only a few strokes of a swim away from the ship was the island they had seen a mere two days before—Nalgordia, its stretch of white sandy beaches leading up to a forest of vines and palms and ferns, what James could only assume was the Jungle of Darkness.

The entire crew had gathered to bid the captive children and bird farewell, and to have some sort of perverse satisfaction, no doubt, at the idea of leaving the four of them behind with the knowledge that they'd soon be killed, either by the Jungle of Darkness if they ventured into it, or by the sharks if they decided to swim away from shore.

Liz and Margot sat on wooden crates, both of them looking tired and scared. Liz still wore the dress she had put on two nights prior. Archit was there too, though James didn't notice him at first. The bird stood nearby, held on what looked like a makeshift leash, though it more resembled a hangman's noose than anything else. The rope was held by a sullen pirate who watched him suspiciously, as if the bird might try to fly away.

Four pirates were already working on lowering a boat off the deck of the ship so that their prisoners could be rowed ashore. No sooner had James been pushed through the doors of the cabin and onto deck than the pirate king himself made a triumphant entrance, sweeping down the stairs at the stern of the ship. He appeared to be dressed in his best. His shirt was crisp, clean linen, his red coat had been brushed, and James was sure that his black goatee must have been freshly braided. Today he was even wearing a black tricorn hat, bejeweled around the brim and sporting two large feathers: one red and the other orange.

"Well," he drawled, with a look of delight. "Is this everyone? Are we all here and accounted for?" He grinned, and James could see the gold caps on his teeth shining in the bright morning sun. Captain Blackcrab lifted his cane and used it dramatically to count his four prisoners. "No use in delaying the inevitable," he said, cheerily. "Put them in the boats and get them to shore."

The pirate who had brought James shoved him toward the rail, lifted him by the armpits, and handed him to another pirate waiting in the dinghy below. Archit was stripped of his leash and handed down as well. James had to admit that they handled Archit far more aggressively.

Before any of Blackcrab's crew could grab Margot or Liz, the pirate king stepped forward. "Ladies," he said, "you know—I wouldn't leave you to be killed in the jungle." He paused, looking from one to the other. "I'm a lonely gentleman, and any company of women I've had in these years at sea has been few and far between. I would be willing to accept both of you onto my ship, if you so desired."

He reached forward to put an arm around Liz's waist, but before he could touch her, Margot shot her hand forward and blocked him. "Thank you," she said coldly, "but my cousin and I will stay with my brother and our friend." To emphasize her point, she pushed his arm away. "We'll go into the jungle."

However disappointed Captain Blackcrab might have been, he also looked surprised to be addressed so fearlessly, and by a woman at that. His expression quickly changed to one of spite. "It would be a shame to see such beautiful women perish, but if that's the way you'd like it to be, then you may tell the Beast of Darkness that the pirate king sends his regards."

He raised a hand to indicate his crew could put the girls in the boat.

Two pirates rowed the dinghy to a sandbar about twenty-five yards from shore. When the rowboat brushed the bottom, the pirates climbed out, splashing into calf-deep water to drag their prisoners out.

James went as willingly as he could, practically climbing out of the dinghy before either of the pirates could manhandle him. He turned back to see one of the pirates taking Liz by the arm.

"When the beast is ripping you apart, be careful not to get blood all over that pretty little dress," he said with a snarling laugh.

He shoved her onto the sandbar, followed by Margot. James went to them, helping them stand up and get their bearings to move out of the shallow water. The pirates laughed at their struggle.

"Bye-bye, children," one of them said. "And good luck."

With that, the brutes rowed away from the sandbar and back toward the ship. James watched them go, trying to quell the mix of emotions coursing through his body. Was he scared or angry? Maybe a mix of both. *Come on, man,* he thought to himself. *It's over now, and you did your best. Did you even know you could be that brave?* Still, it wasn't as if their adventure had started off in a good way.

"Well," he said, turning to Archit. "What now?"

Archit sighed, shaking some of the water from his feathers. "To shore, I guess. No use standing around here on the sandbar."

They trudged through the water, off the sandbar, and toward the beach. "When we get back home," Margot heaved, "I'm going to put on pajama pants, turn on VH1, and eat raw cookie dough straight from the tube. I am so sick of this place."

That was it—James was about to crack. He could deal with everything else, but hearing Margot complain about the adventure was too much. He pushed past her and onto the beach, then threw his bag down onto the sand, swearing. It didn't matter whether he swore or not now. If he were to be completely honest, he didn't care.

"James," Liz said, going near him and putting her comforting hands upon his shoulders. "Calm down."

Archit kicked his leather-shoed talons as he walked up on the beach, trying to get the water out of them. "I'm sorry, you guys. I'm really, really sorry."

"No. No, you have nothing to be sorry about," James said. He didn't want Archit to think that he was mad at *him*, of all things! "We're going to get out of this, and we're going to get to Nalgordia."

"Archit," said Liz, always the voice of kindness, "all right, so things didn't work out like you planned, but we're all still together, and we're all safe for now."

"Don't you understand," Archit said. "There's no hope now. Our only chance was taking a boat down the river through the jungle. That's the only way into Nalgordia. The jungle surrounds it on all sides, and if we set foot in there, we're done for. Otherwise, it's the sharks out at sea or the cannibals who hunt these beaches after dark."

"I'm not cool with the idea of cannibals," Margot said in a flat tone. "I think we're better off going in the jungle. If we meet this beast, the four of us should be a match for some animal. Can I have a sandwich, Jimmy? I'm all kinds of hungry."

James reached into his soccer bag and pulled out the last few sandwiches. He handed one to Margot and offered another to Archit.

"This isn't as simple as all that," Archit said, taking the sandwich from James and handing it directly to Liz. "The Jungle of Darkness isn't an ordinary jungle. There's no telling what could happen to us in there. The plants in there have minds of their own. They spit poison, or else they'll wrap their vines around you and suffocate you."

That was a visual that made James nervous. "You mean...*all* the plants in there?"

"Yes," Archit said. "All of them."

Liz broke her sandwich in half and handed part of it to Archit. "You need to eat something if you're going to keep your strength up."

But Archit was no longer paying attention. He had gone completely quiet, and his gaze was fixed out at sea almost as if he were hypnotized. "Do you guys hear that?"

James looked from Margot to Liz. No, they didn't hear what Archit heard either.

Archit took a step closer to the shoreline, stopping where the waves lapped up against the sand. "No, seriously. Do you guys hear that?"

"Hear what?" James asked.

"Singing," Archit said. He stood ankle-deep in the surf, entranced by whatever it was.

Liz took a step toward him. "Singing?"

"Yeah, don't you hear it?" Archit stepped into the surf, his gaze fixed out at sea.

"No," James said. He looked back at Margot and Liz for affirmation. "No, we don't."

He turned back to Archit just as a large wave crashed forward. Archit slipped and fell into the shallow surf, but another wave rumbled forward atop the first, sloshing and churning. The tide pulled back out, but Archit wasn't there.

"Archit!" James dashed forward. "Archit!"

"Where'd he go?" Margot shouted.

"I don't know," James said. "I didn't see any more than you did."

"Calm down," Liz pleaded. "He couldn't be far."

James trudged into the water and scanned all around, waving his arms under the surf. Nothing. No sign of Archit.

"What was he hearing?" Margot said, starting to sound panicked. "I don't get it. What was he hearing?"

James ducked beneath the surface, looking all around under the water, but he couldn't see anything. He came back up for air and dove back under again.

A face flashed in front of him underwater. It was a familiar face, but it took James a second to recognize it, and by the time he did, he had already sputtered back above the surface, startled.

"Boy," the mermaid addressed him, coming to the surface as well. "I did not mean to frighten you."

She lifted her arms from the water, and in them, she held Archit's crumpled body. Limp, unmoving, and dripping wet, the bird was a frightful sight. Was he dead?

"He is quite safe," the mermaid said. "But I bring grave news with me. Let us get him to shore."

The mermaid swam forward, carrying Archit with her, and James followed. Margot and Liz stood on the shore awkwardly, unsure of how to respond to all of this. Liz made the first move, stepping forward to take Archit in her arms so the mermaid could push herself up onto the sand.

"Where did you find him?" she asked. "What happened?"

The mermaid stretched herself out with remarkable gracefulness for being a creature with no legs. Whenever James had seen illustrations of mermaids reclining on the beach, it had never occurred to him how something with a fishtail could get so easily out of the water.

"He was hearing my people singing below the surface," the mermaid said. "It would seem his bird senses are sharp enough to hear us. I suppose he became mesmerized. A siren song has that power even when we don't intend it." She pushed her wet platinum tresses off her shoulders, displaying bare breasts with no indication of shame. James suddenly felt nervous.

"Thank you," he said, trying to find something impressive to say. "You have no idea how much we appreciate your help."

The mermaid flashed a smile at him. "You're welcome, boy."

"My name's James." He wanted to sound dashing, but it was instead just awkward.

"James," the mermaid said, "I must tell you—the land of Nalgordia is in terrible danger."

"What?" Margot said. "Isn't that where we're headed?"

"What do you mean danger?" Liz said.

"A wicked sorcerer is preparing an assault on all the land, to lay waste to all of it."

This sounded intense. "Mr. Birken, you mean?" James asked. "Is this evil wizard Abaddon Birken?"

"No, but perhaps a lesser wizard at his bidding," the mermaid said. "In only a few days' time, he will have laid waste to all the land. The green plants of the forest will wither and die, snow and ice will envelope everything, and the world will be cast in eternal darkness."

Margot looked as if she were choking on something. "What the...?"

"Dawn Flower awaits your arrival. She must give counsel to Archit and the three of you. But be swift. The sorcerer grows stronger every day."

"Who is this wizard?" James asked. "How many others does Mr. Birken have working for him?"

"That I don't know," the mermaid said. "We merfolk only know what gossip we hear from nymphs and naiiads. I will swim up the Nalgordian River and meet you on the other side."

"You've got to take us up the river with you," James said. "Please, Archit said we'll die if we go into the jungle."

"I've heard many a terrible story about the jungle," the mermaid said, "but it is your only hope. The river's current is too strong for a human swimmer."

"What is it with this place?" Margot said. "Good lord, isn't anything ever simple or safe?"

"Not often," said the mermaid. "And I'm afraid the jungle is your only way. But if you stay on the road through the jungle, the flowers will not strike you, nor will the beast be able to pick up your scent."

James's heart leapt with relief. "There's a road that goes through the jungle?"

"So I've been told," the mermaid said. "Look for a gate not a half-mile from here."

"That's not far at all," Liz said.

"Good luck," the mermaid said. "I will see you in a few days when you reach the other side of the jungle."

She began to push herself back toward the water.

"But what about Archit?" James asked.

"He'll come out of it in a few minutes," the mermaid said. "They always do."

How many times has she had to save somebody from drowning? James thought.

"Goodbye," the mermaid said. "Be safe."

"Thank you again," James said.

The mermaid pushed back into the surf and slid away into the lapping waves, giving her fin a kick behind her as she went.

"I'm never going to get used to this place," Margot said. "Couldn't she at least put on a clamshell bra, for crying out loud."

James laughed. "I don't know that real-life fantasy worlds are exactly the way they're shown in Disney movies."

"I don't know that real-life fantasy worlds are anything I ever thought I'd have to deal with," Margot said.

"This place is definitely scarier than I thought it was going to be," Liz conceded.

James wished he could have said that it was going to get better. But he knew that probably wasn't true.

Suddenly, Archit stirred, coughing up a mouthful of water. He sat up, wheezing and sputtering.

James fell to his knees beside Archit, putting an arm on the bird's shoulder. "You all right?"

"Yeah." Archit seemed to be remembering everything, or so the expression on his face indicated. "But you're never going to believe this. I heard the merfolk singing out at sea."

"We know," James said.

"No, that's the thing. You don't know. I could hear them, and they were singing about an evil sorcerer who's—"

"We know," James repeated. "The mermaid was the one who dragged you out of the ocean. The same one who saved us a few days ago."

"Then you heard everything? That he's planning to destroy all of Nalgordia?"

James nodded, looking at Margot and Liz for reassurance. Were they were taking all of this in the same way he was? The two of them had hardly been able to sit through a Ray Harryhausen movie—he wasn't sure that they actually got what was happening, actually comprehended it. No, not if Margot's biggest concern was the mermaid's being barebreasted.

He looked back at Archit. "She said he might be connected to your uncle."

Archit slowly nodded, a look like dread crossing his face. "I know he is. I didn't even have to hear that part of the merfolk's song."

"But why?" Margot said.

"My uncle is probably panicking that his curse is breaking," Archit said, "so he is going to destroy Nalgordia. To stop me from coming back here."

"So this other sorcerer…" James ventured.

"Lord Iceheart," said Archit. "A wizard fallen from grace, given new powers by my uncle. We need to reach Nalgordia before his strength has mustered. Otherwise, this whole quest will be in vain." He paused, hesitated, then added almost as an afterthought, "And I'll have put the three of you in more danger than I ever intended."

Those last words hung heavy on James. He became suddenly aware of how hot he felt under the scorching sun overhead. He reached up and loosened his tie and undid the button around his collar, then rolled up his sleeves as well.

"Well," Archit said, trying his best to hide his fear, "there are always going to be obstacles, aren't there?"

Liz got up and brushed the sand from her dress. "The mermaid mentioned a gate," she said, "and a pathway through the jungle."

"This way, I think," Archit said, walking down the beach. "We shouldn't be too far."

They trod through the sand along the shoreline for several yards. James looked up at the jungle. He hadn't noticed the iron fence surrounding it until he looked carefully. Green vines, glistening and slimy, wrapped around a rusted iron enclosure crowned with metal spikes. James got an odd sense that this decrepit fence was the only thing that stopped the jungle overgrowing its boundaries and taking over the whole beach.

"I wish I could say the road is still going to be intact," Archit said. "That used to be the way travelers would go. But Nalgordia has been cut off from the mortal world for so long now that the road might be gone."

A chorus of seagulls shrieked in the distance. Everything James normally loved about the beach wasn't much of a comfort to him now. "Archit? Can you explain a little bit more about this sorcerer?"

"In due time, James," Archit said.

Fine, great, it's not as if I'm really freaked out about this, James thought. What a frustrating answer! James had willingly agreed to come with Archit, but he at least deserved to know what was going on.

"Here it is," Archit said, turning toward the fence.

On the rusty gate was mounted a crude sign made from a scrap of driftwood painted with what looked like curdled black blood.

Jungle of Darkness
Go no farther

"Oh, God," James said.

"Is that blood?" Margot said. "Foul."

"I don't like the look of this," Liz said.

Archit nodded. "There are few who would, Liz," he said. "But we don't have another choice."

James peered at the shadowy foliage waiting just beyond the bars of the fence, waiting to swallow them up. They might lose their way. They might be torn to pieces by the beast. Any number of dark, horrific demises awaited them.

"Do you see those red flowers?" Archit said.

James nodded. The flowers looked almost black in the shadows, but where the light made its way through the trees, their petals gleamed like rubies. If

James hadn't known better, he might have thought they were hibiscus. But there was something different about them...something that wasn't quite right.

Before Archit could explain anything about the flowers, a black toucan swooped down from behind them and perched on the gate. It bobbed its head and clucked its large blue bill at the newcomers. Stretching its wings again, it fluttered into the jungle.

It was all over before James even knew what happened. Quick as a pouncing cobra, one of the flowers lunged forward, its stem stretching and its black center opening to reveal sharp teeth. It grabbed the toucan and wrestled it to the ground.

The toucan was dead before it hit the sand. When the flower pulled away from its prey, the toucan's glassy, lifeless eyes were fixed on James. He watched those eyes fill up with red poison.

The flower, its work being done, relaxed its stem and slithered back into place on its vine.

CHAPTER 5
The Jungle of Darkness

The rusty gate opened with a loud, screeching creak as Archit pushed it forward. The sound sent a shiver down James's spine. He still couldn't get the sight of the dying toucan tumbling to the ground out of his head. As he walked through the gate, he tried to avoid looking down at its little crumpled body and lifeless, glassy eyes.

He could feel Margot and Liz close behind him, the sound of their breath restrained as they stepped into the shade beneath a thick canopy of foliage.

"Stay away from the vines," Archit warned them.

"No kidding," Margot said. She sounded bitter, James figured, but at least she sounded as if she understood what they were up against.

Archit let the gate close with another loud creak. "And keep your voice down. They can hear, you know."

"The flowers?" Margot whispered. "The flowers can hear?"

Archit gave a deep sigh. "Come on," he said, leading them forward. "This way. I guess it's best that you all see for yourselves."

James would never forget his first impression of the Jungle of Darkness, an impression of awe and fear. It was beautiful—there was no denying that—but there was something intangibly toxic and dangerous in its breathtaking glory. He couldn't put his finger on exactly why it was so terrifying, but it was. Something about the lush, glistening greenery hanging all around them made him feel claustrophobic and nervous. The air clamped around them with oppressive heat and humidity.

He took a few steps forward, following Archit. Before he could catch up, he sensed movement. Several of the plants were perking up, as if they had taken notice of the strangers.

Archit held up a wing, his eyes going wide. James could read the expression without question: Stop moving. Hold completely still. Try not to breathe.

"They know something's in the jungle," Archit said. "They know we're here."

A wind rushed through the jungle, shaking the leaves. At least, James thought it had been wind.

"They're whispering to each other," Archit continued. "They're spreading word to their master that there are intruders."

"Their master?" James said.

"The Beast of Darkness," Archit said.

"What is this Beast of Darkness you keep talking about?" Margot asked.

"We'll need to go one at a time," Archit said, avoiding the question. "I'll go first. When I usher you forward, James, you follow me. Girls, once we're safely through, you can come through too. All right?"

James nodded and looked to Margot and Liz to be sure they were doing the same. The last thing he needed was for them to chicken out or refuse for whatever reason.

Archit's first few steps into the jungle were reluctant, but then he moved with a little more boldness when none of the flowers seemed to take notice of him. After he was several steps in, he turned and waved for James to follow him.

James took a deep breath and pushed forward despite the pounding in his chest. He took two steps, paused, then took two more. When he reached Archit, the bird waved for Liz and Margot to follow suit.

"How big is this jungle?" Margot hissed as she caught up to them. "We'll never make it moving at a pace like this."

"It's about twenty miles," Archit replied.

"Twenty?" James said.

"But I don't intend to go like this for very far," Archit said quickly, as if to clarify. "There should be that path up ahead where the vines and flowers won't be able to reach us."

"Should be?" James repeated.

"Come on," Archit said, pressing onward.

This was probably going to be another one of those times when Archit refused to provide explanations for anything. Maybe it was because Archit didn't want to scare them, or maybe it was because he didn't understand things quite as thoroughly as he acted as he did, or maybe he thought that a group of humans didn't have enough background knowledge to explain everything without an hours-long seminar-style rundown of everything. Whatever the reason, it bothered James to be denied an explanation.

"Are you kidding me?" Margot said. "This isn't what I signed up for."

James ignored her, instead kneeling to cuff his pants, rolling them once, twice, then up to mid-calf. It wasn't enough in the sweltering humidity of the jungle, but it would have to do. *What I wouldn't give to be wearing shorts!*

Up ahead, Archit turned and hissed back at them, a note of hopeful excitement in his voice. "You guys, wait till you see this! We might be in luck!"

James and the girls hurried forward to where Archit stood, pointing with his wing at a few wooden boards strewn around the forest floor.

"These boards," Archit said. "These look as if they used to be part of the path. We must be getting close."

He looked up, and pointed onward in front of them. "See? There are more!"

About ten paces away, more planks of discarded wood lay in the weedy overgrowth. Some were even still bound and nailed together, and a few even looked as if they were in some sort of order.

"Maybe..." Archit spoke to himself as he walked forward. "Maybe...the path is still here..."

A gasp from Liz behind him nearly scared James out of his skin. "Look!" she shouted, her voice rising. "There it is!"

James followed her pointed finger. She was right. Through the crisscrossing vines and shadows, what was undeniably a rough puncheon built of thick logs weaved through the knee-high undergrowth. The castaway boards they had passed must have been part of the trail leading off the beach, but it had since fallen apart in the years that nobody had used it or maintained it.

"It's a path!" James said. "Oh, hell yes! It's a path!"

Archit hurried forward, and James followed him. "Does this mean we're safe now?" Margot shouted after them as she and Liz caught up.

"As safe as we can be here in the jungle," Archit said, climbing up onto the trail. "The vines and branches won't be able to reach us as long as we stay on the path—and the beast won't be able to follow our scent."

That's a relief, James thought. He stepped up onto the wooden planks. It sounded as if there were something about the trail—something special—that blocked the jungle from having power over those who traversed it, the way hunting dogs lose the scent of their quarry when it passes through water.

Margot pointed into the tall grass alongside them. "What's that?"

James followed her gaze and saw the weather-beaten handle of a rusty axe that looked as if it had been abandoned long ago. He stepped off the path and reached down to lift it up, finding it much heavier than he expected it to be.

"It's an axe," he said, giving it a swing to test out his abilities. He'd never handled an axe before, though he'd watched his grandfather chop firewood several times.

"James, be careful!" Archit shouted.

The panic in Archit's voice caught James's attention, and he turned just in time to duck a venomous vine reaching straight toward him. Liz and Margot both screamed as the vine twisted back and felt around for the prey it was certain had been there but a second before.

James scrambled through the grass and back onto the path, dragging the axe behind him. He collapsed onto the wooden boards, gasping for air with panicked breathlessness.

"That's why we need to be careful in here," Archit shouted. "Got it?"

James sat up, nodding. Had Archit just snapped at him? Archit had never been harsh before. And after James had almost died? Archit didn't even seem fazed or worried about him at all!

"The walkway is the only safe path through the jungle," Archit contin-ued, his tone softening. "If we keep to the path, the plants won't be able to reach us. But if we stray from it..." He looked out into the jungle.

"We won't need to, will we?" James said. "Stray from it, I mean. We won't need to stray from it."

Archit stood silent for a second. "Let's hope not," he said. "Come on."

He began walking and the others followed. His words echoed in James's ear: "Let's hope not." But he didn't know. And the way he had said it! *He sounded almost hollow,* James thought, *as if he didn't even care. And when I almost died, he didn't even seem concerned, didn't seem worried about my safety...he just seemed angry that I'd screwed up.*

For the better part of the day, they made their way through the jungle, and James tried his best not to let his anxiety eat at him. But as the air grew muggier and their surroundings became darker beneath the heavy foliage, it was hard not to worry.

In some parts, the overgrowth was so thick that it blocked out the midday sun entirely. The stifling heat that hung in the air, combined with the weight of the axe, drained James's energy. He didn't want to complain that he was exhausted, partially because he thought it might give Margot and Liz the idea to do so as well, and all he wanted to do was keep morale up. Even more so, however, he remembered how Archit had been so short-tempered with him, and he didn't want to cause any more trouble.

A horrible thought crept into James's mind. He just wasn't up for this—that much he had known from the start, but he had hoped he might be able to hide it while he faked some façade of heroism for at least a little bit of the journey, at least enough to get by.

Maybe Archit could tell he wasn't cut out for adventure. *He probably realizes you're not the companion he needed for something like this. He doesn't care whether you make it out alive because he's better off without you.*

They hadn't been walking for more than an hour before his stomach startled to grumble and he felt the sharp pangs of hunger. With all the excitement they had been through so far that morning, he hadn't felt hungry until then. Their supply of food depleted, he tried his best to ignore the feeling. But with the heat and humidity, he felt increasingly lightheaded and irritable as the day wore on. If any of the others were hungry, they weren't saying anything—not even Margot.

By the time the sun set and the sky through the overhead vines darkened to star-studded blackness, his whole body ached with exhaustion.

"Archit," Liz said, and James could tell she was trying her best to sound gentle, "can't we stop and rest for the night? We've been walking all day." James was relieved that Liz had said something and he didn't have to.

Archit sighed, staring ahead into the darkness before them. "I suppose here and now is as good a place and time as any," he said. "Sure, let's rest."

James took in as much of their surroundings as he could in the darkness. The moonlight gleamed silver on the vines just a few feet away, but there was no motion in the shadows as far as he could tell. Still, he didn't like the idea of stopping to sleep in the jungle, even as tired as he was. He had hoped they'd be able to traverse the whole thing in a day.

Margot and Liz were already stretching out along the wooden beams, so James followed their example. He got to his knees, not quite ready to lie down completely. He was so sore it almost hurt to take any position other than standing, no matter how good it felt to be off his feet.

It wasn't until he was still that he noticed the air had gotten cool and clammy. As if Archit had read his thoughts, the bird said, "I'd suggest we make a fire, but...well, you know." He ran his foot along the wooden beams as if to illustrate how impractical the idea would be.

"It doesn't matter much, does it?" Margot said. "I'm just ready to fall asleep."

"Goodnight," Liz said, lying with the folds of her medieval skirt spread out around her.

A lull hung over them in the dark, and the girls drifted off to sleep in what felt like only a few seconds. James sat and watched them, looking over at Archit every so often. Their fearless leader didn't act as if he were getting ready to sleep anytime soon. Instead, the bird sat, staring off into the darkness beyond their safe little path.

"How many miles do you think we covered today?" James asked.

Archit shrugged. "I'd say about twenty. Maybe a little more. If we get an early start, we might reach the other side by noon."

James nodded, feeling once again the uncomfortable weight of the silence.

"Are you worried?" he asked.

Archit turned to him, his expression blank. "No. Why would I be?"

James didn't know how to respond. *Because you have every reason to be worried,* he thought. *Heck, even I'm worried, and the stakes are nowhere near as high for me as they are for you!*

"I just figured you might be," he replied. From the way Archit had responded, James felt stupid for even trying to be sensitive. "I just thought I'd check," he added. Friends were supposed to comfort each other in times like this, but he always thought that when he had to be brave for a friend, it wouldn't be so uncomfortable. James had always thought that it would be easy, that he would feel confident he was doing the right thing, that his friend would appreciate and welcome the support.

"Nope, I'm totally fine," Archit said, his tone flat, his meaning unclear.

James nodded. "Then what are you thinking about?"

"There's nothing wrong," Archit insisted. "Really, James."

Another lengthy silence followed.

Did Archit really think James didn't care? Did Archit really think he couldn't trust James? That James wouldn't understand? After the ordeals they had just been through together, did Archit think that James was just here for fun, that he couldn't count on James for anything?

Maybe he does feel that way, James thought. *You can't row a canoe or escape from pirates or avoid getting attacked by poisonous plants. Who's to say he can rely on you to be a confidant. You're not the companion he needs on this journey. You are in no way the companion he needs on this journey.*

The uncomfortable moment of quiet felt like the puncheon trail—long and full of the unknown. James tried to swallow the lump that had grown in his throat.

"Well, I'm here to listen," he offered.

"All right."

Archit gave a sigh, one that sounded to James as if Archit were irritated by James's sensitivity. "I'm going to get some sleep," Archit said. "Goodnight."

"Goodnight." James found it hard to say. The word was cumbersome in his mouth because he had so many other questions he wanted to ask, so many worries he wanted to confide in Archit. More than anything, he just wanted assurance that Archit knew he was in this to help, that he wasn't just some burden.

Archit got up and walked a few feet away to an open spot on the puncheon trail where he could stretch out. No sooner had he settled on the wooden beams than he was asleep.

James continued to sit up. Whether he sat for minutes or hours in the quiet darkness, he didn't know. As exhausted as he was, he had found an unwelcome but undeniable energy from his anxiety. He replayed his exchange with Archit over and over again in his head, trying to make meaning out of it.

It didn't help that each of the eerie shapes of the silhouetted plants just a few feet away felt as if they were watching him, as if they were some sort of animal watching and waiting, ready to strike and kill. But he knew the plants couldn't hurt them as long as they stayed on the path. As long as they stay on the path, they were safe.

But still...if they had to leave the path for any reason...

He lay back, staring up at the moon overhead, feeling regretful for the first time that he was on this journey. How could he have been so stupid to think that he was a hero? For the past three days, he had been nothing but a burden. To make matters worse, Archit had—up until that day—been the only person who seemed to believe in him and to count on him. James had just turned out to be the one who messed everything up.

"Welcome to the jungle," he whispered to himself, staring up at the black expanse of sky overhead.

He drifted off to sleep, and his slumber trudged by at an encumbered pace throughout the night, punctuated with tossing and turning, full of frightening dreams that he had completely forgotten about by the time morning arrived.

He awoke to find Archit standing over him. With the bird shadowed by the bright morning sunlight creeping in through the overhead foliage, it took James several seconds to comprehend that Archit had the axe and was holding it up, ready to strike.

James gasped, but he understood what was happening quickly enough to stifle the scream in his throat.

He was lying in the grass just off the edge of the path, possibly having rolled off in his restless sleep sometime in the night. Two vines had twisted around his arms to hold him still. A third vine, this one headed by a blood-red flower, was poised inches from his throat, ready to strike.

Archit must have seen the panic on James's face because his eyes went wide. "Shh!"

The flower turned to Archit, almost as if it were daring the bird to strike, daring him to attempt defending his comrade. James had known somewhere in the back of his head that the plants of the jungle were sentient, but not until this moment had he observed it so perceptively.

The flower turned back to James and hissed. Up close, James saw the blossom had teeth set deep in its eye. Needlelike fangs stared back at him, bared and ready to strike.

In a horrifyingly swift move that took even James by surprise, Archit swung the axe and severed the flower from the vine.

The vines tethering James's arms tightened, and a shout escaped his throat. Archit swung the axe again, chopping at the vine that held James's right arm.

The other vine, the one around his left arm, suddenly tugged at him, dragging James deeper into the grass. Another nearby branch, this one barbed with thorns, swung downward as if it might stab him.

Wasting no time, Archit dashed over and clipped at the thorny branch with the axe, sending its severed end flying.

James reached over and tried to rip the vine binding his left arm, but the grip was too tight. "Archit!" he called out.

The bird swung the axe once more, slashing the last vine that held James. The severed pieces of the plant let loose a stream of black poison that flowed onto the grass like blood. James watched the plant begin to twist and writhe—at first, he would have compared it to a wounded animal in pain, but it was different. It looked more like a person being exorcised, having a demon driven out. James could have sworn there was the faint sound of screaming coming from the plant.

James rolled over and scurried back to the puncheon, followed by Archit. Margot and Liz, the two of them now wide awake, were sitting up with looks of mixed confusion and horror.

"Good God!" Margot exclaimed. "What the—?"

"Are you two all right?" Liz asked.

James collapsed onto the wooden beams and tried to catch his breath. "Yeah...yeah...I'm all right. Thanks to Archit."

Archit chuckled forcedly. "Looks as if you were a restless sleeper last night. I guess you rolled a bit too close to the jungle there."

"Yeah," James said. "I guess I did." He looked up at Archit, registering it all—Archit had saved his life.

"What happened?" Margot said.

"I...I...think some of the vines snuck up on me," James said.

"How awful," Liz said, aghast.

"Archit, I don't like this place," Margot said. "How much longer until we're out of here?"

"We should reach the outskirts of the jungle by midday," Archit said.

"That's noon," James clarified to Margot.

"I know that, smartass."

Archit looked uneasily around them at the jungle. "That is as long as we don't run into any trouble."

"Trouble?" Liz said.

"I mean, if I could foretell what trouble that might be, I'd be sure we'd avoid it," Archit said. "But unfortunately, there's no telling what we'll face as we head farther into the jungle."

James tried to avoid looking at Margot and Liz. *I don't want them to be mad at me,* he thought. *This adventure sure as hell isn't going the way I hoped, but if they give up, then I'm not going to be able to hold it together.*

His eyes wandering, James looked down at the severed vine lying on the floor of the jungle. Something about the large, jagged tooth sticking out of the stem—a tooth as long as a dart, and one he just knew was poisonous—made him nervous. But...

We should take that with us, a little voice in his head whispered. *Having an extra weapon won't hurt.*

What if they did end up meeting the Beast of Darkness? The little voice was right: Having an extra weapon wouldn't hurt.

"Should we try to take that?" James asked, pointing at the dart.

Archit looked at it, seeming to understand what James was saying. "Yeah. Yeah, I think we should."

James bent down.

"It's all right," Archit said. "You can touch it. Just don't stick yourself with it, whatever you do."

James picked up the vine and plucked the poisonous dart out of the end. He held it up and watched it glimmer in the dim morning light streaming through the overhead foliage.

"Wow," James whispered.

"Just be careful holding onto it," Archit said.

James understood. "Sure," he said.

He pulled a bandana out of his bag. If he were going to hang onto the dart, he wasn't going to carry it on his person without wrapping it up in something first. That was an accident waiting to happen.

"Do we have anything left to eat?" Liz asked as she watched James root through his bag.

James had to admit he was hungry too. But the sandwiches were all gone.

"No," he said, shaking his head.

"But look," Archit said with a wave of his wing. "Look! Do you see that there through the trees?"

James and the girls moved close to Archit and stared in the direction he pointed. Just beyond the dense mass of foliage around them, a grove of trees stood bearing what looked like bright blue apples or pears dangling from its branches.

"Is that fruit?" James asked.

"Yeah," Archit said.

Margot didn't look enthused. "Why...why are they blue?"

"They're Nalgordian otaheite," Archit said, as if the answer were obvious.

"Huh?" Margot said.

"They're a type of fruit," Archit said. "But I didn't know they grew in the Jungle of Darkness."

James's stomach gurgled again, and he knew that it might be several hours, if not a whole day, until they found food again. "Should we go and get some?" he asked. At this point, he was willing to risk it.

"It's...it's too dangerous for us to leave the path," Archit said. He hesitated another moment, then said, "I'll go. You all stay here."

With that, he stepped off the path and began to head back into the jungle.

James wasn't about to let him go alone. Not after what they had just experienced. "I'll come with you," he said.

Archit turned back to him. "No."

"James," Liz protested from back on the path, "you almost just got killed by those plants."

"Which is why I'm not afraid to risk it," James said, proud to at least sound a little gutsy if he could. "I can do this."

Archit nodded, almost as if he understood it was useless to argue about it. "Come on, James."

The two of them headed deeper into the jungle.

"James, you'll be careful, right?" Margot said.

For a moment, James thought Margot was worried about him, but Margot wasn't the type to worry or baby him. Margot had always perceived worry as something very not cool.

"No, Margot, I'm gonna try to get shot by a poisoned dart."

His sarcasm wasn't appreciated, or so he saw on the faces of Margot and Liz as he looked over his shoulder when he stepped off the puncheon. They didn't laugh or even crack a smile, too stressed out to be amused.

He trudged through the undergrowth with Archit right behind him, pushing back some of the tangled plants that stood in their way. Some of the flowers growing on vines nearby perked up and took notice.

As they got closer to the fruit trees, James noticed how the black bark of the trees gleamed silver where the light hit it.

He walked up to one of the trees and gaped at the fruit, so bright blue that they seemed to glow. He plucked one of the strange apples. Its soft, plushy body reminded him of a water balloon filled taut.

"Come on," Archit whispered. "Let's fill your bag and get out of here."

James was about to ask why Archit was whispering, but he had a feeling he knew the answer. He felt suddenly self-conscious and looked around.

"Do you...do you think they know we're here?" he asked Archit.

"I don't know," Archit replied. "But let's not draw attention to ourselves."

James grabbed at otaheite with both hands and began to toss them into his bag. Between the two of them, they were able to fill the bag with nearly a dozen pieces of fruit before a distinct rustling came from overhead. James looked up as a vine descended from one of the branches, a cluster of flowers on its end staring straight at him and Archit.

"Don't move," Archit whispered, paralyzed with fear.

James nodded ever so slowly to show he understood.

"Back up very slowly," Archit whispered. "No sudden movements."

As ill luck would have it, James stepped backward directly onto a stick. The cracking sound beneath his foot made his heart jump

Two vines shot toward them from opposite sides, and James had to duck to escape one's grasp.

"Run!" Archit shouted. "Run!"

The two of them took off, sprinting back to the trail. All around, leaves thrashed and vines lurched toward them, nearly grabbing or stabbing them with every step they made.

This was so stupid! Why did I go?! Why did Archit let me follow him? Why?!

By the time they collapsed onto the wooden beams, James was shaking so much he could barely stand up.

"Oh!" he shouted, trying to form words.

Margot and Liz helped him to his feet. "Are you all right?" Margot asked.

James couldn't keep it inside any longer. "What were you thinking?" he shouted at Archit. "Letting us go out there?! What's the matter with you?"

Archit looked completely baffled. "What?" What do you mean? Where's this coming from?"

Hot tears welled in James's eyes. He was angry and scared and embarrassed.

"Why?" James shouted. "You know how dangerous the jungle is. Why did you let me go out there?"

"You were the one who insisted on coming," Archit said.

How could he sound so calm? Didn't he get it? "You should have insisted that I stay," James roared, choking back tears. "You should have tried harder to stop me. I could've been killed."

"But you haven't been killed," Archit said. "You're safe right here."

"That's not the point," James insisted.

Archit's voice sounded so untroubled, so unconcerned. "You're making a big deal of nothing," he said.

"Over *nothing?!*" James screamed, feeling himself lose control of his emotions.

Liz reached out to him. "James—"

"Stay out of this," James said, turning to her and Margot. "Both of you, go on ahead. Archit and I will catch up with you."

The girls looked appalled, but they didn't question him. Without another word, the two of them headed off down the path, leaving James alone with Archit.

For a second, James couldn't form words. He was so stupid for shouting the way he had, but at the same time, didn't Archit understand why he was so upset? It took him a moment to control his crying.

"James," Archit said, "you're letting the jungle get to you."

"What's that supposed to mean?" James said.

Archit looked up, trying to keep his eyes on Margot and Liz. "C'mon," he said. "We should keep up with the girls. Let's not dawdle back here."

"I don't understand why you don't care."

"Of course, I care, James," Archit insisted. "But you're going crazy. It's the jungle doing this to you, and you need to resist it."

"Don't blame it on the jungle!" James shouted.

But maybe there was merit to what Archit said. Anxious, fearful, full of more self-doubt than he ever had, James couldn't figure out which extreme emotions were justified and which ones weren't. Was there really a chance that the jungle was doing this to him? Was it clouding his mind and making him lose touch with sense and reason?

"James, you can't freak out like this," Archit said.

James wiped away his tears with the back of his hand, unsure of how to continue the conversation. *If he's not going to apologize, then there's no sense in fighting about this.* "Come on," he said. "Let's catch up with the girls."

They walked on. The uncomfortable silence hung in the air as thick and unrelenting as the humidity.

"Ssstt...sst," the vines whispered every so often.

"Ignore them, James," Archit whispered, keeping his eyes straight ahead.

"Huh?"

"I said to ignore them," Archit said, his voice still low. "Remember what I told you about the darkness. You can't let it get to you. Don't let them know that it's getting to you."

Easy for you to say, James thought. This quest had all been Archit's idea, and questing was supposed to be his area of expertise! If the jungle were really so powerful, why didn't it seem to have any effect on Archit?

Up ahead, the puncheon curved around a low-hanging branch. When they walked past the curtain of moss and leaves, James felt his stomach turn at what he saw. About ten feet ahead of them, the wooden beams of the puncheon stopped. Scattered planks lay strewn hither and thither for several feet beyond that. Then there was nothing ahead of that but grass and ferns.

James's heart started to race. "What the—I thought the trail was supposed to go all the way through the jungle."

Archit said nothing.

"I thought it was supposed to get us safely to the other side," James said.

Archit avoided his eye. "I guess not."

"You guess not?" James said. "Don't you *care?* I mean, doesn't this mean we're all going to die?"

That triggered something in Archit. The bird gave James a piercing stare. "Yes, I care, but I'm not going to make a big ridiculous scene over it. You're making yourself look like a fool."

Liz put her hand on his shoulder. He pulled away. It hurt to feel her compassionate touch, and he knew why—James had no idea how this was going to end, and he knew the person on the other end of that touch, the cousin whom he loved so dearly, was in danger. His sister too. And it was all his fault.

James looked at Margot, and for the first time in his life, he thought she looked scared. But Margot didn't get scared. Not really.

"We'll just have to face the jungle," Archit said.

James sighed, resisting the urge to tell Archit how angry he was.

"We can do this," Archit said.

James swallowed. *This is a time to be brave. This is a time to trust Archit.* Even if all his self-doubt were screaming inside him, he had to ignore it.

Before he could let himself chicken out, James grabbed the axe and rushed forward to the fragmented end of the puncheon. He took a deep breath and flung the weapon into the air. The axe whooshed as James brought it down and struck at some of the vines that hung in his path. Again, he swung, and again he cut away at the vines. The flowers fell to the ground, their poison spilling onto the grass like blood.

Tiny screams sounded all around him. They were coming from the flowers when he cut them. It was the same eerie scream he had heard earlier, like a demon being exorcised.

Archit, Liz, and Margot followed James off the road into the clearing he had just made. James stared around, horrified by his own bravery, and looked at them wide-eyed.

"Come on," he said. "Let's stay close together."

They pressed on through the foliage and jungle mist, James hacking away at the predatory plants as they went. Several of the flowers seemed poised and ready to strike at him, but as soon as he swung the axe in a fierce show of bravery, they pulled away.

"Why are they doing that?" Margot asked, eying the flowers.

Even Archit seemed confused. "I dunno. For some reason, there's something about James with that axe that terrifies them."

Several of the flowers rose up to shoot forward, but their stingers simply fell from their blossoms and rolled away onto the grass.

"I think they can tell we aren't afraid of them anymore," James said. He began to laugh as he swung the axe back and forth. His fear dissipated with each step and swing of the axe, replaced now by renewed confidence.

They pressed on through the jungle, and after fifteen or twenty minutes, they began to see fewer and fewer flowers. Even the greenery around them felt sparser. Soon enough, the sun was visible through the leaves overhead, bathing them with warm light.

"We must be get getting close to the edge of the jungle," Archit said.

James wiped the sweat from his brow with his sleeve. Why had it never occurred to him that swinging an axe would be such a workout? It should have been obvious in hindsight. And he was so out of shape!

"Look!" Margot said, pointing ahead.

James looked up and saw that they were standing on the fringes of the jungle. Fifty or so yards in front of them, the tangled flora gave way to a clean field overlooking a sloping hill.

"We made it!" James shouted. "We're there!"

Margot laughed for the first time in days, letting out a jubilant shout and throwing her arms around James and Liz.

A crunching sound several yards to their left interrupted their celebration, and the tall grass shook. Something about the ominous sound filled James with sudden dread, and he turned quickly to Archit, whose eyes were fixed on whatever it was approaching them. He looked terrified.

"Archit," James said, "what's..."

But he didn't even need to ask. From behind the brush stepped a creature so strange and terrible there was no doubt it was the Beast of Darkness. It was built like an enormous saber-toothed tiger, its thick greenish-yellow hair hanging all around it in wild tangles. Flaming orange eyes glared at them as it licked its slobbering mandibles and bowed its goat-horned head at them.

"You're trespassing," it growled as it raised its head again. "That's what you're doing, you know. You're trespassing."

Liz leaned close to James and Archit, her voice a hushed, terrified whisper. "Archit, what do we do?"

James wondered the same thing. He exchanged a glance with Archit, trying to read the bird's reaction.

The beast bellowed laughter, its eyes flaring. When it snorted, puffs of smoke erupted from its nostrils. It began to circle the group, its large paws, sharp with ebony claws, pounding the earth as it walked.

James looked toward the edge of the jungle. How far would it be to sprint to the field ahead? Would the beast be able to follow them out of the jungle if they made a run for it? Did they even dare make such a move?

The beast stopped suddenly at James's feet, sniffing them intently. James tried to find his voice, forcing himself to sound brave even though he shook all over and thought he might buckle at the knees. "Please...please, we were just on our way out. Let us go, won't you?"

The beast fixed its orange eyes on James, and he was overcome with an awful sickness in his stomach.

The beast turned its gaze to Archit, as if it knew that Archit was the leader and the reason for their excursion into the jungle. All of a sudden, James forgot his fear in a fit of fierce protectiveness for his friends, and the same mad bravery he had felt when they left the puncheon suddenly possessed him. With one confident swing, he brought the ax down on the beast's head, planting the blade into the monster's skull. The beast stumbled, and for a second, James thought it would keel over. The blade stuck out of the beast's head at an odd angle.

"Oh, no!" Archit shouted.

Maybe this wasn't going to be so easy.

The beast righted itself and shook its head furiously, as if dislodging an axe embedded in its skull were like trying to swat off a few pesky flies. There was James's answer—no, it wouldn't be so easy.

"Run," James shouted. "Run!"

Liz grabbed Margot's wrist with one hand, lifting the hem of her long skirt with the other so as not to trip over it. The girls turned to run, sprinting. Archit spread his wings and rose into the air. James took a few steps, but he turned to face the beast just as the axe fell into the grass. James dove for it and lifted it up again.

"Don't go near them! If you want to hurt my friends, you'll have to kill me first!"

The beast flashed a furious look at him, baring its teeth.

"James, run," Archit urged, swooping overhead.

But James wouldn't break his stare at the Beast of Darkness. The monster's eyes narrowed, and it let out a roar so loud and terrible that he felt the hot breath on his face. The axe disintegrated in his hands, and James found himself standing there empty handed.

"Brat!" cried the beast. "Fool! Do you think such mortal weapons can destroy me?"

With a roar, the creature pounced. In a flash, James felt the hard ground slam against his back; the beast's enormous weight pressed on top of him, its sharp claws digging into his chest. James lifted his head to find himself face to face with a mouthful of gleaming fangs.

James could muster only a pathetic moan of fear.

"What nice carnage you'll make for my shredding claws," the beast growled. Its hot breath reeked, and its fiery eyes hurt to look at.

Archit swooped down from above and grabbed the beast by the hair on the back of its head. The beast growled and turned to swipe one of its massive paws at the bird.

Suddenly remembering the poisoned tooth he'd put in his pocket just earlier that morning, James took advantage of the distraction and wriggled free of the beast's grasp. His hand shook as he reached into his pocket and pulled out the bundled handkerchief.

The beast turned back to James just as he got a firm grasp on the needle-like fang and surged forward. Before the beast knew what was happening, James had plunged the poisonous dart deep into the monster's side.

A mighty squelching sound erupted as the point sank into the beast's flesh. The beast let out an unnaturally loud roar of agony, and the air around them was filled with that same disturbing demonic scream echoing from the flowers.

The Beast of Darkness crumpled limp and soft like a giant stuffed animal tossed onto the grass. James released his grip on the poisonous dart and took a step back, trying to catch his breath. Black ooze flowed out of the wound he had made in the beast's side.

Archit landed beside him. "You all right?"

James nodded, trying to absorb it all, then threw his arms around Archit.

Margot and Liz came running over. They had witnessed everything.

"You guys," Margot said, "that was *crazy*! I can't believe you did that."

James still couldn't form a sentence, so shocked was he by what had just happened. Once he caught his breath, he began to laugh, and the others joined him, letting the excitement of the moment wash over them.

"So we can leave the jungle behind us now?" Liz said. "No more beasts or poisonous plants?"

"Yeah," Archit said. "We're done with this place."

James picked up his bag. "Should we restock before we head out?" He indicated several more fruit trees on the outskirts of the jungle.

"Yeah, I'll go with you," Archit said. "Let's get as much as we can. Girls, we'll meet you up ahead."

Margot and Liz nodded.

James followed Archit toward the trees, opening up his bag as they approached.

"Thank you, by the way," James said.

"For what?"

"For distracting the Beast of Darkness when he had me pinned, of course. If you hadn't pulled his hair, I would've been toast." James hesitated. "I'm sorry I got so mad at you."

Archit didn't even seem fazed. "Don't worry about it."

James nodded, turning his attention to the fruit trees. He began plucking the bounty with both hands, and he and Archit enjoyed a comfortable moment of silence.

"That should be enough," Archit said, surveying the full bag. "At least, it should get us through the day until we reach the hippie commune."

James nodded. "Let's catch up with the girls."

As they passed back by the crumpled corpse of the beast, James paused. "Do you think it's really dead?"

"What do you mean?" Archit said.

"Well, could he just be faking it?" James said. He stared uneasily at the monster's lifeless body. Part of James had expected something more dramatic out of the death—maybe the beast would have caught fire and sizzled into smoke, or else a legion of demons would fly up out of the netherworld to drag the monster's soul back below with them. Either of those things would have assured James that the beast was really dead. Watching it lie there on the grass did nothing for him, not that he had been setting high expectations for the death of the first monster he defeated in combat.

"Who cares if it's really dead? At least it's in no shape to attack us right now," Archit said. "Let's just get out of here. If he's still alive, then he can haunt this wretched jungle for all I care."

James nodded. "You're right." He took two pieces of fruit from the bag and offered one to Archit.

As they walked off to join the girls, they did not even notice how the jungle was changing behind them. The poisonous red flowers and their snakelike vines began to wither away, and brightly colored wildflowers grew in their place.

CHAPTER 6
Rockyland

The four of them had been up for several hours, so it felt much later in the day than it was, but as they walked across the meadow away from the jungle, James noticed the sun was not nearly as high in the sky as he expected it to be. It had to still be morning, and that meant they had the entire afternoon ahead of them.

That meant opportunity. Feeling braver than he had ever felt, James looked forward to the next leg of their journey. It was amazing what killing a monster like the Beast of Darkness could do for a guy! And by nighttime, their journey would be over—and what an amazing story they would have to tell. If only the people back at school would believe any of this.

They came to the foot of the grassy slope where a river ran as far as they could see in both directions. Across the river, a steep hill rose up before them, its entire craggy face covered in rocks and large boulders. It led up to a high cliff that overlooked the countryside.

Archit pointed to the woodland at the top of the cliff. "That's it—just over the cliff, and we'll be in the land of Nalgordia."

James looked up and down the river. "How're we going to cross though?"

The river wasn't wide, maybe only twenty-five meters or a little more, not much farther than the length of a swimming pool. But toward the middle of the river, the current looked fierce. Sure, James was a strong swimmer, and so were Liz and Margot. But all of them were tired and worn out from the past few days, and taking their chances against a rushing current wasn't something James was eager to do.

"I hadn't thought too much about that," Archit said.

James adjusted the cuffs of his trousers and waded into the sandy shallows of the riverbank. The cool water felt good after spending the hot morning in the jungle. He bent down to splash some of the water on his face and behind his ears.

"What about that tree over there?" Liz said.

James looked over in the direction Liz pointed. Down the river a little way, a giant maple tree had been uprooted and fallen across the river.

"Good call," James said.

When they got closer to the tree, James saw it might not have been as great an idea as he thought it was. By the looks of it, the tree had gone down decades ago. Its trunk was all mossy and decayed, and it didn't even look as if it would hold under their weight. He looked at Archit. "What d'you think?"

Archit didn't respond right away, and James knew him well enough to know that meant he had reservations.

"Oh, come on, James," Liz said. "It's fine. After going through the jungle, are you really gonna tell me you're afraid of this?"

James saw a strange expression on Archit's face. Was Archit surprised? Or maybe impressed? James had to admit that Liz's fearlessness sometimes took him aback even after knowing her his whole life.

Liz gathered her skirt carefully in one hand so that she wouldn't trip over it and stepped up onto the trunk.

"Be careful, Liz," Margot said.

"I am." Liz ventured out over the rushing current, balancing herself by holding onto the boughs and branches that stuck up around her.

"Well, would you look at that," Archit said. "She's braver than I would've given her credit for."

Liz was already halfway across at this point. "It's fine, you guys," she said, looking back.

But as she turned, her bare foot stepped onto a patch of moss growing on the side of the trunk, and the branch she was holding for balance broke off, sending her toppling into the river.

"Liz!" the three others shouted together.

Liz disappeared under the water, then emerged again, fighting against the current, struggling to swim in her long dress.

James didn't falter or pause. He dashed forward, running along the fallen tree and leaping onto a nearby boulder sticking up out of the water. If only he could reach her and pull her to safety!

"Liz!" he shouted.

She had caught her bearings, but she struggled against the current. She flailed her arms and tried to push herself toward James. Up and down she bobbed, trying to touch the bottom and push up off it.

She went under again, and this time, she didn't surface. James was going to have to dive in after her, though he wasn't sure what good he would be able to do.

But before he could act, Liz surfaced on the other side of the river, followed by another female figure. It was the mermaid who had helped them twice before.

Liz pushed herself up onto the bank. The mermaid looked from her to James on the other side. "You do get into plenty of trouble, don't you?"

"Hey!" James exclaimed after a moment of incredulity.

The mermaid laughed and brushed her hair coquettishly off her shoulders. "Boy," she addressed him. "James. You've survived the perils of the jungle. Don't you remember I told you I would see you on the other side? And now, here I am."

"But the current," James said.

"It's nothing to a merperson. Do you need help crossing the river, too?"

"I think I can make it," James said, scooting off the rock and dipping into the water. "As long as I'm careful."

"But maybe just to be safe," the mermaid said, stroking through the water toward him. She reached out her hand and took his.

James wasn't able to protest. His eyes met hers—he had never seen eyes so bright before—and he forgot about everything except for her. She was too beautiful to be real. If she hadn't been helping him avoid drowning, he might very well have let her drag him down beneath the surface and hold him there. He wouldn't have protested. No wonder mermaids were rumored to have led so many sailors to their watery graves.

Before he knew it, they had reached the other side, and the mermaid broke eye contact with him. "There, now," she said.

James felt very self-conscious. Had he actually been willing to let the mermaid drown him for a moment there? What kind of power did they have?

Whatever, James thought. *She's our friend regardless.* He pulled himself up out of the water and onto the rocky bank. "Thank you."

The mermaid glided back across the river to help Margot, and James sat down next to Liz on one of the rocks. "You all right?"

"Yeah. Just scared me is all."

"Scared all of us," James said.

James took comfort in knowing that her spirits were still up. He watched Archit fly overhead, circle around, and touch down beside them.

"That was a close one, huh?" Archit said. "Liz, you never fail to impress. You weren't kidding when you said you were braver than you looked, huh."

Liz laughed. "Thanks, Archit."

The mermaid and Margot neared, and James stood to help Margot out of the water.

"It's a real shame I liked this dress," Margot said, sounding only half-bitter. She wrung some of the water out of her skirt.

"Well, that's that, then," the mermaid said. "All four of you are safe, yes?"

They nodded, exchanging looks. The three kids were wet, but besides that, they could have been worse off.

"I must head back downriver now, and back to the ocean," the mermaid said. "My tribe will be wondering where I've been this past day."

"We wish you could come with us," James said.

"As do I, James," the mermaid said. "But that's not meant to be—not for this adventure, at least. I hope that our paths might meet again."

"Yeah," James said. "I hope so too."

"Goodbye," the mermaid said.

"Bye," their group chorused.

The mermaid dove under, flicking her tail up behind her, and disappeared beneath the water's surface.

James watched her go, a little saddened at the thought they wouldn't see her again—or, he figured, at least not again during this adventure, as she had said. Maybe someday though.

"Well," Archit said, "we'll never reach the top of this hill just standing here. We've got to hike."

Admittedly, James had never been hiking before, but he had a feeling this would have been easier if he weren't barefoot and wearing formal clothes, tattered though they might have been. He looked over at Margot and Liz as they began to ascend the rocky hill. The sight of the girls trying to maneuver over the terrain in their skirts made him cringe.

Over boulders and between crags they went, going up the hill one precarious step at a time, one jagged mass of stone after another. The sun was high in the sky by this time, and though there was a cool breeze off the river sweeping up the hill, James's clothes grew damp with sweat.

"What's that?" Liz said as they reached the midway point.

James turned and saw that she pointed at a piece of debris wedged between two rocks. She bent down and lifted it out.

It was a sign, one that must have splintered off and fallen into the crags after years of decay.

Look out for the rockies

"What are the rockies," Liz said.

Archit looked legitimately baffled. "I don't know." He moved over next to Liz to take a better look at the sign, as if she might have misread it. She hadn't.

Something that sounded like laughter erupted from nearby.

"What was that?" James said.

Liz looked from the sign to Archit. "Are these cliffs...are they dangerous?"

"No," Archit said.

Margot huffed. "Look, there was a sign saying that we were supposed to stay out of the jungle, wasn't there? I'm thinking we should listen to these signs that are posted along our way into this Nalgordia place. 'Beware' signs don't seem to be posted without reason around here."

"Oh," Archit said, fumbling for a good retort. "No, we're fine. I've never scaled this hillside before...I've always just flown up...but, y'know, I'm sure it was just some prankster who put that sign up."

"Then what was that laughing at us?" Liz asked.

"I don't know," Archit said. "Let's not worry about it."

"You're right," James said. "It's probably just a big joke, and besides, we're halfway up the hill."

"You're just saying that to agree with him," Margot said.

"C'mon, Margot," Liz said. "Let's just keep going." She set the sign back down. "The sooner we're out of here, the better."

As glad as James was that Liz might have settled that argument, at least temporarily, he got the feeling they were being watched. Every so often, something moved in his periphery, but as soon as he turned, it had disappeared. Maybe it was just his imagination. Still...

He edged close to Archit as they hiked. "You're sure there's nothing that lives on this mountainside?"

"Sure," Archit said. He didn't sound convincing in the least.

Up ahead, James spotted two doll-like figures standing atop a boulder. No more than a foot tall, they were herding what looked like a fold of pet rocks.

"What're those?" James asked Archit, but he was almost sure he knew the answer. They had to be rockies.

The little people had noticed their approach. James overheard one of them whisper to the other, "Should we run and hide?"

"No," the other whispered back. "Who would guard the pet rocks? Stand your ground."

James shifted his eyes to Archit, hoping for an explanation.

"Just walk straight past them," Archit whispered. "Don't make eye contact."

James nodded to indicate he understood.

"Good day," one of the rockies greeted as they passed.

"Aye, how're you?" the other chimed.

"Good day," Archit said in a polite tone. He kept walking, staring straight ahead.

"What brings you to Rockyland today?" asked the first.

"Rockyland?" Liz asked. "Is this Rockyland? Are you rockies?"

James and Archit paused. *No, Liz, don't do that–ignore them,* James thought. But Archit said nothing.

"Aye, we are rockies," said one of the little men. "And what, pray, are you?"

James looked down, taking in the sight of the little men up close. They wore primitive clothes, and their brightly colored hair–orange on one, blue on the other–reminded him of Troll dolls.

Liz bent down next to the rockies. "I'm...I'm a human, I guess," she said. She looked toward James and Archit, as if trying to figure out the best way to describe herself. She had never had to identify her species before.

"A human," said the blue-haired rocky. "As in...an Earthling?"

Liz laughed. "Yes, I guess we're Earthlings, if that's the word you prefer."

The two little men gasped and exchanged amazed looks. "We've never seen one of your kind before," said the orange-haired rocky. "I don't believe that one has ever come through these hills."

Archit leaned close to James. "We'd best get out of here quickly," he said. "I don't trust these guys."

James looked around and saw that the little rockies were appearing from all over–they were crawling out of crevices and from underneath rocks and from inside tiny caves. The throng of them closed in, full of awe, to see the travelers who had wandered into their country.

More and more appeared all around them, and James was surprised to see that the crowd had grown so big that for what looked like the length of a football field, they were surrounded by these little people–men, women, and children. Each had brightly colored hair and was dressed in absurd rag-tag garments. Some of them dragged pet rocks on leashes.

"Earthlings," James could distinguish from the chattering voices. "Have you ever seen an Earthling before? No? Me neither."

"There's too many of them," Archit whispered to James. "If they wanted to hurt us, I think they could."

Liz turned to Archit, a look of discomfort on her face. She had heard what he said.

Without missing a beat, she looked back down at the rockies, ready to force a conversation. "Do you all live on this hill?"

Archit went on. "And that sign told us to watch out for them," he whispered to James.

"They seem harmless enough," James whispered back. After all, he couldn't imagine that the little people were malevolent, what with their plump cheeks and beady little eyes.

"Maybe one or two of them alone might be harmless," Archit said. "But look at this crowd. They don't seem so cute and harmless in such a number."

James felt a little shiver go up his spine. Something about what Archit said made him uneasy. He looked over at Liz, who was still speaking with the rockies. Margot sat down beside her. "Hey, little buddy," she addressed one of the rock herders, trying to sound as friendly as possible. She rustled her hand through his hair.

"Well," Archit announced to the crowd, "it was nice to meet all of you, but we have to be going. We have to reach the woods at the top of the hill by nightfall, and…"

He was interrupted by a shrill scream, followed by frightened cries by other rockies, and the crowd parted to reveal an enormous blackish-brown rodent that had crawled out from under a rock.

"Oh, it's a river rat!" cried one of the rocky women. "Our only enemies—river rats!"

James made a swift grab for the pocketknife in his bag. "This is my fight," he declared to the rockies. "I'll take care of it!"

Margot grabbed at James's arm. "What are you doing?" she demanded.

"Relax," he said, pulling away and flicking the knife open.

He jumped down onto one of the lower rocks and approached the rat with his knife held open in front of him. This was a chance to impress the rockies, to assert dominance.

"Get away," he said dramatically to the rat. "Begone, beast, or perish on my sword."

He waved the knife to make a show. If the rockies had never seen humans before, and were deathly afraid of these river rats, then maybe he had a chance of appearing a divine hero, like the ones in Greek mythology.

The rat looked up at James and stared at the knife glimmering in the afternoon sun. It cocked its head and wiggled his nose in the air.

"I said, 'Begone!'" shouted James, moving forward. At his approach, the river rat scurried and disappeared down the hill between the rocks. With a flourish, James turned back to the rockies. "The monster is gone. He will not return."

Margot and Liz laughed together, rolling their eyes at the whole show.

The rockies, however, seemed genuinely impressed. They gave a collective gasp, and others began to cheer. "You have saved our lives," one of them shouted.

James feigned a sigh of exhaustion, a warrior come home from battle, smiling proudly at his achievement. He swatted the knife shut and put it back in his bag.

"Thank you so much," screamed another rocky.

The rockies were abuzz with chatter, and one of the men—a little being with clownish red hair and a blue tunic—went climbing up to a rock high above the rest where he overlooked them like Mark Antony asking the Romans to lend him their ears. "He has saved our lives. We must crown him king!"

The little people went into a frenzy all at once.

"King! King! King!" the rockies chanted over and over again in their pipsqueak voices. "King! King! King!" They looked at James with eager eyes—not a warm eagerness either, but a dangerous one.

Recognizing the imminent threat, James protested. "No," he shouted, lifting his hands up in protest. "No, that's all right! Thanks, guys."

He looked up to see Archit shifting his feet nervously. If Archit were nervous, then this wasn't good. A lump suddenly formed in his stomach as if he had picked up one of the pet rocks and swallowed it whole. He caught the eyes of Margot and Liz, who were beginning to look uncomfortable too.

The rockies went on chanting and surrounded James on all sides. James spun in a circle, realizing that their entire company was closing in around him, crying out for him to be their king. He looked up and cast a worried glance at Archit. The bird's expression was one that James couldn't interpret, but Archit seemed just as confused as he—and just as scared too.

"Make your way through the crowd," said Archit to the girls, running forward.

The girls responded to his order. The three of them began to press upon the rockies, kicking them out of the way, trying to get through the crowd to James.

But the little men were grabbing at James's ankles and climbing up the leg of his pants. He panicked. What was he to do? Even at their size, the sheer number of them was enormous. How could he get away?

He tried to climb up on a boulder, but they moved swiftly and in an overwhelming number. From where Liz and Margot stood, watching the rockies overpower James was like watching an army lay siege to a tower.

"What are you doing to me?" James screamed, trying to squirm his way out of it.

"We are crowning you our king!" one of the rockies screamed.

Archit saw James buckle at the knees and fall backward. Margot let out a shout and Liz shielded her eyes, thinking he would split his head against a rock. Then what would they do? What aid would they have?

But James's fall was stopped short by the crowd of little people under him. The thousands of rockies who stood at his feet stretched their hands upward and grabbed him. James fought as best he could, but there was nothing to save him from being carried away. The rockies marched like an army of ants carrying a crust of bread or a raisin toward their hill—except that the crust of bread was fighting to get away and losing the battle.

"Let him go!" shouted Margot, running forward, but she was too slow.

The little men and women moved swiftly and easily over the wilderness of stone, taking James with them. Archit swooped into the air and flew after them, but the rockies gained speed.

"Please, stop!" Liz screamed.

"Don't hurt him, you little bastards!" Margot shouted.

At the summit of a boulder above them stood a crowd of rockies, watching in awe at the sight of the capture. They were chanting in tongues, chorusing some indistinguishable incantation that blended with the other shouts of "King! King! King!"

"What are you doing to me?" James shouted, and the rockies began to laugh. Their laughter was a screeching, horrifying sound, the combination of some cartoonish chortle and the sound of nails on chalkboard. James flailed and kicked, but their grip on him was strong.

"Get off him," Archit shouted as he closed in on the crowd. "Get off him, I said!"

As soon as the bird swooped down, a strange and unexpected thing happened—the ground opened up, and the boulders rolled out of the way to reveal a cave tunneling down into the hill beneath the rocks.

The little men and women descended into the darkness, taking James with them. Archit, Liz, and Margot watched in horror as the rockies disappeared into the inky blackness. James's screams were the last thing they heard before the boulders rolled back into place and closed up the cave.

Archit landed where the opening had been. Frantically, he looked around. No, there had certainly been a cave there just a second ago! There was! And now there was no sign of it, no indication whatsoever, no matter how hard he looked, that there had ever been an opening in these rocks!

Liz and Margot came up the hill behind him.

"What happened?" Margot said.

"Where are they?" Liz said. "Where's James?"

"I don't know," Archit said. "The rocks—they opened up, and the rockies went into a cave into the hillside, and then it closed up. I don't know where they've taken him."

"What?!" Margot screamed. She bounded forward, followed by Liz, and they began to push at the boulders as if they might be able to move them out of the way

Archit gave one of the boulders a swift kick. "It won't budge," he said, dejected.

"Did they say a password?" Liz asked. "You know, 'open sesame,' or something like that?"

Archit shook his head. "I didn't hear anything. Nothing except their chanting and their sick laughter."

Margot groaned, sitting down on one of the rocks. "What are we gonna do?"

Liz moved toward Margot's feet. "What's this?" she said.

She grabbed at what looked like a root sticking out from the soil at the base of a rock. She held it up for Margot and Archit to see. It was a rope.

"Pull it, Liz," Archit encouraged.

She pulled, and the boulder behind them swung upward and out of the way. Several other small rocks went rolling to the side. Dust and dirt billowed up around them.

"Oh!" Liz shouted, sounding both surprised and relieved.

Margot stood, her eyes growing wide. She couldn't believe what just happened.

The entrance to the cave had opened before them.

Archit scurried forward, peering into the darkness within. The cavern's mouth opened up into a tunnel with crooked, jagged walls of stone. Stalactites hung from the ceiling.

Archit waved his wing for the girls to follow him. Cautiously, they proceeded into the darkness.

"Oh, man," Margot sighed.

It was pitch black inside, but firelight glowed from around the corner, flickering down a slope of craggy steps. They worked their way through the rocky crevice, then turned right into a long corridor lit by torchlight that cast an orange glow over the grotto.

"What's this?" Archit asked, indicating a bronze plaque on the wall. He grabbed for one of the torches, pulled it from the sconce where it was mounted, and held it up.

The orange glow illuminated the words.

The Underground City of Rockyland

Below that, there were smaller letters: foreign runes and symbols in some ancient language, followed by some Latin Anglo-Saxon lettering. Archit read it to the girls in a hushed voice. His torch moved along the sentences, revealing them as he went.

"All who enter through this cavern, may they be blessed by the power of the unnamed one who slayed the great rat and gathered the stones from the skies above. May our kings always please Eolo, who stands with his father and brother and son, and holds our world from falling into the sea below."

Archit turned back to Margot and Liz. "Their kings!" he whispered. "Did you read that? Just like James—they ask that their kings please their gods."

"Holds our world from falling into the sea below," Liz repeated, gazing at the plaque. "But what do they want with James?"

"Keep your voice down," Archit reminded her. "We're probably in danger here, remember."

"Shh," Margot said. "Do you hear that?"

They stood quiet for a second. A ruckus sounded faintly from far away. Archit looked from Liz to Margot. "Come on," he said.

He led them down the hall, holding the torch out in front of them as they followed the sound of the commotion, which grew louder and louder as they pressed on—voices and stomping and drums.

They reached the end of the passage and came upon a large stairwell that circled downward into a large pit, one that was wide and deep enough to serve as a grand ballroom. From where the three of them stood, they could see the rockies celebrating.

"Oh my God," Liz said.

"What the hell?" Margot said.

The sight below them was so formidable and out of control that the girls could only have described it as being like a mosh pit or a rave—a hedonistic, debaucherous party where no rules applied and touchy-feely dancing reigned supreme.

Three bonfires blazed, and the rockies danced around them. Their tiny bodies were crammed as tightly as they could fit, pressed up against each other as the whole lot of them gyrated and leaped and celebrated. Some of them wore masks, others banged drums or blew on panpipes.

On a platform at the far end of the chamber from the foot of the winding staircase, James sat imprisoned in an enormous golden birdcage. He looked terrified. A jeweled crown perched on his head, and a scepter lay at his feet. He crawled forward, clutching at the bars of the cage and peering out at the crowd of little people. "Please," he called at them, "let me go!"

At the top of the stairwell, Margot stood, furious. "We have to help him," she said.

She moved to push forward, but Liz stopped her. "No, Mar!"

"Why?" Margot said. "Why?! I can take them—they're a foot tall!"

"They managed to kidnap James, didn't they?" Liz said.

"Damn right they did, and now we're going to get him back!" Margot said.

"We need a plan," said Archit. "We're going to rescue him, but we need a plan before we do that!"

Margot sighed, frustrated.

"So help me," she threw her finger at Archit, "if my brother gets hurt because of this damn adventure you've taken us on—!"

"Margot," Liz gasped.

Margot stopped, realizing that Liz was on the verge of tears.

Liz sighed, trying to compose herself. "She didn't mean that," she told Archit, choking back her fear. "She didn't mean it, Archit."

Liz looked at Margot, fear plain on her face. She turned and stormed back down the hall toward the entrance.

"Liz, wait!" Margot said, running after her. "I'm sorry."

Archit followed them, huffing in his frustration. The last thing he needed was for the girls to get in a fight. They had to keep their wits about them if they were going to rescue James.

Margot stomped out of the cavern and back into the afternoon sunlight. "I wish we'd never gone on this stupid adventure!"

"You wanted to come," Archit reminded her. "James tried to stop you, and you insisted. Stop worrying about blame, stop regretting, and let's figure out how we're going to help James out of this mess."

Margot huffed, sitting down on one of the rocks.

"He's right, Margot," Liz said.

"Shut up," Margot said. "I know he is, all right?"

Archit ignored her. "We need to find out as much as we can about these people," he said. "If we know what they're planning to do to James, why they have him locked up, that is, then we might be able to come up with some sort of plan."

"How are we going to do that?" Margot said. "Find out about these people, I mean."

A voice piped up from behind them at the mouth of the cave. "I can help you."

They turned. There stood one of the rockies. He was alone, unarmed, and looking especially small by his lonesome within the gaping entrance to the cavern. He looked up at them with curious eyes and ran a hand through his unruly hair as if he were trying to make himself more presentable while he stood in the presence of human strangers.

"What did you just say?" Archit asked, uncertain. Was this some sort of trick?

"I can help you," the rocky said. "Your companion is in grave danger."

"Danger?" Liz said. "What do you mean?"

"We're not safe to talk here," the rocky said, looking over his shoulder at the open mouth of the underground city, as if somebody inside might overhear them. "We should move farther out. Away from the door."

Archit, Margot, and Liz exchanged suspicious looks, but none of them needed to state the obvious: They had no other choice but to trust the rocky. They were desperate.

The rocky scurried ahead, leading the way down the hillside, moving fluidly over the rocks and boulders with little effort. Liz and Margot moved more slowly, stepping cautiously with their bare feet and trying not to trip.

About twenty yards from the entryway, the rocky stopped. "Before I tell you what you need to know," he said, uneasily, "you must promise me that afterwards you will take me across the river where I can run far away from here. For this treason, my people would surely torture and kill me. There's no question of it."

"First things first," said Archit. "How do we know that you're helping us? How do we know that this isn't a trick?"

"Not to be rude," said Liz, quickly, giving the rocky a smile for good measure, "but—we don't know you. Why are you willing to help us?"

"I'll explain as best I can," said the rocky. "A few days ago, when I was young—a rocky's life is only a few weeks, you see, and our youth goes by in only a matter of days—I was with some friends down by the riverbank. We were being rowdy and adventurous, and I tried to paddle out in the river. To leave the cliffs is forbidden among our customs—we believe that our physical forms are bound to the rocks, that it isn't possible for us to go into the far-off world or else we will cease to exist. But I left the cliffs to swim in the river, and all of my friends assumed me to no longer exist, because they'd seen me stray from the rocks."

"What does this have to do with my brother," Margot said, frustration rising in her voice.

"Patience," said the rocky, "please, have patience. We have time, and I will explain to you why I am obliged to help save your brother."

Margot rolled her eyes. Patience wasn't working for her right now.

"I was caught in the tide and taken far away from Rockyland—I thought myself dead!" the rocky explained. "No rocky had ever left the cliffs before. It wasn't possible, as far as we knew.

"When I washed ashore, I found myself lost in the heart of the Jungle of Darkness. I was come upon by the beast, who took me as his prisoner. I think that he intended to eat me; he carried me back to his cave and locked me up inside a prison made from sticks and bones, where I was held prisoner for three days.

"But just this morning, two creatures who introduced themselves as monkeys came to the cave to ransack whatever treasures the beast had kept there. They set me free, and told me that the jungle had been cured of its dark spell by a bird and three Earthlings who were traveling through. I hurried on ahead to warn you all, but I see that I was too late!

"Understand that I must help you. You've saved my life in having destroyed the Beast of Darkness and setting the jungle free of its curse. Now that I must run away from here, I will return to the jungle, and live amongst the monkeys, eating wild fruit and climbing trees for the rest of my life."

The rocky made a low sweeping bow to show his gratitude. "I am at your service," he added.

"You said you hurried to warn us, but you were too late," Margot said. "You knew what was going to happen here?"

"I arrived just in time to follow the crowd into the underground realm," the rocky said, ashamed.

Sensing Margot's anger, Archit held up his wing to calm her. "What do they want with James?" he asked the rocky. "What sort of kingship is this they've given him."

"As I've told you," said the rocky, "we are a very superstitious people. It is an ancient Rockyland belief that all of the rocks on the hill are held in place by the gods, who demand a royal sacrifice. Tradition states that a king be crowned once every pregnancy of the Giant Star—for a whole day, his coronation is celebrated with drinking and dancing and rabblerousing. But on the morrow afterwards, at dawn, that king is to be burnt at the stake and his ashes offered as a gift to the gods."

"What?" Margot exclaimed.

"No," Liz said. "They're not going to do that to James, are they?"

"They will, my lady," said the rocky. "And they are only too happy to catch an Earthling. It saves us from choosing one of our own."

"So that whole bit about the river rat," Archit said, "that was just a ruse?"

The rocky nodded. "I'm afraid so. They were planning to catch one of you even before his act of valor."

"How awful," Liz said.

"Yes, it is," said the rocky, "but in my travels away from Rockyland, I've learned that there is much to the world besides our country. I don't believe the ways and customs of my people are always right. But please—do what you can with the information I've given you. You have only until tomorrow morning."

"How long does the coronation revelry last?" Archit asked.

"They will be off to bed by midnight," the rocky said. "You'll then have until dawn to rescue him."

Archit nodded, taking in everything that the rocky had said. "Thank you," he said.

"You'll take me over the river, won't you?" the rocky asked.

"Yes," Archit said. "Now, if you'd like."

"I have no possessions to take with me," the rocky said. "I only returned to Rockyland this afternoon, and everyone had assumed me dead. I'll have more of a chance starting anew in the jungle."

"Let's go, then," Archit said. He stooped and allowed the rocky to climb up onto his back. "Margot, Liz, will you be all right until I return?"

The girls nodded. "Thank you," Liz said to the rocky.

"Yeah," Margot said. "Thanks."

"Good luck to you," the rocky said.

Archit took flight and disappeared down the hill.

Margot and Liz looked at each other, unsure of what to make of this new information they'd been given. "I'm sorry," Margot said. "For getting angry, I mean."

"That's all right," Liz said.

Margot sat back down on one of the rocks. "You know I don't mean to be the adult all the time."

"I know."

"I just...I just do it because I feel like I have to. I'm the oldest."

Liz laughed. "Only by a year."

Margot stood and gave Liz a long hug. "I guess now we just need to worry about getting James out of there."

"Archit will get us out of this mess," Liz said. "This might be our first adventure, but it isn't his. He knows what he's doing."

At least, she hoped he did.

The afternoon gave way to evening at an excruciatingly slow pace. At several points, Margot and Liz tried to ask Archit what his plan was, but he evaded the question. "I'm working on it," he insisted. "I'll let you know as soon as it is all worked out in my head."

When the sun had set, he insisted Margot and Liz try to sleep. "We've got our work cut out for us tonight," he said. "You'd better get some rest before midnight."

Margot shook her head, solemn. "I couldn't sleep right now if I tried. Not while James is in trouble."

But Liz managed to talk her into at least lying down, and the two of them soon dozed off, exhausted from the stress of the day. Archit sat awake, looking up at the full moon and waiting until the midnight hour.

He pulled out his pocket watch from inside his vest and took a look at it. It read a quarter to twelve. He stood and crept into the cavern.

Making his way down the passageway, he became aware of how quiet it was. The torches whispered to him as they threw their orange glow upon the stone walls, but the hubbub from deep inside the cave had subsided. When he rounded the corner and looked down the stairs, he saw the chamber below by the dim glow of the dying bonfires. Debris from the celebration littered the floor—food, goblets, carnival masks. Only a few rockies remained, presumably the drunken ones who had passed out atop one another in piles. The others had excused themselves and gone off to bed.

James sat alone in the cage, peering out into the empty rotunda. He looked on the verge of tears.

Archit slunk down the stairs. "James," he hissed. "You all right?"

"Archit!" James whispered, perking up.

"They haven't hurt you, have they?"

"No," James said. "No, nothing serious."

"We're going to get you out of here," Archit said. "I just came to see whether the coast is clear. I'm going to send the girls down together, and then I'll watch the entrance to be sure it doesn't close up on us."

"What's your plan though?" James asked.

"No time to explain now," Archit said. "I'll go get them."

James looked as if he were about to protest, but then he caught himself. "All right," he said. "Hurry."

Archit nodded and turned. He ascended the staircase, crept back down the tunnel, and went back out into the world above.

"Margot, Liz," he hissed as he approached the sleeping girls. "It's midnight. The celebration is over."

The girls stirred and stretched. "So what do we do now?" Margot asked.

Archit pulled a large brass skeleton key from his pocket. "In all my adventures, I've never used this before," he said.

"What is it?" Liz said.

Archit held the ornately designed key up for them to see. "Try this in the keyhole. If it doesn't work, pull it out again and wave your hand over it. The key will take another shape, and you can try it again."

"Show us," Margot said.

Archit winced, a little embarrassed. He waved his wing over the key but nothing happened. "I don't have hands," he said. "Much as my wing might suffice in many situations, this isn't one of them. Birds were made for flying, not unlocking doors."

He handed the key to Margot. She waved her hand over it and watched as the metal teeth molded themselves into a different shape right before her very eyes.

"I've been locked up many times, but I've never been able to use it," Archit said. "Until now. Now that I have human friends who can do it for me."

Margot nodded. "How long will it take to find the right fit?"

Archit shook his head. "I don't know."

"I wonder if your bobby pins will work again," Liz suggested.

"Doubt it," Archit said. "Wait until you see the lock on that cage down there. We're not going to be able to pick that thing." He escorted them to the entrance of the cave. "If you get into any trouble, scream for me and I'll be there in a flash."

"You aren't coming with us?" Liz asked.

"I'll wait out here and stand guard," Archit said. "To make sure the door doesn't close on you." He hesitated. "I wish I could do this myself...but I can't."

Margot took a deep breath. "We'll get this done," she said with clearly feigned confidence. She looked at Liz, then proceeded into the cave.

Through the cavern they crept until the entrance disappeared behind them. Margot grabbed one of the torches from where it was mounted on the wall and held it in front of them to light the way.

The bumpy, rocky ground beneath their feet seemed surprisingly more treacherous than it had earlier that afternoon—or maybe it was just that they were more nervous—but several times, both Margot and Liz stumbled and had to catch each other, trying to make as little noise as possible in the process.

They found themselves at the top of the great sweeping staircase that led into the pit. Margot and Liz stood for a moment, surveying the aftermath of the raucous coronation party. "There's James," Liz whispered to Margot, pointing down below.

The girls went down the craggy steps, holding the torch out in front of them. James saw them and moved to the edge of the cage. "Margot! Liz!" he whispered. "I'm over here!"

"We see you, Jimmy," Margot said.

She and Liz hurried to the side of the cage, relieved that at least the three of them were together again. Even if iron bars prevented her from hugging her little brother, at least she knew where he was and that he was safe—for now.

"Oh, James," Liz whispered. "Thank God you're all right."

"I'm so glad you're here," James said. "You wouldn't believe some of the things they've been doing all day. These little monsters are out of control."

"I know, I know," Margot comforted him. "You must've been scared."

"We're going to get you out of here," Liz said, nodding down at the key in Margot's hand.

Without hesitation, Margot stuck the key into the hole and tried to turn it. No such luck.

"Is it the right key?" James asked.

Margot explained as she demonstrated. "It's a magic key. Archit had it." She tugged the key back out. "You wave your hand over it, and..." The brass again began to shift, reshaping itself like putty worked by invisible hands.

Margot tried the new key, but once again, it was a failure.

"Try it again," Liz encouraged.

"I will."

Over and over, Margot kept going, continuing to change the shape of the key, hoping that the next one would work, or the one after that.

James grew anxious. He looked out at the drunken rockies passed out on the floor behind Margot and Liz. "Do you think the rockies are dangerous?" he asked. It was a fear that had gnawed at his mind all day. "Do you think they...they plan to hurt me or something?"

Margot paused, forgetting to change the current shape of the key. She looked at Liz.

"We have to tell him," Liz said.

"I don't want to scare him," Margot protested.

"Margot, we have to."

Margot gave a hopeless sigh. "James, they're going to kill you," she said. "It's some weird sacrificial rite sort of thing."

James's face went rigid with shock. "When?" he asked.

"First thing in the morning," Margot said. "I wanted to spare you until we got you out of here...but now you get why we have to work fast."

James's chin quivered. "It's all right," he said, his voice cracking. "Just hurry up. We can do this."

Margot went back to working the key. Over and over again, she waved her hand and changed the shape, but each one failed. An hour went by, then two.

"What if—what if you don't manage to find a fit for the lock by morning?" James said, panic rising in his voice.

"James, calm down," Margot whispered. Her patience had begun to wane.

"Don't tell me to calm down," he hissed, trying not to raise his voice in all his fear, trying not to start crying. "You're not the one in a cage. You're not the one they're going to kill."

Margot put her face up against the bars of the cage, locking eyes with her little brother. "Listen, James. I'm going to get you out of here." She was as serious as he'd ever seen her, unblinking, her words slow and deliberate. "But you need to cut that out. I need for you to be strong right now."

Liz reached between the bars and took James's hand. He held it tightly, managing to take a few deep breaths as he tried to regain his wits.

Comforted by Liz's hand in his, James laid his head up against the bars of the cage. In a few minutes, he had calmed down, and unable to resist his weariness, he fell into a deep sleep.

Realizing that James was asleep, Liz gently pulled her hand back from inside the cage. She looked at Margot, who was fumbling with the key. "You're getting frustrated," she said. "Let me handle it for a little while. You relax for right now."

Margot handed the key to Liz, then slumped down on the ground, agitated. "What a piece of crap. Who has the patience for that?"

Liz tried her hand at the key for an hour before returning it to Margot. The night pressed on with the two of them trading the key off between them. When it wasn't her turn, the other sat and waited patiently, letting her frustration wear off.

"Margot? Liz?" Archit's whisper came from the stairs.

"Archit?" Liz grabbed the torch and held it up.

"It's nearly dawn," Archit said. "Half past five. Haven't you found a right fit yet?"

Liz looked back at Margot.

"No," Margot said, suddenly getting angry. "What's your plan now? Your awful key doesn't work."

Liz handed the torch to Archit, then scurried over and knelt beside the cage. "James," she whispered as she reached through the bars to shake him. "James, wake up. It's almost morning."

James sat up, snapping to attention. "Have you unlocked the cage?"

As if in answer to his question, Margot wrenched yet another unsuccessful key from the lock. She waved her hand over it, watched the brass reform into a new shape, then tried it without success.

Liz was trying not to panic. "Archit, how much time do we have?"

"I don't know, but it can't be much. The sky is already getting lighter."

James felt as if he were going to throw up. "What're we going to do?" he whimpered.

Margot's hand shook so badly she worried she might drop the key. She tried to block out the world as best she could, to just focus on what she was doing, as if she might somehow will the magic to work in their moment of need.

She fidgeted the key back out and waved her hand over it. Watching the brass twist itself into a new shape, she felt an odd, inexplicable sense of triumph, and suddenly hopeful again, she shoved the newly formed key in the lock. It slid into the keyhole with ease and turned a full circle. There came a click from inside the lock, and the door swung open.

"Ah!" she gasped, trying to stifle a scream of excitement.

James, suddenly able to breathe again, shot to his feet and stumbled forward into the arms of Liz and Margot.

"Come on," Margot said. "We gotta get out of here."

"Thank you," James whispered as they bolted forward.

Fueled by fresh adrenaline, James and the girls followed Archit up the stairs and back down the narrow passageway. They shuffled single-file down the corridor toward the mouth of the cave. The sunrise poured in, washing the stone gray of the craggy walls with pink and orange.

They rushed through the mouth onto the hillside above. Leaving the dark, terrifying cave was like coming up for air after a deep dive under water. James could breathe again. He looked out over the rocky hillside, taking in the quiet stillness of dawn. He was free. They had escaped.

"Look!" came a high-pitched scream behind them. "There they are! Get them!"

The four of them whirled around to see a crowd of rockies standing at the first bend of the tunnel behind them. What looked like a rocky shaman or priest pushed his way to the front of the crowd, holding out a staff made from a stick mounted with a bouquet of seagull feathers. "Seize them!" he shouted. "Seize them!"

James wasted no time. He turned to Margot, grabbed the torch from her, and chucked it behind them into the cavern. The flames erupted as the torch landed in the middle of the crowd, consuming the bystanders in a small explosion.

"Come on," Archit shouted, signaling them to flee up the hill. "Run!"

James looked over his shoulder to see the survivors of the fire—and there were many—shouting and screaming as they surged forward. He dashed up over the rocks, followed by Liz and Margot. Archit hesitated only long enough to tug at the rope that controlled the entryway, watching the rocks roll back into place. He knew it wouldn't hold them up long, but every second counted.

They bolted up the steep hillside as fast as they could go, scrambling over rocks and boulders as they went, cutting their feet and tearing their clothing.

Behind them, the boulder rolled out of the way and the entrance to Rockyland opened up again. The mob of rockies appeared at the mouth of the tunnel, shouting and cursing and waving their fists, spears, and torches. The savage throng erupted out of the tunnel and up the hillside after their escaped sacrifice and his accomplices.

James couldn't believe their speed. Within a minute, the impish little creatures had nearly caught up with them. He looked up toward the top of the hill. It was getting close, but not close enough.

Liz stopped beside a large boulder balanced precariously against several smaller rocks below it. "Mar," she said. "Help—help me get this rock loose!"

Margot went to her, followed by Archit and James. "No," Liz said, waving James on ahead. "No, you and Archit keep going. Get up the hill as fast as you can. Leave this to Margot and me."

James nodded, realizing that there was no time to protest. Before he turned and pressed on, he paused just long enough to look back and see Margot and Liz grunting and heaving as they combined their strength to send the boulder toppling onto the crowd of rockies below.

"Those girls are so hardcore," he whispered to himself.

He continued upward, feeling more scraped and bruised and bloodied with every step. The hillside seemed to be getting steeper and stonier the higher they went.

"Faster," Archit called, coming up behind him.

James knew that if he were to trip and fall, the rockies would be on top of him in a heartbeat. They would take him prisoner the same way they had the day before, and carry him back to their cave for the sacrifice. Their angry screams and jeers rose through the air as they pursued him. His life depended on his dexterity right now, on his speed, on his ability not to trip and fall and land flat on his face.

Margot and Liz caught up with him, and they put their arms around him to help push him along.

"You got this," Margot whispered to him.

The top of the hill was right in front of them. Clothes torn and dirtied, faces scratched and bloodied, they trudged to the summit and onto the grassy patch of land beyond. Feeling level ground beneath him at last, James took off running, wanting to put as much distance between himself and the monstrous little rockies as possible. Margot, Liz, and Archit kept pace just behind him as they fled along a dirt path through tall grass and ivy, into a flat woodland area where he collapsed, exhausted.

The others fell down around him, all of them heaving collective sighs as they tried to catch their breath. James lifted his head, still panting for air.

The hundreds of little men and women stomped their feet furiously at the edge of the grass.

"Won't...won't they follow us?" he wheezed.

"No," Archit said, remembering what the rocky had told them the day before. "They believe they are bound to the rocks. They won't leave the hill even if they want to."

James lay back down in the grass, his heart still pounding. After a moment, the shouting on the hill dissipated. He sat up to see the rockies turning away to go back to their underground city.

He looked around at Margot and Liz and Archit. To think that a few days ago, they didn't think they could cope with a cocktail party. And here they were, battling pirates and trekking through evil jungles and scaling cliffs. They had proven more resilient than he ever would have expected. They could overcome just about anything.

"Thanks, you guys," he said. "That was a damn adventure, wasn't it?"

"But look around," said Archit, gesturing to the patch of woodland they'd come to. "We've finally reached Nalgordia—journey's end is now in sight!"

CHAPTER 7
The Council
with the Hippies

"You all right?" Margot asked James as they walked along the path through the sparse woodland.

"Yeah," James said. "It all just freaked me out a little bit."

"But," Margot said, "you've probably been through adventures like these thousands of times before."

"Huh?" James said.

"All the stories you write," Margot said, "and all the imaginary games you played as a little kid. And the books you read. You've been through all of this sort of stuff before, in a way, right?"

"I guess." He gripped the knot of his power tie, remembering how confident he had felt when he put it on several days ago. He had loosened it around his unbuttoned collar, but it was still there. "Except...this time, it's real."

Margot laughed and nodded.

The four of them wandered through the woods at a leisurely pace. Finally feeling relaxed again, James looked up at the morning sun streaming down through the trees overhead, covering their surroundings with a patchwork of warm light and soft shadow.

"Dawn Flower and her people won't gather until evening," Archit said as they passed out of the woodland and through a nearby meadow. "We can head to the beach to get some quiet time and rest up a bit."

James wasn't going to say it aloud, but he was excited to meet Dawn Flower and her followers. He had never seen a hippie before, but he knew they had been everywhere in the mortal world back in the '60s and '70s. Nobody had ever spoken of them before as if they were a mythical race or something. They must have been driven away from the mortal world at some point, he figured, the way the fairies and elves were into the Otherworld according to ancient mythologies. Here in Nalgordia, they could live in peace and harmony.

"This way," Archit said. He led them down to a sandy beach just on the outskirts of the woods. As they walked over the dunes, the gentle breeze carried the heavy scent of salty sea air and the sound of waves crashing on the beach. Gulls cawed as they flew overhead.

"How can we be at an ocean?" asked Margot. "I thought you said Nalgordia was an island, and it was surrounded by the jungle?"

"It is," replied Archit.

"Then how can there be a beach and an ocean?" asked Margot. "If we're in the middle of an island."

"Who says there can't be oceans in the middle of an island?" asked Archit.

Margot's brow furrowed.

"Don't worry about it, Margot," James said.

Margot rolled her eyes.

They spent the afternoon on the beach, cooling off with a swim in the ocean and unwinding by building sandcastles and playing tag. When they got tired, the four of them piled together in the shade of the nearby palm trees for an extended nap.

Soon enough, the afternoon drew to a close and twilight set upon them. The air grew a bit cooler, and Archit decided that they'd rested enough and it was time to continue their journey. James, Liz, and Margot washed their faces in the water, and Liz carefully ran the jagged end of a broken seashell through her hair to work out the knots, then helped Margot do the same. Margot had torn the skirt of her dress in their scramble over the rocks, and she fiddled with it endlessly as if toying with it long enough might make it suddenly mend itself. James watched her, slightly amused.

Archit pulled a rag from his pocket and bent down to shine his leather shoes.

"You know, Archit, you seem to like those shoes a lot," James said. "What's your fascination with them?"

Archit looked up. If he were embarrassed, he handled it coolly.

"No, seriously," James said. "What's the deal?"

Archit shrugged. "They're leather. You know, actual skin. Not feathers or fur. They're the closest I'll ever come to having skin."

James nodded. He wasn't going to push the question further.

Liz chimed in. "What about the vest?"

"What about it?" Archit asked, looking up from his shoes.

Liz laughed. "Well, I don't know, it's pretty neat. Where'd you get it?"

"Oh, you know," Archit said, "I stole it from my uncle."

"You mean Mr. Birken?" Margot asked.

James had to admit that he had almost forgotten about Mr. Birken. Talk about an unhappy reminder.

"Yeah," Archit replied. "He had it stored away in the prison tower with a bunch of other old junk, and I took it with me when I ran away. You know, because I needed something to wear, and I might need to carry some money or something in the pockets."

"And then you discovered it was magic?" James asked.

"Pretty much," said Archit. He finished polishing his shoes, stood, and walked up the beach toward the woods. James and the girls followed.

"When I was getting ready to leave, I went through some of my uncle's things," Archit explained, "and I filled the pockets with money and matches and a compass, but no matter how much I put into the pockets, they never filled up or got any heavier. In fact, the pockets felt like they were still empty."

"That's incredible," said Liz. "To think—something that special just getting eaten by moths in an attic somewhere!"

Archit led them past a field of palms and tropical flowers, and they followed a trail up away from shore. Soon enough, the trail disappeared, and the trees grew thicker and closer together. The grass underfoot was soft and mossy. Here and there amid the forest giants were ferns and bushes, mushrooms, vines, and glittering cobwebs dotted with dewdrops. The air smelled of summer, and a gentle breeze whispered through the trees. James couldn't think of any place he had ever been that looked more natural, more as the world was supposed to look. Even when he ventured into the woods around the bike trail at home, it had not been as tranquil and serene.

"These are the western woods of Nalgordia," Archit explained.

Liz was gathering acorns as she went, and after she had a handful she would run on ahead and offer them to chipmunks that passed by. James was amazed to see that the chipmunks actually went up to Liz, took the acorns she offered them, and let her stroke their necks and backs. Liz looked back at them, surprise and joy plainly written on her face.

"Go ahead," she whispered to the chipmunks, offering the acorns. "You can have one."

The chipmunks approached her, taking the nuts right from her hand. James went forward, hoping he might be able to feed the chipmunks too.

"The forest animals are still wild, unlike the animals who live in the village," Archit explained. "The ones here are like the ones you would see back home, but the ones in the village wear clothes and live in houses."

"What?" Margot said. "Animals wearing clothes? And living in houses?"

"That's what I said," Archit said.

"This place is crazy," Margot said.

James ignored her, turning his attention instead to a pair of rabbits that had emerged from the bushes nearby. He pointed them out to Liz.

Archit looked up at Margot. "So, you're still a little skeptical of Nalgordian culture, I guess?"

"I mean, if you're talking about talking animals and all the other stuff we've seen so far," Margot said, "then, yeah. It's just a little tough to believe all of it."

"Well, yeah, if you refuse to believe it, I'm sure it is," Archit said.

"That's just it," Margot said. "There has to be a rational explanation for all of it."

"As long as you keep looking for reasons to doubt, you will doubt," Archit said.

Over by the bushes, Liz gave a few acorns to James. "Come on," she cooed to the rabbits. "He won't hurt you."

Archit looked up at Margot. "But when you let yourself believe, you will."

Margot rolled her eyes. "That's the most pretentious thing I've heard in a long time. My manager at the coffee shop would probably describe it as 'dreck.' Y'know, the manager who's probably firing me for missing so many shifts right about now."

Archit shrugged. "Come on," he said. He called to Liz and James, "Let's keep going."

Twilight settled in. The forests were just as beautiful at night as they were during the day. The silvery light from the moon and the stars shone through the leaves overhead, making the moss and mushrooms and flowers around them light up in a way that James had never seen in the mortal world. They looked like the fluorescent posters under blacklights at the local concert venues he often went to.

"Look!" Liz pointed to what might have been fireflies sweeping through the tree branches. They glowed with vibrant shades of pink, green, and blue. As they flew closer and one of them rested on Liz's stretched-out finger, James saw they were humanoid in shape.

"Fairies," Archit observed. "They're pretty common in the Nalgordian forests."

"Wow," James said.

"You'd find many magical species if you explored these woods long enough," Archit said. "If we stayed out late enough, we'd meet the nightgoblins. They're benevolent little people, but a little ostentatious. They come out of the darkness every night to go streaking. I've never seen them, though, and I've heard some people say that they're strictly legendary."

They pressed on deeper into the woods. The air felt cooler now, but still comfortable—just like the summer nights James used to cherish as a kid. It was probably around nine o'clock, but time seemed to become irrelevant, unimportant, in this world. James liked it that way; there wasn't all of the rush and concern of doing something by an exact hour of the day.

"Here we are," Archit said, stopping in his tracks and pointing up ahead with his wing.

Between the trees up ahead were light and movement and sound. The hippie commune!

"Come on," Archit said, walking forward. He led the way, and James, Margot, and Liz followed, making their way up the slope and stopping behind a tree on the outskirts of the camp.

James gazed in wonder at the scene just beyond the trees. Within the clearing, white candles illuminated a group of young men and women not much older than Margot. The oldest of them could not have been much beyond twenty-five. Some of them knelt on blankets that were spread out on the grass, while others danced barefoot nearby. One of the younger girls sat on a mossy rock, strumming a guitar, while a man sat at her feet, beating a bongo. Others were gathered in little groups, passing a pipe between them, or eating from wooden bowls full of fresh fruit and nuts.

"There they are," Archit said. "The hippies. They are the ancestors and originals of this entire land."

"Which one is Dawn Flower?" James said.

"The one gathering flowers," said Archit, indicating a tall, graceful young woman standing at the foot of a willow tree, picking lilies. "She is the queen of the hippie people. Only she isn't their queen really, because they don't believe in rulers. But Dawn Flower is good and wise, and she serves as the head of their councils and a voice on their behalf."

James nodded. The hippie queen, but not really a queen. She gave him the vibe of a Queen Titania meets Lady Galadriel meets Glinda the Good Witch of the South.

"Is it safe for us to approach them?" Margot said.

"Oh, come on, Margot," James said. "They're hippies, not terrorists."

"The hippies are good spirits, Margot," Archit said. "Some pixies and elves and sprites tend to be a little mischievous, but hippies are pure and good. They wouldn't hurt anyone."

He looked at James and Liz to be sure they got what he was saying. James nodded.

"Come on, then," Archit said.

He stepped out from behind the tree, and James followed, gesturing to Margot and Liz to stay close. A strange sense of calmness and serenity swept over him as he stepped into the soft glow of candlelight that illuminated the grove. The hippies turned to see their four visitors and fell suddenly quiet.

Dawn Flower paused, then stood straight and stepped forward slowly. She was tall and slender and beautiful—James thought she looked like a model, though far more beautiful than any woman he'd ever seen before. Her gossamer robe shimmered as she moved, giving her an ethereal appearance.

"Dawn Flower," Archit said, going down on one knee. James followed Archit's example.

"I know why you have come, your highness," Dawn Flower said, gracefully nodding her head to Archit.

James looked up and caught Archit's expression at her address. "Your highness?" he mouthed at Archit, confused.

Dawnflower nodded at James, then Margot and Liz in turn. "And welcome, children, young Edenites. Please, stand and make yourselves welcome at our gathering."

Dawn Flower's voice was soft, airy, as if it weren't entirely there—but there was a nobility to it, a dignity that no ordinary person would be able to possess. James thought she sounded both dreamy and wise at the same time. He couldn't help hang on her every word, and when she told him to make himself welcome, he was going to do it.

She led them over to the center of the grove where several of her companions unfolded white linen sheets and laid them out on the ground. The hippie queen turned and gestured for the children to seat themselves.

"Sit down and rest," she said. "You've had a long journey and endured much these past days—I know this because I have messengers who've told me. You will have dinner before we have our council."

Real food, James thought. He looked at Archit, who wasn't nearly as responsive to the prospect of a meal as James was. His expression looked nervous, and it dawned on James that this was the moment of truth for Archit. He was about to find out the answers to all the questions they'd had. This was the whole reason they had come here! James felt a little guilty for thinking about his stomach at a time like this.

Several hippies seated themselves on the picnic blankets, so James moved forward, looking at Margot and Liz to see them following his lead.

From out in the woods, a group carried woven baskets and wooden bowls full of food, tin pitchers and glass bottles of drink, and an odd assortment of rustic plates and bowls. They set their goods down on the blankets, and as a group, all the hippies began to partake, passing containers of food back and forth in a communal way.

James accepted a plate from a girl with red curls and a sea-green tunic, and he helped himself. There were loaves of fresh bread, dishes of honey, a large bowl of hummus, and many different kinds of fruit—apples and berries and bananas and avocados. There were bowls of steaming cooked grains, too—brown rice, oatmeal, couscous, and quinoa—as well as trays of nuts and seeds.

"Tell us of your journeys, Adamites," said one of the hippie men.

The four of them all took part in telling about how their canoe broke on one of the rocks as they were coming across the sea, and all of the adventures that followed and the hardships they endured to reach Nalgordia.

The hippies were particularly interested to hear about the little people of Rockyland. There had been no tales of these creatures before, presumably because anyone who encountered them wound up as a sacrifice.

Others of them were much intrigued that James and Archit had slain the Beast of Darkness by the poison of one of his own flowers.

After they'd eaten, the conversation eventually quieted down. Dawn Flower stood to address the group. She walked to the foot of a willow tree on the edge of the grove, where she fetched a worn satchel that lay by the roots. She lifted it and put the strap across her breast, then turned to the children.

"We are honored to have you join us tonight," Dawn Flower said, gazing on them with an expression of favor and warmth.

"Thank you," James said.

Dawn Flower smiled. "To show my blessing, I would like to offer you these gifts."

James turned to Archit. "Gifts?" he mouthed.

Archit nodded, gesturing with his wing for James to turn back around.

The bird must have known that Dawn Flower would start with him, because she said, "James, last born, come forward."

James stood, only half-amazed that she had known his name. Of course she did! She was queen of a mythical tribe—why shouldn't she know more about him than she let on? He straightened his collar and ran a hand through his hair to be sure it was lying flat, wondering for a moment whether he should tuck his shirt in, but he decided to forgo fussing with his appearance anymore. He strode forward with his shoulders back and his chin up. This, he hoped, would make him look strong and mature in front of the queen.

Up close, he found himself once again struck by her beauty. Neither her age nor her race could he really determine, and her eyes were so piercing that he got the feeling that they were able to see straight into his soul.

"Yes, ma'am," he addressed her, giving a bow.

She smiled. "To you, James, I give this stone." She put a hand into the satchel and pulled out a smooth gemstone so clean and polished that James could see his face reflected on the finely cut surface.

"If any curse is sent to destroy you and your friends, this stone will protect you," Dawn Flower explained. "But use it only when you greatly need it, only when you are in grave peril, because it can be used only once."

James nodded. "Thank you."

"That stone," Dawn Flower declared, "was given to me by a witch-priestess, who found it while she was wading in the creek that babbles through the northern forest of the Kaukonen Island, though I do not believe she knew its worth when she passed it along to me. I discovered its abilities from a spiritual session at a bonfire, when a whispering in my ear revealed its power. Use this gift wisely, James."

James thanked her once more and returned to his seat on the blanket next to Archit.

"Elizabeth, middle born, come forward."

Liz stood, quickly straightening out the wrinkles in her princess dress and pushing her hair back over her shoulders. She strode forward but looked much meeker and shyer in front of Dawn Flower than James hoped he himself had looked.

The hippie queen held out a pewter bottle studded with glass beads. "To you," she said, "I give this elixir." She placed the bottle in Liz's hands. "Drink of this elixir and you will adapt to whatever atmosphere you enter, be it under water, into fire, through gas, wherever your journey must take you. But judge carefully when you will need it, only when it is absolutely necessary, because there is only enough for each of you to have one sip."

"Thank you," Liz said.

"That elixir," Dawn Flower continued, "was brewed using the nectar of the elf-flowers that grow on the shores of Iula-Jula, mixed with the sap from the Ahswahth Tree, simmered for seven days and seven nights in a puddle of freshly fallen rain water, and blessed by the tears of a passing doe who had lost her foal—or so I am told. My hippie kin scooped it up with the caps of acorns, in small quantities, and poured it into that very bottle, which had once belonged to a goddess beyond the seas, in which she carried water that sustained her life. Use this gift wisely, Elizabeth."

Liz smiled, and James knew why—the vivid description that Dawn Flower had given sounded like something he would have come up with when they were on their imaginary adventures as children. "Thank you," Liz said to Dawn Flower.

Liz went back to the blanket and sat down, tucking the bottle carefully into the pocket of her dress.

"Margot," said Dawn Flower, "first born, come forward."

Margot hesitated, then slowly stood.

"Come forward, child," Dawn Flower beckoned, smiling kindly.

Margot obeyed, but before Dawn Flower could speak, Margot cut her off. "Please," she said, trying to sound polite, "please, I don't want any present. I appreciate the offer anyways, but I just want to go home. All of us—me and my brother and cousin—now that we're all here and we're all safe."

James felt a twinge of secondhand embarrassment, but if Dawn Flower were at all offended, she didn't show it. Instead, she smiled. "My sweet child, you're needed here."

"But this place is too much," Margot said. "It's all too weird and dangerous. I don't know what you need us to do, but we have to be home. We have things to do and people to see." Margot shrugged, lost for words. "What else do you want me to say?"

Dawn Flower put her hand up and stroked Margot's head. "You've been very brave, Margot, to endure this journey. You've promised Archit that you would serve as his friend and companion on his quest, and you've been true to him."

Margot looked hopeful.

"My gift to you," said Dawn Flower, "is a promise. When Archit's journey is over, and the quest is accomplished, then I will send you home in the blink of an eye, as quick as a heartbeat, all of you safe and unharmed. That is my gift to you."

Dawn Flower leaned forward and kissed Margot on the forehead.

"Will that serve as a fitting gift?" Dawn Flower said.

Margot nodded. "Thank you."

She turned and went back to her seat. She leaned in close to James and Liz. "Once she talks to Archit, she'll get that our journey is over, right?" she said. "And she can send us home?"

James didn't reply. He got the sense from Dawn Flower's promise that maybe their journey wasn't completely over and done with. If there were still a quest to accomplish, as Dawn Flower had described, then maybe the hippie queen had some expectation of them that they didn't yet know about. He looked down at the gemstone in his hand. She was giving them these gifts because she knew they would need them. Magical deities didn't bestow extraordinary gifts with no reason.

The hippie queen's voice drew James's attention back to her. "And now you, Archit," she said. "Your highness."

James looked over at Archit, who stood nervously but put on an air of confidence if James had ever seen one. James could feel the tension in the air around them, all the hippies watching with hushed anticipation as Archit strode forward to Dawn Flower.

"We must have private counsel," Dawn Flower announced to the group, putting her arm tenderly on Archit's shoulder. "Excuse us. We will return within an hour."

She took up a staff of white wood lying on the grass and gestured for Archit to follow her.

The two stepped out of the glen and began to weave their way through the trees in darkness. Archit's stomach had become all twisted all up in knots, and as much as he wanted to ask Dawn Flower to speak the truth quickly and plainly, he knew she did things in her own time and in her own way. But maybe—just maybe—she was about to tell him that his uncle's curse was breaking. It seemed appropriate, he thought, that she was leading him through a dark forest, her robe glowing faintly in the moonlight, as he had felt lost for so long and he was looking to her to provide direction in the darkness.

Dawn Flower stopped in another clearing about a half-mile from the hippie camp. The silver moon peered through the trees.

"Now, your highness," Dawn Flower said, "here we can talk in private. What is it that you have come to ask?"

"Please," Archit said, "why is it that you keep calling me 'highness'?"

Dawn Flower smiled. "You do not know your heritage," she said. It wasn't a question.

"My heritage?" Archit exclaimed. "But I'm a figment of the imagination. I can't have a heritage." He couldn't understand why Dawn Flower, of all people, didn't get that. "I was never born," he continued, "just like I'll never...just like I'll never die."

The realization hit him as the words were coming out of his mouth. "Wait! There's something I don't know, isn't there? Why did my uncle have to curse me to make me immortal if I was already a figment of the imagination?"

Dawn Flower's gaze bore into him. "Why do you assume you are a figment of the imagination?" she asked.

Archit almost had to laugh. Somebody like Dawn Flower wouldn't actually be messing with him like this, just screwing with his mind as if this were all some big joke. "Why do I assume? Look at me!" He spread his wings out, as if she couldn't already see him standing there in front of her. "Nalgordia is the only place where I've ever fit in and seemed normal. I'm not like all the creatures of my father's world, of James's world."

He paused. "Or am I? Am I real?" It seemed absurd, but Dawn Flower seemed to be actually insinuating this. "I used to age," he said. "I remember it vividly, even after all these years." The childhood that he had long suppressed, the happy memories he had relayed to James, Liz, and Margot only a few nights before, all blazed anew in his mind. "I had birthdays and I grew,

157

back when I lived with my father, back before I was cursed. Does this mean I'm real?"

Dawn Flower crossed her legs and seated herself on the ground. "I think it is time you hear the full truth, Archit," she said, patting the grass next to her to tell him to sit down beside her. "I am sorry that I did not tell you a long time ago."

Archit trembled as he took a seat next to the hippie queen.

"Before I begin," she said, "I will tell you this: Yes, your uncle did *try* to curse you to be a fully imaginary creature. And no, figments of the imagination do not age or grow or even die. But you are only half-figment, Archit. Your mother was an animal from Earth, though she was not one of the progeny of Adam. In fact, I am sorry to say, your mother and her kingdom met their death at the hands of mankind."

"My mother?" Archit said. This was the first time he had ever heard mention of either of his birth parents. "And her kingdom? Killed by humans?"

"Yes," Dawn Flower said. "Your mother was a dodo bird, an extinct species—"

"I know about the dodos," Archit said. "I've heard of them."

"Native to the island of Mauritius," Dawn Flower said. "And your mother was their princess."

"Why have I never heard this story before?" Archit asked. He wasn't angry, just confused.

"Because it didn't matter until now, at least not as far as I could tell," Dawn Flower said. "I wanted to spare you the painful story of what happened to your mother and her subjects."

"Am I the only one left?" Archit said.

"Yes," Dawn Flower said. "Your grandfather and grandmother, the king and queen of the dodos, were not alarmed when a group of excited young fledglings came to their nest one morning, each of them shouting about the great sea creature perched on the waves and swimming toward them. None of them could have known that this sea creature was called a ship, and it carried a crew of white sailors from Europe, explorers and treasure seekers who were out to conquer the world.

"But the dodo kingdom knew no enemies, not pig nor lizard nor wildcat. Its idyllic home in the jungles of the island was so undisturbed that they contented themselves to build their nests low to the ground.

"'When this creature reaches our shores, we will greet it as a friend and welcome it,' the king declared.

"Your mother, Princess Avis, was a curious and headstrong young dodo. She felt compelled to greet this newcomer before any of the others. She thought if she asked her parents for permission to go see it arrive, they would never agree. She decided she had to go without asking them.

"So, the princess snuck away from the nest and headed out to the beach. The ship was close by then, anchored only a few yards from shore. Men had come off the ship in rowboats to make their way to the island.

"The princess looked joyfully at the rowboats full of men. 'Why,' she said, 'the sea creature has come close to shore to give birth. How wonderful!'

"The princess watched the men push their rowboats ashore and climb out. They came toward her. How strange and interesting they were! They were big to be babies—the largest of them was twice the height of any dodo bird—but then again, they would have to be big if they were to grow up to be anywhere near the size of the full-grown sea creature.

"'We will be great friends,' said Princess Avis, still hidden in the foliage and watching the men walk onto the beach.

"She emerged, eager to make acquaintance.

"'Welcome,' she said, brightly, 'welcome to Mauritius! I am the daughter of King Raphus, and my name is—!'

"But as she went to hug one of the men, he bent over and his two big, leathery hands closed around her neck and lifted her with such force it was a miracle her neck didn't break.

"'Look at this bird!' shouted the sailor to the others in a gruff voice. 'Look at how big and fat it is! How long it's been since we've had meat. Won't one of these make a tasty dinner tonight.'

"'Put me down, please' said the princess. 'Please, sir. What are you doing?'

"'It doesn't even resist you,' laughed one of the other sailors. 'They must be stupid creatures.'

"'Stupid creatures are an easy capture,' said another.

"'Sir, you are welcome on our island,' said the princess, 'but please, put me down. This is most uncivil of you.'

"But to the men, her words only sounded like a blunted caw. 'Do-do! Do-do!'

"The men all laughed to hear her caw. 'Listen to it,' one said, 'calling *dodo, dodo!* That's right—dodo-brained creatures they are, without a doubt!'

"For the next three hours, the men ravaged the island. Every last one of the fat, happy birds was torn from its content life, never to know peace or comfort again. They were led and pushed back to the beach, where the men loaded them onto the rowboats and took them back to the main ship. Imagine their horror as this happened. They did not even know to run or hide or defend themselves. In one afternoon, their beautiful kingdom was raped of its people, who had now been made prisoners.

"That was the end of the dodo birds. They were rounded up and imprisoned on the ship, and for days upon weeks they endured abuse in their captivity as the ship sailed back to Europe. Every night, the ship's cook would choose one of the birds, kill it, and cook it for the crew's dinner. King Raphus was the first to be killed, and after him, each of the biggest and fattest of the remaining birds went one after the other. Their flesh was devoured by hungry sailors every night for dinner.

"Princess Avis cried and wept for many hours every day, even though she knew it would do her no good. Her father was dead, eaten by the sailors. Her mother, Queen Columbidae, had starved herself to death in grief. Many of her friends had been beaten to death or eaten as her father had been. She was all alone with nobody to comfort her. Every night, she would curl up in a cold corner of the room where the birds were kept. Amid the stink of rotting flesh and the groans of the dying, she would pray that if she herself were not killed, she might find hope for the future somewhere.

"She was the only one to survive the journey. By the time the ship returned to Holland, all of the other subjects of the dodo kingdom had met some grisly, horrid demise.

"'Only one!' said one of the sailors in disbelief as he stepped over several corpses toward Princess Avis, who cowered before the men.

"'What's been happening to all of them?' asked another.

"'We've not been feeding them proper,' observed a third. 'And the captain's dog has caught a few of them. I've seen it happen.'

"After all of that, Princess Avis's horrors were still not over. She was locked up and imprisoned in the London zoo, where people could travel from all over to see her, make a spectacle of her, gaze upon the prisoner, the captive princess from the late-discovered kingdom.

"Within only a short time, much of mankind had heard of this exotic and queer creature brought back from a faraway land, and those who traveled to look at it were amazed by its shape and size. Still, many people refused to believe—both those who had only heard of it, as well as those who had laid eyes on it. They declared the dodo bird to be a strange mythical beast concocted by delirious sailors, and there was no way that they could possibly exist.

"After weeks of misery in her prison of a zoo cell, Princess Avis died. The year was 1681, and with her ended the entire species of the dodo bird.

"She was stuffed by a skilled taxidermist and put on display at the Ashmolean Museum in Oxford. For years, the dead body of Princess Avis, with her glassy eyes and melancholy expression, would display itself as just another curiosity of the museum's collection. In time, her race faded into legend.

"'Preposterous-looking birds,' people would say when they saw depictions of the dodo in paintings. 'And you expect for us to believe that such a monster once walked this earth? And a stuffed figure of it in an Oxford museum? What are we coming to? They'll be telling us that dragons and mermaids are real, and they deserve their own places in the history books and museums.'

"That was until 1775. That was the year the curator of the museum discovered the stuffed body of Princess Avis had lice. 'She'll have to be burned,' he said. 'Such a shame. That's the last remaining example of this creature. See that it's removed no later than tomorrow.'

"On this night, the stars must have aligned, for that was the same night that my people assembled in the moonlit clearing of the western woods of Nalgordia. The giant oaks, all covered with ivy even back then, stood around us in a circle. I sat upon a rock to address the others.

"'I am feeling inspired tonight,' I said. 'Let us create something.'

"'Perhaps we shall weave a magic cloak,' said one.

"'Or make an enchanted candle,' said another.

"'Or a charmed drinking goblet,' said yet another.

"I considered their suggestions. 'As special as all of those may be, I have a better idea. Let us create an animal, a creature, something that is as attractive as it is mystifying and exciting.'

"The other hippies murmured their excitement over this idea.

"'Let it have feathers so vibrant that they make a king look like a peasant in comparison,' I continued, 'and a mane of hair that would humble a lion.'

"'Give it a gold beak, and pearly eyes,' said one of the hippies.

"'It will be able to fly as well as swim and talk,' said another.

"We talked all night, and in our wild imaginations, we invented a beast so beautiful and unique there was no question we wanted to see it brought to life.

"'Well, here is a thought,' said I. 'The Adamites of far-away Earth have slain off one of the animals with whom they share their world.'

"My announcement was greeted with expressions of disgust and horror.

"'It will be a long time before the Adamites understand the error of their ways,' I continued. 'They are foolish, blundering creatures, and lay continual waste to the beautiful world they've been given, and very seldom do they recognize that they share it with other animals. But why do we not do this: We shall let our little bird creature be born through one of the dodo birds. That way, he shall be brought to life, and the bloodline of the dodo kingdom shall not be lost to extinction.'

"A strange idea it was, but nobody questioned it.

"At midnight that very night, I traveled to the mortal world. I went to the Ashmolean Museum, where Princess Avis waited. Through my magical arts, I was able to give her life once more just for that night. Her last night. She laid an egg, and within that egg slept our little figment of the imagination.

"'But who will raise my child?' asked Princess Avis when she gave the egg to me. 'I cannot raise it.'

"'He shall be raised by the hippies in Nalgordia,' I told her.

"'I have a better idea,' Princess Avis gently said, 'for he is my child, and

I think I know the man to father him.'

"I gave her a look of curiosity and she continued.

"'There is a man who comes to this museum every day, a bachelor, I believe, for I never see him with any wife or child. He is quiet and kind in his demeanor—I have seen him treat the curator and the other visitors with grace and respect. He come frequently and looks at the exhibits, taking notes, making sketches. I do not know much about humankind, but this man strikes me as a worthy one. He pursues knowledge for the sake of knowledge, and he is kind for the sake of kindness. If only more humans were like him. I know he is the man to raise my baby.'

"'These are the words of a wise mother,' I observed.

"That night, I helped Princess Avis slip out of the cold museum and we went to the home of George Birken—the man whom you knew as your father, Archit. Princess Avis left her egg on his front step, wrapped in a blanket and tucked in a wicker basket with a note explaining everything."

As Dawn Flower finished her revelation, Archit found his breath stopped up in his throat. He stared, blinking at the hippie queen. This account, combined with revisiting the memories of childhood the other night, had opened up wounds he thought healed long ago.

"So..." Archit began slowly, "I am part animal and part figment."

"Yes," Dawn Flower said. "The last of an extinct species, and of royal blood at that. Some humans never believed in dodo birds, and would never acknowledge a social hierarchy among animals could resemble their own."

"But I'm not entirely imaginary," Archit said. "That's the important thing. I'm not entirely imaginary." He paused and sighed. "Well, this explains a lot."

Dawn Flower looked up at the moon. She seemed to consider her words carefully. "Your uncle tried to change that though. He tried to make you fully imaginary."

"Tried," Archit said, hanging on her words. "He tried but he didn't succeed."

"No, he did not. Not entirely."

"Why not?"

Dawn Flower reached forward and put a comforting arm around Archit.

"Do you recall what your father told you about your uncle? Back before you met him, when he was only somebody you knew of through your father's stories and explanations?"

Archit thought for a moment. "Only that he was evil, but Father still loved him. He was his brother after all."

"There it is," Dawn Flower said, a note of triumph in her voice. "No matter how hard your uncle tried to shuck off his humanity, to make himself an immortal warlock and join the monsters of the Night Scourge, he would never become fully immortal as long as there remained somebody who loved him. Your father's love stopped his brother from becoming an imaginary villain, and it wasn't until your father was dead that Abaddon truly became the evil wizard he had long aimed to be."

Archit stood, shaking his head. None of this made any sense to him. "So what? You mean, all these years there's been somebody out there who loves me? And that's why my uncle's curse couldn't fully take hold of me?"

Dawn Flower nodded.

"Who?" Archit asked.

Dawn Flower smiled. "I think you know."

There was nobody else Archit had known except his father and Dromio, and both of them were long gone. At least, that's what he had always thought. He was almost afraid to ask lest he might be wrong, but maybe... just maybe there was a chance. "You can't mean Dromio, can you?" he ventured.

"Of course," Dawn Flower said.

"But Dromio's destroyed," Archit said. "He's been destroyed for many years, for centuries."

"Why is it that you think he's destroyed?" Dawn Flower asked.

"My uncle told...oh!" The realization hit Archit like a bolt of lightning, one that ever so quickly illuminated all the darkness and fear he had carried around for centuries. "Oh, why didn't I realize it before? It's so obvious."

"It would not be the first time your uncle lied about something," Dawn Flower said. "Deception is in his nature. He can justify it if it gets him what he wants. Those in power always think the truth is of no consequence as long as the lie satisfies them."

"Do you think Dromio is the one who will be able to break the curse?" Archit said. "If he was able to protect me from the spell in the first place, and stop it from fully having effect, then reuniting with him again will be able to free me from it entirely."

He looked at her, waiting for a response. She remained silent, weighing her words.

"There's more to this wish than you are letting on, I think," she said. "Tell me, why is it that you wish so badly to be real? Life as a figment of the imagination might suit you. You would live forever, never knowing fear or sadness or anger, never made a victim by your own faults or foolishness, never having to choose a side in the great battle of good and evil that has always plagued the mortal world."

Archit shook his head. "No, that's not exactly right," he replied. "You said 'live forever,' but figments of the imagination don't really live. They just exist."

He hesitated, wondering how much he should confess to her. It wasn't just about being real or imaginary. "If I were to become real, then I might be able to make some sort of difference in that great battle of good and evil, and then find peace and respite in the life after this one. My father always taught me that even though humans live in their world for only a short time, their souls go on living forever in another life long after their human bodies have turned to dust."

Dawn Flower pondered what Archit had said. "It sounds to me as if you don't merely want to be real. It sounds as if you want to have a soul."

"Yes," Archit said, unable to resist smiling, so grateful that Dawn Flower seemed to understand and didn't dismiss what he said as folly. "I want to have a soul."

"There are plenty of creatures that are real but do not have souls," Dawn Flower said. "Only humans have souls."

"I want to be human," Archit said. "Just like my father, and just like my new friends." To admit it was embarrassing and a relief all at the same time.

Dawn Flower again did not dismiss him, instead giving him an approving look as if she were impressed by what he said. "It is interesting," she said, "that you should want to be like humans when they are the ones who brought your kingdom to ruin."

Archit nodded. "That's the strange thing about humans. They are capable of tremendous evil," he said. "I mean, you need only look at their history of wars, of oppression, of greed and slavery and prejudice and terror. But they are also capable of incredible good. I've read some of their ancient scriptures, particularly the ones revered by those who worship the Nazarene carpenter, and he said that no human being is as evil as his or her worst deed. All their faiths point to the hope that love will triumph, even when hate and malice seem so prevalent. That's a powerful thought."

"It is," Dawn Flower said.

Archit kneeled down beside her. "So is it possible?" he said. "Is it possible for a figment of the imagination to become human?"

"If it were ever possible, then this might be the one way," Dawn Flower said. "Your uncle cursed you because he wanted to corrupt you to be like him. By putting a curse on you when you were only a half-figment, your uncle inadvertently gave you the choice for greater glory, because now you must decide whether to be real or imaginary, to break the curse or not. Being half-mortal is an existence to which you can never return. If you break this curse, you will become fully mortal."

"By reuniting with Dromio?" Archit asked.

"Yes," Dawn Flower replied. "His love protects you. That is why your uncle tried to separate you from him."

She stood, putting her hand on Archit's shoulder. "By defying your uncle's hatred and demonstrating an act of love, you might prove yourself worthy of being human."

"Where will I even start?" Archit asked. "I wouldn't even know where to look for him."

Dawn Flower shook her head, a smile on her face. "You would. Your uncle might have abandoned Dromio, but Dromio would never abandon you. He will still be at the amusement park all these years later, waiting for your return. You needn't doubt it."

"Then we'll set out tomorrow," Archit said. "We'll have to find him by my birthday. James overheard my uncle's oracle say that on my next birthday, I would turn sixteen. That gives us only three days."

"The amusement park is a week's journey from here on foot," Dawn Flower said. "The only park you would find would be a ruin. You must first defeat Lord Iceheart if you're going to seek out Dromio."

Archit's stomach dropped. "Lord Iceheart. I'd almost forgotten."

"He has been sent by your uncle to thwart your mission."

Her words confirmed what Archit had suspected. "But why? My uncle is far more powerful than any minion sorcerer."

"Don't you see why?" Dawn Flower said.

Archit thought for a moment. "My uncle is afraid to kill Dromio."

"Afraid?" Dawn Flower said. "Or simply knows better? Of course, no imaginary creature can die, but they can be destroyed beyond all measure. To kill one of Dromio's kind carries a dreadful condemnation. Your uncle needs a powerful servant to do it for him."

"What do you know about Lord Iceheart?" Archit asked.

"He was once Janus, the sorcerer of the east," Dawn Flower said. "A good and just ally of my people. He was not an Earthling, but he looked like one, and he spent many years trying to find a way to restore Nalgordia to everlasting peace and harmony, to shut out evil forever. But he never found the answers he sought. When your uncle came to him, offering him great power in exchange for his loyalty, he was easily corrupted. Your uncle changed him from a creature of good to a creature of evil, and gave him new sources of magical powers."

"And has commanded him to destroy all of Nalgordia?" Archit said. "All of Nalgordia, just to stop me?"

"In only another day, his power will be strong enough to launch an attack on the entire land," Dawn Flower said. "I am sending the human children with you to defeat him."

"Us?" Archit said.

"You," Dawn Flower said. "The humans will have the power to destroy Lord Iceheart, and I think that you will learn from them exactly what your wish—to be human and to have a soul—truly requires of you."

Archit didn't know how to reply. It was all too much. "But—"

"Listen to me, Archit," Dawn Flower said. "This is the quest that you are destined to fulfill. Don't you see the fault that your uncle has committed?

He separated you from Dromio. He sent Lord Iceheart to destroy Nalgordia. In doing both acts, he has given you the chance to prove yourself worthy of a soul. A virtue untested cannot be praised, and if you remain untested, you will never be more than a figment creature. Only by resisting this evil can you prove yourself to be something more. Resist it."

Archit nodded. "All right."

Dawn Flower lifted her staff. "Will your human friends go with you?"

"Yes," Archit said. "Yes, I know they will."

"Then you know what you must do."

"I do."

Dawn Flower took a step toward the edge of the grove. "Let us return, shall we?"

They walked back through the woods in silence.

When they arrived at the grove, his three companions were deeply engaged in conversation with the hippies. James lay on his back, looking up at the stars as he mused philosophically aloud. When he saw Archit return from the woods, he sat up.

"Hey," he said enthusiastically.

"Hi," Archit replied.

"So...?" James said.

Archit put on a brave face. "Everything is going to work out. I'll tell you guys everything in the morning?"

"So, we're not going home right now?" Margot asked.

"You'll sleep here tonight," Dawn Flower said in a voice that James found overwhelmingly comforting. "My people will watch over you until dawn. You will be safe in our company."

James wanted to protest. They had just arrived, and he finally had a chance to hang out with actual hippies. He didn't want to go to bed yet! He wanted to stay up late and have a long philosophical talk about searching for the meaning of life, breaking away from rigid social restraints, out-of-body experiences, and harmony with the rest of humankind! "But..."

"Let's go to bed," Archit said. "We have a big day ahead of us tomorrow."

James looked at Margot and Liz, recognizing the uneasy look on their faces. Despite how they felt, he trusted Archit. Archit knew what was best.

He lay down on the picnic blanket, and Margot and Liz lay down beside him. Archit joined them. "Good night," he whispered.

"Good night," James whispered in reply.

The hippies went around the grove, putting out the candles. The night was full of the sound of crickets praying and leaves rustling in the breeze. Some of the hippies continued to strum their guitars, playing soft lullabies.

One by one, the children—as well as Archit, with all of his worries—floated off to dreamland. Their adventurous day had finally drawn to a close, and even heroes needed sleep.

CHAPTER 8
The Mountain
of Sinacshin

James woke to see the faint glimmer of dawn through the trees. The stars faded into the lightening sky, and he rolled over, knowing that his time of rest was drawing to a close. He wished he could sleep for only a few more minutes, but if it was daybreak, then Archit would likely be waking them up soon.

He sat up. The hippies had departed, along with any sign they had ever been there to begin with, except for a last remaining picnic blanket spread out with breakfast—fruit, nuts, a carafe of tea, and a large bowl of steaming oatmeal gleaming with dribbled honey. Archit sat alone with his back up against a tree, watching the sun rise through the trees overhead.

James climbed to his feet and went to Archit. He knelt down. "Morning."

"Morning," Archit replied, his eyes still on the sky overhead.

"Did you sleep well?" James asked.

Archit shrugged. "Not especially. You?"

James felt a little guilty. "Yeah. I practically passed out."

"You were tired."

"I guess so." James sighed. Something was bothering Archit, he could tell. "What kept you up?"

Archit was silent. "Dawn Flower just told me an awful lot last night," he said. "So I had a lot on my mind."

James nodded. "We're not done, are we?" he said. "I mean, it's not time for us to go home yet?"

"No," Archit said. He reached for a piece of fruit from the platter on the blanket. "We have another task to fulfill. This one might be the most dangerous of all the things we've done."

James felt a sinking feeling in his stomach. More dangerous than what they had just been through? What could this one possibly entail?

"We should wake the girls," Archit said. "I can explain it all to you together."

He started to get up, but James stopped him. "Hold on," he said. "Explain it to me first. The girls won't be so crazy about staying here in Nalgordia, but I promise you, no matter what they say, I'm with you on this. All the way. Even if they decide to go home..."

"I can't send them home," Archit said. "Not now. They're going to have to come with us."

James bit his lower lip, contemplating. "What is it we have to do here?"

"I need your help," Archit said. "Dawn Flower told me to take you with me to do this."

"Do what?" James didn't like the enigmatic nature of this conversation.

Archit shifted on the grass. "There's an evil sorcerer named Lord Iceheart, the one the mermaids were singing about," he said. "He's been commissioned by my uncle to destroy all of Nalgordia." Archit hesitated. "Dawn Flower has instructed us to go destroy him before it's too late. If we don't—and he does destroy all the realm—then I'll never break my uncle's curse, and I'll never become human myself."

The last part of this rant was not lost on James. "So that is possible?" he asked. "For you to break the curse?" He wasn't even going to ask about the whole part of what Archit said about being human. Not yet.

"Yes," Archit said. "The only way is to reunite with Dromio, who's been waiting for me all these years on the grounds of the amusement park."

"Dromio?" James said. "But I thought he was..."

"No," Archit said, shaking his head. "My uncle lied to me."

James couldn't stop himself from gasping, dumbfounded. "Sonnoffa..."

"Dawn Flower said we'll never make it to the amusement park in time," Archit continued, "and even if we could...well, I have an obligation to save Nalgordia."

James's confusion must have read on his face, as Archit tried further to explain. "James, don't you see. It's all because of me that Lord Iceheart is doing this. He's in the service of my uncle, and if my uncle weren't hunting me, then Nalgordia would still be safe." He cast his gaze down, avoiding James's eyes. "I need your help if we're going to do this."

James almost felt stronger hearing those words. "I'm with you all the way. Just as I said."

Archit smiled. "Good."

The leaves overhead shook. James couldn't deny that the once summery air around them had given way to a terrible chill. He crossed his arms around him. "Is it getting cold?"

"Yeah." Archit looked up at the trees overhead. "And look...the leaves seem to be...well, dying..."

James's gaze followed where Archit pointed with his wing. The green leaves had changed to autumnal shades of orange and red, and with the slightest push of the breeze, they withered and fluttered into the air.

"It's started," Archit said. "This is Lord Iceheart's doing. Nalgordia is a land of eternal summer, or so it has been up until now."

James didn't like the fear he heard in Archit's voice. *Eternal summer,* he thought. But it definitely looked like fall in the forest now. "Let's wake the girls," he said.

Archit was on his feet. "There's not a moment to lose. I'll wrap up some of this food so we can take it with us."

James hurried over to where Margot and Liz still lay, stretched out on a blanket under the willow tree.

"Margot," he whispered as he kneeled beside her. "Margot, wake up."

His sister stirred, stretching one arm upward and the other across her face, rubbing the sleep from her eyes with her biceps. "What is it?" she groaned.

Oh, James thought, *if only I could be this apathetic to the danger we're in.* "C'mon," he said. "Archit and I can explain on the way."

"Is it time to go home?" Margot asked as she pulled herself up.

James ignored her question. "Liz?" he whispered.

Archit approached just as Liz was waking up. "Ready?" There was a sense of urgency in his voice.

"Yeah," James said, standing. "Let's get going."

Margot looked at each of them, casting her stare from one to the other. "We're not going home, are we?"

James avoided Margot's gaze. He halfway hoped that Archit might answer, but he also knew that it would be better if Margot heard it from him. "No...no, I'm sorry, we're not."

"Why not?" Margot said, pulling herself to her feet.

"We're needed here," James said.

"We're needed back at home, where we have places to be," Margot said, "like school and work."

"This is bigger than that, Margot," James said. "Don't you get it?"

Archit stepped forward between them. "Maybe," he said, putting a wing up to James, "if I put it in a little perspective..."

The heat of Margot's and Liz's stares bore down on him, and he suddenly seemed very self-conscious. "Let's walk and talk though," he said.

Margot rolled her eyes as she extended her hand and helped Liz to her feet. "I can't wait to hear what this is about," she grumbled as Liz stood.

"Maybe it won't be so bad," James heard Liz whisper back. "What else could be left for us to do here?"

They left the grove and set out through the woods, winding between trees and around patches of thick undergrowth. Archit explained everything as best he could, handing them pieces of fruit and nuts that he had wrapped up in one of the napkins with the hope that they might be less inclined to berate him if their blood sugar were stable.

They emerged from the trees on the edge of a mossy cliff that overlooked the beautiful countryside below, which was lined and dotted with what looked like cobblestone streets and rustic cottages, sprawling fields, towering trees and cool ponds.

"This is it," Archit said, "this is Nalgordia."

James looked uneasily at Margot and Liz, hoping that they might be feeling a sense of excitement again. Their expressions gave no indication.

"See those mountains in the distance?" Archit said, pointing at the majestic peaks that crowned the horizon and disappeared into the clouds overhead. "That's where we're headed. There's a sinacshin named Balthazar who lives in the pass between the mountains, and he'll be able to send us in the right direction to find Lord Iceheart."

James had to admit he understand only half of that. "What's a sinac-shin?"

"A dog," Archit replied, but then quickly backpedaled. "Or, at least, what looks like a dog. But they're something greater than a simple animal."

Archit began to head down the hill as he continued speaking, and James and the girls followed. "In the olden days, the sinacshin served humankind as its protectors and guardians," he said. "I mean, that was how it was originally. But in the many years since sinacshin protected humankind, there have been increasingly fewer sinacshin in the mortal world—many dogs, yes, but far fewer sinacshin—and increasingly fewer humans in magical worlds."

James nodded. "And Balthazar is...?"

"Sinacshin to Lord Ophir," Archit said.

"Should we know who he is?" Margot asked.

They reached the foot of the hill and set off across the field in the direction of the village up ahead. The air still had a cool nip to it, but the morning sun shone warm and welcome on their faces as they walked through the tall grass.

"Lord Ophir was revered throughout Nalgordia as a demigod, but he was pure human through and through," Archit explained. "He is the only human to have ever set foot in Nalgordia...well, until you three."

"What an honor," Margot quipped.

"What happened to him?" Liz asked.

"He died many years ago," Archit said. "But the legends say that another human would come again."

James had a gut feeling he knew where this was going, and he didn't like it. "You don't think that's us, do you?"

Archit didn't answer but kept on walking ahead through the field. That didn't help assuage James's sense of self-consciousness. If the Nalgordians were expecting the return of a demigod, or some powerful humans who could stop Lord Iceheart, then they were going to be disappointed. There was no way that he, James, could be expected to fill those shoes. As far as the others were concerned, Margot seemed to be weirded out by everything she came across in Nalgordia, and Liz was going along with it just for fun, but James knew she was hoping to head home soon, too. What sort of heroes were they supposed to be?

As they drew closer to the stone wall surrounding the village, Archit spoke again. "I think you'll soon get a sense of how Nalgordians perceive humans," he said. "We're headed into one of the villages here, and we're bound to meet several civilized figments that have heard about your kind in stories and legends."

"Stories and legends?" James asked. He couldn't help feel a little amused by the thought of humans being the stuff of stories and legends.

"Just keep an open mind," Archit said. "Openness is always the best policy."

"I thought that was honesty," James said.

Archit shrugged. "Sometimes, they can be one and the same."

He stepped onto a cobblestone walkway that led up to the wall surrounding the village. "This way," he said.

Now that they were closer, James could see the houses in the village stood in all shapes and sizes, some nearly as small as dollhouses, and others so large that James would have had to stand on his toes to reach the knob to the front door. The hodgepodge of architectural styles and bright colors all throughout gave him the impression that the world of Nalgordia wasn't tied to any specific time or culture from human history—at least, not as far as James could tell. It gave him the impression of what would happen if Norman Rockwell and Dr. Seuss had collaborated on a project together.

"Come on," Archit pulled open the brass gate that led through the wall into the village and held it open for his companions.

"What the heck?" Margot said, trying to point subtly ahead of them.

A tiger had come out the front door of one of the houses, dressed in a business suit and walking on his hind legs. He clutched a briefcase as he made his way down his front walk and through the white picket fence that surrounded his yard, then headed along the street.

"Whoa!" James said.

"Good morning," the tiger called to one of his neighbors.

"Good morning!" greeted his neighbor, a velociraptor in a housedress who was out watering her flowers.

James looked at Archit. "What kind of village is this?"

"Were you expecting something more like Annapolis?" Archit asked.

"Well, no, but...I guess I just wasn't expecting this."

"I haven't expected a lot of what we've seen these past few days," Margot said.

They continued down the street, first passing a kangaroo who was escorting her little joey on his way to school and fussing with his little bowtie as they walked, then passing a groundhog who was carrying bags of groceries as he hurried down the street.

The oddity of it all wasn't the uncomfortable part though. The villagers were staring at them, straight-up goggling in a way that James would almost consider rude. One female brontosaurus peered her head forth from the upstairs window of her house, not even trying to be inconspicuous as she watched them walk along the street. A koala bear who was trimming his shrubs even stopped to gape openmouthed at them.

As they headed into the downtown area of the village, which hustled and bustled with more humanoid animals, dinosaurs, and figments, James picked up on snatches of conversation.

"Look, that's him," said a bear engaged in conversation with a dragon. "That's the purple bird."

"And see," the dragon said, pointing with one of his claws, "he has humans with him."

Across the street, another conversation hummed between a rabbit and a fuzzy green monster. "Are those indeed humans? I've never seen one before."

"Preposterous," the monster said. "Everyone knows that humans are simply made-up creatures."

James felt very aware of the dozens of eyes staring at them from all around, and the unmistakable whispers that came with them.

"Humans?"

"No, they can't be."

"I've never seen one before."

"I thought they were the stuff of myth."

Despite how awkward he felt, he kept quiet. Margot and Liz probably felt just as uncomfortable, maybe even more so—but he knew that whispering to them about how weird he felt would just make all this even more embarrassing. He kept staring straight ahead.

When they reached the village square—a large paved area surrounded by shops and other merchant buildings centered on a large fountain and manicured shrubbery—one of the dragons approached. The beast stood on its hind legs, bearing itself nearly seven feet tall, and its wings stayed tucked in behind him as he lumbered forward.

Archit stopped, and James and the girls followed his lead. The dragon didn't look as frightening as a dragon might have—friendly, almost.

"You are welcome, noble humans," the dragon said, his eyes ablaze and several rows of gleaming teeth visible when he opened his snout, "to the Village of Caprice in the land of Nalgordia."

The hustle and bustle of the town around them has stopped, and all eyes were bearing down directly on them. *Noble humans*, James thought. That sounded weird.

"And you, your highness, Prince Archit," the dragon said with a bow of his head.

"Thank you," Archit replied.

A puff of smoke came from the dragon's snout, and the beast smiled wide. "Pray, introduce us to your friends."

Archit must have noticed, as James had, that the entire town had stopped to hear this introduction. The bird raised his voice as he named his companions. "This is James and Liz and Margot," he said. "They've come with me from the mortal world, and...and, as I'm sure you've heard, the sorcerer Lord Iceheart means to cast Nalgordia into eternal winter."

Gasps and murmurs swept through the crowd. If the villagers had heard, then they certainly had not believed it until now.

"We have been sent by Dawn Flower of the hippies," Archit continued, "to face Lord Iceheart and put a stop to his plans of destruction."

The dragon, whom James was beginning to think might have been some sort of mayor, seemed humbled. "To think we should see this day when the first Adamites since Ophir himself should come to our lands and even stop in our village to greet us," he said. "All of us in Nalgordia have heard stories of the champions from your world."

"Champions?" James said before he could stop himself. Maybe he had spoken out of turn.

A rabbit piped up from the sidelines, coming forward as he spoke. "We have heard the stories of the Adamites who fought the evil in your world," he said. "Some of them kings, some of them peasants. Some of them old, some of them young."

"Some of them are even said to have been subject to terrible weaknesses themselves," said a tiger, the same one they had seen earlier.

"Yes," the dragon concurred, nodding to the rabbit and tiger in turn. "But they all took stances against the evils of their world and sought charity and wisdom and hope, even when it wasn't easy."

James had always pictured valiant champions to be like the characters he had read about in his fantasy novels—brave knights, powerful wizards, benevolent kings. There weren't any people like that in the mortal world. "Who are these heroes you're talking about?"

Voices came from throughout the crowd. "Mother Teresa," said one.

"Dr. Martin Luther King," said another.

"Leonardo da Vinci."

"Anne Frank."

"Nelson Mandela."

"Gandhi."

"Stephen Hawking."

"Harriet Tubman."

"Galileo."

"Princess Diana."

The dragon laughed. "We could go on all day. We've heard stories of all of them."

Margot did a double take at the dragon. "You're expecting us to live up to the reputation of some of those peeps?"

James wouldn't have put it exactly that way, but he had to admit that Margot had a point. He hadn't considered some of the people who had indeed changed the course of the world, and none of them had done it by riding steeds into battle. "Those are big shoes to fill if that's what you expect of us," he said.

The dragon raised his snout in the air. "The legends say that every human has the potential if put in the right circumstances."

James shook his head. "Not every human. If every human were that brave or that selfless, then those people wouldn't have left such an impression."

Before the dragon could respond, a voice from the crowd shouted. "What's that?"

James looked up. A swirling mist of gray clouds had blocked out the horizon and was steadily approaching the village.

"It's the work of Lord Iceheart," Archit gasped.

"Run!" cried out one of the villagers, just as the clouds swept over the sun, casting everything in a sort of dim twilight.

Chaos ensued. Creatures of all shapes and sizes pushed past them in panic, knocking them back and forth. James felt a sudden shove from behind and fell forward onto the cobblestone floor. He looked up to see all kinds of feet running this way and that.

Liz knelt to help him up. "You all right?" she asked.

"Yeah," James said, hugging her tight. He didn't want to get separated from the others in the madness. He felt Margot come up behind him and put an arm around him and Liz. He looked at Archit, feeling his anxiety turn to panic. "What's happening?"

"They've never known danger before," Archit said. "They've never had any reason to be afraid before this."

"Not with them," James said. "With that storm."

Archit looked up at the clouds overhead. "I'm not sure, but...but it can't be good."

"Is this dangerous?" Liz asked.

"It might be," Archit said.

James watched the villagers running amuck all around them, screaming and crying as they went. He turned back to Margot and Liz, then to Archit, who seemed just as lost for a plan as he was. If Archit didn't have any idea how to fight this magic, then...

Suddenly, the thought occurred to James. "Wait! I have it!"

He fumbled in his pocket for the stone that Dawn Flower had given him only the night before, remembering she had told him the stone would protect them from any curse. If there were ever a time when he needed it, this was it. He pulled the stone out and held it in front of him for the others to see.

"Hold tight," he shouted over the escalating howl of the wind and the shouts and cries of the frightened villagers. "I've got this," he said as he and the girls and Archit drew close into a huddle. "I think."

He had no idea how to use the stone. Dawn Flower had given it to him, told him of its power, but made no explanation of how to work the magic.

Feeling stupid but hoping for the best, James held the stone up over their heads. "I command this stone...to protect me and my friends," he shouted. He felt Margot's arm around one side of him and Liz's around the other. Trying to summon up as much courage as he could, he shouted for good measure, "You have no power over us!"

It was snowing then, and the blizzard raged so hard that all James could see was blinding whiteness. The wind burned at his cheeks and ears, tugging at his hair and clothes.

"You have no power over us," he whispered once more.

For a minute or two, the storm continued—but then it dissipated almost as quickly as it began. The wind died down, and when he realized what an eerie quiet remained, James lifted his head from where he had buried it into Liz's shoulder and opened his eyes.

What he saw was devastating.

All around them, the once lively and happy village was dead, desolate, frozen. It was all white as far as the eye could see. The trees stood bare of all their leaves, the bushes had shriveled up and died, and a thick coat of ice covered all of it. The villagers had frozen in place, transformed into ice sculptures that were swiftly vanishing beneath the falling snow as it piled higher and higher.

"What the hell!?" Margot gasped, sounding both terrified and appalled.

James looked at Archit, hoping for some word of encouragement, but Archit looked completely dumbfounded. "This is bad, my friends," he said. "And I doubt it's going to get any better."

A gust of wind howled, nipping and burning James's ear. This was no ordinary winter weather. "What do we do?" he asked.

Archit looked ahead. "We start walking."

"Huh?" Margot said.

"The snow is piling up," Archit said, "and we have to reach the mountains. Come on."

Archit set off down the cobblestone walkway, now slick with a thick coat of ice. James and the girls followed, and as they started walking, James realized that he was trembling. He looked at the morbid, shimmering white display all around them. The blizzard had frozen all of the villagers right where they had been when the storm struck, and the whole scene looked like some arctic Pompeii: lives interrupted, cut short, their final devastating moments preserved with eerie perfection. Some of them looked as if they were cowering in fear, and others were running, or moving to protect children or loved ones. The sight of all of it disturbed James. All of a sudden, this mission felt terribly personal.

They left the village behind them, heading into an open expanse of white that stretched out as far as the eye could see. The snow swirled around them, swiftly growing so high that it was difficult to walk. Overhead, the clouds clustered thickly, blocking out the sun.

"Stay close together," Archit said. "The last thing we need is for one of us to get lost in this snowstorm. You hear that, Margot?"

Margot had strayed away from them a few feet, and was standing pensively in the deep snow. In her sleeveless cocktail dress, with only her long hair to protect her shoulders from the harsh wind, she was shivering. She turned at the sound of Archit's voice.

"I heard you," she said. "Stay together, right?" She moved closer to the group.

A particularly strong gust of wind blew against them, and Margot gasped loudly. She crossed her arms in front of her chest, shivering.

"We're going to freeze to death," James said to Archit.

"No," Archit shook his head as he pushed ahead through the blizzard. "The magic you cast with that stone protects us from the elements. We can't die in this snow."

"But it's so cold," Liz said.

"Well, it doesn't protect us from being cold," Archit said. "It doesn't protect us from pain, just from perishing."

"That's comforting," Margot snarked.

James glared at her, biting his tongue. He was getting real tired of her cynicism. He didn't want to upset her more, and he had a feeling that if he opened his mouth, there was no telling what would come out. He wanted to remind her that she'd insisted on coming on this adventure, even though he told her she wouldn't like it. As they walked forward through the tundra, the snow fell more thickly, and all they could see was whiteness. After hours of trudging through the snow, it began to grow dark, and with the dark, it got even colder.

The snow eventually tapered off. They were left alone in a desolate white wasteland illuminated only by the moon and stars overhead. On the horizon, they could make out the mountains silhouetted against a slate-colored sky.

They arrived at the foot of the mountains, soaked by the snow and in pain from the cold. The slopes loomed before them, stony and gray, strangely ominous in the pale moonlight. The shadows cast by the moon were long and velvety on the undisturbed snow.

"Here we are," Archit said.

"Right," Margot said. "So what now?"

"This way," Archit said.

He moved up the slope of the mountain and between two large jutting crags. "Come on."

Inside the mountain pass, the slopes blocked out the wind, making it slightly cozier—but only slightly. James took an inexplicable comfort in having these stone walls around them.

"Where to?" he asked.

Archit looked up and down the path in both directions. "I'm not sure, but I think if we explore long enough, we'll have some luck."

James didn't like that response. "Some luck?"

Archit shrugged. "I don't know these mountains any better than you do," he said, sounding defensive. "All I know is that Dawn Flower told us we would find Balthazar's den here somewhere."

"This is hopeless," James said.

Archit didn't reply. He just looked at the ground as if he were avoiding James's eyes.

"No, it's not," Liz said, quickly. "We've figured everything out so far, haven't we?"

"We sure couldn't figure out how to go home this morning," Margot said.

"Come on," Archit said. "Let's not dawdle here."

They moved through the mountain pass, heading along the upward slope. The night grew darker around them as clouds rolled in overhead, blocking out the moon and stars, and the trees grew thicker and closer together.

Up ahead, the light of a fire emanated from inside a cave on the hillside. "That must be it," Archit whispered. "That's Balthazar's house."

The light in the cave indicated that warmth and dryness awaited, and that somebody was still awake, sitting up to welcome them. Still, it was a cave.

"You mean that's Balthazar's home?" James said.

"You were expecting something more elaborate?" Archit said.

"Well..." In all honesty, James had pictured a house of some kind. After seeing the animals in the village living in houses, he thought that all Nalgordian animals must live in houses. But maybe it was just that the creatures of the village were villagers, and the creatures of the forest were wild. Just because sinacshin were supposed to be wiser than others, it didn't necessarily mean that their homes would be elaborate.

They stepped inside the cave, moving in the direction of the flickering light until they came upon an alcove where a small fire set the walls with a dancing reddish-orange glow. James peered toward one of the alcove's dark corners to see an enormous English sheepdog emerge from the shadows.

"Welcome," Balthazar said. His voice sounded almost grandfatherly. "Welcome, Archit, and children."

"Thank you," Archit said.

"Come close to the fire," Balthazar said. "You must be tired from your long journey."

"I'm afraid it wasn't just the distance that tired us," Archit said, moving closer. "Winter—a snowstorm—everything to the east of here has been frozen."

Balthazar looked long and hard at Archit. "Then it has begun, I'm afraid."

James took a step forward. "You mean," he said, "the destruction of Nalgordia?"

Balthazar nodded. "And if you don't stop it—"

"Us?!" Margot said incredulously, as if she had not been hearing it all day long—or had at least been hoping somebody would intervene and relieve them of the responsibility. "I think you owe us an explanation." She looked at Archit. "Both of you."

James didn't like where this was going. "Margot," he hissed.

"Why can't we go home?" Margot said, throwing her arms up. "We agreed to come with Archit to meet the hippies, and he has."

"And they told me that my journey isn't over, Margot," Archit said. "I told you this morning. All of Nalgordia is under threat."

"More than under threat," Balthazar said. "If Lord Iceheart's snowstorms have already struck, then this land is under siege. Within another day, Lord Iceheart's power will have grown strong enough to trap all of Nalgordia in eternal winter."

"What does this have to do with us though?" Liz asked. "Is this why the animals in the village were so eager to meet us? They were talking as if being human made you some sort of hero, and that they were expecting us to save Nalgordia." She looked from Margot to Balthazar to Archit, and James knew from her expression that she was trying to play the peacemaker. *Such a Liz thing to do.* "We don't mean to be rude, Balthazar," she went on, "but I think what my cousin means is that this has nothing to do with us."

Balthazar sighed and slowly circled back into the depth of his cave. "It has everything to do with you," he said. "You're the only ones who can stop it."

James took a few steps in Balthazar's direction. "I thought so," he said. He turned to Archit. "Did you know about this? Why didn't you tell us right away?"

Archit looked down at the floor, avoiding James's gaze. "This is the mission Dawn Flower assigned to me," Archit said. "She told me this is what I have to do if I want to be human. The three of you will know how to do it, and you'll show me. It's all my fault that Nalgordia is in danger, because my uncle has commanded Lord Iceheart to stop me. My uncle thinks that if Lord Iceheart destroys Nalgordia, then it will stop me from reuniting with Dromio, and if he stops me from reuniting with Dromio, then the curse will be fulfilled and I'll never be real."

James had never seen Archit so honest before. In a weird way, it almost hurt to see his friend so exposed emotionally.

Balthazar sighed. "I think it would be best if you all sat down around the fire," he said. "You are wet and cold."

James looked at the girls, giving them what he meant to be a pleading expression. He didn't want them to be resistant to any of this, or begrudging, or reluctant, or whatever it was that they were being. He stepped forward and sat down at the edge of the fire. Its heat felt good against his cold, frostbitten skin and damp clothes, and he held his hands out to its dancing flames, watching his fingers glow orange in the firelight.

Margot and Liz sat down next to him, and he didn't have to look at them to feel the tension in the air. Archit walked around to the other side of the fire and sat down so quietly and nervously that it gave away any brave façade he might have been putting on.

He's scared, James realized. *I can't be. I have to be brave. Remember? For Archit's sake.*

He remembered how he had felt when he was holding the magic stone out in the face of the blizzard. He had been so scared, so full of doubt—but he had known deep down what he had to do. Once he started to actually do it, the sense of fear had lessened.

"We find ourselves faced with a struggle between good and evil," Balthazar said, standing before the fire. His black eyes sparkled when they caught the firelight. "Unfortunately, no Nalgordian creature can stand up to Lord Iceheart."

"Why not?" James asked.

Balthazar paused, and the quiet was overwhelming. "I don't exactly know."

Archit looked up. "Because figment creatures are either good or evil," he said, as if he had been struggling to understand it. "Oh, sometimes they're mischievous but benevolent, like gnomes, or they might be ethically solid but still malicious, like djinn, but they're either on the side of good or the side of evil."

James understood what Archit meant. "Some creatures can still be good but chaotic, and others can be evil but still lawful," he ventured, remembering the concept of alignment in Dungeons & Dragons.

"Right," Archit said. "You humans are different though. You're not so neatly categorized. You're not always one side or the other."

"That still doesn't mean we know how to fight an evil wizard," Margot said.

Balthazar turned his gaze toward her, then on James and Liz, his eyes bearing down on each of them in turn. "If you don't, there is no hope for Nalgordia."

James felt as if his whole spirit were squirming inside his skin. *This isn't how it's supposed to be*, he thought. In fantasy novels, this was the part where the hero received some sort of counsel or guidance from the wise figure assigning the task, and then the hero was supposed to stand up and accept the challenge. But if that were the case, then why didn't Balthazar have anything valuable to offer them, and why did he, James, feel so scared?

Still, they couldn't refuse. They just couldn't.

"We'll go," he said, feeling the words force themselves out of his mouth before he could stop them.

"What?" Margot turned to him. "James, you can't be serious."

"I am serious, Margot," he said.

"If I could solve this problem myself, I would," Archit said. "But Dawn Flower sent you with me for a good reason."

James saw how helpless Archit looked. Somehow, the sight of that strengthened him instead of scaring him. Archit, along with all the creatures of Nalgordia, was counting on him to be a hero.

"Might I suggest," Balthazar said, "that you rest here tonight." He looked at James, and this time it was a comforting look. "Creatures of flesh and blood need sleep just as they need food and drink if they're going to function."

"Yes," Archit said in a soft voice. "Yes, I do know something about that, at least in part."

James couldn't deny how tired he felt. His muscles ached from their trek through the deep snow, and the warmth of the fire had overwhelmed him with a comfortable lethargy that he didn't think he could resist much longer. "Is that all right?"

"It's probably the smartest thing to do," said Archit.

James lay back on the carpet of moss and dead leaves that covered the cave floor, turning his face away from the glow of the fire. Staring out of the mouth of the cave, he could still see the faint stars in the sky.

His eyelids were heavy, and he could barely keep them open anymore. He closed them, just for a second, as he listened to the others whisper in the dark.

"Won't it be dangerous for us to sleep?" Margot said. "If there are, y'know, bad guys out there."

"I will stay up and keep watch," Balthazar said.

"All night?" Liz asked.

"Yes," Balthazar said. "Not to worry, my dear. You're safe."

That was the last James remembered before he slipped off into a deep and dreamless sleep.

CHAPTER 9
The Flight to the East

Morning came too quickly. James drifted slowly back to consciousness to see the soft light of dawn pouring through the opening of the cave. He wanted to close his eyes and fall back asleep for only a few minutes more, but he could hear the whispered voices of Archit and Balthazar behind him.

"You'll never be able to make it on foot," Balthazar said. "You'll need to seek out the flying bison."

"The flying bison," Archit said. "But they—"

"They'll appear to those who need them, and I believe you and the human children qualify."

"How do I call for them?"

"The horn that summons them has not been seen in Nalgordia for many years, but if it's to be found anywhere, I think I know where it would be."

"Where?"

"Seek out your old underground hideout. Since you left, the kobolds have taken up camp there. They are notorious treasure hoarders, and anything of value that is ever lost in Nalgordia often ends up in their possession."

James couldn't deny—at least on some weird, subconscious level—that every time he started to feel comfortable in Nalgordia and acclimated to all its otherworldly culture shocks, they were introduced to some imaginary creature that threw his whole sense of reality back out of whack. Flying bison and kobolds? Is that what today held for them?

"They won't give it up willingly," Archit said.

"Perhaps not."

"What do you suggest I do?"

"There are some problems here that you're going to have to solve your-self, Archit." Balthazar's voice was kind but firm. "I can't undertake this quest for you."

"That was rude, Balthazar."

"A sinacshin's duty is to guard and protect. We were not created to lead."

"I know." Archit sighed. "Maybe I should wake the humans."

James snapped his eyes closed and pretended to still be asleep. He didn't want Archit to look over at him and know that he had been eavesdropping.

"James," Archit whispered, and even though James's eyes were closed, he could sense that Archit was drawing close. "James, wake up. It's time for us to get going."

James opened his eyes to see Archit kneeling next to him. He stretched and nodded, watching as Archit went to wake the girls. "Margot," he heard Archit whisper. "Liz."

James got to his feet and did the best he could to brush the dust and dried leaves off his clothes. He looked down at what had once been his semiformal party attire. It was now tattered and stained from the many days of hard adventure. The knees of his trousers were ripped open and the hem of his shirt hung untucked. Even his necktie, the green silk tie he had been so proud of, was torn up at the end. But he didn't want to take it off just yet. It was still his power tie, messy though it had become.

They collected themselves and wasted no time getting on their way. "Thank you for your hospitality, Balthazar," James said as the group made their way toward the mouth of the cave.

"Yeah, it was nice to be able to rest and know that we were safe," Liz said.

"You're most welcome," Balthazar lowered himself to the ground in an odd sort of bow. "My best wishes go with you on your mission."

Archit gave the dog a wistful look. "Thank you, Balthazar."

"Best of luck to you, your highness."

Archit knelt to wipe some of the dirt off his shoes. "It won't be luck that gets us through this," he said.

"Very true," Balthazar said. "Until we meet again, Archit."

"Until then," Archit replied with a nod.

Archit turned to head out the mouth of the cave.

"Margot," Balthazar said. "Hold on, dear. Before you leave, I have something for you."

James saw that Margot looked surprised to have been called out individually. She gave a look at James and mouthed, "Me?" It was one thing for Balthazar to address Archit because he was the leader, or even James because he was the human who seemed to understand this fantasy world, but Margot—what could a talking dog have for her?

Balthazar went to a pile of blankets on the far side of the cave and dragged out a mass of heavy fabric that he carried back to Margot. "Wear this," he said, dropping it at her feet. "It's cold out there."

Margot lifted it and held it out. It was a wool overcoat, a heavy one that went down past her knee, sort of like the one her father wore over a business suit during the coldest parts of winter. Her face lit up.

"Thank you!" she said. "You're the best! You have no idea how much I appreciate this."

"I have an idea," Balthazar said. "I can glean only from how blue and windburned your shoulders were last night that the sleeveless dress you're wearing is doing nothing to keep you warm."

Margot laughed as she swept the coat around herself and pulled the sleeves over her arms. She snuggled into it, drawing the lapels up to warm her cheeks. "Thanks!" She paused, then looked down at Balthazar, as if unsure of what to say next. For a moment, James saw something strange in her expression, a sense of understanding she had just discovered.

"Thank you," she said again.

"Take care of your brother and cousin," Balthazar said. "And your friend Archit. They need your strength."

Margot nodded. "You got it."

They walked along the pathway between the mountain slopes, back to the expanse of frosty whiteness that remained of Nalgordia. Looking out at the snow-covered countryside, James remembered what they were up against.

He couldn't shake the thought of all the villagers—frozen, inanimate, their faces fixed in expressions of fear and pain.

"So...uh, Archit," he said as they trudged through the snow, "what's our plan for today?" The bits and pieces he had overheard from the conversation between Archit and Balthazar needed some explanation if he were going to make full sense of it all.

"We've got to get far away to the east before the day is over if we're going to face Lord Iceheart," Archit said. "But it's a long journey, so we'll need to seek aid from the flying bison."

James had remembered hearing that. He nodded. "The flying bison."

"Yes, they'll heed the orders of whoever summons them with a magic horn," Archit said. "Balthazar thinks he knows where it might be hidden. Only problem is that the ones who are guarding it might not be easy to deal with."

They carried onward, the snow piled up so deep it reached their knees in some places, and they struggled to push through it. The wind no longer blew violently the way it had the night before, but the bitter chill still hung in the air. The misty gray clouds were so thick they blocked out the morning sun, leaving everything in what felt like continual twilight.

"Look, there!" Archit called out at last, gesturing with his wing several feet ahead of them where, almost indistinguishable from the rest of the white surroundings, a frozen tree stood slanted over the slope of a small hill.

James was about to ask what was so special, but he had a feeling that this was the hideout Balthazar had mentioned. The tree's curved trunk gave it an unmistakable quality, turning it into an easy landmark, and James was glad that they were finally having some progress after wandering through snow drifts all morning.

"This is it, you guys," Archit said, approaching the tree. "Help me clear away some of this snow from the base."

He made a pathetic effort to shove some of the heavy snow away from the base of the tree with his wing. James stepped forward and plunged his bare hands into the drift, and together they were able to work enough of the mound away to reveal a small door built into the base of the tree.

"Yes," Archit said in triumph.

He pulled at the knob and swung the door open. The entry dropped down into what looked like an underground fort accessed by a rickety wooden ladder propped up against the inside of the doorframe.

"This is your place, Archit?" James said.

"Yeah," Archit said. "How'd you know?"

James shrugged. "Just a hunch, I guess."

Archit nodded, giving James a sly look, one that said to James, "I had a feeling you were awake when Balthazar and I were talking." He didn't seem mad though. Relieved, if anything.

"Well, you're right," Archit said. "C'mon."

He stepped down onto the first rung of the ladder and began to lower himself.

"Shouldn't one of us wait up here?" Margot said. "You know, just to stand guard?"

"Maybe it'd be best if we all stuck together," Liz said.

James looked at Margot. "You're not afraid, are you, Margot?"

Margot scoffed. "Are you kidding me? Please. I'm just trying not to go foraging in underground hideouts if I don't have to."

"Then wait up here," James said. "Liz, you stay up here with her. Archit, I'll go down there with you." He felt a little bit better knowing that they weren't splitting up entirely. Margot and Liz were enough for any danger that might come along while he and Archit were bargaining with the kobolds underground. *That's not something I ever expected to be on my to-do list*, he thought. *Bargaining with kobolds. After this, buying a car should be a piece of cake.*

He followed Archit down the ladder into a small room. When his eyes adjusted to the dark, he looked around to see that its walls were supported by tightly packed stones. The tiny space was crammed with a ragtag collection of old furniture—a bed, a chair, a table—and furnished with shelves of books, clothes hung upon pegs, and odd collectables set here and there on every horizontal surface.

"Sweet place you got here," James said.

Archit nodded, his eyes narrowing. "Except I don't think it's quite empty." He looked around, then called, "Hello! Is anyone here?"

A voice responded from down near the floor. "Who goes there?"

Another voice from the other side of the room: "Identify yourself, stranger."

James felt his skin prickle as small figures emerged from hiding places all around the room. At first, he thought they were raccoons, but at second glance, their eyes and ears were humanlike. Their ears were even pointed the way elf ears looked in picture books.

Archit wasted no time mincing words. "I could demand the same of you," he said. "I am Archit, prince of the dodo birds, and this is my home."

"Prince of the dodo birds," mocked one of the kobolds.

"Archit!" screeched another.

Several of them drew close, drawing their clawlike hands up from where they'd been hidden in the tatters of the little tunics they wore, and taunting Archit.

"Welcome home, little bird."

"Welcome home."

"Welcome home."

James didn't feel comfortable with any of this. He almost wished he had stayed up above ground with Margot and Liz.

"What do you want from us?" one of the kobolds croaked.

"I seek the horn that summons the flying bison," Archit said.

"And what makes you think we have it?"

"Because you are the most admirable collectors in all the land," Archit said. "And—"

The kobold slashed at the air with one claw. "Spare us the pretty words, bird."

Archit glared at the kobold heatedly. "All right," he said with a sigh. "Because you're greedy little hoarders and everyone knows it. If anything is lost in the land of Nalgordia, there's a good chance you have it."

The kobolds erupted into laughter. "There's some honesty for us," chortled the one who seemed to be the leader.

"I think I know what horn he's talking about," shouted a kobold from the back of the crowd, a particularly fat and slightly cross-eyed one.

"Silence!" another hissed.

"But I think I do," the fat kobold insisted.

"Shut up!" the leader shouted.

Archit stepped forward. "So you do have it." When there was no immediate response, he added, "Don't feign ignorance. I don't have time for it."

The leader of the kobolds clicked his tongue. "Even if we did have it, what makes you think we'd give it to you?"

James heard movement behind them and turned to see Margot descending the ladder. "Oh, what fresh hell is this?" she said, looking around.

Archit seemed to take no notice of Margot and continued to address the kobolds. "You will give me the horn because it is rightfully mine," he said.

"Finders, keepers."

"And I need it to get to the east if I'm going to save Nalgordia," Archit said. "Otherwise, you'll be destroyed when the next ice storm sweeps through here."

The lead kobold paused, considering what Archit said. "If we were to give it to you," he said, "what would you give us in return?"

That was enough for Archit, whose patience was nearly gone. "How dare you!"

Margot had hesitantly stepped off the ladder and approached the scene. "What's going on, James?" she whispered as she sidled up next to him.

James tried to whisper back as discreetly as possible, choosing his words carefully in case he was overheard. "The kobolds have Archit's magic horn."

"Why's it so important?"

"He needs it if we're going to fly east and stop this whole mess."

The kobolds took no note of whatever side conversation James and Margot were having, but instead drew tighter in their close around Archit. "Come now, your highness," said the leader. "You know we wouldn't give anything away without some treasure traded in return."

Archit was getting visibly frustrated. "But—"

"We didn't ask you to argue. We asked you to barter."

This raised a chorus of laughter from the rest of the kobolds. The sound of their chortles and guffaws was so shrill and heinous that it hurt to hear it.

Margot stepped forward toward the cluster of kobolds. "Here, take these." Her hands were already at her ears, plucking her studs from her earlobes, then unclasping the necklace around her neck. She knelt down and held them out to the leader of the kobolds. For a moment, he looked long and hard at the jewelry in her hand, a greedy look overcoming his face.

"What are they?" he said, a note of suspicion in his voice.

"Diamond," Margot said.

The kobold looked closer at the jewelry, then up at Margot. "Eh..."

Margot sighed. "All right, they're crystal. But they're Swarovski. That's gotta count for something, right?"

If this meant anything to the leader of the kobolds, he didn't show it. He took one of the earrings from her hand and held it up, examining it. "They're pretty," he said in a perverse tone.

"I know," Margot said. "And you can have them if you give Archit his horn back."

The rest of the kobolds waited in a hushed silence for direction. The leader of the kobolds deliberated, clutching the earring as if it were his own infant child.

"This offer doesn't last all day," Margot said.

The kobold sneered. For a second, James thought the little thug might refuse, but then he called over his shoulder to his compatriots, "Bring out the bird's horn."

James heaved a sigh of relief as he watched the leader of the kobolds grab at the other earring and the necklace from Margot's outstretched fist. Meanwhile, several other kobolds disappeared under the bed and emerged a few seconds later, dragging a battered bronze horn strung on a braided cord.

"Take it," the leader huffed as the other kobolds handed the horn out to Margot. She grabbed it by the cord, trying to avoid making any contact with the kobolds as she took it, then stood and slung it over her shoulder.

"Nice job, Margot," Archit commended as they turned to go up the ladder.

"You bet," she said.

Before ascending, she stopped and turned back. "And as for you, you greedy, materialistic little punks," she said, "I hope you get what's coming to you."

With that, she climbed up the ladder, leaving Archit and James to bring up the rear. Archit gave James a look of surprise, as if to say, "Has she always been this cool and we just haven't noticed?"

It was a relief to be back up above ground, where Liz greeted each of them with a sigh. "I was beginning to get worried," she said.

"I should have known we would run into trouble," Archit said. "Kobolds can be like that."

Margot laughed. James could only assume she was exhilarated from the rush of confronting the kobolds the way she did. "Here," she said, handing the horn to Archit.

Archit shook his head. "No, it's yours. You were the one who bought it from the kobolds. You're the only one who can rightfully use it."

Margot looked down at the horn. "What do I do?"

"Just blow into it," Archit said.

Margot lifted the horn up to her lips and leaned into it. When she blew, the sound that erupted from it shook the frozen branches on the tree nearby, sending little flecks of broken ice down upon them. James jumped.

"Whoa!" Margot said, lowering the horn.

"The cloud," James said, looking upward toward the sky. "See that cloud?"

A fluffy mass of white had broken away from the other clouds in the sky and was drifting downward toward them. When it touched the ground, James expected it to dissipate into mist. Instead, it looked surprisingly solid.

Archit moved toward it. "Let's go."

"Is it safe?" Liz asked.

"Of course," Archit said, looking back at her. "They're just clouds. They won't hurt you."

James wasn't sure if Archit were aware of the irony in the statement or not. "I don't think that's what she meant, but..."

"Come on," Archit said, hopping up onto the cloud. His feet sank into the white puffiness, but for the most part, it seemed to support his weight. James followed his lead and stepped up. He perceived a strange sensation underfoot.

Liz lifted her long skirt with one hand and gave the other to Archit so he could help her up, and Margot followed suit.

"See," Archit said. "This isn't so bad."

The cloud ascended as easily as an elevator. James was amazed by the weightlessness he felt as they rose higher into the sky. Still, looking down and seeing the ground becoming farther away made him a little nervous.

"So, Archit," he asked, steadying himself where he stood, "are clouds always solid in Nalgordia, or just when you blow this magic horn?"

Archit looked confused. "I'm not really sure. Are they not solid in the mortal world?"

"No," Margot said. "They're just water vapor."

Archit nodded, registering the fact in his mind. "Gotcha."

For someone who has spent most of his existence in the mortal world, he seems to understand very little of it, James thought. Not as if that were a bad thing!

They floated upward, finally reaching a cluster of cumulus clouds that hovered around them like white islands on a sea of sky. Their lift came to a gentle halt alongside one of the larger masses.

James watched Archit hop off onto the cloud with an air of nonchalance that James still couldn't accept. It seemed that maybe Archit had gone cloud hopping before, if that were a legitimate pastime in Nalgordia.

"Whoa," James murmured as he stepped from one cloud to the other. "This is crazy!"

Liz laughed as she moved through the billows. "I've always wanted to do this," she admitted.

James trudged around the white fluffy billows, a strange tickling feeling in his feet. *I wonder what makes it feel like that,* he thought. *It's only water vapor after all, just as Margot said.*

Archit stood at the edge and stared off pensively toward a patch of clouds in the distance. "Here they come."

James followed Archit's gaze. It shouldn't have surprised him. He had heard Archit and Balthazar talking all morning about them. Still, he had to blink several times just to be sure that he was actually seeing what he thought he was seeing.

A mass of brown rounded the edge of one of the clouds, and as it got closer, James could see it was a herd of flying buffalo moving swiftly through the air, each of them carried by enormous chicken wings that sprouted from its back.

"Would you look at that," James said.

"Are those...winged buffalo?" Margot asked.

"Yeah," said Archit. "Don't tell me you've never heard of a winged buffalo before."

"I...I've eaten buffalo wings before," Margot offered as if that counted for something.

Archit gave her a dry look. "I wouldn't tell them that."

The herd of buffalo drew close and, as a group, landed on the surface of the cloud with such grace that the entire act seemed a little surreal to James, like a bit of animation that had been synchronized for a clip in a music video or something.

One of the buffalo stepped forward and bowed low. When he lifted his head again, James found himself amazed by the creature's large, black eyes—they were so emotive.

"Who summons the flying buffalo?" the animal bellowed in a deep, James Earl Jones voice.

Margot hesitated. James had never seen her this nervous before. She was normally so effortlessly confident, so cool that nothing seemed to bother her. Here in Nalgordia, she had been nothing but tongue-tied and sheepish in every situation.

"Um...that would be me, I guess," she said, raising her hand.

The herd of buffalo bowed in unison, then raised their heads again.

"And where do you wish to travel?" asked the speaker of the buffalo.

Margot looked at Archit. "Uh..."

"To Cocytus," Archit prompted her.

"To Cocytus," Margot said.

"The dominion of Lord Iceheart," Archit continued in a hushed voice, "the sorcerer of the east."

"The dominion of Lord Iceheart," Margot said, "the sorcerer of the east."

Several buffalo reared, their eyes growing wide. For a moment, James was worried that this request would be denied. There was something about Cocytus that frightened these beasts.

But the leader of the buffalo grunted and tossed his head from side to side, glaring at his subjects and telling them to silence themselves. He turned back to Margot. "We hear and we obey." He looked from Margot to James and Liz. "Come, children, we will carry you."

What an awkward invitation. James wasn't crazy about the idea of mounting one of these buffalo and riding bareback through the open air. He looked over at Archit, unsure of what to do.

"Go on," Archit said.

James resisted the urge to shake his head. It was easy for Archit to act so casual about it, but Archit wasn't the one being asked to mount some strange animal and ride it in a not-so-safe manner. James wasn't about to admit that he was scared, though.

He moved forward toward the leader of the buffalo. "Does it matter which buffalo we go with?" He hoped that he might be able to ride the leader of the buffalo, thinking that maybe the leader would be a little more reliable.

"Climb on," the buffalo said. "I would be honored to carry the right-hand man of the purple bird."

A little surge of pride went through James. Did the creatures of Nalgordia really consider him Archit's right-hand man? That counted for something, as far as he was concerned.

He hoisted himself up on the wooly back of the buffalo. The beast was much larger than he ever pictured a buffalo to be. He couldn't help wondering whether all buffalo were this big or just the flying variety, just as he had wondered whether all clouds were solid or just magical Nalgordian clouds.

He looked over at Margot, who was struggling to mount one of the buffalo in her long overcoat—unlike Liz, who had swung herself up with impressive gracefulness, even in her flowing medieval dress.

"You having some trouble, Margot?" James asked, trying to lighten the mood.

"I'm fine," she growled, teetering like an ill-balanced turtle. Each of her limbs poked out stiffly in a different direction. "Don't worry."

Archit swooped over and helped her right herself.

"Thanks," she said.

"No problem," Archit laughed as he turned to mount a buffalo himself.

"Mind if I ride?" He added in a lower voice. "My wings aren't good for carrying me much more than a few feet from the ground."

The buffalo nodded and Archit climbed on.

"Well, then," said the leader of the buffalo. "Let us fly. We will see you in the eastern land."

James didn't even have time to brace himself before the entire herd took off. The next thing he knew, he felt the wind rushing through his hair. His stomach lurched as the buffalo swooped up and sank down, then rose up again.

He dug his fingers deep into the buffalo's fur, trying to hold on as tightly as he could. The air whipped around him as his steed soared through the clouds. "Whoa!" he shouted. He regretted it immediately, feeling stupid.

They surfaced above the clouds, and the wind quieted. James looked out over an expanse of blue dotted with white. Far below, the snowy landscape stretched out all around them.

"Is that better for you?" the buffalo said.

"Huh?" James asked.

"Is that better? You seemed nervous."

"Me?" James said quickly, his voice cracking. "No. Never."

The other buffalo were ascending all around them, their wings flapping up and down as they bobbed over the clouds. James could see Margot and Liz, not far from where he was.

"Wow," he said, taking in the sight. "Who would've ever expected I would be riding a flying buffalo?" He laughed. "Who even knew there were such a thing as flying buffalo?"

"Who knew there were such things as humans?" the buffalo observed.

James paused, wondering whether his initial observation had been rude. What the buffalo said, though—he couldn't ignore it. It was just like what all the other Nalgordian creatures had said back in the village the day before.

"Are we that foreign to Nalgordia?" James said.

"Not that foreign, no. There were once humans among us. Lord Ophir was a human, as I'm sure you've heard."

There was that name again. All these Nalgordian creatures seemed to revere Lord Ophir, but none of them seemed to really understand who he was. "Yeah...Archit mentioned something about him, but...he didn't go into detail."

The buffalo needed no further prompting. "Under his rule, Nalgordia knew nothing but peace and harmony. He was said to have a magic horn, given to him by the good wizard Yima. It was a unicorn horn, the most sacred of all substances. One end of it served as a drinking flute, and the other end served as a spear tip."

"Sounds like a strange device," James said.

"As long as Lord Ophir drank from the horn, he would never die, and as long as he used the spear tip to defend himself, he would never be vanquished."

"So it's like the Holy Grail," James said, "and the bleeding lance?"

"I'm afraid I'm not familiar with the relics you mention," the buffalo said.

Sheesh, James thought, *I'm even too nerdy for people in fantasy worlds.* "In our world, there's a legend about this guy named King Arthur. His knights go out to seek this chalice called the Holy Grail, which..." James hesitated, unsure of how he was going to summarize everything appropriately. "Basically, there's a sacred drinking vessel that offers eternal life, and there's a bleeding lance that can heal wounds—or at least, that's how it works in some of the later versions after the pagan legends got Christianized."

"It sounds as if what you mention might be like Lord Ophir's horn," the buffalo said.

"Anyway," James said, "I'm sorry to interrupt. Go on. What happened to Ophir?"

"Some strange illness came over him," the buffalo said, "and it was as if the horn had lost its power."

"You mean..."

"Maybe it had to do with humankind," the buffalo said. "No offense."

"None taken."

"I mean only that Nalgordia is a world of human dreams and hopes and wishes. Humankind has...well, for the most part, given up on their dreams and hopes in exchange for temporal powers and luxuries. They have abandoned all that is good in their world for selfish desires—materialism, greed, indifference, ignorance."

"That sounds like the mortal world, all right."

"Many doctors and wizards came from throughout the land to tend to Ophir, but he withered away. Not even Yima knew what to do, and Yima was his right-hand wizard. After weeks of suffering, Ophir closed his eyes and went into an eternal slumber. Balthazar ordered the palace closed up—"

"Wait," James said. "What does Balthazar have to do with all this?"

"Why, Balthazar belonged to Ophir. He was his sinacshin."

"That's right," James said. "Archit mentioned that too." But why hadn't Archit mentioned how significant Ophir seemed to be in Nalgordian history?

"After Ophir's death," the buffalo continued, "Balthazar retreated to the mountains to den there, and Ophir's palace—along with the sacred horn—disappeared forever, along with the wizard Yima. It was said that neither the palace nor the horn would be found again until another Earthling came to claim them."

James remembered Archit saying something similar the day before, and he had a feeling he knew what the implication was. "Another Earthling...like me and my sister and cousin."

"Exactly," the buffalo said. "We look to you to make this world right again."

James didn't want to admit it, but all of this was beginning to sound a little...well, trite. To make matters worse, he didn't like the way they were being spoonfed all this exposition one little bit at a time by different counselors they met along the way. "We knew about this whole other-humans-come-to-be-Lord-Ophir's-successors thing that all the Nalgordians seem to believe. I got that impression, at least. But they didn't tell us about Lord Ophir's horn. Why wouldn't Balthazar tell us that?"

"A sinacshin's role is to guide and protect, not to lead," the buffalo said.

James remembered hearing those words before—Balthazar had said them to Archit earlier that morning.

"But," the buffalo continued, "there are privileges granted to us creatures of the air that the creatures of the ground do not have."

There was nothing to be gained by tiptoeing around the subject, James knew. "What would we need to do?"

"If you are the humans come to save our land, and you mean to defeat Lord Iceheart, then I would tell you to seek out Ophir's palace and take up his sacred horn."

Again, this was an answer that led to another question, much to James's chagrin. "Where is his palace?"

"It disappeared after he died," the buffalo said. "It faded into the mist, and nobody has seen it since. The legends say, however, that an Earthling will be able to find it."

"Oh, that's convenient," James said, and he realized he was sounding like Margot. "That's what my sister would say if she heard all of this, and I honestly think I agree with her."

"Do you?"

James couldn't bring himself to concur with what he had just said. Sure, these prophecies that the buffalo spoke weren't exactly straightforward, but what magical prophecies ever were? Besides, it all made sense as far as James understood it. "You really think we would be able to find Ophir's long-lost palace?"

"If you are the rightful heroes of Nalgordia, it will reveal itself to you."

The rightful heroes of Nalgordia, James thought. "I wish I could promise you that we were." He had always wished that he could one day be the hero of some fantastic adventure, but there was no way he was cut out for this. Maybe Margot or Liz would be able to do it. Margot was tough, headstrong, never daunted by anything nor disrespected by anybody. Liz was more mild-mannered, but everyone had always regarded her as perfect, without any shortcomings whatsoever, and if this were the sort of relic that would reveal itself to somebody who was pure of heart, then there would be nobody better than Liz. But in no way was *he* cut out for being this hero that Nalgordia needed. No way.

He felt a sense of doubt so strong and overwhelming that it sent a shiver through him. It was beginning to get dark. *Wasn't it just morning?* Had an entire day really gone by already? Or were the days just shorter because of Iceheart's curse.

"We are getting close," the buffalo said. "Let's descend."

He leaned forward and began to swoop downward. When they emerged from the clouds, James could see the countryside below them spread out under a frozen blanket of snow that was bathed in the murky haze of twilight. As they neared the ground, James could see two more buffalo fly down alongside them, Margot and Liz clinging to their backs with nervous expressions on their faces.

The buffalo touched down in the snow, and it wasn't until James felt solid ground beneath them that he realized how nervous he had been up in the air. He looked over to where Margot and Liz were dismounting nearby.

"Margot," he called. "Liz."

Margot came hurrying toward him, followed by Liz.

"Where are we?" Margot said. "This place gives me the creeps."

James looked around and couldn't deny that he felt the same way. "I don't blame you," he said, taking in the sight of endless snow stretching all around them as far as the eye could see, punctuated by twisted, bony trees, their frosty branches shining in the dimming light of evening.

"What about Archit?" Liz asked.

James looked up, hoping to see some sign of movement in the clouds. The thought hadn't occurred to him what they would do if any of them had ended up separated from the others. There would be no way of finding him now, not with night setting in.

"There he is!" Margot shouted.

Another buffalo appeared out of the mist overhead. James could see a blur of purple bobbing up and down on its back, teetering this way and that as he struggled to hold on.

"Whew," James sighed as the buffalo descended and touched down.

Archit stumbled to catch his balance as he climbed down off the buffalo's back. "Sorry, got caught in a crosswind," he said. "This weather is awful."

Before they could reunite too warmly, the leader of the buffalo spoke, drawing their attention back to himself and his brethren. "You will find the entrance to Cocytus only a quarter-mile off," he said, "but we dare go no farther than where we are now."

"I don't like the sound of that," Margot muttered.

204

"Thank you," Archit said, making a courteous bow to the buffalo.

James and the girls echoed his thanks, and followed Archit's example of bowing.

"Your humble servants," the buffalo said, giving a nod of his head. "Should you need us again, you need only sound the horn."

With those words of parting, the leader of the buffalo spread his wings and leaped upward, followed by the others. James watched them fly higher and higher, disappearing into the sky above the clouds.

"And just like that, we're all alone again," James observed, crossing his arms to block what little chill he could.

"We're not alone," Liz said. "We've got one another."

James looked at her and couldn't resist a smile. Liz always had a kind word to say, even in the darkest of times. She was right, though—they weren't alone as long as they had one another. *I doubt I'm worth much*, James thought.

A rush of wind blew across the arctic wasteland, pushing up billows of freshly fallen snow and swirling it around in the air. It came on so suddenly that James turned, startled, and then felt sheepish as he looked back at the group.

"Come on," Archit said. "This way."

They trudged onward in the direction the buffalo had indicated was the way to Lord Iceheart's domain.

Should I even bother bringing up the topic of Lord Ophir? Up in the air, when the buffalo first told it to him, it sounded so inspiring to James. Now that they were back on the ground, he had his doubts. It was all a little too far-fetched. Still, he felt it would be a betrayal if he didn't at least suggest it.

"Archit...the buffalo told me that he thinks...well, he thinks that we might be the humans who...I mean, he thinks we're...we're the successors of Lord Ophir."

The look Archit gave him said it all—Archit didn't believe any of it. He even seemed a little offended James would suggest it. "Really?"

"That's exactly how I reacted," James said. "But what if—and I know it's a big *if*—but what if he's right."

"You heard Balthazar," Archit said. "You three are humans. That's supposed to be power enough. You're supposed to be able to do this. That's the whole reason Dawn Flower sent you with me."

"I don't have any other ideas," James said. "I'm sorry."

"It's not too late for us to turn back," Liz said.

Archit stopped and shook his head. "Don't you understand? If we turn back now, the hopes of all Nalgordia are lost. And so is all hope for me...any hope of becoming human..."

James and the girls were silent. The only sound was the howling wind sweeping over the snowy landscape.

"All right then," James said at last. "We can do this. We can figure it out. Let's go face us an evil wizard."

CHAPTER 10
Lord Iceheart

They huddled close together to stay warm as they worked their way through the snow. Night had fallen, and the expanse of white around them glowed under the hazy moon. The landscape was flat, unbroken except for a strange, low, round form several feet ahead of them.

"Look," James said. "What's that?"

As they approached, they saw that it was what looked like a well, only much wider, its stone border standing only about two or three feet high, circling about eight or nine feet in diameter, full to the brim with black water as flat and shiny as obsidian.

"That's the entrance to Cocytus," Archit said. "Just below that water, I think, we'll find the domain of Lord Iceheart."

"We actually have to go in that water?" Margot said.

Archit didn't answer.

"Who's going first?" James said after a moment.

A heavy silence hung over them again. "I think..." Archit said slowly, "...it's only right that...well, that a human lead the way."

James could feel all eyes hanging on him. Margot and Liz weren't volunteering. "I guess that would be me," he said.

He stepped forward, looking at the black water. He could tell just by the sight of it that it was cold, and for all he knew, there was something evil lurking just beneath its surface.

He climbed up onto the wall and dipped his legs in. He shuddered. "Oh! It's *freezing*." The icy cold was so intense that it burned.

He lowered himself to his waist and took a deep breath, preparing to go under.

"Wait, James!" Liz cried.

He turned to see her moving her hand around in one of the pockets of her flowing gown. She pulled out the phial that Dawn Flower had given to her. Stepping forward, she held the little bottle out to him.

"Drink this. Remember? Dawn Flower said that it would let us pass through different elements. I think that means it will help you breathe underwater."

James held out his hand and accepted it. "Is there enough for all of us?" he asked, looking down at it. The bottle was so small.

"She said there's just enough for us to use once," Liz recalled. "So...small sips, I guess. Right?" She looked around to Archit and Margot for affirmation. Archit shrugged.

James uncapped it and touched it to his lips. He took a little sip, and the sweet, flowery flavor spread over his tongue and down his throat. Nothing extraordinary happened as far as he could tell, but there was no way of knowing for sure until he was down underwater. He handed the bottle back to Liz.

"See you all down there," he said.

He took a deep breath and plunged downward. When he opened his eyes, he saw nothing but darkness. He kept swimming downward, lower and lower, to make room for the others to follow him. Reluctantly, he drew a breath. The potion had worked. *It actually worked!*

Feeling braver now that he could breathe, he kicked and swam deeper into the pool.

There was some light down at the bottom, but what it was exactly, he couldn't tell. He pulled himself down toward it, watching as the ghostly specter rose out of the darkness, glowing with an eerie whiteness. It was a fortress, built from what appeared to be slabs of ice.

James came to rest on the stony floor, touching down first with one foot, then the other. He bobbed forward, moving with surprising ease across the floor of the lake.

He sensed movement overhead and looked upward to see Archit swimming through the water, followed by Margot and Liz.

"I guess that's it, isn't it?" he said, indicating the fortress in front of them.

Archit touched down and gazed with open beak at the ominous sight. "Would you get a look at that," he said.

"This Lord Iceheart sure knows how to make company feel welcome," Margot said.

Archit looked up at James. "You ready?"

"Ready as I'm ever gonna be," James said.

"Girls?" Archit asked.

"Yeah," Margot said.

"Let's go then," Archit said, moving forward.

The fortress loomed over them. It reminded James vaguely of one of the monuments he had often seen in Washington, D.C.—except there was something more sinister about it, something more than the simple gothic touches to the architecture.

They approached the front doors, two large slabs of ice. Archit reached up and grabbed the cord of bones that hung nearby. When he pulled it, an eerie melody of bells echoed from inside the fortress.

"Margot is right," James said. "Lord Iceheart sure knows how to make people feel welcome."

The doors swung open, leading into a cavernous foyer with shimmering white walls. All was still.

"Do we just walk in?" James asked.

Archit held his breath, unsure of how to respond. "Yeah," he whispered at last. "Let's go."

The four of them moved in unison over the threshold. Inside the foyer, everything was dry but drafty. Some enchantment must have been placed on the threshold to keep the water from flooding into the palace. The four of them huddled close as they stepped into the middle of the foyer, looking around for some sign of life.

"Who is it?" came a voice.

James turned and saw a group of what looked like snowmen cowering in the shadows of a hallway that led out from the foyer. He could see three of them, but there might have been more hiding just around the corner.

"It is the purple bird," one of them whispered, "and he has come with three humans."

"Are we to introduce them to the master?" asked another.

James leaned close to Archit. "Do they know we can hear them talking about us?" he whispered.

"I wouldn't suggest such a thing," Archit whispered back. "I would hate to be rude, especially when we are guests in such an uninviting place."

Two of the snowmen emerged from the hallway, followed by two others, then one more. If James hadn't been so nervous, he might have been amused by how each of them waddled from side to side on the mound of snow that formed its base.

"Come forward," one of them said. "What is your errand?"

"We have come to see Lord Iceheart," Archit said.

That must have been offensive to the snowmen, because they all looked shocked to hear Archit speak. "I was not asking you," snapped one. "I was asking the humans."

Now it was James's turn to be offended. "You will address my friend with more respect," James said, trying his best to sound polite but firm.

The snowmen gasped in unison. "Brazen, are you?" said one.

James couldn't believe himself. He had no idea where this forwardness was coming from, but it was as if there were a fire inside him that was apt to flare up when barely provoked.

"Hardly," he replied. "I'm hardly brazen, as you put it, but I think that everyone deserves to be treated politely." He swallowed. "My name is James, and—"

"And you have come to see Lord Iceheart," the snowman said. It wasn't a question.

"Yes," James said.

The snowmen exchanged looks with one another.

"He is not the one the master needs to fear," one of the snowmen murmured. James had a feeling the snowman didn't think they could be overheard as they whispered among themselves. "The one in the greatcoat, I think—only a bold hero would wear such a garment, someone who is ready to take action and fight an enemy. And it is a girl who wears it! She must be especially forceful, to be a woman dressed in such a coat."

"No," another whispered. "It is the other girl—see how sweet and innocent she looks in her blue gown, a sainted maiden, maybe even a princess. It is always the pure of heart who are the greatest threat."

"Silence," said the chief snowman. "We will let the master decide what he wants to do with them."

With that, the snowman looked back at James. "Right this way," he said, hopping forward. He gestured with his stick arm.

He led them through a narrow doorway into an even narrower corridor. The foursome followed the snowman, traversing a labyrinth of white, frosty passages. They turned this way and that, heading deeper and deeper into the heart of the fortress.

Even the snowmen don't think I'm cut out for this, James thought as they went. *They think it's Margot or Liz. Even they could tell just by looking at us that Margot is headstrong and capable, and that Liz is perfect, and that I'm just a pathetic nobody compared to the two of them.*

They reached the end of a hall where an archway led into an expansive chamber. The snowman paused at the entry and turned to them.

"Right this way," he said. "Through here."

He held his stick arm out, ushering them to go through.

James glanced at Archit. "Here goes nothing," the bird's expression said.

They stepped forward, the girls right behind them, into a cavernous throne room. At the far side of the chamber stood a white dais, elevating an illustrious white throne upon which sat a sullen-looking young man not much older than Margot.

"Well, well," the young man said. "What have we here?"

With a haughty raise of his head, he gave a toss of his platinum blond hair. Something about him gave James the impression of the spoiled son of a wealthy white-collar professional, like one of the countless boys he went to school with, whose good looks and life of pampering had instilled in him a disregard for any rules that didn't suit his own selfish desires or ambitions.

Lord Iceheart stood, sending his silvery robes billowing around him, and surveyed his audience with a cruel look in his green eyes. "Bow to me," he commanded.

Archit moved to bow, but James spoke up first.

"We will not."

That sent the entire throne room into a frenzy. Archit stood up straight, looking at James with a fearful expression on his face. "James!"

Lord Iceheart snapped, furious. "How dare you!"

Now was not the time to back down. "Pardon me, your excellency, sir," James continued, speaking as respectfully as he could, "but I will not do something that is not right." He swallowed, realizing how forward he was being. It was a little exhilarating.

Lord Iceheart looked slightly angry and slightly amused. "You are bold, aren't you," he said with a grin. "Hold your tongue for just a moment, or else you will spoil my intimidating introduction. If you will not bow to me, the conqueror of Nalgordia, you can at least cower while I boast about my plan."

James tried his best to hide his distaste as a heavy silence filled the room. The sorcerer stepped down from his dais, approaching the small party of heroes that stood before him. His heeled boots echoed on the smooth white floor.

"Well, well, well," he said, his mouth twisting into an ugly grin, "Earthlings sent to me from the farthest reaches of Nalgordia on the command of the hippies and the talking dogs." He turned and went back to the dais. "Why is it that you come?"

James looked to Archit for support as he began to speak again. "We...we have come to command that you relinquish your hold on Nalgordia."

Lord Iceheart sat himself on his throne. "What pretty little words you have there," he said as if he were almost impressed. "And it's so very rare that Earthlings are delivered right into my clutches. What a very nice claim you would make for me. Very well, if you wish for me to relinquish my hold on Nalgordia, perhaps we can play a game. I did not realize that this world meant so much to a group of petty little humans."

Feeling strengthened now, James didn't hesitate this time. "What's this game you propose?" He had half a mind that Lord Iceheart was all pretense and did not really have so much power as he pretended.

"Come with me," Lord Iceheart said, standing and giving his cape a dramatic toss. He stepped down from the dais and headed toward a side door.

Archit moved forward, and James stayed close by his side. He could sense Margot and Liz just behind him, and it was a comfort to know that they were there to have his back—and Archit's back—should anything bad happen. There was no way of knowing whether they were walking right into a trap.

Lord Iceheart paused on a balcony overlooking a series of white hallways below, a labyrinth of passages that were each indecipherable from the others. "See here," Lord Iceheart said, "I will give you free rein of my castle. There are a hundred rooms and a thousand passageways, and much magic to be discovered. Explore all of it as your heart desires, and see whether you might be able to find some secret weakness of mine. I will come after you in time, and when I do, you best be prepared to face me. We will square off and see which of us is the more powerful."

His mouth twisted into a smirk, and he lifted his head as he surveyed the group. "If you win, I will set Nalgordia free. But if I win, then you all belong to me as my lawful prisoners for all time."

James stared at Lord Iceheart, confused. This was not what he was expecting. The sorcerer had offered up this game without any sort of protest, and he seemed a little too eager to partake in it. What was he planning? What was it about this game that he wasn't fully disclosing to James and the others?

"I could destroy you all right now if you prefer," Sir Iceheart said, as if he could read the questions in James's head. "But I thought it would be more fun this way." He strode along the edge of the balcony, brushing the rail with the tips of his fingers as he looked out over the hallways below.

Archit leaned close to James. "What else can we do, James? He's a very powerful sorcerer."

James felt a nervous tingling in his stomach. Archit was leaving this decision up to him.

"So let me get this straight," James said, trying not to look suspicious but trying desperately to understand, "you're willing to square off with us?"

"Oh, yes," Lord Iceheart said. "It seems only appropriate that if humans come to challenge me, I should give them that chance."

"And you're willing to give us a head start?" James said. "A chance to explore your castle and develop a plan?"

Lord Iceheart flashed a smile. "Naturally. But I think you will find my palace just a bit more dangerous than you might be expecting."

James nodded. "That makes sense. But why are you offering to do this?"

Lord Iceheart put his arm around James, and he was shocked by how cold the sorcerer's touch was. "Because, James," Lord Iceheart said, "as I told you, it will be more fun this way."

He leaned in close. James hated the cruel expression on the sorcerer's face. "Dominating a world just wouldn't be the same without somebody trying to stop you," Iceheart continued. "And since you don't seem to know the first thing about challenging a sorcerer, I thought I would make it easy for you."

James still sensed there was something Lord Iceheart wasn't telling him. But everyone—the villagers and Balthazar and the buffalo—had all talked about humans having the power to defeat Lord Iceheart. Maybe there was a chance the sorcerer knew this, and he was just as afraid of them as they were of him. Maybe this whole game was just a ruse to distract them.

"Or," Lord Iceheart said, "I could send you back to your own world. I do have that power, you know. And when you are back in the mortal world, you'll remember nothing of Nalgordia, not even in the dreams of your deepest sleep."

James hesitated. It was tempting. Lord Iceheart must have known it was tempting! But they couldn't turn back now. This mission was Archit's only hope, and they were the only hope of Nalgordia. Still, if they lost...

But Archit was right—they had no other choice.

"All right," James said. "We accept."

Lord Iceheart flashed a broad smile and clapped his hands. "Good. Come, follow me back to my throne room."

He brushed past them, and they followed. Upon returning to the chamber, Lord Iceheart seated himself upon his throne with a haughty apathy that James thought seemed almost catlike. That was appropriate—they were about to play a game of cat and mouse, or so it sounded.

Lord Iceheart raised his hand and an hourglass materialized in front of him, floating in the air. With a wave of the sorcerer's hand, the hourglass flipped over, and its sand began to fall.

"This marks your headstart," Lord Iceheart said. "When this hourglass is finished, I'll come find you, and you best be ready."

James found himself staring at the grayish green sand as it fell from one end of the hourglass to the other. It didn't look as if it would last very long.

"You can go anywhere within my palace," Lord Iceheart said. "But you may not leave. If you do, you forfeit this game, and I claim the right to destroy you."

"You have our word," James said.

Lord Iceheart sneered. "Then go." He gave a wave of his hand. "The hour is yours."

James looked at Archit, waiting for him to lead the way. He could still feel Lord Iceheart's gaze bearing down on them.

"Do we just walk out of here?" James asked.

Lord Iceheart stood, seeming annoyed that they weren't leaving. "Perhaps you need a little nudge. Allow me."

He waved his hands, and the walls around them began to shift. Lord Iceheart's throne and the dais it stood on slid away, and as the walls moved to new positions, the foursome found themselves standing in a bare corridor.

"Whoa," James said. "I guess he's not screwing around, is he?"

No response.

"Just trying to lighten the mood," James said.

"So, what now?" Archit asked.

Why's he expecting all this from me? James had not quite warmed up to the thought that he had somehow become the leader of this quest. Up until they had reached Cocytus, James had counted on Archit for everything.

"I thought you had a plan," he said to Archit, hoping that maybe he was just misinterpreting all of this. "Look, I proposed what I think: We go off looking for the long-lost palace of Lord Ophir."

"James, I told you that's ridiculous," Archit said. "Besides, it's out of the question at this point. That would require us to leave the castle, and that's against the rules of Iceheart's game. And all for a stupid myth that may or may not be true?"

Liz chimed in. "What's this myth you two keep talking about?"

"Yeah," Margot said, "I mean, maybe you should let Liz and I be the tiebreakers."

Liz and me, James thought, despite the precariousness of the situation, but he resisted the urge to correct her grammar. "You remember how Archit was telling us about Lord Ophir yesterday?" he said. "He was this human who ruled over all of Nalgordia? And he died because, well, humankind is going downhill, but according to ancient Nalgordian myth—"

"Emphasis on *myth*," Archit said.

"—humans would come again and restore peace and harmony to the world," James concluded.

"And that's supposed to be *us*?" Margot said. "The humans?"

"Well, yeah, if the legends are true, but that's a big if," Archit said. "What reason do you have to believe that?"

James couldn't form a response to that. Why was it so preposterous to believe all the other fantastic things that happened in Nalgordia, but this story somehow crossed the line? Just because some of the creatures of Nalgordia had never seen a human, that didn't mean they were some abstract concept or made-up creatures. More importantly, it all made sense to James—it made sense that Lord Ophir's legacy would have to be carried on by humans who sought to restore what was lost.

Margot and Liz kept silent. If they weren't buying it, then maybe James's faith was misplaced. After all, it would be one of them, not he, who would be able to fulfill the prophecy. Even the snowmen had observed as much when the four of them first entered the fortress. The girl of action in her long coat, or the girl pure of heart in her princess gown. Not the pathetic little nobody in his tattered power tie.

"So what's our back-up plan?" James asked.

"I don't know," Archit said. "You're the one who challenged Lord Iceheart. You're the human. I thought you knew what you were doing?"

"Well, I..." James looked at Archit and couldn't quite figure out his expression. Fear? Confusion? Whatever it was, he was counting on James to step up and handle this. There wasn't time to be afraid anymore.

"Come on," James said.

He turned and began to lead the others down the hall.

For the next several hours, they wandered aimlessly through the labyrinth of shining white walls. Each turn gave way to another icy, expansive passageway, with no discernible difference from the one before it. After a while, it was difficult to tell whether they were exploring new parts of the castle or just wandering through the same portions over and over again.

"Come on! What are we even doing here?" Margot said. "We've just been wandering around for hours."

James couldn't argue with that. It seemed as if something should have happened by this point, either some major discovery on their part or a troublesome obstacle that they hadn't expected. "This doesn't seem right," he agreed.

"It's not what I was expecting either," Archit said. "But then again—"

He stopped talking abruptly. As if by some unseen force, the floor started to vibrate. The walls leaned to the left, then right, and left again. The force threw James back and forth before he could regain solid standing.

"What—what's happening?" he exclaimed.

The stones that formed the floor suddenly loosened, then slid out from under them, opening up a rift in the ground. Archit grabbed James by the sleeve and pulled him back. A black expanse of nothingness spread out underneath the floor, and the stones that fell away plummeted downward until they disappeared into the abyss below.

Margot screamed. "Holy—!"

The bottomless chasm expanded as the floor on both sides of it crumbled. Archit and James were on one side, and the girls were on the other.

"Run!" Archit shouted. "Run!"

The split in the floor had separated them, and James saw the look of dread on Margot's and Liz's faces as they realized what was happening.

Archit tugged the hem of James's shirt, pulling him down the hall to flee the falling floor. James looked over his shoulder to see Margot and Liz running in the other direction.

"But the girls—"

"We'll have to find them later," Archit shouted. "For now, we gotta get away from this."

The floor stones fell away faster and faster, and James and Archit picked up speed.

"What the hell is this?" James screamed as they continued to sprint.

"I guess this is what Lord Iceheart had in mind," Archit replied. "Wait until we're off guard and..."

They turned a corner, and the collapsing floor followed them. "At least we know what we're up against now," James panted through his breathlessness.

At the end of the corridor, they dashed up a short flight of stairs. James looked behind them with half a hope that the falling floor would not pursue them upstairs. No such luck.

"Keep going," Archit urged him.

Onward they ran, turning this way and that through the labyrinth. A stitch burned in James's side. *How are we going to escape this? We can't keep running like this all night?*

The torches on the walls flickered, casting the passageway in darkness, then illuminating it again.

When they turned the next corner, they found themselves faced with a dead end.

"Oh, what the—" James shouted. "We're done for!"

Archit stared blankly at the wall. He was lost for ideas.

James looked at the dead-end wall, then back at the crumbling floor. *This can't be happening! No, this isn't how this is supposed to end!*

The torches flickered again. Once, then a second time.

When the flames rose a third time, they revealed the hallway completely restored, as if none of the trickery had even happened. It was over.

James had to take a moment to register what he was seeing. "What just happened?" he said.

Archit seemed just as shocked and speechless as he. "The spell...something must have blocked it."

"Something we did?" James looked up and down the hall, first at the dead end, then at the expanse of hall behind them that had been crumbling away only seconds before. With his legs shaking so badly they could barely support him, he leaned up against the wall to catch his breath.

"I dunno," Archit said.

"But what could have stopped that? It doesn't make sense. I thought we were goners."

"So did I," Archit said. "But I definitely get the sense that Lord Iceheart feels threatened by us."

"You do?" Admittedly, James had gotten the same impression. Something about the way Lord Iceheart had acted so buddy-buddy with them, then so easily agreed to present them with a challenge.

"Yeah."

Something in the gray shadows over Archit's shoulder glinted in the flickering torchlight.

"What's that?" James said.

He stepped past Archit and walked toward it, discovering a large oval mirror hanging on the wall. Unlike the rest of the palace, it was neither icy nor frozen. The glass was speckled with warm spots that gave it an antiqued appearance, and the copper-lined wooden frame stood out against the white wall.

"It's a mirror," Archit said.

"But what's it doing here?" James said, running his hand over the ornate carvings in the gleaming wooden frame. Something about the mirror excited him, gave him a good feeling, but maybe that was just his being optimistic and trying to find some hope in this dismal place. "Why does it look...I dunno, normal?"

Archit shrugged. "Who cares? It can't be anything important. Let's go."

"No, wait," James called after him. "Archit, hold on."

"James..."

"Archit, I'm serious," James said. He looked back at the mirror, holding his breath as he studied the antique glass. It almost felt warm as he leaned up close to it, as if the glass itself were heated. "Archit, look!"

The reflection had shifted. No longer was James staring at a distorted version of himself; instead, he was staring straight into what looked like an ancient study. Shelves stacked with books and apothecary jars lined the walls, and a desk sat in the center, scattered with scrolls and loose sheets of parchment. The whole room was shrouded in smoke from the cauldron set over the fire.

An old man hobbled into view. Ancient and withered, he leaned on a tall staff, his long white beard nearly brushing the floor as he bent over. He turned and cast two shining black eyes up at James and Archit through the frame where the glass had been.

"Hello," he croaked. "Hello. Come forward, young sirs. Come forward."

"Us?" James asked.

The old man chuckled. "Are there other young sirs to hear me?"

"No," James said. "I...I guess not."

"Come forward," the old man said, pulling himself up a little taller. "The portal won't hurt you."

James hesitated.

"Go on," Archit urged. "Don't wait for me to make the first move. You were the one who wanted to examine this mirror."

James lifted himself up and climbed through the wooden frame into the study. He stumbled as he dropped down onto the wooden floor below, and the old man hobbled forward to help him to his feet.

"Careful, my boy, careful," the old man said. He extended a gnarled hand out from the sleeve of his oversized blue robe and pulled James to his feet. He was surprisingly strong for his age.

"Thank you," James said. He breathed in the heady scent of whatever potion was brewing on the fire. It smelled of patchouli oil and tobacco, like the record store back at home. It was much warmer than the rest of the fortress as well, and James had a feeling that they had somehow entered another time and place altogether.

Archit flittered up and through the portal. James felt better knowing that Archit was there by his side, even if Archit were counting on him to take the lead.

"Who are you?" James asked the old man. "Sorry, I hate to be rude, but—"

"But you don't have any reason to trust an old man appearing out of nowhere," the man said with a toothy grin. "Very wise, my young man, very wise. I invited you into my study because I would appear to you only if there were a reason. I have been waiting for you, you might say. You are an Adamite, yes?"

James nodded. "Yes."

The old man looked triumphant and clapped his staff on the wooden floor. "Then that is why I have appeared to you. My name is Yima, and I am—"

"The servant of Lord Ophir!" James exclaimed, remembering the name from the buffalo's story.

"Yes," the old man said, laughing again.

James felt a rush of thoughts and feelings go through him so fast that he didn't have time to register any of them. "Then the legend is true."

"Of course it is true," Yima said.

Maybe that offended him. "Sorry, but...we had our doubts," James said quickly.

"Did you though?" Yima said, leaning on his staff and staring pointedly at James. It almost felt as if the old man could see right through him, could hear all the secrets going on inside his head.

"Why are you appearing to us now?" James asked. "Why is this mirror in Lord Iceheart's palace?"

Yima looked confused. "Lord Iceheart?"

"The sorcerer of the east," James clarified.

Yima looked as if he understood.

"I hid myself away in this mirror for a rightful human who could find me," he said. "Janus spent many years seeking me, but never did I appear to him. He was not an Adamite after all, though he might have looked like one, and I would appear only to the rightful heroes of Nalgordia."

"You mean that's us?" James said.

"Do you doubt that?" The old man's reply was quick, straightforward.

"No," James said. "No, of course not."

"Good." Yima nodded. "Good."

James got that sense of nervous excitement again. "What do you need us to do?"

The old man pointed a finger toward James, smiling. "I think you already know that."

James couldn't resist smiling himself. "Yes. Yes, we do."

Yima circled back to the table and sifted through the piles of parchment. From within one old leather-bound portfolio, he pulled out what looked like Da Vinci's Vitruvian man, except the center depicted a unicorn instead of a human.

"Seek out Ophir's palace," Yima said, holding up the sketch. "And take up the chalice-spear. You know the story, do you not?"

James nodded. "Sure," he said. "It's made from unicorn horn, the most sacred of all material." He knew he was just showing off now, but he didn't care. Everything the flying buffalo had told him was just rolling off his tongue, and he was excited to think that they had actually found the answer to how they would defeat Lord Iceheart. "One end can be used as a drinking flute, and whoever drinks from it cannot ever die. The other end can be used as a spear tip, and it grants its bearer unlimited power."

Yima slapped the sketch down on the desk and clapped. "Right you are, my boy. I gave that horn to Ophir, and only when another human takes it up will all be right in Nalgordia."

James felt that pang of self-doubt prod him again. "I don't understand any of this," he said. "Why us?"

Yima came back around the desk. "Do you know why Ophir grew ill and died?"

James hesitated. "I heard it had something to do with humans being... y'know, bad people."

"Because Nalgordia is a paradise of dreams and fantasies," Yima said, "but humans had begun to lose hope in the ideals of a better world. Tell me, James, do you believe that good will always triumph over evil?"

"Yes," James said.

"Why?"

James hadn't expected that he was going to get grilled in philosophy and theology tonight. "Well," he said, "in a world like this..."

"In any world, James," the wizard said.

James swallowed, trying to think how he could best phrase all of this.

"Before I came here—to Nalgordia, I mean—I read a lot of fantasy novels, and in them, there were always clear-cut heroes and villains, and in the end, the heroes would always be victorious. It isn't always like that in the mortal world, you see."

Yima gave him a skeptical look. "So you do not believe?"

"No, I'm not saying that at all," James said. "On the contrary, I think what's so important about fantasy novels is that they tell us good will always triumph over evil. But I'm just saying it isn't always that simple. A villain isn't always going to look like a fire-breathing dragon, and a heroic act isn't always going to be about swinging a sword in battle. It's hard to tell who is good and who is evil, and sometimes they can overlap, which makes it even harder, because nobody is really fully one or the other."

Archit was looking at James with an expression that James had never seen on the bird's face before, as if he were trying to make sense of all of this.

"The villagers of Nalgordia told us that they had heard stories about the humans in the mortal world and some of the heroic acts they had done," James said, hoping he made sense. "None of those humans defeated an evil wizard or monster. They just did what was right, even when it wasn't easy. They did charity for those who suffered from illness or poverty, or they sought justice in a culture built around prejudice, or they helped those in need of sanctuary, or they cared for those who were sick, or maybe they just wanted to better understand human nature or science or the world around them. I know none of them were perfect, and they all had their own flaws, but when it came down to what mattered, they weren't going to let evil prevail."

If James were on to something, he couldn't tell. Yima's expression gave away nothing.

"So, yeah," James said, forcing himself to feel more confident in his response. "I know that good will always come out triumphant in the end as long as good people stick together and don't give up. It's what we need to do."

"A wise observation," Yima said. "Do you truly believe it?"

James nodded.

"Then I think the horn will appear to you," Yima said.

James turned to Archit. "We've got to do as he says. We've got to go seek out the lost castle."

"How will we know the way?" Archit asked Yima.

"It will reveal itself to you," Yima said. "Just as I revealed myself to you." He lifted his hand and held out a piece of chalk to James. "Take this."

James accepted the offer, looking at the chalk curiously. "What do we need this for?"

"You'll know when the time comes," the old man said. He leaned on his cane and hobbled across the room toward one of the shelves. "And I must say, a guide would not hurt, eh? To lead you in the right direction."

He reached for a small wooden chest and lifted it off the shelf, then swiftly threw open the golden latch. When Yima opened the lid, three orbs of glowing light—one red, one blue, and one green—rose from inside and circled around the old man's head. James looked closer and realized there were tiny humanoids inside the lights. They must have been sprites or fairies!

"Let them guide you," Yima said. "Let them guide your way to the castle."

The old man's voice sounded far away, and James thought for a second that the smoke from the fire was getting thicker. In a moment, the study had faded away. James and Archit found themselves once again standing in the white hallways of Lord Iceheart's fortress. The mirror on the wall had returned to normal, its speckled glass merely showing their distorted reflections. If it hadn't been for the three fairies hovering in the air next to them, James would have worried that it all had been a hallucination.

"Holy guacamole," he said. "Can you believe this?"

Archit had been reserved about the whole thing up until then, but he began to laugh with relief and excitement. "No! No, this is crazy!"

"We have to find the girls," James said. "Oh, cripes, they could be anywhere."

"There's no telling how many hallways are in this castle," Archit said. "We could spend all night looking for them."

An idea hit James. Yima had referred to the fairies as guides. "Hold it," he said to Archit, then looked up at the hovering orbs of colored light. Now that they were close, he could distinctly see the figures of the tiny women inside them, their wings beating like those of little hummingbirds. "Would you know how to seek out two other humans in the castle?"

Their glows shimmered, and they spoke in a twinkling of chimes that James could only interpret as an affirmative.

"Help us find them," he said.

The fairies looked among one another and chattered in their chimelike language. The blue one took off down the hall, darting in a zigzag, then disappeared behind the corner. The red and green one circled around James and Archit, twinkling to get their attention.

"All right," James said. "You have our attention."

Green and red then took off down the hallway in the same direction blue had gone. Archit and James ran after them.

"I guess we have to trust them on this," Archit said.

The fairies sped around a corner, then down a spiral staircase. James hadn't realized fairies could fly so quickly. He and Archit had to run to keep up with them.

The spiral staircase led down into another hallway that fed into the rotunda, just within the main entryway. The fairies hovered in the air in the center of the chamber.

"Well," James said. "Here we are. Back where we started from."

Everything was eerily still. He wondered whether this might have been some sort of trick, a trap of some kind. The idea hadn't occurred to him earlier when they were talking with Yima, but there was always the possibility that the old wizard was some traitor who would lead them right into Iceheart's clutches.

No, James said. *That's ridiculous.* If Lord Iceheart had been trying to trick them, his agent likely would have looked a little friendlier and have given off a vibe that was not as honest and earnest. Yima had seemed a little creepy at first, but everything he had said made sense. They were just going to have to trust their instincts on this one.

The sound of chimes came from atop the stairwell at the far end of the rotunda. James looked up just in time to see the blue fairy appear at the top of the stairwell and zoom down into the chamber. Margot and Liz followed, and when they saw James, their faces lit up. "James!" they cried in unison.

James ran forward, relieved to see them alive and safe. The girls rushed down, taking the stairs two at a time, and buried him in a group hug.

"Are you all right?" he asked.

"Yeah, yeah, of course," Margot said. "You?"

James nodded.

"Thank God you're safe," Liz said. "We were losing our minds." She turned from James and went to Archit, kneeling down to hug him as well.

"Come on," James said. "Archit and I have so much to explain to you, but we need to get out of here first."

Liz stood. "Leave?" She looked worried. "But I thought we had to stay inside the castle."

"We have a new plan now," Archit said. "We have to leave this place and go find the palace of Lord Ophir."

"Don't you get it?" James said. "This whole game was just a distraction, to get us under Lord Iceheart's power. He doesn't want us to go off searching for the horn, so he made up this whole cat-and-mouse game. But we've figured out his weakness." He turned to Archit. "You feel sure about this, right?"

"Don't you?"

"Yes," he said. "Yes, I do."

"Then so do I," Archit said. "You're the leader here now, James."

The leader now. James didn't quite feel up to that responsibility. If Archit were counting on a human, then he should have been counting on Margot and Liz. Even Lord Iceheart's servants had been able to observe as much. The savior of Nalgordia would either be perfect like Liz or resilient like Margot. It only made sense.

But they would figure all that out when the time came. For now, James was going to ride this wave of adrenaline-based confidence for as long as he could. "Let's go," he said. "Archit and I will explain everything on the way."

He headed toward the main gate and paused only long enough to figure out how to open it. When the double doors swung open, their group found themselves staring at the black water just over the threshold.

"I'll go first," James said. "You all are right behind me, right?"

"I'm not hanging around here any longer than I have to," Margot said.

James took a deep breath and stepped through the doorway, feeling the piercing cold wetness soak all around him. His body suddenly became weightless in the water. He turned over several times to catch his bearings, then began to swim toward the surface. He could make out the glow of the fairies just below him—they must have followed him through the doorway.

He burst up from beneath the surface, feeling relieved to be out of the depths of the pool.

Pitch-black night surrounded him, almost overwhelming in its darkness. Something seemed wrong, but he couldn't quite figure out what it was.

Reaching for the stone wall that surrounded the pool, he hoisted himself out of the water and rolled over onto the snow. Everything was so cold it burned. His fingers and his toes were already numb.

Margot and Liz sprang up from beneath the surface, the two of them scrambling to drag themselves out of the water. James leaped to his feet to help them. Their hair clung to their faces in dripping wet tangles. The three fairies popped up one by one behind the girls.

Archit brought up the rear, pulling his sopping body from the depths of the pool and shaking himself to rid his feathers of the heavy water. "Ugh!" he moaned.

Liz was looking all around them, an expression of fear on her face. "What happened?" she said. "Something's not right."

"So it isn't just me?" James said. He was glad he wasn't the only one to notice something wasn't right. "I can't figure out what it is though."

"There are no stars," Archit said. "And no moon."

A shiver ran down James's spine. Archit was right—the stars and the moon were gone. Inky blackness surrounded them.

"This is more of Iceheart's magic, isn't it?" he said.

"Eternal darkness," Archit said. "His curse is growing stronger."

James looked at the fairies hovering just over their heads. Their light shimmered, and he heard the familiar sound of their twinkling voices. "This way," he said to Archit and the girls. "We'll follow the fairies."

The fairies led them across the snowy landscape, bobbing orbs floating through the blackness. They were the only source of light in all of Nalgordia. If James had possessed the energy to worry, he would have done so—but running through the snow in wet clothes while a wintery wind howled all around rendered him unable to think about anything except putting one foot in front of the other.

He looked at Margot and Liz blearily. Liz had the hem of her flowing skirt in one hand so that she didn't trip over it, and Margot was hugging the sopping wool coat tightly around herself as she ran. Archit had taken flight, but he was struggling against the wind.

"How far is it to this castle?" Liz asked.

"I'm not sure," James said. "I don't think anyone knows."

A cracking sound thundered from overhead, and two giant luminous eyes opened up in the dark dome of the sky.

"To Palace Ophir, are you?" Lord Iceheart's voice boomed from the sky above. James knew with sudden dread—he just knew in the pit of his stomach—that those eyes belonged to Lord Iceheart. By some inexplicable magic, the sorcerer was spying on them. "Then you have forfeited," the echoing voice continued. "Prepare to meet your doom, and then all of Nalgordia will be mine!"

The eyes closed, casting the sky back into darkness.

Archit began to panic. "Run!" he shouted. "Run! We have no time to lose!"

He circled around them, urging James and the girls to move faster. James knew that this wasn't the time for him to be weak. It was time to run, or else their mission would be futile.

They summited the hill ahead and were about to descend as a group when James paused. "Wait!"

The girls stopped, and Archit hovered in the air. All eyes were on him.

"Do you feel that?" James said.

By the puzzled expressions on their faces, he could tell they didn't. "Feel what?" Liz said.

James couldn't explain it. For whatever reason, he felt a sense of relief. He looked up, staring at the expanse of blackness ahead of them. Maybe he was just being ridiculous. Now wasn't the time to be going with inexplicable instincts or nervous reactions.

Something was moving in the sky, and his heart leaped. It was a cloud rolling away from a silvery full moon. There was still some light left in Nalgordia after all!

The moon shone down on the countryside around them, illuminating a white palace standing on the hillside across the valley. Its turrets and towers jutted into the sky from a magnificent curtain wall.

"That's it!" James shouted. He didn't have to ask Archit—he just knew. "That's the palace. We've found it."

"Yeah," Archit said. "Let's not waste all night savoring the moment, all right? Let's go."

They took off across the valley. Maybe it was the rush of adrenaline or maybe it was just because they were going downhill—whatever the reason, James moved with renewed speed and vigor. They pushed through a deep patch of snow at the foot of the next hill, then rushed up the slope and through the open gate into a courtyard.

James slowed down again, looking around. There was no way of knowing who or what might be lurking there. The wave of courage and determination that he'd been feeling for the past few hours was beginning to dissipate. Was he actually up to this challenge? Why had it been so easy up until this point, and when was that about to change? It had to change. There was always some sort of final confrontation in scenarios like these. He looked over at Archit, wondering whether he were thinking the same thing.

"Would you look at this place," Liz said, staring around. "You mean to tell me that this place has just been *missing*? For years?"

"Yeah," James said. "That's what they say."

"Disappeared into mist, or so the story goes," Archit explained. "It would only reveal itself again when humans return to Nalgordia."

"And what exactly are we supposed to do here?" Margot said, looking up at the main entryway.

"Go to the topmost tower, I imagine," James said. "That's usually where long-lost sacred relics are kept."

"Right," Margot said. "Go to the topmost tower in a hidden castle, and find the sacred relic. Why didn't I think of that?"

They stopped outside the main gate, and James examined the great slabs of ornately carved mahogany hanging in the stone frame. Nowhere did he see a latch or a handle or any other way of opening the door. He looked at Archit. "Well, what are we supposed to do?"

As if on cue, the door lurched forward. James jumped back, startled. He watched, half-amazed and half-afraid, as the doors creaked outward, revealing a shadowy chamber within. A gust of warm air swept out and curled around them, ruffling their hair and clothes and feathers.

"So," said Margot, "I'm guessing that's how doors are supposed to open for predestined heroes from another world?"

"You're finally catching on," James said.

For whatever reason, James had always thought that the palace would be a lot more welcoming. He didn't expect the castle to seem so abandoned and...well, creepy. "Who's going first?" he said. "I guess it's me, isn't it?"

They didn't reply.

James took a deep breath and stepped forward into the great hall, the others following slowly. They stared around the shadowy depths. By the light of the moon shining through the windows, they could see a heavy, velvety carpet spread out along the floor, and opulent banners hanging on the walls.

With their next steps came popping sounds from all corners of the room. Torches hanging in the wall sconces had burst alight, filling the chamber with a warm orange glow. At first, James felt a little bit relieved to have some light—but then he could clearly see exactly how thick the dust was on everything, and make out the gleam of numerous spiderwebs all over the place. Long, skeletal, spidery shadows fell on the floors and the walls.

"I guess there's not much cleaning that gets done in an abandoned castle," Margot said.

James stared up and down the hall in either direction. Neither seemed more promising than the other.

"Which way?" Archit asked the fairies.

Their voices chimed low, and their glow dimmed ever so slightly. James didn't have to speak fairy fluently to know what that meant.

"They don't know," he said. "It's up to us."

"Then which way?" Archit said.

James felt as if his head were spinning. The wave of adrenaline that had carried him since they left Yima's study came crashing down. *I can't do this,* he thought. *Why is this up to me? Why does Archit seem to think I'm the one who's able to do this? I'm the last one of us who should be leading this expedition!*

He looked at Liz and Margot. "Well, does one of you know? Why is everyone expecting me to be the hero here?"

Margot and Liz looked lost for words.

"I mean, really," James said. "I'm nothing. I'm not perfect like you, Liz. And I'm not tough and fearless and invincible like you, Margot."

"What?" Margot said.

"Why can't one of you figure this out?" he said. "It's got to be one of you! I'm not cut out for this!"

Liz looked almost hurt. "James, you don't really think I'm perfect, do you?" she said. "I'm not! I know it sucks to admit that, but I'm not."

Margot huffed. "And I'm so far from brave it's not even funny. You're the brave one, Jimmy. Look at who you are! You've always just been *you*, and you've never cared what anyone else thinks. Even when the world is full of jerks and idiots."

James shook his head. "I can't do this," he repeated. "It has to be one of you."

"Are you kidding me?" Liz said. "Who was the one who knew what we had to do from the start, and challenged Iceheart, and led the way for everything we've had to do tonight?"

"You *can* do this, Jimmy," Margot said. After a moment of thought, she added, "I believe in you."

"And so do I," Liz said.

Archit stepped forward and put his wing on James's arm. "And so do I."

James heaved. "Look, I'm sorry," he said. "I'm not trying to have a moment of weakness here, but—"

"That's all right," Archit said. "But this is up to you. We need you to do this. *I* need you to do this. I can't do it myself. It's like Liz said—you've been the leader of this mission from the beginning."

That was all James needed to hear. He remembered what he had said to Yima only an hour or so before. "Listen. We're not perfect or invincible. We're just human." He looked at Margot and Liz. "But if we stick together, then nothing can stop us."

"It's that simple?" Archit said.

James felt a small rush of pride. "You think that's *simple*? Do we make it look simple?"

"Yeah," Archit said.

James shook his head. "Far from it," he said. "But for right now, we have an evil sorcerer to defeat and a kingdom to save. Come on."

He took a step down the hallway to the left, then looked back at the hallway in the other direction. One way was just as good as any other, he figured. He pointed to the left. "This way!"

He took off running, knowing that the others were following him. At the end of the hall, a grand staircase rose up in front of him, curving around to a hallway above. "Come on," he called back to the others. "This way.

Taking the steps two at a time, he ascended into another long hall, this one lined with magnificent stained-glass windows and ornate French doors. He ran down the hall, pulling at each of the doors to see whether any of them would open. They were all locked.

He ran back to the stairs just as the others were reaching the top. "If I were a secret entrance to a secret tower," he wondered out loud, "where would I be?"

"Do you think we should split up and cover more ground?" Margot said, coming to the top of the stairs.

"No," James said. "We all need to stick together if we're going to win this."

The sound of broken glass tinkling to the ground caught them all off guard. James turned to see one of the windows had shattered. A gust of wind swept through the hall, carrying a burst of snow with it. The wind stung cold across his face as the frost swirled around them, coating the floor and walls with a thick, shimmering coat of ice.

"This is it," James said. "This is the end. We're running out of time."

Wasting no more time in contemplation, he stepped forward and kicked one of the French doors. The glass shattered and the wood splintered easily against his foot. He gave it another swift kick with his heel, knocking the last of it from the frame. "This way," he said.

He stepped over the broken remnants of what had once been a fancy door and went through. The others followed.

They made their way through a series of rooms, each opulent and lavish but long forgotten and left to decay. As they made their way through one extravagant parlor, James paused and looked upon a giant oil painting hanging over an empty fireplace. The portrait depicted a young man—about his own age—seated on a throne, a sheepdog puppy at his feet.

"Lord Ophir," he observed.

It sent a tingle down his spine, as if Ophir might have been with them, right then, right there. But the thought of it didn't scare him. He felt almost comforted, even braver, as if he were where he was supposed to be and doing what he was supposed to be doing.

Rushing winds roared from behind them, and all four turned together. A billowing wave of snow came through the door they had just entered.

"The snow!" Archit said. "I think—I think it's *following* us."

James didn't want to admit it, but he thought so, too. Something about the way the wind howled seemed malicious, and he could see the frost clinging to the walls like some sort of monster latching onto its prey, as if it had a mind of its own and it had been sent by Lord Iceheart to destroy them.

When he looked across the room to the other side, he saw someone standing near the door. The moonlight pouring in one of the nearby windows illuminated the slender form, and James recognized him. It was the same young man depicted in the painting: Lord Ophir, dressed in velvet and satin, his gentle-looking face framed by his silky hair.

"Hey!" James shouted. It was a stupid greeting, but it was the first thing that came by instinct.

The ghost turned and went out the door.

"Hey," James shouted. "Hey, wait up!"

He took off toward the doorway and the others followed. "James, who is it?" Liz said.

"I..." James realized how stupid he would sound if he'd been mistaken or, worse yet, if what he thought was the ghost turned out to be just an illusion. "I'm not sure, but I think I know."

He bolted through the door and turned the corner, but he was faced with an empty hall. There was no sign of the ghost. The corridor dead-ended with a blank wall. He paused, staring at the empty corridor. That inexplicable feeling of excitement returned as he approached the end of the hall, feeling as if something good were about to happen. *What's going on here?*

Margot, Liz, and Archit followed him into the corridor. "James?" Archit said.

"This is it," James said.

"Is what?" Archit said.

James took a deep breath, reluctant to say it out loud in case he were wrong. "The way to Ophir's tower."

"That blank wall?" Archit said.

"Yeah," James said.

He put his hand up against the wall. It wasn't cold like the rest of the castle. On the contrary, the stone was warm under his palm. Then he remembered.

"The chalk," he said, looking back to the others.

He reached in his pocket and pulled out the fragile piece of white chalk that Yima had given him. He had to draw a door. That must have been why he'd been given the chalk. He stooped and pressed the chalk against the wall at the floor, then drew it upward, tracing the shape on the blank wall. When he was done, the outline on the stone began to glow—dimly at first, then brighter and brighter. He stepped back. "Whoa!"

The glowing patch in the stone faded, and a doorway stood in what had once been plain stonework. In the shadows beyond the archway, James could see a stairway spiraling upward.

"Come on," James said to the others. "Let's go."

He hurried through the doorway and ascended. Around and around the staircase went, and James knew something special must await them at the very top. He sprinted, taking the steps two at a time.

"James, wait up!" Liz called out behind him.

He reached the top of the stairs and entered a small solarium. All around the room, the windows looked out on the countryside beyond. His heart leaped to see that the gray clouds were turning forth to hazy light. It was nearly dawn, and if night were turning forth to dawn—well, maybe that meant there was some hope for this terrible situation after all.

The room was sparsely furnished with shelves of books and artifacts. James scanned the walls, hoping to spot the horn quickly. *It's got to be in here somewhere.*

He had never seen a unicorn horn before, but he was confident he would recognize one if he saw it. He had seen plenty of illustrations of what unicorns supposedly looked like.

The others came up the stairs, first Margot, then Liz, and finally Archit. James looked back at them. "Look around. See if you can find the unicorn horn."

Scarcely had he given the instruction when a cold voice came from the darkness outside one of the windows. "Oh, yes, the unicorn horn."

James spun on his heel to see Lord Iceheart stepping through one of the windows, almost as if he had been hovering in the air just outside and waiting for them.

"The unicorn horn," Lord Iceheart repeated, standing on the sill and surveying the room. "It's got to be here somewhere, hasn't it?"

James didn't know what to say. He stared at Lord Iceheart. For whatever reason, he had thought it would be a lot more one-sided in his favor when he finally confronted the enemy of Nalgordia. But here he was, defenseless and powerless, and Lord Iceheart was about to destroy all of them.

"My, my," Lord Iceheart said as he stepped into the solar. "What bold little adventurers all of you are. I must say, I'm quite impressed to see such initiative, seeking out the lost palace of Lord Ophir, as if there might be something here that could save all of you."

James let out an uneasy breath.

Lord Iceheart continued. "But you have broken the rules of my challenge to you, and that means you are now mine to destroy."

A noise erupted from above them, pulling their attention away from Lord Iceheart. A blinding light opened up overhead and shone down. James threw his hand up over his eyes to shield them from the overwhelming brightness. Something floated downward through the light, but what it was, he couldn't tell for sure at first. But he had a feeling he knew.

"What's happening?" Margot shouted.

James could now see the object descending from the light above. It was a platinum-white horn, long as his forearm and textured with delicate ridges like a seashell. James reached up and grasped the horn in his hand.

"A unicorn horn," Lord Iceheart spat. "Fools! This is your great weapon against me?"

James held the horn out as if it were a sword, hoping he looked stronger than he felt. Lord Iceheart threw his head back in a fit of maniacal laughter.

Margot leaned close to James. "Jimmy, what do we do now?"

Lord Iceheart began to circle their huddle. "Yes, what do you do now?" He lifted his chin with a terrible grin on his face. "You've come all this way, and you've found the lost palace and the lost horn inside it. Do you think that by doing all of this you would defeat me?"

James tried to find his voice. "I..."

"Perhaps," Lord Iceheart snarled, taking a step back to survey all of them, "if you drop to your knees and admit your defeat, I will not be quite so harsh with you."

James's hand holding the horn was sweating and trembling. He tried to steady himself.

"James..." Archit said, and James had a feeling he knew what Archit was about to say. Maybe they should accept Iceheart's offer. Maybe they had been wrong and this wasn't the salvation they had hoped for.

"You have no other choice," Lord Iceheart said. "The night is over. Your time is up. Nalgordia is conquered."

James found his voice at last, along with that same groundless confidence he'd had back in the underwater fortress. "And yet you still have not destroyed us. What is it that holds you back, Iceheart?"

It was so obvious! This was why Lord Iceheart had needed them to agree to the game in the first place! He had no real power over them.

Lord Iceheart's eyes flashed with anger, turning almost a silver color, and he threw his arms up with violent fury. Snow billowed around him, and James could feel the frosty cold blow on his face.

"You can't hurt us as long as we stick together," he said. "As long as we stick together in the name of goodness and love."

Something about that word seemed to make Lord Iceheart angry, repulsed even. "Love?"

"Love!" James shouted back. "The love I have for my sister and cousin, and the love I have for my friend."

Lord Iceheart shouted as if he were in pain and stumbled back. "Do not speak of this!"

James felt renewed confidence—Iceheart was weakening. He couldn't stand to hear talk of love! It was so simple, and yet—who would have thought it?

"You don't get it, do you?" James said. "Love is always what motivates people to do good. Love over selfishness. Love over indifference."

Behind Iceheart, through the window, James could see the sky turning lavender, and the clouds glowed with orange edges.

"Isn't that the sunrise behind you?" he said. "Don't tell me your endless night has come to an end?"

The snow that Lord Iceheart had conjured up began to dissipate into the air. The sorcerer looked over his shoulder, wincing at the lightening horizon as if the sight of it were as painful to him as the sound of the word *love*. He stumbled to the side. "No!" He tried to raise himself up, holding his cape out to look intimidating. "No, I still have power here."

"No, you don't," James said. "And you never did!" James suddenly remembered what he had shouted back in the Nalgordian village, when he had held up Dawn Flower's magic stone in his first act of defiance against Iceheart's magic. "You have no power over us!"

As James said those words, the sky outside the window lit up with a blaze of orange and pink. The first light of the rising sun appeared over the horizon.

"You have no power over us!" James repeated. "You have no power over love!"

The light from the rising sun flooded through the window, casting orange light over the solarium's walls. Lord Iceheart screamed, lifting his cape as if it might be able to shield him from James's talk of love and from the light of the sunrise. His cry sounded pathetic and appalling all at the same time.

James stepped forward, holding out the unicorn horn, but he knew he didn't have to say any more. Lord Iceheart's body began to deteriorate into mist as he stumbled backward toward the window. James watched with mixed feelings of triumph and horror as he realized what was happening. Lord Iceheart was dying.

"No!" the sorcerer cried. "No!"

A gust of warm spring air breezed through the window into the room. Lord Iceheart doubled over, his cape billowing around him, and he suddenly burst into a flurry of snowflakes that fluttered through the air before sublimating right before their eyes. With that, Lord Iceheart—the evil sorcerer and the enemy of Nalgordia—was destroyed.

James stared at the empty space where Lord Iceheart once stood, breathing heavily. He lowered the unicorn horn, still in disbelief.

"He's gone!" Archit said. "You've defeated him."

James turned to Archit and the girls. "We," he emphasized, unable to resist a smile. "We defeated him."

Archit rushed forward to the window. "Nalgordia! It's saved."

James followed Archit to the windowsill and looked out over the land. As the sun rose over the horizon, it illuminated a world fresh and new, a world where the snow had melted away and left a land green and lush. James couldn't believe it. When they'd run across those hills and fields only an hour before, they had trudged through knee-deep snow, and now it was all lush green grass and flowering trees as far as the eye could see.

Margot threw her arm around James. "Jimmy, that was brilliant!"

Liz put her hand on his shoulder. "You were amazing! How did you know what to do?"

James shrugged and had to laugh. He didn't really know how else to respond. "I guess I just knew it all along," he said. "I just had to trust myself and be brave enough to follow through with it."

CHAPTER 11
The Amusement Park

"So, what do you suppose I should do with this?" James asked Archit, holding out the unicorn horn. It wasn't every day that he found himself in possession of such a rare and powerful object.

Archit shrugged. "I dunno. I guess it would be irreverent to just leave it here, wouldn't it?"

"Yeah, but I don't want to take it with us," James said. "Where it might get lost."

He wandered over and placed the horn on the center of the shelf above the mantel. "There," he said. "If we ever need it again, we know it's here and we know how to find this tower."

Archit nodded. "Good."

With the warm morning air breezing in through the open window, Margot shucked off the wool coat and laid it on the floor. She stuck her head out the window, relishing the sun on her face. "It smells like summer," she said.

"What's next, Archit?" Liz said.

Archit stared around the room as if he were looking for something. "We're going to need to move post haste to the amusement park, but we'll never make it there on foot," he said. "And without the flying buffalo..."

Margot turned back from the window. "The trumpet!" A look of shock went across her face. "I must have dropped it somewhere back in Lord Iceheart's palace. I don't even remember putting it down."

"No matter," said Archit. "I noticed you didn't have it. We'll just have to find another plan."

"How far do we have to go, Archit?" James asked.

"To the far north," Archit said. "It would be at least a few days on foot, but..." He eased across the room to study an ornamental rug rolled up beside one of the shelves. "I think we have options."

He lifted the rug and gave it a toss to unroll it. Instead of spreading across the floor, the carpet drifted languidly in the air.

James stood dumbfounded. "Is that...?"

"A magic carpet?" Archit said. "Yes. Yes, it is. This is how we can travel to the other side of the realm." He flapped his wings, lifting himself into the air and coming down to rest on top of the carpet. "The wind will follow our demands and carry the carpet wherever we want to travel—and swiftly, too. Why, if we wanted, we could have breakfast in Damascus and dinner in Media." James felt as if Archit might have quoted that from something, but he wasn't sure what.

"Well, that'll be something," Margot said. "If I ever want to have breakfast in Damascus."

"Come on," Archit said. "Climb on. Don't dawdle."

James stepped forward first and climbed up onto the carpet the way he would climb up onto a platform. Underneath of him, he could feel the air moving, and the fabric rippling ever so subtly.

Liz and Margot climbed up after him.

"Ready?" Archit said.

The carpet didn't seem inclined to wait. The next thing James knew, the rug had dived through the open window. Then they were flying, wind rushing through their hair as they soared over fields and forests. The greenery looked lush and vibrant, dotted with patches of flowers and lined with babbling creeks.

James stretched back and lay down, putting his arms behind his head. "Ah," he sighed. It was good to relax after the stress of the night before.

"You tired?" Archit asked.

"Yeah," James said, closing his eyes for just a minute.

"It wouldn't hurt to take a little nap," he heard Archit say to Margot and Liz. "Go on...I'll sit up and keep watch."

With the carpet bobbing gently in the air, and the sound of the wind rushing past them, James slowly drifted off to sleep—only to be awakened what felt like a few seconds later by Archit patting him on the shoulder.

"James! James, wake up, we're nearly there."

James stretched and sat up to see that the carpet was descending, and spread out below them was the most magnificent amusement park he had ever seen. "Whoa!"

Margot and Liz were awake, too. "Would you *look* at this place?" Margot said, amazed.

James looked from the roller coaster tracks crisscrossing high above the ground to the rocking ship moving up and down, back and forth, then to the swings that were spinning so fast they stood out nearly parallel to the ground, then to an expansive lake in the center of the park, and then up to the Ferris wheel, towering at the far end of the park.

But something was off.

"Archit," James said. "Where are all the people?" Not that he expected human people, of course—maybe figments and talking animals and other Nalgordian folk—but Archit knew what he meant. Where were all the visitors?

"Oh," Archit said, "about that. I guess I should probably explain."

The carpet descended to about two or three feet off the ground just outside the park gate. Archit stood and hopped off.

"The park is...well, I guess it's abandoned," he said.

James climbed off the carpet, staring in through the gate at the bright colors and flashing lights of the park. "It doesn't look abandoned," he said. He would have expected an abandoned amusement park to look far eerier, not so well maintained. An abandoned amusement park would have been out of operation, covered with spiderwebs and rust and overgrown plants, sort of like the abandoned greenhouse where James and Archit first met.

In fact, as far as he could tell, everything was operating even as they spoke. Just without passengers. He could even smell popcorn and funnel cakes and cotton candy.

"Well, everything is still in operation, if that's what we're talking about," Archit said, helping Margot and Liz climb down from the carpet. "That's all a natural part of the park. You know, like how a flower blooms or a river flows, the park is going to operate itself whether there are guests or not. But nobody comes here anymore."

"Why not?" Liz asked.

They left the carpet and headed toward the gate. "Because," Archit said. "They think this is where my uncle..." He took a deep breath. "You know, this is supposed to be where Dromio was killed, except I guess my uncle didn't really kill him. He only separated the two of us, and left him to die. But that's still a dark offense, and one that everyone in Nalgordia might fear."

The thought hadn't occurred to James until then that there was still some danger they were going to have to face that day. He had been so excited about their success from the night before and feeling so sure that they would be able to reunite Archit with Dromio that he had forgotten all about Mr. Birken.

Archit pulled open the gate and held it for the others to head inside. James didn't want to be the first one in the park, but he figured it was better he go first rather than the girls, just as he had been the first to go into the waters of Cocytus.

"It's sort of like a haunted forest, you know," Archit said. "I think the stories might be a little exaggerated, but still. Everyone in Nalgordia knows this is where my uncle separated me from Dromio so that he could curse me. 'Whatever you do,' people say, 'don't go near the old park. Something bad once happened there, and you don't know what danger might still be there.'"

James's skin prickled. He remembered the magic he had seen Mr. Birken conjuring, and he knew that it wasn't something he'd ever want to see again.

"Come on," Archit said, leading them along the walkway through the park grounds. "Just keep an eye out. I don't think we're in any danger, but we can't be too careful. Just be vigilant."

"Where will we find Dromio?" James said.

"Somewhere," Archit said. "But where exactly...well, it's a big amusement park."

"Should we shout for him?" Margot said.

"No," Archit said. "I don't think that would be smart."

James got an uneasy feeling they were being watched, as if somebody were lurking just out of sight and following their every move.

No, he thought. *You're just being paranoid.*

An hour went by as they weaved their way along the path through the park grounds. When they reached the lake, James realized they must have worked their way to the center of the park.

He had observed Archit was keeping quiet but keenly aware of what was going on around them. As they approached the concession stands and game booths that lined the lake, Archit scanned his eyes over the scene.

"What do you see?" James asked.

"Nothing," Archit said. "I just...I want to be aware of our surroundings. If there are any clues as to where Dromio might be hiding, I don't want to miss them."

"Maybe if you would tell us what you're looking for," James said, "we could help you keep an eye out."

"He's right, Archit," Liz said. "You haven't even told us what Dromio looks like."

That's a good point, James thought.

"Oh, right" Archit said. "I guess I should tell you that he's—"

But Archit's words were cut off by a deafening explosion from up ahead of them. James jumped back, watching black smoke billow up from between two structures about fifty yards away.

Archit froze, staring at James and the girls. The look on his face went beyond startled, beyond worried. He looked downright *disturbed.* "Come on," he said and took off running.

James and the girls went after him. As they turned the corner around a bumper car track, the air grew suddenly warm. The sound of crackling flames met their ears.

"Oh, no!" Archit said.

A concession stand stood ablaze, orange and yellow flames licking at its side and dancing above its roof. Black billows of greasy smoke roiled into the air. The shutters on its windows shriveled up right before their eyes, crumbling to ash.

"This isn't good," Archit said. "This isn't good at *all*."

"What could have caused that?" Margot said. "A grease fire?"

"That's no grease fire," Archit said. "This is black magic."

"What?" James exclaimed.

"This is my uncle's doing," Archit said. "And that's going to spread."

"Oh, cripes," Margot said.

"We have to get out of here," Liz said.

"No," Archit said. "Not without Dromio. Hang on."

He spread his wings and flapped up into the air, perching on the roof of a nearby ticket booth. "It's no good," he said, looking around. "We need to get higher up."

"Higher up?" James said. "For what?"

Archit hopped off the roof and fluttered back down to the ground. "To get an overhead view of the park. Maybe we'll see Dromio if we can look down at everything from overhead—and we can see whether anything else in the park is on fire." He shook his head, then added, as if he were admitting some awful weakness, "I'm not strong enough to fly up that high."

James looked back at the smoldering concession stand and saw that the wind had already blown embers to a nearby circus tent. The tent's canvas walls began to blacken and disintegrate in the flames.

"We can go get the magic carpet," James suggested.

"No," Archit said. "We don't have the time. We need to act fast, I think."

He ran back the way they had come and stopped at the edge of the lake. "Look, there!"

With his wing, he gestured at a roller coaster track rising high above any other ride in the park. Its highest slope ascended directly above the lake.

"From that height, we'll be able to see the whole park," Archit explained.

Something about that plan didn't sit well with James. He couldn't exactly figure it out, but he knew right then and there that something was wrong. This wasn't a plan that was going to work out exactly the way they expected it.

"Archit..." he said.

"Do you have a better idea?" Archit asked. James could detect the hint of desperation in his voice.

"No," James said, looking at the girls.

"Then come on," Archit said.

They raced around the edge of the lake toward the boarding platform for the roller coaster. As they approached, James watched an empty cart inch toward the top of the highest slope, far above the rest of the park. It lingered for a few seconds at the apex, then plunged down, gaining speed. No doubt about it—from up there they would be able to see the entire park. But still...

James climbed into the cart first, and Archit beside him. The girls climbed in the back.

"Buckle up," Archit said, pulling his seatbelt around and clicking it in place.

James tugged on his seatbelt, making sure it was secure. "All set," he said, trying to ignore the bad feeling he had.

The cart lurched forward and moved steadily along the first length of track before sloping steadily upward. James had that trembling uneasiness he felt before every rollercoaster—but this time, it was far worse.

"Keep your eyes peeled," Archit said as they moved higher and higher over the park.

The entire park spread out for miles around them, and a billowing cloud of black smoke rose from the fire across the lake. It looked as if it had spread significantly. Now the bumper car track was burning up, as was a nearby miniature golf course.

"Hang on, Archit," Liz said. "You didn't get a chance to tell us before—what does Dromio look like?"

James looked down and let out a moan of dread. It was like a worst nightmare come true. His seatbelt had completely vanished into thin air, and all that remained was an old silk scarf draped over his lap. He grasped at his waist in disbelief, hoping that maybe he was crazy, that maybe his seatbelt was actually there and he was just imagining things.

"Guys!" he shouted, holding up the silk scarf. "My seatbelt—"

The others looked at him, and he waved the scarf, trying to formulate words in his state of panic. "There's no seatbelt! It's just—just—"

Archit gasped. "This is witchcraft if I've ever seen it. The park has been hexed."

"What do I do?" James said, looking ahead to see that the cart was approaching the apex.

"Here," Archit said. "Take my seatbelt." He reached down to unclasp his, but it wouldn't budge. He jerked at it. "It's stuck."

"James, get off the ride," Margot screamed, fear in her voice. "Climb down along the tracks."

He jumped to his feet, knowing that what Margot said was the only option he had. He would have to climb down the tracks as if they were a ladder. Standing, he looked down; seeing the park so far below made the reality of the situation hit him like a truck. He felt paralyzed with fear for a moment. His legs went completely numb. All he could do was sway back and forth, mesmerized by the ground so far below.

The others were screaming, but he couldn't hear them. He could see their lips moving, but their shouts of terror were like hazy echoes in the distance. He blinked, then leaned forward to crawl over his seat and across the girls, moving to the back of the cart.

When the cart reached the track's peak it hovered there, suspended for just a second. All of them forgot to scour the park in search of Dromio. Instead, they were too busy screaming and staring at each other, not knowing what to do. Then it happened.

The cart plummeted down the hill. James felt a lurch, and he was thrown into the air. He locked eyes with Margot for just a second as he went up. Then everything whizzed past him faster and faster as he plummeted toward the lake below. The last thing he remembered before he hit the water was the rumbling rush of the cart along the track, and Liz screaming his name in horror.

When he slowly drifted out of unconsciousness, he opened his eyes to see darkness all around him. *Where am I?* He felt his heart begin to race with panic.

As his eyes adjusted to the dark, he realized he was in an attic, or maybe a loft. There were thin slivers of light around the cracks where the sloping ceiling met the floor, as if the structure were poorly constructed. Maybe it was one of the buildings on the amusement park grounds.

He was pushed up against some pole, and his arms were pulled behind his back and bound with rope. He tugged at them, but he had no luck. Who had done this to him? He remembered how Mr. Birken had tied him up in the storage closet. *Is he here now?*

Something moved in the dark off to the side. He turned, trying to make out who or what was lurking in the shadows.

"Hello?" he called. "Who's there?"

A circle of candles illuminated around him as if they'd been lit by some unseen hand. The room was filled with dim, flickering light zigzagged with shadows.

A growl erupted from the darkness, and James could see some large, four-legged beast prowling just outside the light. Another one appeared from the other side of the room. James held his breath as he watched it step into the light—it was a gray wolf, larger than James would have ever imagined the animals to be, and it licked its lips, a hungry tongue sloshing over its giant jaws of glistening teeth. Another one appeared, and then a third.

James drew his knees up to his chest and swallowed hard, feeling their hard stare.

Something else was moving in the shadows. James looked past the wolves to see that there was a person standing in the darkness as well.

The shadow of a teenage girl's figure approached. Tall, slender, dressed in a flowing black dress, she stepped into the light, and something about her face was eerily familiar.

"Well, now, James." Her voice was cold and sullen. "This is a pleasant surprise."

She came closer, her black eyes bearing down on him. James remembered where he had seen her before. She went to his school! She was a senior with Margot, and her name was Miranda Audley. She spent third period as an aide for the science department, so she had assisted Mr. Birken during several classes.

"Miranda?" he exclaimed.

"That's Lady Miranda to you," she said. She raised her chin, and the sight of her standing there in her long black robes with her hair pulled in a tight bun gave James the impression of a wicked witch. "Lady Miranda of the Carnage Heart, high order of the Night Scourge, in service to the dark lord, and huntress of Dromio." A crow descended from the rafters to perch on her shoulder. She drew a pale hand from within her robes and stroked the head of a wolf that had come to stand by her side.

James felt a lurch in his stomach as he started to piece it all together. She must have been in the science wing one day after school, or during Mr. Birken's planning period, and she—

"Oh, God!" James shouted. "You're possessed! He's got you, hasn't he?"

"If you're referring to Abaddon, Lord of Night Scourge—"

"He's got you under his spell!" James began to kick his legs and wriggle his arms, but it was no use. The cords were tight.

"There's no use calling for help," Miranda snapped. "There's nobody who can hear you."

James continued to shout, tugging his arms against the ropes so hard that his skin began to burn.

"If you continue to scream, I'd rather see you killed," Miranda said. At her words, the wolves drew near James, glaring at him with their hungry eyes. Their paws made heavy thuds on the floor as they moved closer.

James stopped screaming, but his heart continued to pound. He looked up at one of the wolves, watching how the creature's saliva shined in the candlelight.

"A wise decision, I commend you," Miranda said as she watched him try to stay calm. "I must say, it would have been quite a show to see you ripped to shreds, and your blood lapped up as if it were water. Or perhaps you would have preferred to be pecked to death by the crows, and they could have saved the wolves the effort of killing you rather than just scavenging your carcass when the crows were finished."

James couldn't believe he was hearing this. "You wouldn't do such a thing."

"You think that Lord Birken has commanded me to show mercy?"

The wolves were now so close that James could feel their hot, stinking breath on him as they sniffed him up and down. Miranda raised one of her hands and snapped her fingers, and the wolves backed away at once.

"Why do you look so sullen, James? Lord Birken gave you a choice—you could have joined his army and served him. Such a future you would have had. But no, it was far more suited to you, you thought, to have been noble and heroic." She cackled, throwing back her head. "Noble, heroic! See how that turned out?"

We're still in the park somewhere, James realized as he looked around the room. *She couldn't have taken me too far, so we must be up in one of the crawlspaces in one of the buildings.* "Do you know the park is on fire?" he asked. She had brought him here as prisoner, but if the park were going up in the flames, then she'd be in just as much danger as he, and now she'd have to relocate him.

"I'm well aware that in a matter of hours the amusement park will fall to ash, for it is I who controls the flames," she said, raising a hand and shooting sparks of fire from her fingertips. The burst of flame lit up her face, then vanished into smoke. "And it is I who will be rewarded when Dromio is killed."

"You know about Dromio?" James said. How much else did she know?

"Of course I know about that miserable beast," she exclaimed. "For centuries, it has been his existence that has stood in the way of Lord Birken's great destiny—it has been his existence that has prevented Lord Birken's curse from taking full effect, the curse that has long made Lord Birken revered among the Night Scourge." She spoke as if she had actually been around for all of that and not just brainwashed into believing it after Mr. Birken possessed her.

"But when I have hunted down that miserable creature and slain him, Archit's fate will be sealed," she said. "He will be a figment creature forever—immortal and unreal. And then Lord Birken will have kept his promise to the monsters of Night Scourge, and he will be their king, and I will be his queen."

"Don't you dare hurt Archit," James shouted. "Or I'll—"

"I do not intend to hurt Archit," Miranda continued, pacing around James now. "I intend to take him to his uncle, safe and unharmed, but he will see no reunion with Dromio, not now that we have you as our hostage.

Don't you understand, James? You will now be a part of a glorious rescue. With the amusement park falling into flames, and there being no time to search for both you and Dromio, Archit will have to abandon his quest to come help you."

"No, he won't," James shouted. "He wouldn't be so stupid! Not after all of this! He has to rescue Dromio!" James swallowed. Was he trying to convince Miranda or himself? "You might think you know Archit, but you don't. This quest means everything to him."

"Well, well," Lady Miranda said, turning away from James. She raised a hand and snapped her fingers. The three wolves drew near, looking up at her with obedient expressions. Four or five crows descended from the rafters and began to circle.

"Go! Hunt the park!" she commanded. "Search for the purple bird and the two girls. Tell them that we have James here, and that if Archit turns himself over to us, we will see the boy set free."

The wolves howled and the crows cawed. "No!" James shouted. "No, don't you do that!"

But it was no use. The wolves and the crows disappeared into the darkness across the attic.

"No!" James shouted one last time.

"Are you afraid that Archit will become all noble? That he'll turn himself in to us? I thought you believed Archit's search for Dromio was more important."

James swallowed, feeling himself made bold again by sheer determination. He blinked his eyes, trying to shake off the tears, and bit his lip. After everything they had been through, he wouldn't let this be what undid them. But how they were going to get out of this mess, he had no idea. He kept his mouth shut though—it had already gotten him into too much trouble.

Miranda took a step back, looking James up and down with a cruel smile. "Much as I enjoy staying here to taunt you, James, I do have other duties that I must see to in the name of Lord Birken of Night Scourge." She took her skirt in one hand and lifted the hem so as not to trip. "I'll leave you here alone with these happy thoughts. If it starts to get warm, don't worry—it will all be over soon. I hope you are good at holding your breath."

She snapped her fingers and all the candles extinguished at once. James could still see her shadow standing there in the dark. She left, the clap of her heels growing quieter as she descended after the wolves and crows. She was gone, and he was all alone now.

He sighed, pounding his head against the pillar. *What am I gonna do now? How are we gonna get out of this one?*

He remembered once reading in an Edgar Allan Poe story about a prisoner who'd been tied up in a pit and had freed himself by rubbing meat grease along the coils of rope binding him so that the rats would gnaw at them and set him free. That had always seemed to be an ingenious escape plan, and he wished he could do something like that now. But there were no shreds of meat and, so far as he could see, no rats.

"Think, James," he told himself. "You can do this."

He sniffed, and he could detect the unmistakable putrid smell of smoke. It wasn't strong, but it was definitely there.

The room felt stuffier too, warmer. And the floor—suddenly, the floor surged with heat. Whatever was below him must have been on fire.

He jerked at his hands furiously, trying to undo the knot. Then he felt a furry snout up against his wrists, and he recoiled, tightening his hands into fists. Was it a wolf? Had the wolves come back to tear him to pieces?

"Hold still," came a kind voice from behind him. "I won't hurt you." There was something comforting in the voice—something like a mix between an older brother and a guardian angel.

James could feel teeth gnawing at the ropes, and in less than a minute, the grip around his wrists loosened and fell away. James pulled his arms free, heaving a sigh of relief and rubbing his shoulders.

He turned to see a dog step into a shaft of pale light. It was a tri-color corgi with big black eyes.

"Follow me," the corgi said. "We have to get you out of here."

James stood. For a moment, his legs felt as if they would give way from sitting so long. He had to catch his balance. "Thank you," he said.

The dog turned and moved across the room through the dark, trotting toward the staircase. James followed. "Wait," he hissed after the dog, "Who are you?" That sounded rude, he realized. "I'm sorry, but I don't know who you are. Are you a sinacshin?"

The dog paused at the top of the stairs. "Shh! You must keep your voice down. Yes, I am a sinacshin, but we must get out of here before I explain any further."

They headed down the stairs, and James realized the staircase was steeper and longer than he'd originally thought. It was also getting hotter the lower they went.

"Where are we?" he whispered.

"The attic above the funhouse," the dog replied, "where the electrical equipment is housed."

They soon reached the bottom of the stairs. Before they could step into the darkness of the room below, they were met by four pairs of glowing red eyes and low, guttural growls. The wolves!

"Back the other way!" the dog shouted. "Hurry!"

James turned on his heel, nearly tripping, and bolted back up the stairs. He could hear the wolves close behind.

"This way!" The dog bounded across the tiny room in the dark, then circled something on the floor. As he got closer, James could make out the shape of a trap door. He lunged for the handle, tugged it open, and looked down a short drop into what appeared to be a narrow passageway below.

"Jump down," the dog barked.

James did as he was told. He landed on a rickety wooden floor, and when he picked himself up, he saw that the walls were covered with dust and grime.

Ferocious barks, snarls, and growls came from overhead, followed by claws scraping against the floor. The dog was somehow managing to hold off the wolves, but for how long?

He fumbled through the crawlspace a few feet, trying to get his bearings. *Which way am I supposed to go if I want to get out of here?*

He felt a sudden surge of heat behind the walls on both sides and looked up to see they were beginning to glow a dull, angry red. Some sections were already melting into black ash and crinkling away. The fire raged all around him in seconds; he could see the wooden pillars holding up the ceiling were blackening, shriveling in the engulfing flames. He coughed, the air around him thick with smoke.

James stumbled forward, his eyes watering. "Help me! Help!"

Just then, the floor gave way and he tumbled into the room below. His fall was broken by a ball pit, an eerily absurd reminder that he was running around the back end of a funhouse. He flailed around, knocking plastic balls in all directions as he tried to get to his feet again. The charred remains of walls were being consumed by the fire. They looked alarmingly lacy at this point.

"James!"

He turned and saw the sinacshin standing in a circular tunnel just behind him.

"This way!" the dog barked.

James ran forward and crawled into the tunnel after the dog. They emerged into what looked like it had once been the hall of mirrors, before the fire destroyed it.

"Come on!" the dog shouted, leading him down one of the halls. "The exit's this way."

James felt dizzy from all the smoke, and had to hold his arms out in front of him keep from tripping. He squinted, unable to see very much.

"Follow my voice," the dog called from up ahead.

The next thing James knew, he was stumbling forward through a doorway into daylight, drinking in the wonderful taste of fresh air. He bent over, trying to steady himself.

"Are you hurt?" the sinacshin asked.

"No," James heaved and coughed for a moment, shaking his head. Standing upright again, he wiped his sooty hands over his sweat-drenched shirt. "No, I'm fine. You?"

Before the dog could respond, shrill cackling broke through the air overhead. James looked up to see Lady Miranda, flying overhead on a broomstick, her black cape swirling behind her. *How clichéd*, he thought, despite the danger. She circled them like a vulture.

"Think you've escaped, have you?" she shrieked.

Towers of flames shot up all around James. He stepped back, startled, feeling the immense and terrible heat upon his face.

Lady Miranda glided down to the ground and stepped off her broom. "Very well done, James," she said. "Very well done. I do commend you." She took a step forward, and it wasn't until then that James realized she seemed inexplicably taller than she had whenever he'd seen her in school. Maybe it was just the high-heeled witch boots she wore.

"You have thwarted Lord Birken's wolves," she said, "and braved my fire, and escaped the funhouse. But this isn't over yet."

Having no other weapon or means of defense, James threw up his fists. "Let me pass!" he shouted.

She threw her head back and cackled. "Give me that dog and I will spare your life."

He had no idea what move he should make next. The fire raged around them, growing stronger every second. There wasn't time for a face off. "Don't make me hurt you," James shouted. "Miranda, I don't want to do this." He knew how pathetic he must have sounded, but he didn't care. He wasn't afraid of some apprentice witch given half-developed magic powers by his fat science teacher. At least, that was what he told himself.

Miranda drew her wand and turned, swishing it toward the burning structures to their left—a concession stand, a game tent, and a small video arcade—sending the flames rushing to consume them.

James looked around. He was surrounded on all sides by towering fire. Faces emerged from the flames—lizardlike, crowned by goat horns—and gnashed their teeth at him.

Lady Miranda raised a hand, speaking to the faces. "Gently, my pets," she said. "Do not destroy him right away."

The heat intensified, and James looked down at the sinacshin for an idea. "Have courage, James," the dog said. "They are only magic, and your power is stronger than theirs."

James looked back up at the demons to see two of them lunging their pillar-of-fire necks down toward him, hissing at him. He stumbled backward and felt something jab into his back. He whirled around to see he had walked into a counter of one of the game stands, and he brushed something with his elbow as he turned.

"At your feet," the sinacshin barked.

James looked down to see what he had knocked over—it was a slingshot, one that must have been used to shoot marbles at glass bottles on the other side of the counter. James stooped to grab it. Lying right next to it in the grass was a smooth stone. He took the slingshot with one hand and the rock with the other.

"A slingshot and a rock?" Miranda shouted. "*This* is your great weapon against my hellfire?"

James didn't care. She could laugh all she wanted, but if he'd been able to stand up to Lord Iceheart, then he could definitely stand up to her.

He pulled taut the sling and released.

The stone sailed through the air and disappeared into the flames. As if they could actually feel the impact of the blow, the demons let out a chorus of hideous shrieks, their heads bending backward in agony. The flames began to die away, black smoke spewing from the shrinking forms of the demons as they disappeared.

"No!" Miranda's eyes went wide as she watched the demons disappear into the fire. She turned to James, seething. "Then I will finish you myself."

She stepped forward, but hardly had she raised her hands to cast a spell than the sinacshin rushed forward, barking and growling, and sank his teeth into her ankle. She stumbled backward, howling in pain, and fell right into the fire behind her. The flames spread hungrily across the hems of her black gown and cape.

"Run!" the dog shouted to James, and the two of them took off. James gave one last look over his shoulder, and the last thing he saw of Miranda was her engulfed by flames, burning, screaming.

"She'll be all right, won't she?" James asked. Even if she were possessed by Mr. Birken, she was still just a teenager and someone he knew from school.

"She'll be fine," the dog said. "The fire will break the possession on her, and she'll be able to find her way out of trouble."

James couldn't deny that. By the age of high school, anybody—especially someone as accomplished as Miranda Audley—should know how to stop, drop, and roll.

They wound their way through the park. The dog was leading him back toward the lake, James realized. With any luck, the others would still be waiting for him there.

All around them, the fire blazed. James had a sinking feeling in his stomach. There was not much time left. The park would soon be nothing more than a smoldering wasteland of ash and charred ruins.

On the other side of the park, Archit was edging closer and closer to despair.

"Where could he be?" he asked Margot and Liz. "If he swam to the edge of the lake, we would have found him by now."

He looked up the hill to watch the Ferris wheel, still revolving despite the fire devouring it, slowly crumble into a blaze of orange and a cloud of black plumes.

A howl caught his attention, and he turned to see a wolf bound out of the surrounding smoke, followed by four others. Margot and Liz shrieked in unison and drew back, clinging to each other.

"Archit," the alpha wolf growled, baring his glistening teeth and looking up at Archit with red eyes. "So good to find you safe despite these conditions."

Archit had no time to waste on trivial greetings from his uncle's servants. "Where's James?"

"We have him captive," said the wolf. "You shouldn't worry. He is safe... that is, as long as you follow our commands."

"What do you want?" Archit asked. He looked over his shoulder at Liz and Margot, then back to the wolves. "You won't hurt these girls, or you'll be dealing with me."

"We've no use for the girls," growled the wolf. "And we will see to it that they—and the boy—are delivered home safely. On one condition. You will turn yourself over to us."

Archit nodded. "All right."

"No!" Liz screamed. She lunged forward, but Margot held her back.

Archit looked at the girls. "There's nothing I can do. They have James."

Margot shook her head as if she didn't accept that answer. "Archit..."

Liz had tears in her eyes. "Archit, there has to be another way!"

Archit took a deep breath and addressed the wolf. "What about Dromio?"

"What about him?" sneered another wolf.

"I demand you see him safely into the company of my human friends," Archit said. "You will deliver James to his sister and cousin unharmed, and you will lead Dromio to them so—"

"You are in position to argue, Archit," the leader of the wolves snapped. "I can easily give word for my pack to spring upon you and tear you to pieces instead."

Archit didn't reply. He was stalling, trying to think of something to say.

"Dromio is dead," another wolf said. "He was consumed by the fire and killed. We saw it happen."

"You lie!" Archit shouted. "Do as I say! Promise me that Dromio will go with my friends."

The black smoke thickened all around them. It swirled over their heads, blocking the setting sun.

The lead wolf turned to his companions. "Kill the girls!"

The other four wolves bounded forward, leaping with unexpected speed and dexterity. They surrounded the girls, crouched and ready to pounce. Margot and Liz grabbed each other, huddling in a tight embrace.

"No!" shouted Archit. "You have my surrender."

A terrible, familiar voice thundered behind him. "A wise decision."

Archit and the girls turned in the direction of the voice. Even the wolves looked startled.

Mr. Birken stood at the top of the nearby hill, silhouetted against a backdrop of black smoke streaked with orange lines of fire. His black robes billowed around him like flags waving in victory.

"At last," he hissed. Mr. Birken stepped down the hill, leaning on a black staff topped by an obsidian sphere. "At last, I stand before my nephew, and he is to be delivered into my clutches."

The wolves let loose and began to howl. Archit edged closer to Margot and Liz, ready to defend them if his uncle tried anything. He was ready to surrender, but he would not let his uncle hurt them.

"Come, Archit," his uncle said. "Or it will be too late. The fire grows stronger every minute."

Before Archit could respond, another voice interrupted. "No! No, wait!"

James came bounding through the flames, running at full speed.

Archit's face lit up. "James!"

It wasn't until then that Archit noticed the corgi running alongside James, moving with surprising speed and dexterity on his short legs.

"Dromio!" Archit shouted. "Dromio!"

James stopped in his tracks, the realization dawning on him. *The sinacshin*, he thought. Why hadn't it occurred to him earlier?

Archit came bounding toward the two of them. If he had ever feared his uncle, there was no sign of that fear now—only excitement to see both James and Dromio alive and safe. Empowered, James rushed forward.

"No!" Mr. Birken shouted. "I said no!"

But he was too late. Archit was on his knees, scooping up the dog in his wings and hugging him close.

"Then I will stop this myself," Mr. Birken shouted, whipping his staff up into the air and pointing it in their direction. James felt his heart stop as he saw the obsidian orb light up and a burst of silver light shoot out of it.

Margot must have also realized what was happening, and before James could act, his sister had already rushed forward, throwing herself in front of the shaft of light.

A cracking sound erupted as the bolt hit her. She crumpled to the ground like a ragdoll.

"Margot!" James rushed forward, falling to his knees.

Mr. Birken cackled, spinning his staff over his head with a crazed look in his eye.

James pulled Margot's limp body into his arms. "No," he whimpered, not wanting to think the worst. Hot tears welled up in his eyes. "No, no, no!"

Liz rushed forward, and Archit and Dromio were beside him now, too. *Can't somebody help her?* James thought. *Archit, we have to do something!* But his voice was gone.

"Margot!" Archit cried, falling down beside James.

"Is she...?" Liz couldn't find the words.

"Attack them!" Mr. Birken shouted to his wolves. "Have at them!"

James's eyes flashed from Margot, wilted in his arms, to Mr. Birken, who still held his staff above his head. The wolves closed in around them.

"James."

The sound of Margot's voice made his heart skip with relief. He looked down to see her eyes were open. She tried to lift her hand to touch his cheek, but she was still too weak. Her arm dropped back onto the grass.

"Margot!" Liz exclaimed.

"It'll be all right." Margot's voice was soft but unafraid. "It'll be all right."

Suddenly, a cool breeze swept over them, ruffling their hair and clothes. The heat of the surrounding inferno lessened as well. Even the wolves noticed something was not altogether right.

James looked at Archit. "What's going on?"

The heavy black smoke was giving away to cool white mist, growing thicker and thicker every second.

"Attack them!" Mr. Birken shouted, but his voice sounded faded.

The wolves howled, and they, too, sounded far away.

Margot pulled herself up, and through the mist, James could recognize the energy in her expression. She was all right!

Relief washed over him, followed by exhaustion. The mist was so thick he couldn't see anything anymore.

That was the last he remembered.

CHAPTER 12
The Fall of Archit's Uncle

Drifting out of unconsciousness, James looked up uncomprehendingly at the hazy, dark sky. He sat up and looked around, feeling as if he were coming out of a deep sleep. Everything was shady in the dim, pre-dawn light, but his surroundings were unmistakable. He was home.

The others were nearby—Margot, Liz, and Archit, and even Dromio. All of them were sleeping in the grass at the foot of the hill where Archit and James had left the pumpkin cab just before the family reunion, and where they would later duck in the shadows as they ran away like vagabonds into the night.

That Friday night seemed like so long ago. It was strange to think that it had only been a little more than a week. It felt like a year.

James sighed and looked up at the house. All the lights were off, and the house stood silhouetted against the dark sky, which was already starting to turn pink and lavender with morning's imminence.

How did we get here? It felt like waking up out of a dream, but there was no way he could have dreamed all of their adventures in Nalgordia, could he?

Dawn Flower's promise! He remembered what the hippie queen had told Margot that night in the forest. When Archit had fulfilled his quest, they would be transported back home, safe and unharmed. Dawn Flower's magic must have saved Margot from Mr. Birken's spell in the process. Here they all were, the others still sleeping peacefully like little kids who'd been lost in the woods and lay down to rest, only to have fairies and guardians of the forest carry them to safety while they slept.

But what about Archit? He was still a figment creature, still a purple bird with shaggy purple hair and yellow beak and talons. *Why isn't he human? What did we do wrong?*

He sighed, tracing his eyes around the scene.

They weren't alone! Two glowing white eyes watched them from across the street. The shadowy figure stood beneath a tree, leaning on a black staff. He stared at James with malice.

"Ah!" Mr. Birken said. His mouth twisted into a malevolent grin.

"Guys," James said to his sleeping companions. "You guys, wake up!" He kept eye contact with Mr. Birken, bracing himself for whatever might come. There was no way of knowing what an evil wizard had up his sleeve.

Archit stirred from sleep first and let out a gasp. As the girls sat up, Archit drew himself close to them. "No quick movements," he whispered. "We're going to have some trouble getting out of this one."

James took a step forward, ready to put himself between Mr. Birken and the others.

"I must commend you on a job well done," Mr. Birken growled with an air of cruel sarcasm. He stepped out from under the shade of the tree and began to walk across the street toward them. "What pathetic little heroes you all are. To think you would dare cross me and defy my evil plans! But I must say you have done an excellent job."

He clapped his staff on the pavement and the obsidian orb flashed with red light. James felt himself jump, and the sight of his fear made Mr. Birken laugh.

"So, Archit," Mr. Birken continued, looking to his nephew. "Reunited with the sinacshin and still not a human. Where has your defiance brought you? What have you gained from crossing the dark lord of Night Scourge, may I ask? Has the prophecy come true? You have crossed me in vain, dodo prince. And now, you're mine."

Goaded to action by his loyal and protective nature, Dromio bounded forward, barking wildly, and with unapologetic forcefulness, he sank his teeth into Mr. Birken's leg. Mr. Birken roared in pain.

"Run!" Archit shouted.

James and the girls took off, sprinting up the hill toward the house. James hadn't the slightest clue what they might do once they got inside, as shutting and locking the door didn't seem like something that would keep Mr. Birken at bay for long—and Mr. and Mrs. Shannassy wouldn't be able to protect them from an evil wizard any better than they could themselves.

Dromio caught up with them, barking to get their attention. "Be careful," he said. "He's calling for backup."

Archit stopped and turned. Something must have been very wrong.

Mr. Birken wasn't chasing them. Instead, he had his arms spread wide and his head tilted back, muttering something under his breath.

"This isn't good," Archit said.

A dark cloud appeared over the tops of the trees behind Mr. Birken—or, at least, what looked like a cloud at first glance, but as it came closer, individual shapes came into view: a mass of demons and spirits, all flying and chattering as they hovered through the air.

Some hubbub to his side drew James's attention away from the dark mass of spirits, and he turned to see several monstrous forms crawling forward from behind trees and cars and houses.

"It's the Night Scourge," Archit said. "All the dark and midnight creatures at my uncle's service."

James understood what he meant. These must have been the same creatures who had stood by and watched with wicked delight when Mr. Birken first aimed to curse Archit in the dungeons of Gehenna, and the same creatures who had hunted Archit for the past two centuries.

Dromio circled around their group, barking and growling at the approaching miscreants.

For a moment, the monsters and demons hesitated, looking at little Dromio with dread on their faces.

"They're afraid of a sinacshin," Archit observed. "They're afraid of Dromio."

Mr. Birken waved his staff. "What are you waiting for?" he bellowed to his servants. "You are many more and much bigger than that stupid dog.

Kill the children, and bring the bird to me!"

The horde growled and hissed, baring their claws and gnashing their fangs at Dromio. Motivated and encouraged by Mr. Birken's demands, they lumbered forward again.

"Don't just stand there," Dromio said to Archit. "I can't hold them off for long!"

Archit nodded. He looked to James and the girls. "Come on."

Their feet found purpose again, and they went running up the hill. But just as they reached the peak, Margot's bare feet slipped on the dewy grass and she stumbled forward, just as she and James had on the night they ran away. Her knees broke her fall, and she threw her hands out to catch herself.

It must have been fate. It was far too great a coincidence that she had tripped and fallen in exactly the same place she had on Friday night. As her hand fell into the grass, she felt something under her fingers and rolled over, holding up her discovery in triumph. It was her key ring.

"Guys! Come on!" she shouted to the others, rattling the keys over her head for them to see. Jumping to her feet, she turned and bolted down the hill toward her car, still parallel parked on the street.

It wasn't a great escape plan, but what other choice did they have?

Margot fumbled with her keys and unlocked the car, then hopped into the driver's seat. James and Archit piled into the backseat, and Liz ran around to the passenger door.

James pulled the door closed and locked it, feeling a little better to know they were safe inside the car. Outside the window, monsters closed in around them. Dromio barked and bit at their legs to stall their approach.

Margot jammed her keys in the ignition and started the car. How strange the engine sounded after so many days of being in a world where there was sorcery and magic instead of motors!

At the sound of the engine roaring to life and the sight of the headlights flashing on, several of the monsters jumped back in surprise, confused or even unnerved by the sight of this hulking block of metal and glass that the humans had just crawled into, and now it had come to life.

"You cowards!" Mr. Birken shouted. "After them! After them!"

Margot put the pedal to the metal and took off down the street.

"Where are we going?" Liz asked.

"Anywhere but here," Margot replied. "For cripes' sake, where is everyone?"

She had a point. Even at dark o'clock in the morning, the neighborhood was unusually still. James tried to do the math in his head. "It's Sunday," he said. "Everyone must still be asleep."

"Through all this commotion?" Liz asked.

"If they're adults, it might not be real to them," Archit reminded her. "They might not be able to hear it."

"We can't just drive in circles around the neighborhood," James said. "We gotta go get help."

Margot's car veered around a turn, running a stop sign. There was only one road that led into the neighborhood, but if they could access that street, then they could get into town and maybe get to some sort of help.

"Do we go to the police with something like this?" she asked.

"Yes," Archit said. "They might not believe in monsters—"

"But they'll believe in Mr. Birken," James continued, realizing how simple it all was. "He's a madman, and he's a madman employed by the public school system. They've gotta lock him up."

"Yeah," Archit said, but he sounded only halfway sure.

Silence hung in the car for a second. They had no other option.

"Do you think Dromio will be all right?" James asked.

"He'll be fine," Archit said. "We don't need to worry about him."

"*Margot, look out!*" Liz shrieked.

Coming around a bend in the road, they saw Mr. Birken just up ahead of them, standing right in the middle of the street, as if he had been waiting for them.

Margot accelerated, spinning the wheel to go around him, but Mr. Birken swung his staff in their direction. A sudden crack of red lightning erupted from the end of the staff.

The car skidded sideways, then spun over and over, round and round, before a sudden impact from slamming into something stopped it almost as quickly as it started.

James looked around. His seatbelt had locked up, and he lay at eye level with the street outside the window. The car must have been on its side. "Is everyone all right?"

"Yeah," Margot shouted.

Margot's purse had been tossed just within James's reach. He reached for it and fumbled around. If he knew Margot, there might have been a corkscrew in there, and if it were the corkscrew she usually carried...

There it was! He pulled the wine key out and flicked it open, first the screw, then the knife on the other end, and began sawing at the seatbelt.

Archit had wriggled himself loose from the seatbelt and was helping Margot and Liz.

Outside the window, several clawed feet approached on the pavement. Time was short!

James felt the seatbelt give, and he was free from its binding. He pulled himself out and began to clear award the shards of broken glass at the window overhead so he could crawl out onto the street.

A horde of goblins surrounded the car with their spears pointed right at him. Mr. Birken stood only a few feet away.

"Catch them!" Mr. Birken shouted.

James hopped from the car and helped Margot and Liz out behind him. Archit brought up the rear.

"Come on!" James shouted as he took off running down the street.

"After them!" he could hear Mr. Birken shouting. "After them, I said. Don't let them get away!"

James looked left and right and could see other members of the Night Scourge descending on them, not just the goblins but hags and demons and beasts. From overhead swooped giant bats with humanoid heads. He could hear Margot and Liz running behind him, and he could see Archit flying in his periphery. If they stuck together, they'd be able to outsmart these miscreants. He knew the neighborhood well, and he knew all the smart and shifty getaways he had learned from nights of dark tag as a kid, when he had run with flashlight in hand through neighbors' yards to seek out hiding spots and escape routes.

"This way," he hissed to the others as he veered off the street and into a nearby yard. Margot, Liz, and Archit all followed.

He went around the side of the house, hoping that they wouldn't make so much noise that anyone inside would notice them. Up until two years ago, this house had belonged to Mrs. Strithers, but since her family had moved her to a nursing home, a new owner had moved in, and he didn't know who they were.

"C'mon," he whispered to the others as he ducked into an alcove between the brick stairs leading to the house's back door and the lean-to where the gardening tools were kept. There was just barely room for all four of them to squeeze.

They waited a moment, all holding their breath. Soon enough, they heard the rumble of heavy feet on the sod a few feet away. James pulled his head away from the huddle just enough to watch the army of monsters run past them, completely unaware that the objects of their hunt were so close.

When the crowd passed, James heaved a sigh of relief. "Come on," he whispered.

"How did you know about this hiding spot?" Margot asked.

"All those games of dark tag as a kid," James explained. "This is where I always used to hide. This way."

They tiptoed out of the yard and scurried across the street, avoiding the gleam of a nearby streetlight. They probably had only another five to ten minutes until full daylight. Some streetlights had automatically shut off already.

"Look there!" Archit whispered, throwing his wing out to indicate three burly figures coming down the street. Long, shaggy hair hung down from their lumpy bodies, and each one carried a massive spiked club. "Ogres," Archit said under his breath. "Back this way."

Archit headed into a patch of woods just off the street, and James and the girls followed.

"Here's the plan," Archit said when they were back far enough. They were knee-deep in ivy and other weeds, and James was sure that there must have been snakes back there. "James, you and I will create a distraction. We'll get the ogres' attention and run back off the way that we came. Liz and Margot, you two will need to go get help."

"Get help?" said Margot. "How are we supposed to get help?"

"We aren't leaving you," Liz insisted.

"Look," said Archit, "you two need to get out of the neighborhood. Get to a police station and send help."

"We can't just leave you and James here," Margot said. "There are monsters all over the neighborhood."

"We can handle this," James assured her. "I'll make sure nothing happens to us."

"There's no time to waste," said Archit. "Come on, James."

Without waiting for a reply from Margot and Liz, he jumped out of the bushes. "*Heyyy!*" Archit shouted. "Hey, numbskulls! Over here, ugly!"

James took Archit's cue and began to jump up and down, waving his arms over his head. "Hey, we're over here! We're over here, you tools!"

If there were one thing about distractions that James could never quite understand, it was why people continued to fall for them—at least, for simple and stupid ones like the one they were currently creating. When people jumped up and down and shouted, "Hey, I'm over here," it should have been a red flag to anybody that they were being distracted from something.

But the ogres fell for this ploy—before James knew it, the beasts were charging, ready to catch him and Archit. They came running with footsteps that shook the ground, their weapons raised over their heads.

"Yeah, that's right," shouted Archit, "we're over here! Come and get us!" He waved his wings and hovered a few feet off the ground. "Wooo!" he cheered.

"They see us," said James. "They're coming!"

"I know! Run!" said Archit.

They sprinted down the street, the sound of heavy footsteps pounding behind them. James looked over his shoulder to see the ogres gaining on them, waving their spiked clubs over their heads.

"This way," James said, grabbing Archit by the vest and swerving into a neighbor's yard.

They ducked along the side of the house, stumbling through bushes and undergrowth as they went. Around back, the shrubbery opened up to an expansive backyard centered on a brick firepit. A forested area stood just beyond.

"That woodpile," James hissed, indicating a tall tower of freshly chopped logs stacked beside the firepit. "Behind there."

"Good idea!"

The two of them slipped behind the woodpile, peeking out only to watch the ogres continue running through the yard and disappear into the trees at the edge of the property. The sounds of their footsteps thrashing through the foliage soon faded away.

James stepped out from behind the woodpile, still a little breathless. "That was close."

Archit didn't respond. James turned back, a little uncomfortable at Archit's quietness. He looked pensive, as if some terrible thought had just entered his mind. "Archit?"

Archit avoided his eye. "I'm going to have to turn myself in to him."

James felt the words like a blow right in the stomach. "What? No—Archit, you can't!"

"There's no other way, James!" Archit said. "Don't you get it? If I don't, then he'll kill you. And Liz and Margot, too!" Archit paused for a moment, and then added, "It's me he's after, not you. And once he has me, he won't have any more reason to come after you. And as long as Dromio lives, remember, he can't seal the curse."

"No, Archit, listen to me!" said James, realizing his voice was growing a little too loud. Then, he whispered, "We'll find a way out of this—we have found a way out of every problem we've been in!"

"This isn't as simple as all those other things, James."

"So what if it isn't?!" James said, trying to control his voice. He wouldn't let himself get emotional. Not now, not when he had to be brave. But he realized that if he didn't argue quickly enough—if he didn't come up with some other viable alternative—then he was going to lose Archit. Their whole quest would have been in vain.

"James," Archit said, "I can't continue to be this selfish. It's like you said in Ophir's palace—sometimes doing what's right isn't what's easy. But if giving up myself to keep you and the girls safe is what I need to do, then I'm damn well going to do that!"

James struggled to find the words in his throat. Archit—their fearless leader, the one who had believed in him and counted on him from the start, the one who had stood by his side through countless dangers—was going to give up this easily. And for what? So that Mr. Birken might leave them alone? "No," James said. "No, please, Archit—you can't!"

"Take this," Archit said, shucking off his vest and handing it to James. "Whatever magic is in it, maybe it will bring you more luck than it did me."

"No," James said, shaking his head.

"Take it, James."

James reached a trembling hand forward and accepted the vest. Maybe if he put it on, maybe if he had the vest's magic to protect him, then Archit would let him go along to confront Mr. Birken with him. James couldn't let him go alone. "You're my friend and I won't let you—I'm going with you," he said, pulling the vest over one arm, then the other.

"No. I need you to stay here," said Archit. "When you meet back with Margot and Liz, tell them what happened."

"Archit..." James stammered, not knowing what to say. He could feel tears welling up in his eyes.

"Stop it, James," said Archit. "I know this is hard, believe me, I'm terrified—but this is the only way."

The two of them just stared at each other. James couldn't accept this. For a moment, his insides shook and he was unable to breathe as he racked his brain for something to say.

Was there no talking Archit out of this? James needed to prolong the farewell as much he could, holding onto each last word of the exchange, valuing each moment more he could spend with Archit by his side before they parted—possibly forever.

Archit slowly spread his arms for a goodbye hug. James fell into him, unblinking or else he would tear up.

It was the most difficult hug James had ever experienced.

"Goodbye, James," said Archit, pulling out of the hug. He avoided James's eye.

"No, no—!"

"Goodbye," Archit said with a note of finality. He turned and ran.

James stood, paralyzed, watching Archit run off. His arms that had once hugged his best friend fell empty down by his sides.

He had let Archit down! He had failed him.

He couldn't control his emotions anymore. Salty tears rolled out of his eyes and slid down his face, and he reached up to brush them away with his muddy hands. They had failed!

For a moment, he howled, then choked again.

"No!" he said, slamming his hands against a nearby tree. "No!"

This wasn't how the adventure was supposed to end! He wasn't sure, exactly, how he had imagined it ending—but for whatever reason, he had always counted on the thought that they would defeat Mr. Birken and Archit would be free. And when James returned to normal life with the girls, it would be as heroes whom his peers and parents would admire. As if any of that mattered now! No, the only thing that mattered was that they save Archit.

He stumbled to his feet. His legs were shaking so hard he could barely stand. His arms fell against the woodpile, trying to steady himself.

I'm not letting him go alone. I don't care what Mr. Birken might do to me. I'm not letting Archit go down without a fight!

"Be brave," he said to himself through gritted teeth. "Be brave for Archit!"

He didn't care—he damned well didn't care now! Not any more—not at all! Let the Night Scourge do what they would! James wasn't going to let their quest fail while he still had life in his body.

He took off running through the yard in the direction Archit had gone. He was no longer being cautious or wary that any of the nearby monsters or miscreants might attack him. He ran from one yard to the next, making no effort to be stealthy in his course.

As he crossed through one of the yards, he found a metal baseball bat leaning up against somebody's back porch. He grabbed the bat, swinging it back and forth in front of him as hard as his pathetic unathletic arms could manage. If any of the goblins or ogres tried to capture him before he could catch up with Archit, then he would beat them senseless. He didn't know where this heedless aggression had come from—he knew only that he didn't care about anything except the fact that he still had some strength left, and as long as he did, he was going to fight for Archit.

Strength returning to his legs, he began to run. He knew that Mr. Birken would be waiting at the street corner back at the house, where they had all arrived from Nalgordia.

The sky was rapidly brightening, and James realized there wasn't much time left. The civilized world would be waking up by now, and people would be coming outside soon. That very likely meant that whatever Mr. Birken needed to do, he would have to do it quickly. James picked up speed, no longer feeling as nervous as he had before.

As he approached his house, he ducked behind the row of bushes in a neighbor's yard across the street, taking in the sight before him. All his fear and dread returned when he saw the massive crowd of monsters that had gathered to witness Mr. Birken's victory.

Archit stood in front of the nightmarish throng, his head hung low as he stepped forward. Several of the villains closest to him hissed and snarled at him; others merely cackled and jeered.

The crowd parted, giving Archit room to approach Mr. Birken, who held his staff up above his head in a sort of victory pose.

"Ah, what have we here?" he cawed. "Come to give yourself over to me, have you, Archit?"

Archit lifted his head. "If I surrender to you willingly," he said, his voice sounding broken, "and end this obscene chase, will you leave my friends alone and not hurt them?"

Mr. Birken gloated. "It seems you have no choice."

"Promise me!" Archit shouted, his voice cracking. "Promise me that you won't hurt them! Ever since you killed my father and separated me from Dromio, they are the only ones I have ever loved. I'm giving myself to you—you can do what you will with me! You can work any sort of curse you want, just don't hurt James or his sister and cousin."

Hearing this gave James the courage he needed to step forward. Still a little dizzy from nerves, he stumbled out into the street, regained his footing, and walked forward. "You won't be working any curse on Archit," he said.

Mr. Birken looked up and took in the sight of James. "What have we here? Two self-sacrifices right in a row?" He gave a long, terrible, drawn-out evil laugh. "How disgustingly noble!"

Archit turned and looked over his shoulder at James, giving a subtle shake of his head and a pleading look. James noticed that the bird's eyes were misty with tears. "No," Archit mouthed at him. "Go back."

James took a deep breath. "If you dare hurt Archit," he said, a little more bravely this time, "you'll have to deal with me." He took a few steps forward, holding the baseball bat out in front of him.

Some of the monsters looked ready to move or pounce, but Mr. Birken lifted his hand. "Do not lay a tooth or claw upon that boy," he said. "He will watch as I have my triumph, and then I will deal with him myself."

With those words, Mr. Birken swung his staff around and pointed it at Archit. The obsidian stone flashed again, and a swirl of black smoke shot through the air toward the bird. Roiling like a storm cloud, the mist struck Archit right in the chest, sending him backward. He skidded along the pavement several feet.

"No!" James shouted, starting forward.

Mr. Birken swung his staff in James's direction. The staff ushered a cracking sound, and James felt his feet under him slipping backward as if the street were greased with thick butter. He tried to gain his footing, but the power of the curse was too strong, and he was sent sliding into a neighbor's yard and straight into a tree trunk, where he dropped to the ground.

His back stung from the impact, but he picked himself back up. Mr. Birken stood over Archit, and the black mist that he had issued from his staff engulfed Archit's crumpled body on the pavement. It was taking form, wrapping Archit in thick binds the way a spider would wrap a fly.

James sprang forward, but as he approached, one of the monsters leaped from the crowd. A lizard-like head perched on a jaguar body leered at him. "You will not come between our master and his victim," the beast spat.

James looked to the rest of the mob. Several of the demons hovering in the air had turned their red-hot iron spears in his direction. They bared their teeth and cackled. He took a step back, looking from the lizard-jaguar to the demons and then with agonizing dread at Archit, who was quickly disappearing beneath the wrapping of black cords.

"Stop!" James shouted. "Stop it!"

Mr. Birken looked up but kept his staff fixed on Archit. "Silence the boy!" he shouted to his minions.

The next thing James knew, there was a knife at his throat, a long stone blade wielded by a scaly-skinned caveman. James took a step back.

"Help, help," mocked Mr. Birken in a high-pitched whimper. He laughed at James, looking directly into his eyes.

A jolt of rage ran through James. "You shut up!" James shouted at Mr. Birken. "Let's see how brave you are without your army."

Before Mr. Birken could respond to that, there came the unmistakable rumble of a vehicle speeding down the street, and Margot's car swerved into sight around the corner. How Margot and Liz had managed to overturn the battered car after it had been wrecked so thoroughly, James didn't know—but he couldn't have been more grateful to see it tearing down the road in their direction.

The car slowed as it approached the scene, but it never fully stopped. Liz leaped from the passenger seat, and it was then that James realized the brakes must have given out in the crash. Somehow, the rest of the car was working just fine. That was the way it always worked in action movies, James knew, but he had never expected it to be that way in real life!

Liz started to move toward James, but he pointed her toward Archit. "I'm fine! Help him!" he shouted.

Liz nodded and turned back to Archit. Whatever spell Mr. Birken had cast, it was working. Archit lay limp, growing less and less resistant to the smoke swirling around him. "Archit," Liz cried out. "Archit, can you hear me?" She kneeled and shook him.

Mr. Birken cackled. "*This* is your great defense?" he roared with another laugh.

Margot's car continued to skid and came to a stop several feet away. The driver's door burst open, Margot emerging from it with a fearless determination.

James looked back at Mr. Birken, who still held his staff fixed in Archit's direction. If he didn't stop Mr. Birken right now, it was all forfeit.

In one swift move, James stomped the caveman's foot and pushed his knife away, then grabbed the baseball bat from where he had dropped it on the street. He surged forward, gripping the bat tight with both of his fists. He swung the bat over his head as he charged. By the time Mr. Birken turned to see James coming toward him, it was too late. With a forceful swing, James brought the bat down on the end of Mr. Birken's staff.

There was a flash of light, and black smoke filled the air as the dark crystal on the end of the staff shattered under the bat's force. The end of the wooden shaft splintered into thousands of pieces. When James lifted his eyes again, he saw Mr. Birken holding only a broken pole. Shards of the destroyed glass lay at his feet.

Mr. Birken seethed, his eyes flashing from the broken end of the staff to Archit, who was no longer shrouded in black mist. The bird lay cradled in Liz's arms, and his eyes opened as the black bindings dissolved away.

All action around them seemed to freeze. James looked at the army of the Night Scourge, and he was surprised to see that they looked dumb-founded, even frightened. Their master had just lost all his power, and they knew it.

James heaved a deep breath. He realized what he had done. When he had run forward, he had been thinking only of stopping Mr. Birken's curse on Archit, but he knew now that he had stripped Mr. Birken of all his magic powers!

Mr. Birken stood fuming, his nostrils flaring, his eyes wide with fury. James took a step back, fully aware of the gravity of the act he had just committed. Mr. Birken could no longer perform magic, at least not until he acquired another staff, and who knew how an evil sorcerer went about getting one of those?

Mr. Birken lifted his broken staff and hurled it forcefully into James's abdomen. He felt a stab of pain. Though the broken splinters of wood were not sharp enough to do anything more than tear his shirt and leave a few scratches in his skin, the blunt shock as the pole of wood went into his stom-ach was enough to rob him of air. Mr. Birken drew the staff back again, then struck James across the face. James fell backward, feeling not only the blunt force but also the burn of the splintered wood against his cheek. *Oh, God!* he thought. *Mr. Birken's going to kill me! He's going to beat me to death!*

Both James and Mr. Birken were staring at each other so intently—James with terror and Mr. Birken with anger—that neither of them heard

Margot approach.

"Hey!"

Mr. Birken turned.

Margot hauled off with a tightly made fist and landed Mr. Birken a punch right in the nose. If she hadn't caught him off guard, she might not have been so successful, but Mr. Birken would never in a million years have thought this girl capable of such strength. He had not yet recovered from the first punch before Margot gave him a second, this one across the jaw.

"Oof!" he moaned out loud as her fist cracked against his chin.

"That's right," Margot jeered. She lifted a hand with a tube of pepper spray that she must have found in her purse when it spilled all over the inside of her car. She spewed the fiery aerosol right in Mr. Birken's eyes, smiling as she watched him wince in pain. Mr. Birken doubled over, reaching for his eyes as if he might be able to rub the pain away. His staff clattered to the ground.

Margot kept pressing the little tube of pepper spray until it was expired. "You mess with my little brother..." She dropped the pepper spray and gave Mr. Birken another punch to the face. "And I'll *kick–your–ass!*" She emphasized each word with a punch, then finally a swift kick between his legs. Mr. Birken stumbled backward. His nose was bleeding, as was his mouth. She surveyed him with a broad smile on her face. "Not so tough now, are you?"

The sorcerer staggered to his feet. He was stripped of his magic and had just been beaten up by a teenage girl. He raised a hand to his face and wiped the blood from his nose, leaving a dark red smear across his face. "Oh, you have really got it now!" he growled at Margot and James.

He looked out at his crowd of monster and miscreants, all of whom stood nearby with apprehensive expressions he had never seen before. They did not know what to make of the display of courage they had seen from Margot and James, nor the kindness and compassion of Liz, who kneeled on the edge of the street with Archit in her arms.

"Destroy them!" Mr. Birken shouted.

The monsters would not obey. They shrank back. Their once-master had been disempowered, and he no longer controlled them. He had no authority over them anymore. Who was he to give commands to the Night Scourge?

"Obey me!" shouted Mr. Birken. "Destroy them, I said!"

His voice was so loud that it seemed to echo down the empty residential streets. For a moment, silence.

Then they heard it ever so faintly. Sirens.

The sirens grew louder as they approached, and everyone present—good or evil, human or monster—looked around. The authorities were coming.

James caught Margot's eye. She smiled and lifted up one of her hands. In it, she clutched her cellphone. She must have found it inside her car, just as she had found the pepper spray.

Margot. James really had to admit that she was the coolest person he had had ever known. Even under pressure, she always knew what to do.

All the creatures of Night Scourge screeched and looked around. They knew what those loud whirring sounds meant. Not only had their master lost his power, but he was now about to meet his punishment at the force of Adamite law.

"What is that?" James could hear some of them hissing.

"It is the call of the law," others replied.

"The law?"

"They're coming to enforce order! Run!"

The monsters and beasts began to scatter, retreating into the yards nearby and disappearing behind trees and bushes.

"No," Mr. Birken screamed. "No!"

But his minions ignored him. He no longer had power over them.

"Destroy them!" he ordered. "I command you to attack them!" His voice broke as he realized it was no use. "Obey me...defend me...kill them..."

He stood utterly alone. The horde that had once surrounded him was gone, leaving him abandoned with no defense—no magic, no army to command. He looked around as if he didn't know what to do. It was almost a little pathetic, James thought with a shake of his head.

The whir of the sirens had grown deafening by the time two FBI vans and police cars turned the corner and tore down the street with their lights flashing, followed by three others from the opposite direction.

Liz and Archit came running over to James and Margot, and the four of them stepped aside as they watched the FBI agents jump out of their cars with their guns drawn.

"Abaddon Birken, put your hands in the air!" one of the agents shouted.

Mr. Birken stifled a sob as he looked around, almost as if he expected his minions to return at any second. "Why won't you destroy them? Why won't you destroy them?"

James watched the agents close around his science teacher. It shouldn't have satisfied him as much as it did. To think that Abaddon Birken, who was responsible for centuries of evil scheming and plotting, was being brought to justice—and by a group of kids at that!

As his sense of panic lifted off him and was replaced by relief, he felt Margot's arm around him. "You okay, buddy?" she said. She sounded remarkably casual for having just beaten up a two-hundred-and-fifty-pound evil wizard.

James couldn't help smiling.

"You were awesome," he said, looking from Margot to Liz. "Both of you!"

Archit gave James a playful swat with his wing. "And what about you, huh? I told you not to commit any acts of selfless valiance."

James laughed. "Good thing I didn't listen, right?"

He bent down and buried Archit in a hug. They had won!

"Get off me!" Mr. Birken shouted behind them. James turned. How satisfying it was to see the investigators shoving his chemistry teacher into handcuffs!

"I command you! I am a dark lord! Don't you know what that means!?" Mr. Birken shouted.

James shook his head. "I never thought about a dark lord getting arrested. I guess he picked the wrong world to mess with."

Two police officers approached them. "Hey, are you kids all right?" one of them asked.

It hadn't occurred to James how awkward they must have looked, all scraped and bruised, he and Margot dressed in their tattered formalwear, Liz in her blue princess gown, and Archit standing there with them. "Yeah," he said, then, "I mean—yes, officer. We're fine."

"What happened here?" the other officer asked.

"You're never going to believe any of this," Margot said.

Before the agents could reply, a flash of light erupted around them, so bright and sudden in that gray autumn dawn that James was momentarily blinded. He blinked several times, then saw a familiar figure standing there where the light had been. It was Dawn Flower the hippie queen, dressed in the same ankle-length kaftan, her mahogany-colored hair dotted with white flowers.

She strode forward. "Do not gape, gentle Adamites," she said. "Do not be surprised or startled by my appearance."

A hush fell over the crowd. James had never imagined a group of FBI agents and police officers could look so...well, stupefied. Even those who held Mr. Birken in handcuffs paused to hear from this hippie who had just appeared in a blaze of white light.

"I commend you on your hard work bringing this villain to justice," the hippie told them. "A tyrant and a criminal not only in this world but in others as well. Here, he was a murderer, a kidnapper, a plunderer, a grave robber, a torturer, and in other worlds, he was the leader of all creatures nightmarish and foul."

Mr. Birken looked as if he wanted to reply but had not the energy. All the fury and rage that had once possessed him seemed to have left him along with his magical powers.

Dawn Flower turned to James and the others. "These children," she said to the agents, "are your real heroes. Step forward, Adamite youths."

James could feel the confused stares of all the agents and officers bearing down on him, but the warm look from Dawn Flower empowered him. He did as she said and stepped forward.

"These Earthlings have fought evil in my world of Nalgordia and re-stored the harmony that was once lost many years ago," she explained. "Now they have led you, the enforcers of justice, to capture Abaddon Birken."

James could see that the agents holding Mr. Birken were lowering him into the back of a car.

"James has thwarted the master of Night Scourge by breaking his staff and ending his magical powers," Dawn Flower explained. "Now all that you gentlemen must do is see him imprisoned forever without ever an opportunity to return to his craft."

Hearing James's name out loud, one of the officers looked suddenly alert. "James? As in James Shannassy? You three are—"

"Yup," Margot said with a nod. "I guess we've been reported missing for the past few days?"

"Ten days," the officer said. "No sign of you. Where in the world have you been?"

"Not in the world, good officer," Dawn Flower chimed in. "Not this world, at least. They have completed their journey, and now, at last, they are home again."

James ran forward to the hippie queen. "But," he said, "what about Archit?"

Dawn Flower looked down at him. Her expression was so gentle that James forgot any inhibition he might have had. "We fulfilled the prophecy, didn't we? The journey, and the reunion? We did everything just as you said, and by the day that would have been his sixteenth birthday. Why is he still not human?"

Dawn Flower smiled. "My precious child." She lay a hand on James's shoulder. "Bless your sweet heart. Do not worry. Yes, the reunion did indeed come to pass on Archit's birthday, but though the prophecy foretold when, it did not say how Archit would become real. Only by proving himself kind, brave, and honest, of good will and noble action, pure of heart, self-controlled, both humble and merciful, and, most importantly, selfless and able to love others as he would love himself—then he would be granted an Adamite body and soul." She gestured with her staff. "Look you now upon the purple bird."

James turned and was amazed. Whatever sort of transformation had taken place, he'd completely missed it. Where just seconds before a figment had stood, there was the slender figure of a young man, without wing or feather or beak or talon. His hair and skin were light and fair, and he was dressed in a shirt and pants made from linen that were shining as white as virgin snow.

Archit ran forward, eager, his face lit up as though this was the first real moment he'd set eyes on the earth and was so eager to experience all of its wonder. "I'm—" he exclaimed, "I'm human!"

James ran forward and hugged him. "Oh my God," he exclaimed. "Look at you! Oh my God!" Margot and Liz ran forward as well.

"Cripes," said Margot with a joyful laugh. "I can't believe it."

They turned and looked at Dawn Flower, who was standing next to a group of truly wide-eyed and open-mouthed FBI agents and police officers who were still trying to put everything together in their heads.

"How?" asked James of Dawn Flower.

"I told you," said Dawn Flower. "It was Archit himself who proved he had a soul. He has proved to be selfless, good, and true. He has proved himself to be real."

Archit gave an embarrassed laugh, and looked to each of his companions. "Thank you, guys. So much." He looked at James. "Especially you, James. You're a real hero."

James laughed. "Y'know—heroism isn't all it's cracked up to be. I thought it was about being fearless, but...but I think it's just a lot easier to face your fears when it's someone you care about who's at risk."

Margot and Liz hugged Archit in turn. "You're the best," Margot said to him.

Archit sighed deeply. "I couldn't have done this without you," he said, looking at each of them. "I love you all."

By this time, the excitement out on the street was drawing attention from the neighbors who were waking up. Several of them were peering from their windows or front doors to see what was going on.

A voice called from the top of the hill. "James! Margot! Liz!"

Mrs. and Mr. Shannassy had come out the kitchen door and now tore across the lawn and down the hill toward the crowd on the street. Though dressed in their pajamas and bathrobes, they looked as if they hadn't slept in the days since the family reunion.

In a flash, Mrs. Shannassy had her arms around all three children at once, then hugging each of them in turn and burying them in kisses. "Oh, my darling children," she said. "I've been worried sick. Where have you been?"

Mr. Shannassy looked them up and down, taking in the sight of their tattered clothes, dirtied faces, and greasy hair. "Are all of you all right?"

"We're fine," James said. "We're better now that we're home."

"Go get some blankets, dear," Mrs. Shannassy said, and with a nod, Mr. Shannassy ran back toward the house.

"You're never going to believe half of what we tell you," Margot said. "It's like something out of one of James's stories come to life."

Mrs. Shannassy looked at Margot, speechless. James couldn't help smiling—if Margot could testify to all of it, who was Mom to question anything? "We've been in the land of Nalgordia," he said. "And this is Archit."

James turned and urged Archit forward. "Nice to meet you," Archit said, holding out his hand to shake Mrs. Shannassy's. There was something in his gestures that still reminded James of his having wings, even if they had now been replaced by arms.

"He's a friend of ours," James explained. "He's the one we've been away with, and...well, is it all right if he stays with us for a while?"

Mrs. Shannassy smiled. "Oh, James...well, I'm sure we can figure something out."

One of the police officers approached. "Well, ma'am, after everything I've seen this morning, I imagine your kids have got quite a story to tell you." He looked over his shoulder to watch the car holding Mr. Birken drive off. Mr. Birken pressed his face up to the window, glaring, a mix of fury and fear on his face.

"I'm just glad to see that they're safe," the officer continued, looking at James, then at the girls. "What do you say you get yourself settled. Let the kids go in and get cleaned up and rest a bit. I hope you don't mind if we ask the kids to come down to the station this afternoon to answer some questions for us."

Mrs. Shannassy shook her head soberly. "No, not at all."

"All right, then," the officer said. "We'll be giving you a call later in the morning."

He turned and went back to his squad. Some of the FBI agents were departing the scene, but others were staying to collect the shattered remnants of Mr. Birken's staff, as if they might be using it as evidence against him.

"Come on," Mrs. Shannassy said. "Let's get you all inside. I'll put the coffee on, and I'll send Dad out to get bagels. How does that sound?"

James smiled. "It sounds great."

"It sounds as if you're getting ready to listen to everything we have to tell you," Liz said. "This is going to be a lot for you."

As they began to walk up the hill, James looked at Archit. "We did it," he said. "I don't know how, but we actually did it. You're human, and your uncle is gonna be in prison."

Archit smiled. Even in human form, the smile was recognizable. "You did it, James. I meant what I said. You were the hero here."

"You really were," Margot said.

"Yeah," Liz said. "You kicked butt today."

James shook his head, and all the memorable moments of the adventure seemed to flash through his mind. The pirates, the jungle, the rockies, all the dangers that had instilled in him more confidence and bravery he had never known. And then there was the quest to stop Iceheart, and the confrontation they had had up in the tower of Ophir. Finally, the danger they had faced in the amusement park as it went down in flames.

A bark came from behind them, and James turned to see Dromio bounding toward them. "Dromio!" he exclaimed.

The dog's tongue hung to one side of his gaping mouth as he looked up excitedly at Archit, James, and the others, but he didn't say anything.

"He'll wait until we've explained everything to your mom," Archit whispered to James. "We don't want to startle her."

James nodded. In that case, all was right. What could possibly be left to worry about? Well, except for the fact that his mom might not believe any of this, but who really cared about that? They had triumphed over evil, saved the land of Nalgordia, won a mortal soul for Archit, and brought down Mr. Birken. It had been a pretty successful adventure, as far as he was concerned.

Mrs. Shannassy proceeded up the hill in front of Margot and Liz, and James and Archit hung back for a moment.

"So you're part of our family now, right?" James said. "If my parents are willing to adopt you, that is. Right?"

"I dunno," Archit said. "There's so much of the world I need to experience and see. I might be only sixteen years old in human years, but..."

"But what?" James said. "A normal adolescence would do you well. After hundreds of years, do you really know everything there is to know about the world? Couldn't you still learn something from a few years in high school? As my older brother?"

"I guess you're right," Archit said.

James sighed. "Will there be more adventures in our future?"

"Undoubtedly."

"Well, I guess we'll face those when they come up," James said. "In the meantime, let's be proud of what we accomplished."

Archit nodded. "Yes. Let's."

James stopped, watching Margot and Liz follow his mom into the house. He looked at Archit and threw his arms around him once more. He hugged him close, breathing in the scent of patchouli and sandalwood that hung on his white linen shirt. It felt overwhelming to know that he had accomplished a victory like the ones he had read about in fantasy novels, like the ones he thought were meant for knights greater than he, like the ones he thought he would only have through games of Dungeons & Dragons.

"You know," he said as he and Archit went into the house, "maybe one day there will be people who talk about a figment of the imagination who dreamed of being human, and some will say that it was just a fantasy tale or a legend. But we'll know the truth."

"Yeah," Archit agreed with a smile. "We will."